I'll
EAT
WHEN
I'M
DEAD

Barbara Bourland

riverrun

First published in the USA in 2017 by Grand Central
First published in Great Britain in 2017 by riverrun
This paperback edition published in 2018 by

riverrun

an imprint of
Quercus Editions Ltd
Carmelite House
50 Victoria Embankment
London EC4Y 0DZ

An Hachette UK company

A CIP catalogue record for this book is available
from the British Library

Paperback 978 1 78429 857 9
Ebook 978 1 78429 858 6

10 9 8 7 6 5 4 3 2 1

Book design by Marie Mundaca
Illustrations by Peter Bernard

Printed and bound in Great Britain by Clays Ltd, St Ives plc

To all my friends: I wrote this for you.

I'll Eat
When I'm Dead

Praise for I'll Eat When I'm Dead

'I can't put *I'll Eat When I'm Dead* down, I LOVE it. Bourland's debut ... e *The Devil Wears Prada* meets *American Psycho*'

Louise O'Neill

'An one who has opened up a woman's magazine and despaired at the ontent should **read this book**' Rhiannon Lucy Cosslett

'A **hip-smart** New York fashion magazine-set crime novel with mo edge than all the haute couture shows put together'

Sarra Manning, *Red*

'A s ire, a murder mystery and an exaggerated exposé of the industry peo le love to make assumptions about . . . If you want **an Agatha Ch stie update**, this is it. We look forward to Bourland's next quir y outing' *Stellar*

'An itious but far more brutal**. This murder mystery takes a satirical ook at the world responsible for bombarding us with destructive ima es' *Big Issue*

'A s nart, satirical** take on fashion and media that will have readers snor ing with laughter' *New York Post*

'Sex Drugs. Dries van Noten. *I'll Eat When I'm Dead* **skewers Trib Fashion with wit and wicked intelligence**. From Finnish toast only restaurants to kobe-beef hide bikinis and grandiose faux femi sm, Barbara Bourland makes you laugh out loud and keep turn g the pages. A deft, smart, and hilarious debut'

Wednesday Martin, author of *Primates of Park Avenue*

'A s nart feminist fashion manifesto** packed with pulpy, sexy, mur erous intrigue. Highly entertaining!'

Elizabeth Cline, author of *Overdressed*

Prologue

It was not *impossible* for a thirty-seven-year-old woman to starve to death in Manhattan, less than a mile from the nearest Whole Foods, though it *was* unusual.

When the NYPD opened the locked workroom at the offices of *RAGE Fashion Book*, where Hillary Whitney's body lay dead on the floor, most of the officers placed their bets on a cocaine overdose. The still-perfect hair and makeup, the bleach-white Dior pumps, the long, manicured red nails; it could all have been part of one of the magazine's photo shoots, if not for the way her limbs sprang—unnatural, *akimbo*—from her mint-colored dress. It was the officers' collective experience that women who died at work in clothing this expensive were partying themselves into eternity.

Yes, cocaine was a solid bet, but still: one optimist had chosen aneurysm. "She looked like a nice girl," he'd said, "and her skin was in *great* shape." Another risk-taker bet meningitis, "because you never know."

Yet, in the end, Carol, Midtown South's senior secretary and most enthusiastic bookmaker, was the sole profiteer: the coroner's autopsy reported that Hillary Edith Whitney had experienced a fatal coronary as the end-stage event of starvation, which no one had thought to bet on. In a zip code where the average net worth topped a million dollars, starvation hadn't been recorded as a cause of death for an able-bodied woman under sixty since the previous century.

The unmistakable signs of a lifetime of disordered eating, chronic malnutrition, and various muscle tears and strains from an intense daily exercise regimen—along with a clean standard toxicity screen—buttressed the coroner's conclusion, and so the precinct's detectives saw no reason to dispute his theory that with the right combination of stress and a diet of alkaline-only green juices, a fatal heart attack could've happened anytime.

Clues, too, were in short supply. The only things discovered in the workroom with her were one half-empty juice bottle, an over-sized and overturned box filled with thirteen yards of "luxury" ribbon, a pile of blank index cards, and a pen. It appeared she'd suffered the heart attack before she had the opportunity to write anything down. An attorney for Cooper House, *RAGE Fashion Book*'s publisher, confirmed that Hillary Whitney was working on a shoot involving ribbon. He helpfully offered that she was proba-bly taking notes on the texture and provenance, which he insisted was a "low-stress" activity—though Cooper's reputation as a high-stakes workplace preceded his remarks, but that in and of itself wasn't technically a crime—and so, the case was closed in eleven days.

Eventually, like all things do, the death of Hillary Edith Whitney faded out of public consciousness.

Two months later the odors of new paint and new carpet were almost gone from the workroom where she'd died. The funeral was long over, her ashes scattered in Old House Pond on Martha's Vineyard, when her boyfriend went back to his wife and her par-ents stopped crying first thing in the morning. Her estate was processed, her apartment was put on the market, and an interim fashion director was hired to replace her. It seemed to everyone that the ripple of her death had run its course.

Naturally, they were wrong.

Part I

July

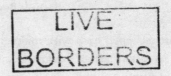

Chapter One

Every weekday morning, as the sun rose above Sixth Avenue, a peerless crop of women—frames poised, behavior polished, networks connected, and bodies generally buffed to a high sheen—were herded by the cattle prod of their own ambition to one particular building. They streamed as if by magic from all over Manhattan and Brooklyn, through streets and subways teeming with sweaty crowds and heavy traffic, to work at Cooper House, the only remaining major magazine publisher in New York.

Some, like Bess Bonner, a twenty-eight-year-old associate editor at *RAGE Fashion Book*, arrived earlier than others. Though her colleagues frequently staggered in around noon after long nights spent drinking fistfuls of sponsored celebrity vodka in yet another chartered barge or pop-up school bus, never Bess, who took pride in being punctual. Monday through Friday she stuck to the same routine: First, she walked her bike, a large Dutch commuter, through the West Village streets to pick up her coffee at Joe. Second, she stood on the sidewalk and drank half the cup, no matter the weather; finally, she took diligent mental notes on the outfits of pedestrians who were, like her, freshly pressed to meet the promise of the day.

One Monday in July, in attire that was stylish but functional (trousers clipped back with midnight-blue leather bands, her buttery navy kid-leather backpack stuffed in an orange milk crate affixed firmly to the back with neon cable ties, and a waterproof oilcloth bag that held an emergency poncho tucked beneath her seat), Bess drank her coffee, took her notes, and hopped on her bike, pedaling toward Cooper. After a few minutes of glorious, uninterrupted speed through Chelsea, a rush of adrenaline kicked in, and she smiled; that final mile of her morning commute both boosted her mood and set the tone for the long day ahead, working at the magazine she'd worshipped her entire life.

Today, that work meant sorting bracelets into velvet trays.

She hung a left on Thirty-Ninth Street, crossed Broadway, and pulled smoothly into the Cooper garage. Gina, the usual attendant, took her bicycle and wheeled it into the rectangle of her personal parking spot, a privilege for full-time employees, as Bess took off her helmet and shook out her tangled mess of dark blonde curls.

Shouldering her backpack, she walked up to the aluminum post outside the service elevator and waved her phone in front of it. A large blinking *F* appeared briefly on a previously invisible screen. Ten seconds later, the *F* disappeared and the post became a mere metal column once more.

Bess walked into the elevator and examined herself in its mirrored walls. *Not too bad*, she thought, looking down at her electric-blue Pappagallo flats for rips, tears, or smudges, smoothing her ankle-length silk tuxedo trousers, and tucking her deliberately threadbare men's white V-neck into the side of the waistband. Her jewelry today was simple and bright: a stack of rose-gold pyramid-stud bracelets from Hermès covered one wrist, and a pair of dangling yellow-gold earrings—from the Egyptian section of the gift shop at the Met, purchased long ago with her fifth-grade allowance—hung casually from her ears.

When the elevator stopped on the forty-sixth floor, Bess walked into the main entrance of *RAGE*'s offices. The reception area still gave her a thrill every time she entered: *RAGE*'s front lobby walls were made of a creamy-white marble, shot through with jagged bolts of mint and lavender, seamlessly paneled between a polished black concrete ceiling and floor. RAGE *Fashion Book* was etched in three-foot platinum-leafed letters across the wall opposite the elevator bank.

The front "desk" was a sculpture by the architect Maya Lin, made of stacked gradient disks of a now-extinct ash tree suspended on four thin wires. There was a silver rotary telephone in place of a receptionist, as Margot Villiers, RAGE's editor in chief, had decided long ago that the first face of RAGE should never, *ever*, be a person—just this empty, Lynchian room with a single telephone, through which you could dial a two-digit extension for any of the seventy-five women in the office.

There were no obvious doors save for the elevators. Bess crossed the floor and waved her phone again, this time in front of a brass plate set into the far-left corner of the back wall. The north and south walls of the lobby were made of marble so thin that the light shone through them, and when prompted by an authorized phone like Bess's they split down the middle, slid back on tracks, and functioned as automatic doors. Margot called them the Beinecke doors, after the rare books library at Yale, walled in the same tissue-thin rock.

The walls slid away, revealing the magazine's offices—open plan, like a newsroom. Bess made a beeline through the custom black Lucite cubicles for the southwest corner. Her own cube was stacked high with boxes, jewelry, invitations, gift bags, flowers, and a precariously perched laptop, on which she recorded who sent what object where and whether or not it was featured in a shoot. She tossed her backpack behind her chair and set her phone on top of the contact charging dock wedged into the corner of her desk.

Today, a Monday, was an accessories day for Bess. A total of 342 bracelets had been sent in the weeks before—solicited and unsolicited—and she had to account for each one in a spreadsheet, giving it a genre, a color-coded price point, a possible assignment for any of the upcoming shoots scheduled in the next five months, and then, finally, handwrite a thank-you note to the jeweler on *RAGE* stationery before putting the bracelet in one of the velvet trays that would eventually wind up in the office of Catherine Ono, her boss, close friend, and senior editor at *RAGE*. She sighed, thinking, *I need more coffee for this*. Bess walked over to a vintage Coca-Cola dispenser, popped in a quarter, and pulled out a squat, sweating black bottle of cold-pressed coffee. After diluting one-third of the bottle in a glass of ice water, she walked back to her desk and set her phone to silent. It was time to get to work.

Bracelet, rose gold, hinged band, with raised white enamel dots.

Very Julianne Moore in *A Single Man*.
Price point: Green ($5,000+).
Possible shoots: **Day Drinking**, January issue; **Astronauts'
　　Wives**, December issue; or **Dotty for It**, the Sylvia-Plath-in-
　　a-mental-hospital-themed feature for the October issue,
　　shooting in three weeks.

Bangle, lavender Lucite and bronze, laser-cut etchings à la **Stargate.**

Pat Cleveland goes to a garden party in 2035.
Price point: Mint ($10,000+).
Possible shoots: **FUTURAFRIQUE**, November issue; **Gone
　　Yachting (A Gowanus Story)**, October issue.

Bracelet, chartreuse ½-inch-diam. rope and platinum Monopoly playing pieces.

Rich children.
Price point: Yellow ($15,000+).
Possible shoots: **Tea Party All Night: A Celebration of Suri
　　Cruise**, October issue; **1% (and Rising!)**, December issue.

Bess was so focused that she hardly noticed the office filling up around her when the clock struck eleven o'clock. The Beinecke doors parted over and over as *RAGE* staffers spilled onto 46, their near-uniform of summer silks in post-neon colors filling the office with little glowing blocks of color and activity as they poured into their Lucite cubes. That summer, the women of *RAGE* favored filmy sundresses with modish hems and lurid accessories; the shorter girls stomped around in oversized sandals, soles heavy and dense, while the taller ones, like Bess, leaned toward slipper-style flats. Makeup was out this year, so no one wore any. Skin care was in. The only embellishment Bess had on her face was a thick set of individually applied mink lashes that cost $900 per application, giving her the look of a soft-focus Twiggy.

Intern Molly eventually whirled in on a pair of six-inch leopard-print calf-hair pumps, their two-inch baby-blue platforms trimmed in red and gold. Her royal blue minidress had an extended trompe l'oeil collar in black, and her pile of hair was tinted in shades of the same baby blue as the platforms on her pumps.

"HiBessI'mSoSorryI'mLateIMissedTheTrainAndThereWereNo Cabs," blurted Molly as she hung her Céline handbag—this season's, Bess noticed—from a hook on the side of Bess's cube.

"That's fine, Molly," Bess replied kindly. "You can stay a bit later. Cat and I have to leave early. We'll get a to-do list to you this afternoon. For now, please finish addressing those envelopes from last week."

Molly visibly relaxed. Her hairstyle—an intricate series of plaits that ended in an extension-boosted fishtail—must have taken at least two hours at Barrett's Braid Bar, and she was grateful that Bess didn't comment on it. *Bess knows that it's more important to look right and be a little late*, Molly thought, *than to be ugly and be on time*. This was a certainty that Molly would carry with her throughout her entire life.

Bess, indeed, had no intention of embarrassing Molly or anyone else, under any circumstance. The middle child of four, Bess adjusted cheerfully to the people around her, and going out of her way to make others more comfortable made Bess more comfortable in turn; she was the rare Manhattan native who grew sweeter with each passing year instead of more calcified. Still, it was true that some part of her natural ease came from her family's astonishing resources, a fact she rarely, if ever, admitted. Bess instead devoted a significant amount of time each day to calculating the exact ratio of basic to bitch—placing the threadbare cotton T-shirt, for example, next to the Hermès bangles—in a misguided attempt to tone down the gleam of her family's wealth.

After studying peace and world security at Hampshire College, she'd once intended to join the State Department, but her first job out of school—a paid internship at the teen magazine *Filly*, another Cooper title—set her on a different path. Bess had worked her way up to senior editor at *Filly* before taking a title cut two years earlier to work at the far more prestigious *RAGE Fashion Book*, where, like everyone else, she was more than overqualified for the general responsibilities of her position.

But Bess didn't mind, for *RAGE* was so much more than just a magazine: it was the most successful women's title in the history of print publishing. Distributed in thirty-four countries worldwide through seventeen international editions, with four million domestic subscribers, it was the gold standard for women's lifestyle publications, print or digital, and held a moral high ground that few others could claim: all the apparel featured in *RAGE* was manufactured by living-wage workers. Yet it was as high-fashion as any quixotic editorial in *W* or *Harper's Bazaar* had ever been—before their parent companies had gone bankrupt, anyway.

Bess came to the office every day with a serious commitment to the work they did there, no matter how trivial, but she didn't expect everyone else to have the same energy; certainly not an unpaid intern like Molly, so she let the girl's lateness slide, just as she would the next day, and the day after that.

Besides, after what happened with Hillary, everyone in this office could use a little slack.

Catherine Ono opened her eyes. *Fuck*, she thought. *Fuck you, morning*. She fumbled around in her sheets until she found her phone and held down a button.

"SIRI, WHAT TIME IS IT?" Cat asked, unable to read the clock until she had her contacts in.

"It's 10:25 a.m.," Siri replied.

Cat bolted out of bed. She looked around her apartment—an unrenovated loft off the Morgan Avenue stop in Bushwick—and scanned the room for a pack of cigarettes. A yellow box came into focus nearby. She grabbed the pack off the nightstand, popped one in her mouth, and pulled her hair back into a loose ponytail in a lame attempt to keep the smoke out of her hair. An old book of matches from the long-defunct Mars Bar was tangled in her sheets and she lit the cigarette, then strode quickly across the cold, dirty floor to the bathroom. She set the cigarette in an ashtray, spritzed her face and arms with a large spray bottle marked "CARIBBEAN SEA WATER DO NOT DRINK" in permanent marker, squirted more in her hair, grabbed the cigarette again, took a deep drag, then rooted around in a jar on the sink for a black liquid eyeliner to distract from the bags under her eyes. Two quick swipes later, she grabbed a pair of thin, gold-framed vintage Oliver Peoples eyeglasses from a selection of spectacles on a shelf she'd installed next to her bathroom vanity. She peed, brushed her teeth, and applied deodorant before springing out of the bathroom and diving into her closet.

Cat's closet was the only part of her apartment that was actually a built-out room with walls. She grabbed two black silk tank tops, a pair of perforated black lambskin pre-Galliano Margiela leggings, her black leather cowboy boots, and a set of large, ultra-oxidized heavy bronze bracelets from Nigeria that always left her with little bruises. She pulled a large leather tray off the closet's top shelf and fished a white grosgrain ribbon out of it, which she wove into her hair in a plait. After snaking into her clothes, she stubbed out her cigarette and sprayed herself down with an industrial-strength bottle of Febreze stolen from the maid's cart at The Standard Hotel. Cat had tried electronic cigarettes for a few years, just like everyone else, but after people everywhere had gone bald overnight in an epidemic of vape-related hair loss, she'd decided it was safer to stick with regular old carcinogens and gone right back to American Spirits. So had millions of other ex-smokers, and now, in a regulatory mea culpa, cigarette prices were almost reasonable again.

Finally, she grabbed the paperback copy of *Welcome to the Desert of the Real* that she was halfway through and shoved it, along with her cigarettes, into a black leather Alexander Wang shopper with pointed rose-gold feet on each corner.

"Cigarettes, phone, wallet, metro card, keys," she said out loud as she reached the door, a recitation she made every time she left the house. Check check check check check: all still in her handbag from the night before. She shut the door, locked the heavy dead bolt, and booked it for the subway.

At 12:45, Cat finally stood on the four-story showboat main escalator. Huge, nearly prehistoric ferns salvaged from a Cooper scion's overgrown Great Neck mansion surrounded her in a humid wall, and she tried not to sweat as she rode up to the elevator bank. Although the $112 million lobby was meant to inspire the legions of employees tasked with channeling the zeitgeist each month, it just reminded Cat of the infinite escalators in London tube stations, where the urge to slide down the center railing was

almost overwhelming. *Someday*, she thought, letting her fingers drag off the edge of the rubber banister. *When I quit this place in a blaze of glory.*

But today, the very thought of sliding made Cat dizzy. Late. Sweaty. Tired. *Today is going to be r-u-f-f ruff*, she thought. She looked down and took a long, thirsty gulp of her iced Trenta Red Eye from the Starbucks around the corner, then fished an Adderall out of her purse's side pocket, broke off half into a sugary orange chunk, and crunched it between her teeth. *Please kick in soon*, she thought.

"Kit-Oh!" yelled out a Sloaney voice behind her. Boots clomped up the escalator steps ten yards below, and a tousled head of expertly colored and blown-out caramel-blonde hair ascended in double time. Cat hoped it looked like she was coming back from coffee and not showing up two and a half hours late to work, for the immaculate hair and boots belonged to Whig Beaton Molton-Mauve Lucas, an oft-photographed socialite, clotheshorse, and twice-divorced mother of two, known simply as Lou, who was a temporary fill-in for Cat's now-dead boss and close friend, Hillary. Among other affectations, like dropping most vowels and willfully mispronouncing even her own surname, Lou thought calling Catherine Ono "Kit-Oh" was hilarious. Cat disagreed.

It was their second month working together, and while Cat was doing her best to be friendly, she was still trying to figure out what she and Lou had in common. So far, it was just tequila—but in some cultures that was plenty to forge a lasting work relationship. When Lou got within a foot, Cat smelled faint traces of jasmine and honeysuckle, a subtle smell that dozens of women in the *RAGE* office had adopted over the past few years. *Lou is trying to fit in every way she can*, Cat realized, and she suddenly felt appreciative of the gesture, however small.

"Hi, Lou. Love your color," Cat complimented her, pointing to Lou's hair.

"Oh thaaaaank you!" Lou smiled. "Jane has been in the sun all summer and she has such amazing color, we just chopped off a lock of it and brought it in to Tricomi."

"That's brilliant, Lou. If she ever wants to look like Mia Farrow, you could sell the whole mop to Rusk and make a custom color blend...just think: *Lucas Blond Balayage*."

Cat wasn't joking. She'd seen the Lucas daughters the week before when their nanny brought them to visit the offices, and their perfectly healthy little-girl hair—seasoned only by the sun from sailing in Cap d'Antibes, Montauk, and the Dutch Antilles with their father—was a tone that Cat was sure every old bag of bones in New York would pay through their hollowed-out noses for.

Lou roared, a big, horsey Lou-laugh. Whenever she laughed, spoke, or really made *any* kind of noise with her mouth, it was as though her jaw nearly detached from her face and became a separate object. It was all Cat could do not to stare openly at Lou's enormous, perfectly capped white teeth as her words boomed out through them.

"We'll just have to pray one of them goes through a Sinéad period before hitting puberty. God, Kit-Oh, you must be broiling in those leggings."

Cat looked down. *Oh—right*. In her hangover rush, her body confused by the industrial air conditioner in the loft, she'd worn leather leggings in July.

"Oh, no, I'm fine, Lou—they've got tiny holes for air," she said.

"So is Margot in yet?" Lou asked nervously as they stepped into the elevator, referring to *RAGE*'s venerable editor in chief.

Cat desperately tried to recall if Margot was even in town that day. "I feel like she's in Milan for the rest of the week, but let's check with Bess—she's the only one who actually listens to Paula, anyway."

Paula Booth had worked for Margot Villiers for nearly thirty years. They ran *RAGE* together with a pair of iron fists. Though it was Paula's title, "Assistant" was hardly her job description; in truth, she was somewhere between a deputy and a surrogate. She had two assistants of her own *and* a personal secretary but, for some reason unknown to Cat, never had an editorial title tacked before her name on the masthead. Yet Paula led each Tuesday's big edit meeting where she often ran through Margot's schedule toward the end, when Cat usually had stopped paying attention altogether. Bess tended to write down everything Paula said, because the sixty-year-old—known for always wearing black, never smiling, being semipermanently attached to the telephone, and having a short temper—didn't like repeating herself *ever*.

Lou, as a temp, a newcomer, and a genuine publishing outsider, was still terrified of both Margot and Paula. A socialite and friend of Hillary's who had been on the pages of *RAGE* dozens of times, she'd been recruited—rather quickly—into Hillary's job after the accident because of her experience as a *subject* in magazines, not as a writer or an editor.

At Hillary's funeral, a photographer for *The New York Times* had taken a photo of Lou as she gave her condolences to Margot and featured it on the cover of the Styles section's tribute to Hillary. Two days later, Paula and Margot offered Lou the job. Cooper had needed to hire someone who understood, instinctively, what *RAGE*'s customers would covet, they'd explained, and Lou in turn thought it might be glamorous to work—especially at a job that so many people would have killed for. They'd settled on an interim contract position naming Lou as contributing fashion director for six months. Paula and Margot assured Cat behind closed doors that they'd *wanted* to promote her into Hillary's job, but, being an EU citizen, she'd need a full green card—her current visa wouldn't support the types of travel required for the job—and they needed more time to get Cooper's approval. Lou's interim role was just a part of the process.

Cat hadn't resented their decision. Hillary had been one of her closest friends, and she would have felt disloyal lobbying for the position. Lou's stepping in allowed Cat some real time to grieve and search for balance in her life, and no one at *RAGE* expected that Lou—who'd never had a paying job before—would want to stay beyond her six-month contract, anyway.

As she and Lou walked together to their offices, the new crop of interns stared, openmouthed, at the ghostly pale six-foot-one half-Japanese, half-Belgian senior editor dressed like an off-duty model at a dive bar and the five-foot-two alarmingly tan semi-famous blonde Brit beside her who wore mud-encrusted riding boots, dark khaki microshorts, and a white linen trapeze top with ropes of turquoise and topaz around her neck.

Constance Onderveet, the magazine's managing editor, peered through the glass wall of Margot's office, her eyes narrowed and critical, a look Cat tried to defuse by smiling and waving. Constance smiled uncertainly back, while Paula, on the phone in her own office next door, mercifully kept her back to Cat's entrance. *Constance is calculating* exactly *how late I am*, Cat thought, realizing that she'd crossed some kind of invisible boundary. Thankfully, Bess looked up from her desk a moment later and smiled her sunny grin at both Cat and Lou.

"Hi!" she said, pausing from her bracelet sorting. "I'm on bracelets all day, but let me know what you need. Margot is out in Paris, but she's back tomorrow. Paula's on a rampage. Constance is reworking **Judy and the Technicolor Housecoat,** so we will have to pull more brooches—it *was* Havisham, but *now* it's more early Cindy Sherman throwing eggs on the floor. I put a tray in your office, Cat; and Lou, we need picks for the blue page for September's NEEDS. Molly is feeling *very* blue today so she'll help you."

As always, Cat was awed by Bess's organizational skills. Lou looked over at Molly, the blue-haired intern.

"Moll!" Lou called out with delight. "You ARE blue today. I love it. If Boots says so, then it must be done. Blue's the thing for *Book*, then. I want a coffee and then let's get started."

Lou chucked her striped linsey-woolsey tote—custom-made for her by female prisoners in Uzbekistan through a collaboration with

Barneys, a project cut sadly short by the elaborate pleas for help sewn into many of the final product's linings—at the doorway of her office and marched over to the Coca-Cola coffee dispenser. Molly stood there awkwardly, unsure of whether or not she should have gotten the coffee *for* Lou. Lou also seemed unsure whether or not she should have asked Molly for it, like she would a maid or a flight attendant. Lou was a bit lost in the working world, still, and in that sense, intern and boss were perfectly matched. Molly was glad that at least Lou was kind, even if it was in that ropy British backslapping kind of way. And had she really just called Bess "Boots" and *RAGE Fashion Book* just plain "*Book*"?

Later that night, on the phone to her parents in Los Angeles, Molly would casually refer to the magazine as simply "*Book*," thinking she sounded sophisticated. After she hung up, Molly's father would say, "I think she gets dumber every year."

When Lou returned from the Coca-Cola machine with a cold press and a single glass filled with ice, Molly followed her into her nearly bare office, formerly occupied by Hillary. Molly sat down in the sky-blue Le Corbusier swivel chair in front of Lou's desk, Moleskine and purple jelly pen in hand, ready to take notes, while Lou sat behind the desk on a shiny exercise ball she'd swapped in for the existing Aeron chair. She expertly popped the cap off the bottle of cold press using a monogrammed gold Dunhill lighter and poured the coffee into a glass and slid it across to the intern.

"Mummy's little helper," she woofed at Molly, who smiled nervously.

Molly didn't think you were supposed to drink cold press straight, but she didn't want to be rude, so she took a sip. *Jesus, that's bitter.* She looked up to see Lou gaily swigging from the bottle as though it were water.

Lou stared at the laptop left open on the desk in front of her, displaying a completely blank spreadsheet in CoopDoc, Cooper's in-house, cloud-based version of Excel.

"So," said Lou.

"Yes," said Molly.

"How many."

"How many . . . what?" asked Molly.

"How many bloody *blue* bits do we need for NEEDS September?"

"I think twelve. But it can be fewer than that if we shoot some really big."

"All right. *Twelve*. We can do that. Twelve blue things you just absolutely fucking need. Well. Okay. Yves Klein, let's start there. Can you call Zoe at YSL? Let's see what they're doing with everything from the Marrakech house this year—I know they do a home line based off Majorelle for spring every year. Tell her I want six things in *bleu*. We can use two of those, probably. Then I want you to call this place I went to last year in Nah-miii-biii-ah. It's this eco retreat and elephant sanctuary and this sort of wonderful yogic cleansing place that you heli into and they have these blue harnesses for their elephants, for their little baby elephants, and they make the dye out of some kind of Namibian flower, so let's get a few of those. You could repurpose it for a large dog or child, or maybe you could wear it like a vest. And, hmm, more blue, maybe we should go to some showrooms. Oh—AND I've been thinking about tiling the upstairs bath blue so we'll need some blue porcelain tiles anyway, maybe a blue toilet to match. Let's find an Italian one. Is it too kitsch to have a cerulean potty? What do you think?"

Molly was still scribbling furiously, trying to write down the correct keywords for further googling. *What time is it in Namibia, anyway?*

In her own office next door, Cat stared at the wall of windows behind her desk, which she'd painted over last year with an enormous white rectangle that blocked the view of New Jersey. The rectangle—known as Plus-Minus Sign, or PMS—was how Cat documented the Roman winds of her aesthetic favor upon the world's objects. The left column had a large black plus sign painted at the top; the right column, a minus sign. Cat added or subtracted a new item from each column every week using a black erasable marker. Today the PMS read:

+	—
sailing instead of driving	"luxury"
human ivory	woodworking
dread	the 1920s
eating raw meat	self-help
butt-tight overalls	new safari anything
painted cinderblock walls	strappy shoes
charm bracelets	shorts

Although Lou's outfit invoked at least two of Cat's current minuses, she reconsidered Lou's shorts. They were basically a large pair of underwear, which Cat approved of wholeheartedly. You had to be really courageous, really narcissistic, or the usual industry combination of both to wear underwear as pants to work. *Perhaps*, Cat considered, *I can genuinely work with Lou after all.*

Cat didn't like any outfit, accessory, aesthetic, or genre that reduced women to what she considered to be traditional female prisons: the happy homemaker, the sexy librarian, the bitch in a power suit, the carefree athlete, the sophisticated socialite, the bad girl, and so on. These tropes were not only done to death, but they weren't, she felt, *modern*; they didn't account for the global diaspora of cultures and pressures that affected how women chose to present themselves each day. All those old hats did was show a woman how to occupy a place she'd already been hundreds of times before.

A woman draws attention everywhere she goes with everything she does—whether she wants to or not, Cat knew. The management of that attention was the full-time focus of the fashion industry, and she was heavily invested in the conversation. Every look she created and every reference she styled was seen, appreciated, and digested by millions of women around the world. Magazines were where women watched themselves being watched; where they learned how to *be*. Cat was passionate about delivering a complex version of female identity politics to everyone—or to *anyone*, she acknowledged, who had the fourteen bucks to buy a copy of *RAGE*.

When Cat had dropped out of her doctoral program in art history at the University of Chicago, her parents had been deeply disappointed. *Hell, I was disappointed, too*, she remembered, but the best position she could have gotten as an academic was as a mere adjunct: the job market was simply too crowded. By the time she'd started writing the second chapter of her thesis, two whole cohorts ahead of her were still unemployed, milling around campus with tragic, unwanted-puppy looks on their faces. They would never get full-time jobs—not when they were already marked with the scent of failure. Cat was no better and deep down she knew it, so when she ran out of funding after five years, her thesis far from complete, she decided to throw in the towel. The stars hadn't aligned, and she gave up, surrendered without protest, for the very first time in her life, feeling like a complete and total failure, an outlook that she didn't reverse until years later. Academia was the first career she'd ever tried and the first thing she'd ever quit. Three months after her funding appeal had been rejected, with her credit card maxed out and her checking account in overdraft, she'd prayed for a miracle and texted Sigrid, a close friend from boarding school, to lament her condition.

Suddenly Hillary Whitney—a graduate of the very same boarding school and one of Sigrid's former roommates—was on the phone, asking Cat to be her assistant at *RAGE* and promising that

Cooper could turn her student visa into a work visa. Cat had jumped at the opportunity to work for the magazine and for Margot Villiers, a woman she'd long admired. Margot was the only public feminist Cat could think of who wasn't painted with the word *bitch*; instead, newspapers, journals, magazines, and history books described her using words and phrases otherwise reserved for men. *Legendary, futurist, visionary, perfectionist, creative genius, hard-nosed leader*; never *difficult, high-strung, radical*, or *temperamental*. No woman, including President Warren, had ever managed that.

Cat found herself in New York four days later, suitcase in hand, knocking on Sigrid's door.

Right away her responsibilities at *RAGE* felt relevant to her academic work, although her parents—a practical-minded pair who lived happily on their hobby farm in rural Belgium—rolled their eyes at the connections she insisted were obvious. *You're too smart to work at a magazine, Katteke,* her mother had chided at first, *and you are too old to start anew. Choose something you can excel at or you will have a crisis at thirty, and then where will you go?* Yet, six years later, now thirty-three, Cat truly felt she was still practicing, on an *exceptionally* macro level, the theories and arguments she had made all through her master's and doctoral research on the feminist aesthetic practices of fine art. When asked to explain to others why she'd left academia for a women's magazine, she often referred to poet and art critic John Berger's observation on the historic depictions of women's bodies in photography and painting from his book *Ways of Seeing*:

> To be born a woman has been to be born, within an allotted and confined space, into the keeping of men. The social presence of women has developed as a result of their ingenuity in living under such tutelage within such a limited space. But this has been at the cost of a woman's self being split into two.
>
> A woman must continually watch herself. She is almost continually accompanied by her own image of herself. Whilst she is walking across a room or whilst she is weeping

at the death of her father, she can scarcely avoid envisaging herself walking or weeping. From earliest childhood she has been taught and persuaded to survey herself continually...

One might simplify this by saying: *men act* and *women appear*. Men look at women. Women watch themselves being looked at... Thus she turns herself into an object—and most particularly an object of vision: a sight.

She'd had a short, slightly truncated quote from *Ways of Seeing* screenprinted over a photograph of one of Egyptian artist Ghada Amer's embroideries of a woman pulling down her underpants. In rose-colored paint, it read: "A woman's presence defines what can and cannot be done to her."

Cat had the screenprint framed in blue and hung it next to her desk, where visitors to her office could get a nice long stare at it without having to crane their necks. The opposite wall held an enormous metal bookcase filled with all of her books from graduate school lest her peers forget, even for a moment, where she'd come from.

Still, every day at *RAGE* was a personal challenge for Cat to figure out how to apologize for the ads, the actual and unfortunate bulk of the magazine's pages, the quantity of which grew every month. With a staff of seventy-five in New York, seventy in Los Angeles (though only a third were full-time with benefits), and the enormous cost of the lobbyists and attorneys they employed to ensure the accuracy of their claims that the featured apparel was, in fact, made by living-wage workers, *RAGE Fashion Book* was beyond expensive to publish.

The previous decade's watershed declines in print advertising rates meant that *RAGE* was profitable only when domestic newsstand sales matched domestic subscribers, a total monthly goal circulation of eight million. The international editions merely broke even, their continued existence a reflection of only Margot Villiers's negotiating skills and the importance of the *RAGE* brand; it was the domestic subscriptions and sales that mattered to Cooper. But it was getting harder every day to be popular, *and* ethical, *and* profitable. Their numbers had fallen short every issue of the last twenty, and so they took on more ads for fewer dollars every single month.

The editorials that Cat worked on for each issue served two purposes: to attract the advertisers on the opposing pages and, more to *her* point, to dispute them. Cat thought that fashion and beauty advertising preyed on the basest human insecurities, showing only legions of poreless, polished dolls serving as human shelves for handbags and perfume, their mouths set into dick-sucking Os and their legs splayed open, slack and lifeless. *Buy this bag*, the advertisements in *RAGE* screamed, *and you'll be someone's princess, so wealthy you don't need to eat, so successful you don't need to work.*

Those advertisements paid her salary, but they haunted her dreams, too.

She'd spent the last six years working harder than she ever had in school to ensure that the women of *RAGE's* editorial pages were aspirational in their strangeness, in their danger, in outfits that very specifically said *I am not a woman for sale*. Cat was determined that the next generation of little girls would *not* want to grow up and look like a dictator's mistress—fake tits pouring out of bandage dresses, feet shoved into bindings, literally immobilized by their roles as living, breathing decoration. She wanted them to grow up to want to look like Isabella Blow or Anna Piaggi: women who wore watermelons on their heads and carpets as skirts, women whose self-presentation was so complex that no stranger could ever presume to know what could or could not be done *to* them but only immediately consider what those women might *be doing* to the world.

Today's challenge: choosing the accessories for **Dotty for It**, the Sylvia-Plath-in-a-mental-hospital-themed spread for October shooting in three weeks. Bess had placed a tray of possibilities on her desk next to the tray for **Judy and the Technicolor Housecoat**, Margot's inspired shoot for the November issue about a bored suburban housewife who decides to eat a fistful of magic mushrooms and Scarlett O'Hara some clothes out of every god-damn upholstered object in the house.

Cat cracked open her laptop and started sorting through the **Dotty for It** tray, snapping pictures with her phone. Bess had chosen several large bangles covered in enamel polka dots; six pairs of clip-on earrings in solid gold, set with both paste and real gemstones; three silver collar necklaces that looked like chain-mail dickeys; a sterling rope with an enormous triangle that hung down to the belly button; and fifteen rings that sat above the knuckle in thin bands. Cat logged into the company's private badge board, used to organize shoots across departments, and examined the clothes Margot and Paula had approved: simple shifts with barely there net-textured polka dots from Stella McCartney; tapered cigarette pants and doctor's-coat-length felted-wool cardigans from Jil Sander; and overstarched French-striped tieback cotton dresses that looked like stiff hospital gowns from Marc Jacobs. The shoot would be on location at Scoria Vale, the venerable and picturesque rehab in Connecticut that had been treating the mental health and addictions of rich New Yorkers since the 1930s. The clothes suggested a quiet kind of mania, and Cat thought that Tilda Swinton would look amazing in all of them.

As she was adding shots of the big silver triangle necklace to the board, her desk phone rang. The caller ID read lobby security.

"Catherine Ono," she said automatically; her friends often stopped by unannounced, eager to peruse the magazine's free table, where unsolicited items lay out for the taking.

"Good afternoon, Ms. Ono," said the deep voice on the other end of the line. "There's a detective here from the NYPD. He'd like to speak with you as soon as possible. May we send him up?"

Cat was startled but didn't protest. A sinking feeling lodged in her chest as she prayed she hadn't somehow jeopardized her work visa. "Of course, absolutely," she said quickly. "I'll meet him in the lobby on 46." She hung up the phone and felt her entire body break out in a nervous sweat.

Chapter Two

After being escorted through a vertical greenhouse to the Cooper House elevator bank by two teenage mutes in navy tuxedos, Detective Mark Hutton formed the professional opinion that he might be in an elaborate theatrical production of *Gattaca*. There was no one else in the mirrored elevator—it was lit only by some kind of handwritten neon sculpture that read "Cunt Love"— yet he was sure he was being watched closely. *Seriously? Well*, he thought, *I'm watching you, too.*

Getting into the building had been easy, so far. Catherine Ono's status in the Homeland Security Database had indicated that she was likely to comply with his requests unless the company explicitly asked him to leave, but he suspected she wouldn't tell HR he was here; foreigners on work visas almost always cooperated without hesitation.

Hillary Whitney's death over two months prior, after suffering a heart attack on the forty-sixth floor of this building in a locked and windowless room, had been suspicious from the very beginning. Hutton had been at another crime scene when the body was found, but he'd been assigned to review and eventually close the case. He knew the 911 call was made at 11:30 p.m. on the fifteenth of May, a weeknight, by a hapless intern named Molly Beale. The girl reported that she'd tried to access the room much earlier in the day, found it locked, knew Hillary was inside and had been "for a while." After waiting *six hours* for a reply to her knocks and emails, Molly had finally called 911 from the office's landline.

By the time the paramedics had been waved through security and the door was knocked down, Hillary had been dead for at least eight hours, and Cooper's attorneys had swarmed the room where her body lay sprawled on the floor in an expensive-looking dress. A single bloodred fingernail was curled as if to beckon for help, and a very large box of ribbon was overturned behind her. She had no laptop or cellphone, only the stack of index cards and a felt-tip pen.

She must have begun to smell toward the end of the day, Hutton was sure of it, yet *RAGE* employees had simply gone about their business on the other side of the door, later insisting they'd been none the wiser to the grotesque scene within. As the corpse lay still, Hillary's blood had settled into the bottom half of her body, changing the left half of her ivory face into a bloated, rotten raspberry, though her green eyes remained open, looking toward the door.

Molly told the officers who handled the initial investigation that Hillary Whitney's behavior—locking herself in a windowless closet with her work and refusing to reply to any form of attempted contact—was "normal," and that the only reason Molly became concerned was because the deceased hadn't opened the door even once to go to the toilet, apparently surprising because she was on a "juice cleanse."

It had reminded Hutton of a start-up case he'd worked on a year earlier. A twenty-four-year-old man had died in a nap pod after a seventy-two-hour coding marathon for an app that was being pitched as GrubHub meets Tindog. No one had noticed the body was cold until the following day. What kinds of workplaces let employees lock themselves in closets for half-days and routinely kept interns until near midnight, so paralyzed by the fear of being fired that they wouldn't disturb their coworkers for a perceived emergency?

The only clue had been the overturned box of ribbon. Still, Hutton couldn't buy the idea that a box of thirteen yards of "luxury" ribbon would be a sufficient cause of stress to kill anyone, no matter how trivial or oppressive the workplace.

How high, honestly, could the stakes really *be at a fashion magazine?* At least in the start-up case, there was money on the table; but magazine employees made practically nothing, and in any case, she'd come from money. It had *all* seemed odd, he'd thought—right from the very beginning.

But it hadn't really mattered what he thought—not back in May. After the coroner's report, the department ruled her death a fatality by natural causes and removed the case from the investigative queue. There were several reasons for this: One, Hillary's boyfriend—the married owner of a popular cocktail bar in Carroll Gardens—was on a pickup basketball team with Detective Sergeant Peter Roth, Hutton's superior, and pressured them to stop the investigation, lest any more details emerge that might derail a reunion with his wife. Two, Hillary's next of kin, a brother in San Francisco, expressed absolutely no surprise that she'd stressed and dieted herself into a coffin, and Cooper's reputation as a stressful workplace seconded that theory. Three—and this had been the most substantial reason—in New York City, the department had bigger fish to fry, fish that flopped on the precinct's doorstep, bleeding in suspicious places, or fish weighted to the bottom of the river. The biggest fish embezzled hundreds of millions of dollars, and the angriest fish murdered their girlfriends in broad daylight at Soho House. An upper-middle-class single woman who had probably dieted herself to death was not an NYPD priority.

So back in May, Hutton had done his job as required. He reviewed the notes from the reporting officers, appended the coroner's ruling, transcribed the verbal testimony of the next of kin, and closed the case. He'd moved on, until yesterday, when a bike messenger had shoved an envelope into his hand.

Earlier that week, Rupert Whitney, Hillary's brother in San Francisco, had traveled out to the family's cabin in Idaho, closed up since the end of ski season in April. In the stack of mail he found a postcard addressed to Hillary, postmarked May 15, from the same zip code as Cooper House's offices. In Hillary's own spidery cursive, the postcard—actually a college-ruled white index card—read:

the ribbon is the key to everything

Rupert had overnighted it to Hutton, whose own business card, Hutton now realized, must have been appended to the death certificate; a phone call to Rupert had confirmed that he was officially petitioning the department to follow up. The petition consisted of a potential donation to the policemen's union that would put new, high-def televisions in every single precinct breakroom in the city, for which Hutton could take credit.

Though he had his doubts about the value of the note, the opportunity was too good to ignore. He walked directly to the nearest newsstand and opened a copy of *RAGE Fashion Book* to find a list of names under the dead woman's on the masthead. He punched those names into the precinct's Homeland Security Database and pulled the Whitney file. This was his shot to crack the case back open and solve something on his own—maybe the only chance he'd get all year. This was his chance to move up.

He took it.

When the elevator doors finally opened onto the forty-sixth floor, Hutton found himself even more disoriented. He walked into a dark room walled in faintly glowing white marble with no apparent doors and a table hanging upside down from the ceiling. He'd read about this room before; it was variously described in cultural publications as "nightmarish," "dreamlike," "a luxurious tomb," "utterly gestational," "a Fashion Week pop-up in Bergen-Belsen as imagined by Matthew Barney," and "a horrifying display of the aesthetic urges of a truly tin-eared 1%." The only available seating in this now-infamous lobby was a plain, inhospitable black wooden bench set firmly in the center of the room. Visitors new to the space— i.e., tautologically without membership in fashion's ruling class— were supposed to feel helpless, trapped, and confused. But Hutton kept calm, and after a moment, his eyes adjusted to the dim lighting and found the ghostly woman seated in front of him.

With her waist-length black hair braided into some kind of horror-film little-girl plait and a tall, angular body wrapped in black silk and leather, the woman looked like she'd been born in this room and appointed its terrible eternal guardian. She stood, uprooting herself from the hard black bench, and walked toward him, growing taller with every step. As the distance closed between them she stuck out a long, wraithlike limb with a narrow hand at the end of it.

"Hi, I'm Catherine Ono," she said. Though her voice was soft, her handshake was strong. He noticed that her fingernails were painted navy blue and had been filed into extended points, like fangs, almost. *Weird, blue finger teeth.* He cleared his throat and tried to sound businesslike.

"Detective Mark Hutton, NYPD," he said, his native New York accent peeking around the corners of his vowels. "I have some questions about Hillary Whitney. Is there somewhere we could speak privately?"

Catherine Ono looked up at him, through spiderweb-thin gold eyeglasses, with an absolutely enormous pair of brown eyes. Her skin was so pale it was nearly transparent, with some kind of dewy finish on it. She smelled like Rockaway Beach. *Does she live in a cave?* he wondered. *Is this a real human being or an elaborate joke?* He was momentarily held in an honest-to-god trance as they stared at each other. *Is this woman murderer material? Maybe*, he thought.

"We can sit in my office," she said briskly, turning those huge brown eyes to the floor. "Follow me." As she waved her phone across a brass plate set in the wall, the marble walls split open. Sunlight spilled into the lobby cave, and the spell was broken. He stood tall, lifted his shoulders, and turned to follow her, determined to regain a professional bearing.

His newfound decorum didn't last long. Her purposeful strides pulled him through a maze of dark plastic cubicles filled with a series of beautiful young women, each one more so than the last. Their eyelashes had been transplanted from dolls. Their clothes were all so delicate that if there was a gust of wind he imagined they'd all suddenly be naked. He smelled perfumes, cupcakes, steaming hot coffee. He wanted to stop at each cube and touch their glowing faces, their soft pink lips, the floating halos of their hair, see them up close. But after the first glance, Hutton kept his eyes to the ground and used all his composure to keep moving; if he wanted this woman to cooperate, he couldn't show vulnerability, not any variety, not for a moment.

Finally Catherine Ono opened a huge steel door, its surface engraved directly with "CATHERINE ONO // SENIOR EDITOR." She gestured for him to follow her through. Grateful for the end of the gauntlet, he rushed to sit in the nearest available chair.

Cat's heart was racing as she closed the door behind Detective Hutton. When he'd come out of the elevator, she'd been shocked. Cat had been expecting a barrel-chested swath of heavy blue polyester, the same type of men who came through in droves the night Hillary died. Instead, an impossibly tall, big-jawed man with brownish-blondish hair, thick glasses, and a scruffy beard stepped through the doors blinking sweetly in mild confusion. She'd taken automatic stock of his clothes: an unstructured linen-muslin sport coat, a rumpled white button-down, navy slim-fitting summer trousers over battered brown oxfords. No tie; no wedding ring. He looked like he'd just been released from an Italian library—nothing like a New York City police officer.

Now, she walked around to her own side of the desk and sat down to face him. Upon closer inspection of his nose, an oversized Roman affair, she could see a scar, and his hair had some gray in it. He was her age, maybe older, and he sat upright in his chair with his arms and legs folded up, in the awkward way tall people always seem to arrange their bodies.

He stared back at her dispassionately, with what seemed like an almost scientific curiosity, and flashed a quick smile—*more professional, detached, than anything*, she thought.

"I need just a second to get myself in order here," he said. "Do you have coffee?"

She turned to her computer and summoned coffee from Molly. Detective Hutton pulled a flip-top notebook and a felt-tip pen out of his breast pocket and turned the pages, staring intently, almost as though he was deliberately refusing to look at Cat or her surroundings, so she opened her email and pretended to read something important. Irrational panic forced her into racking her brain: *Is this really about Hillary, or something else?* Had she messed up her taxes? Missed a credit card payment? Did they send the *police* for that? She'd gotten a traffic ticket on a bicycle, but it had been paid; if that was what he was here for, she'd just write a check. *Don't freak out*, she told herself. *You're just mildly hung over. Get a grip.*

Ninety long seconds later, Molly opened the door and placed a steaming mug of French-pressed coffee in front of Hutton on a black soapstone coaster before wordlessly exiting. Cat expected him to turn his head and check out Molly's nearly exposed baby-blue rear end, but he kept his head down, flipping the pages for another agonizing minute. He seemed surprised when he looked up and saw the cup of coffee in front of him. Cat grabbed a fountain pen and a rose-colored legal pad from a pile next to her computer to keep her hands busy.

"Thank you," he said, finally taking a drink of the coffee and looking up at her. "I wanted to speak with you regarding the death of Hillary Whitney."

"Why?" Cat asked, confused.

"I wasn't here with the reporting precinct's officers when"— he paused, searching for a tasteful word—"Ms. Whitney was *found*... and I like to get my own understanding of the people involved."

"No, I mean, why now? We already did this. I spoke with the police months ago."

"We're reassessing some of our own conclusions. It's something we do from time to time."

"I don't understand," Cat said slowly. "I don't understand what that means."

"This is... not yet a formal investigation," he said, his voice even. "I'm trying to determine whether it's worth department time and resources, in a city that has over four hundred murders each year, to reinvestigate a death that was already determined to be from natural causes."

Detective Hutton used a measured cadence. His vowels betrayed an accent; *something local*, she thought, but being foreign-born herself, she couldn't quite be sure. Still, his tone was the exact opposite of every previous NYPD officer she'd spoken to: Hutton really and truly didn't act like he was trying to intimidate her. His syntax hinted at an educated upbringing, he seemed intelligent, and his *sprezzatura* clothes indicated that he wasn't just some blue-collar cop from Staten Island waiting for his twenty.

"We're simply... having a conversation," he said with an insistent, deliberate ease. "I want to know what you think."

"Why?" Cat asked again.

"You worked for her for six years. You told the reporting officers you were friends from boarding school. You came back to the office when they found her body even though it was the middle of the night. I think you care," he said. "I think you want to talk to me."

Cat paused and tried to ignore how condescending he now sounded. Unlike Bess, Cat had a hard time making other people comfortable, knowing what to say or how to say it; she'd always told herself it was a language issue, a cultural issue, and that her abrasiveness and attitude was a price her friends occasionally had to pay to be close to a woman who was at heart very bright and very thoughtful. Hillary had been the only one in Cat's life who had simply told her, flat out, what the right thing to say would be, trying to train Cat from a sharp-tongued know-it-all into someone gentler. Cat wasn't sure how honest to be with this man, and she wished desperately that Hillary were here to tell her. She elected to speak her mind.

"Why do you care *now*?" she asked, curious and outraged. "You didn't care before. Hillary died, and some guys with badges wearing too much Paco Rabanne showed up here, looked at our boobs, asked us about her eating disorder, and then told the *New York Post* she'd starved to death and sold the crime scene photos. New York's finest. It wasn't much of an investigation. And even if it *was* true, she was humiliated by the police for no reason at all."

"So you don't think that's how she died," he replied immediately, his tone encouraging her to continue.

"I was as shocked as anyone that her body was in such bad shape, but she didn't *always* look like Karen Carpenter. I mean, she was an *athlete*, she skied, she ran, she kayaked. She looked like a *socialite*, like a well-dressed fashion editor. That's *who she was*. She was *never* one of those people who talked incessantly about being vegan or gluten-free or corn-free, but she did drink a lot of juice I guess, and she did get a weekly colonic. She was thin, but here"—Cat gestured to the office around her—"it did not stand out as a capital-P *Problem*."

Hutton nodded with an understanding that read as sincere. His big eyes peered out from behind his glasses, with a little thicket of eyelashes—*like a baby deer's*, Cat thought—that brushed against the lenses when he blinked.

"Did anything about Hillary's behavior stand out as a capital-P Problem to you?" he asked.

It certainly had. Over the past year, Hillary had become obsessed with her job, with double- and triple-checking their work, insisting everything be completed well before it was due. She arrived early and stayed late, worked hard at the gym, became overly concerned about her appearance in every possible way. Cat had brushed it off as the motivational paranoia of a single, childless, thirty-seven-year-old woman in a going-nowhere relationship with a married man—the kind of fire under the ass that occasionally builds empires.

But last month, when the estate probate hearing was held, it became apparent that Hillary had owned her apartment outright, had savings in good standing, and maintained positive relationships with her friends and family. The married man turned out not to be the only beau; two or three more men had shown up at the funeral, claiming to have been casually dating her, and to have been already, instantly, *maddeningly* in love with her.

Cat picked up her phone's charge cord. She looked down at her hands and found that she'd woven part of it through her fingers into a net, a cat's cradle. Until this very moment, she hadn't admitted that the whole thing sounded *very* strange; that it *wasn't* right and that it *didn't* feel like an accident.

"She did . . . *starve*, I guess, if that's what the coroner said," Cat offered. "For six months before Hillary died, though, it seemed like she was upset about something, but she never told me what it was. And she did get super thin last year, but she died alone in a room with a box of *ribbon*, which didn't make any sense at all. And

I honestly don't believe she was *able* to starve to death. That's just crazy."

Hutton drank his coffee, put down his pen, and looked directly at her. His eye contact was steady but not invasive.

"Ms. Ono, I appreciate that you work in an environment where excessive thinness is the norm. But there is absolutely no question that Hillary Whitney suffered from a physically devastating eating disorder that badly damaged her heart. The coroner saw *years'* worth of damage to her arteries. Eating disorders don't always result in excessive thinness," he pointed out.

"Look around," Cat snapped. "This isn't a building full of bulimic teens getting rid of cookies. We're grown women whose profession is deeply vested in excessive thinness. If *that* were what Hillary wanted, she'd have been a skeleton for much longer than the last six months, and she would have done it safely, honestly, probably with surgery. I knew her for *twenty years*. I am telling you, it doesn't make sense," Cat insisted.

"I'm not the coroner," he said plainly. "I can't argue with you. I do think that the stress...is *unique* to this situation. I agree with you that *ribbon* for a"—he checked his notes—"'holiday shoot'...seems profoundly trivial, though I admit I don't completely understand how fashion magazines work. Why would that be stressful?"

"I don't *know* why. That's what I'm telling you. It *wasn't important*. We do try to satisfy a select group of major advertisers with placement in our editorials, and using background elements—like textiles or ribbons and other kinds of notions made or licensed by advertisers—tends to meet that requirement in a way that doesn't force us to change other, more major, parts of our editorial vision. But this wasn't urgent, obviously. I don't even know what the shoot was. I think it was scrapped after she died."

He was still taking notes when she stopped talking. As she waited for him to ask another question, she eyed his hair, cut short on the sides, and the shape of his neck, his broad shoulders. He looked up and caught her staring. She dropped her eyes and looked back to her computer, trying to act like she'd been looking at the screen instead of evaluating him, her cheeks burning with embarrassment.

"What's that?" Hutton lifted his head and asked, pointing at the PMS board.

"That's the Plus-Minus Sign," she said. "Cooper doesn't believe in whiteboards—because they're too 'LinkedIn,' you know what I mean?—so I painted the window."

The detective raised an eyebrow. "Aren't you going to get in trouble for that?"

"No," Cat said, looking at him like he was the dumbest man on earth. "If I wanted to wallpaper this room in vintage pornography and replace the carpeting with jet-black Astroturf, they wouldn't care, as long as we closed our issues on time. This is a *creative* workplace. Cooper is not like other companies. We don't have BlackBerries, if you get my drift. We have stock options vested after six months because if you stay that long you'll generally stay for a decade. Not many people actually make it to six months. We *are* expected to work hard. And there aren't that many staffers anyway, people like me who can paint the windows if they please—a lot of the people you see out there are permalancers."

"What's a permalancer?" Hutton asked.

"They're freelancers on an open-ended contract, and they make up over eighty-five percent of the people who work here," she said impatiently. "They are contract employees of a separate company, exactly like temps. They're not allowed to work more than thirty-five hours per week, even though they all do. On the masthead they're denoted by the word 'contributing.' It's extremely competitive to become a staff employee here. The permalancers know that and tend to work extra hard, unless they're interim, you know, *truly* temporary, and then they're usually straight nine-to-five, hour lunch, no-bullshit kind of people."

"Was Hillary a permalancer?" Hutton asked.

"No. *Of course* not," Cat said. "She was on staff here for eight, maybe nine years. It could have been longer, actually. You'd have to check with Cooper HR."

Detective Hutton straightened up in his chair. "Thanks. I'm meeting with them on my way out," he lied. "What can you tell me about her replacement?"

"Lou Lucas? She's interim. It's temporary."

"Temporary until what?"

"Until they promote *me*, I think, but Cooper would have to sponsor my green card because of all the travel involved . . . it's kind of complicated. I don't know what's going to happen."

"Don't you think they should give you the job?"

Cat sighed. "I didn't come to work for *two weeks* after Hillary died. They think I need time, which is decent and human of them, and probably accurate, and Lou . . . she's a good distraction for everybody. It's a big job, and it's a hard hire. They're right to be skeptical."

When she finished talking, it was as though someone had let the air out of Cat's body; she transformed. The silk and leather swaddling, the pointed fingernails, the horror-movie hair, the extra-sharp eye makeup—it all fell out of focus. Mark Hutton found himself staring into the face of a young woman, someone who could be one of his own friends—in *pain*. Her grief was unmistakable. It filled the room.

"How did you meet Hillary?" he asked.

"At boarding school—Miss Sawyer's School in Connecticut—when I was in seventh grade and she was in tenth. She treated me like a sister. When I moved to New York six years ago, she hired me as her assistant. Then about two years ago, Bitsy, I mean *Joan*, *Joan* Peters, who *used* to be the fashion director, decided to open her own store and so she left, and then Hillary was promoted into her job and I was promoted into Hillary's and we hired Bess, who also went to school with us."

"Did Hillary Whitney have her own office, like this one?"

"Yes. Right next door. Why?"

"Why would she lock herself in a windowless closet when she had a perfectly functioning office with a perfectly functioning door?"

"Oh." Cat laughed. "I guess that does seem weird. That's... completely normal here. When we want to just put our heads down and work—and make ourselves unavailable—we use the workrooms. That way no one can disrupt you by knocking or ringing your landline or whatever. It gives us *real* privacy, in case we need to plan something that needs total secrecy, or whatever, because there are always a billion people coming through our own offices. It's in our handbook. Hold on, let me find it."

Cat swiveled around and pulled open a filing cabinet, then rooted around until she found a lavender suede binder labeled *RFB HANDBOOK*, and turned to the page titled "Managing Your Workflow."

"May I have a copy of that?" Hutton leaned toward her to examine the pages.

Cat frowned. "I think you probably need to get that from HR," she said.

Hutton leaned back and nodded. "Cooper has not been particularly helpful."

"They wouldn't be," she agreed. "I should probably stop there, I guess." She tried not to sound strained. "Not that it matters."

"You don't think it matters?"

"I think the damage is done." Cat sighed. "Hillary's death was undignified and humiliating. I guess emotionally, I do appreciate being able to complain about it to your face, but I know you won't actually *do* anything."

"Why won't I?" He looked puzzled, but not insulted.

"It's not personal," she said apologetically. "I'm sure you're a great detective. But I know this isn't a priority. The other cops told me that two months ago."

He looked at her, his mouth unmoving, holding his pen. A *gaze*, that's what it was. He was *gazing* at her. Abruptly he dropped his eyes. *Well*, she thought, realizing she felt disappointed, *that didn't last long*.

"I'll be in touch." Hutton stood up and tucked his pen in his pocket.

Cat grabbed a business card out of the drawer and wrote her cellphone number on the back.

"Here's my number, if you need it."

He took the card, nodded, and handed her one of his own before turning toward the door. Cat got up to follow him out. Right before he reached the handle, he turned around.

They were less than eight inches apart. He smelled like something clean and sharp—grass, maybe. *Does he smell like cut grass?*

"For what it's worth, I'm sorry for your loss," he said with genuine compassion.

Cat's mouth dropped open with surprise. She meant to say "Thank you," but she couldn't get anything out. Her heartbeat sped up, a deafening wave of sound cycled through her eardrums, and her mouth fell open, but she said nothing. Seconds passed while they stared at each other in silence.

And then Molly knocked.

Hutton opened the door. Before Cat could compose herself, he'd already walked out the door and closed it behind him.

Bess was finishing up for the day. She had cataloged 184 bracelets—not too shabby—and tonight she was going to dinner with her friends. Lou had already left to pick up her daughters from school, and Molly was trapped on a long-distance phone call with a factory in Shanghai, tracking down electric-blue slub silk made from an ultramarine dye that had to be buried underground for months to reach its pigment potential. Bess grabbed her helmet, unplugged her phone, and walked over to Cat's office.

"You ready?"

After a beat, Cat looked away from her laptop and nodded.

"Yes. Okay. I'm doing it. Closing computer." She closed her laptop and grabbed her bag.

"I'm dying to know," said Bess as Cat closed her door and they walked in the direction of the elevators. "Who was that guy? He looked *really* familiar, but I honestly couldn't place him. Is he from Barneys?"

"No. I'll tell you later," Cat whispered as they passed a gaggle of permalancers. "Are you going to take the train with me?"

Bess shook her head. "Bike. I need the exercise."

They stepped into the elevator and chatted idly about the bracelets Bess had been working on that day. Cat seemed closed off and distracted when she got off on the main floor.

"See you at Sigrid's in a bit," said Bess.

"Yeah…see you there," Cat mumbled quietly as she walked away.

Bess set off down Thirty-Ninth Street before turning south, riding all the way to Canal where she hung another left and pumped her way up and over the Manhattan Bridge, all the while dodging the city's crazy traffic, occasionally smacking the hood of a taxicab with the bottom of her fist.

Once she hit Grand Army Plaza, she let out the tension she was holding in her shoulders and turned off into the park to cruise downhill, riding countercurrent over to Lincoln Road. There were no cars allowed in the park during this time of day. The summer evening was hot, its steamy air settling around her like a duvet, but Bess didn't mind: she was, as always, just happy to be moving forward. *What was up with Cat?* She was *dying* to find out about the handsome—and vaguely familiar—stranger who had sat in Cat's office for almost an hour. Both women consciously tried not to get too personal at the office. They didn't want to look unprofessional, or inadvertently share too much of their lives with their colleagues; Cooper was simply too competitive of an environment to take the risk.

Bess turned down Ocean and coasted for two blocks until she reached Sigrid's five-story limestone, walking her bike inside the familiar gate at 170 Ocean Avenue and locking it to the fence with a heavy Kryptonite chain before bounding up the steps. She rang the bell, a round, filigreed pewter button, and waited.

Until about two years ago the neighborhood had been genuinely terrible. The surrounding blocks were littered with mansions whose once open-air porches were all bricked in, first to protect from the seventies riots, then for the eighties riots, and, finally, the nineties riots. The eastern section of Prospect Park that the Gunderson family town house overlooked had been riddled with crime for years. But like the rest of Brooklyn, the neighborhood had changed, importing young, self-consciously hip, mostly white professionals seemingly overnight, shipped in from Ohio or Minnesota or Colorado via Sarah Lawrence or Colgate or Swarthmore. The B and Q trains were now fully stocked with WNYC tote bags and Warby Parker eyeglasses, and the prewar apartment inventory, always gorgeous, had been renovated by eagle-eyed landlords. Something was in the air, and this neighborhood felt safe, even if the police blotter said otherwise.

Sigrid answered the door in her usual attire: a white silk tank tucked into black high-waisted cigarette pants and little red pull-on sneakers from France. A joint was balanced between her clean, bare fingernails; her only makeup was a large swoop of black liquid liner. The four dots tattooed across the cheekbone under her left eye moved up in a half-moon when she smiled. Her brown hair was tied back and teased at the crown in a fifties' ponytail. Sigrid's toothy grin was the friendliest thing Bess knew.

"Bessie, helloooo, you're here!" she trilled, gracefully exhaling pot smoke out the door as Bess stepped through it.

In the tenth grade, while Sigrid was boarding at Sawyer's, her

musician parents and two younger sisters had died in a train accident on the Hudson Line. There were no survivors, and Sigrid
Gunderson was left all alone in a matter of moments.

A friend of the family, a painter named Matt Keyes, was named
as her legal guardian. Matt gave up his rent-controlled studio in
SoHo and moved into the downstairs garden-level apartment and
watch over Sigrid. The mortgage had been paid off—and then
some—by the Gundersons' life insurance policies and a settlement
from Metro North, leaving Sigrid with money left over to cover
Sawyer's, college, and maybe graduate school someday, but she
wasn't rich by New York standards. Some would have sold the
house during the insane highs that the real-estate market brought,
even to this part of Brooklyn, but Sigrid was a city girl with
nowhere else to go. She knew what this house could be: it could
give her a life if she put some life back into it. The house had become Sigrid's livelihood and lifelong project.

Throughout the remaining summers of high school and college,
Sigrid finished the renovations her parents had started in 1990
when they'd first bought the giant town house. Matt remained in
the basement to watch over her and her friends. Hillary had been
Sigrid's Big—the older girl responsible for mentoring her, a Sawyer
tradition over a hundred years old—and she'd moved in after graduating from college, helping Sigrid to figure out right away how to
turn the place into a boardinghouse for Sawyer girls. They worked
on different rooms between waitressing shifts and acting auditions
and Hillary's job at *RAGE*, repairing floorboards and sourcing antique fixtures, and slowly the house had become perfect.

Bess, in turn, had been Sigrid's Little, and by the time she graduated, moving into Sigrid's was a path already forged by a dozen
girls before her, a tangled litter of Bigs and Littles making their way
together until one by one, they struck out on their own. Bess had
lived here for five years, until her family had given her a brownstone apartment.

She pulled a metal stool up to the breakfast bar at the back of the kitchen. Sigrid handed her the joint and they took deep drags, cranking open the leaded multipaned window and exhaling out into the summer air, chatting about everything and nothing at all. Sigrid, an actress, had recently finished filming an indie movie on the North Shore of Long Island she was sure no one would ever see; her tenants were a whole new crop of recent Sawyer girls, fresh out of college. Bess's latest housemate at her brownstone in the West Village was doing a *lot* of coke and wearing a *lot* of unfortunate outfits when she showed up to work three hours late. They laughed over her 5:00 a.m. tweets reading "I love tacos." They admired each other's jewelry. They finished the *NYT* crossword and eventually stubbed out the joint.

The sound of a key turning in the lock finally interrupted their reverie, and Cat walked in with an enormous, clownlike scowl on her face.

Chapter Three

"The subway could not be more disgusting," Cat complained as she tromped through the parlor. "The train took forever, the AC was broken in my car, the guy sitting next to me threw his chicken bones on the floor, and at the DeKalb stop *a rat actually got on the train*, picked up one of the bones, then exited at Atlantic—presumably to share his bounty with whatever rat king is balled up underneath the platform. Also, I stopped at Whole Foods."

"I got here almost an hour ago," Bess pointed out.

"I would've CitiBiked, but I was *so* hung over today," she said, shifting from scowl to grimace to smile as she turned to Sigrid. "Sig! What's *up*!!"

The women hugged and tumbled back into the kitchen. Sigrid pulled some extra-large mason jars down from a shelf, filled them with ice and halfway with vodka, and sliced a cucumber. As she pulled a bottle of rosemary-infused seltzer out of the refrigerator, Bess turned on the stove and Cat pulled two raw organic chickens out of her Whole Foods tote. Once a month since they'd moved out of Sigrid's house, the friends returned to drink vodka and roast chickens in the oversized Gunderson Dutch oven. Bess chopped and crushed herbs for the butter, Cat rinsed and patted the chickens dry, and Sigrid mixed the drinks. It was a routine that brought them back to the easy years of their mid-twenties, when Bess had just graduated and was working at *Filly*, Cat was an assistant editor at *RAGE*, Sigrid had been in the corps of a cheesy Broadway show, and Hillary had been joyfully shopping for apartments in the wild west of the postcrash market.

Sigrid raised her drink. "To vodka," she began, a familiar toast.

"To chicken," Cat continued.

"To friendship!" they said together, clinking their jars.

Cat pulled out her cigarettes and seated herself next to the window. "Okay, so, today's story, and I know Bess is dying for me to get into this: a hot, and I mean *so, so hot*, guy came into my office today."

"And?" Bess asked.

Cat lit a cigarette. "He's a police detective who's looking into Hillary's death."

Sigrid, shoving pats of herbed butter underneath the skin of the chickens, stopped short with her hand halfway up one of the birds. "What?" she asked.

Bess looked horrified. "*Seriously?*"

"Yeah," Cat said. "I know. It's crazy."

"*Why?*"

"He wouldn't say. He said it wasn't official—he just wanted to know what I thought."

"I bet *you* held back," Sigrid said sarcastically.

"I wasn't a *huge* asshole, actually," Cat said. "I merely pointed out that they didn't *have* to call the newspapers or sell the pictures of her dead body. Her life didn't have to end in ridicule."

"What did he tell you?"

"Not much. I felt so upset about it all day, so unsettled, but on the way here, I just thought, *You know what, this is what happens*. People die and there's a million details to handle. It never ends. And I'm so sick of being sad."

"I'm sick of being sad, too," Sigrid admitted. "Hillary wasn't a sad person."

Bess sighed. "I know."

"At first I had this totally irrational childish principal's-office panic, that he was going to arrest me for that bike ticket and throw me in jail and I'd get fired and my life would be over," Cat admitted, "and then I had a whole series of terrible thoughts about Hillary, like oh my god, what if someone *killed* her? And we live in a *horror movie*? And then I thought, *That's ridiculous*. It's the same pantomime police bullshit they pulled before. It's more pointless paperwork. They never actually *do* anything."

"I paid the tickets on Friday," Bess said. "It's all taken care of."

"Why are you paying Cat's bike ticket?" Sigrid asked.

"Because I insisted it was fine for her to learn to bike on the sidewalk, and I was wrong," Bess explained. "Annnnd...I kind of already owed her fifty bucks."

Cat nodded.

"Okay, whatever," Sigrid said, waving her hands. "But how exactly did the cop get into your office?"

Cat lit a cigarette, rearranging her body in a storytelling perch. "He walked into Cooper, no appointment," she said approvingly, "flashed his badge at security, and asked for me. He asked how I knew her, what our history was, and why she was so stressed out over a box of ribbon...obviously, the million-dollar question. I said she'd been acting weird for five or six months and that, you know, I didn't know, I didn't get it," Cat said. "His questions were basically the same as the cops' before, and I gave him my number, and he gave me his card. Honestly, he was...nice and easy to talk to."

"You mean he's *hot*," Bess pointed out. "Wedding ring?" Cat shook her head.

"Let me see his card!" Sigrid demanded. Cat dug it out of her bag, and Sigrid immediately typed his name into her phone. "Okay, Mark Hutton...is...an insurance salesman's name. I assume he's not this doughy guy in a crewneck. Detective Mark Hutton NYPD gives us...nothing. There's an NYPD listing with his name, but...there's no photo. Huh." She switched the phone over to image search and flipped the screen to face Cat. "Is he any of these guys?"

Cat scanned the thumbnails. "No...no...no."

"He's a million feet tall," said Bess, "and I think he was wearing all Rag & Bone."

"When a man's outfit is composed of a single brand, he's either divorced or gay, right?" Cat asked.

Bess and Sigrid both shrugged before nodding their assent.

"He's probably divorced. But he could also be lazy and have female friends," Bess offered. "And he's *definitely* attracted to women," she insisted. "He was blushing when he walked out of your office. The man couldn't look at any of the women on the floor, he was so mortified. It was like seeing a teenage boy in a women's locker room. He just looked so...shocked." All three women cackled with delight. It was refreshing to think of a heterosexual man who didn't automatically view a crop of young professional women as a desperate geisha buffet there for the taking.

Cat sighed. "I mean, whatever, I'll probably never see him again. What's tomorrow, Tuesday? Is it weird to ask him out? Should I wait until Thursday?"

Sigrid's face clouded over as she slid the chicken into the oven. "I keep thinking on Thursdays that I have to meet Hillary for a drink on Twenty-First Street." On Thursday nights in Chelsea, rivers of free wine flowed gently from most major galleries, and Hillary had loved to trip from bottle to bottle, canvas to canvas, cheek to cheek.

"I know what you mean," said Bess. "We keep having weird moments at work where we realize before we make a decision that we're waiting for her input instead of just moving forward. I feel bad for Lou. We don't really *need* anything from her, you know? She's just kind of doing her 'small bones, hearty breeding, expensive upholstery' thing on two or three pages per issue."

"Are people still talking about it?" Sigrid asked.

"Kind of," Cat replied. "The workroom where she died was totally redone, new carpet, new paint, new furniture. No one really talks about it to us, although I've definitely heard some 'don't stress or you'll die' kinds of jokes. In theory we have to hire someone new once Lou's contract is up in December. But I'm pretty sure they'll promote me." She smiled at Bess, an expression both sad and proud. "Then I can promote you."

Bess gave her the same sad, proud smile back.

Sigrid yelped and hopped up. "I almost forgot. I found a handbag of Hillary's! She left it here after that dinner party we had in April. Anyway, when I emailed her about it she said there were 'just cigarettes in it' since 'we'd done all the cocaine.' And she'd get it next time."

All three women looked briefly heartsick.

"But...I didn't check inside," Sigrid continued. "So make more drinks and I'll get it!" she yelled, walking backward through the hall before bounding up the staircase.

Cat and Bess doubled the vodka. Sigrid returned with a diminutive black Perspex cube dangling from a solid-gold handcuff strap. "I cannot believe she left this here. It is so *b-a-double-d*."

"Me-ow," said Cat. Bess purred. They both reached for the bag. Cat snatched it first and popped it open.

"Well, Hillary was definitely wrong about the cigarettes and cocaine," she said. "There's cocaine and something else, but no cigarettes." Cat pulled out a small brown glass bottle, half-full of cocaine, and a clear plastic bottle with a handwritten label reading only "Bedford Organics."

Sigrid pounced on the cocaine. "I'm hiding this from the ducklings," she announced, referring to her tenants, as she popped open a plastic bottle labeled "Glucosamine" and buried it inside. "I have never seen *anyone* open this. I think they're dog vitamins. Don't forget where I hid it."

Cat, meanwhile, was examining the bottle and smelling its eyedropper. "I wonder what this is...maybe it's MDMA?"

Bess laughed. "Don't test that. We have to go to work tomorrow."

Sigrid was already typing <u>Bedford Organics</u> into her phone. "This is an actual company. They make some kind of organic skincare bullshit in Williamsburg. But I don't see anything in this shape and size . . . maybe it's custom?"

"Probably, but . . . does it make sense to bring cocaine, cigarettes, and face oil to a party?" asked Cat.

"Yes!" Sigrid said. All three girls laughed.

Cat grabbed a saucer and squeezed out some drops to examine them. "It doesn't smell like anything. It doesn't look like oil, either. Should I lick it?"

"It'll probably taste disgusting, but yeah, I dare you," challenged Bess. Cat pinched her nose, pulled out the dropper, and dramatically lowered a drop onto her tongue. She suddenly tasted a sharp, clean numbness, followed by an intensely bitter aftertaste.

"Guys, this is *definitely* drugs." But by the time Cat was done with her sentence, the slight numbness had already vanished. "It doesn't seem to be very strong. I estimate . . . one cocaine per drop."

"Catlock Holmes, on the case," Sigrid cracked. "By 'one cocaine' do you mean *one dust speck* of cocaine?"

"Yeah. A particle. There's something else in it, too, something bitter. It's gross. I don't think it's for eating. Maybe it really is a skin oil. I bet there's some process whereby the cocaine acts—"

"Like capsaicin?" asked Bess.

"Exactly!" responded Cat.

Sigrid looked at them quizzically.

"Capsaicin comes from chili peppers. It's included in skin creams and ointments meant to relieve muscle pain, arthritis, stuff like that. The burning sensation overwhelms the nerves and temporarily blocks them from feeling pain," Bess explained. "Maybe you can use cocaine in the same way."

Sigrid was nodding. "Okay, but . . . what was *wrong* with Hillary?"

"Neck pain?" Cat proffered. "Eye twitch?"

"Teeth grinding?" posed Bess.

"It has to be something small, because this bottle is small. I like teeth grinding and eye twitch; maybe . . . ear infection?" Sigrid's face rose with excitement. "Who wants to take it on the gums? Either of you have a toothache?"

"I don't taste anything," said Bess after placing a drop in her mouth. "It's just bitter. Also I veto ear infection. She'd get Cipro."

"You don't taste anything because you only smoke pot, Bess. You don't have the vocabulary for it. Let me try." Sigrid motioned for the bottle and dropped some on her own tongue. "Oh . . . that's really subtle. It's kind of sharp, then bitter, then nothing. *Weird*."

"Why don't we just Photogram them and ask what it is?" asked Cat. "I don't really want to put this inside my ears or my eyes. At least now that I know I can't really get high from it, anyway. Use Bess's account, though."

Sigrid moved the bottle into a clean spot on the counter so Bess could snap a photo; in no less than thirty seconds, they'd sent it from @loch_ness_bess and @ragebeauty with the caption:

@bedford_organics: found in our beauty ed's pile of magic ointments.
label long gone—what's inside? #RAGEdetectives

"I love it when you can't google something," said Sigrid with glee. She drained her mason jar and raised the vodka bottle. Cat and Bess nodded and slid their glasses toward her.

Before she had a chance to pour another round, they heard a key turning clumsily in the lock. After a brief struggle, three of Sigrid's tenants reeled through the doorway singing "Hakuna Matata."

Birdie, Helen, and Lottie were hammered. Birdie's poppy-tinted lipstick was smeared all over Lottie's face; Helen's unlit cigarette hung from her mouth and white paper flowers dangled haphazardly from her afro.

"*Please* tell us there's chicken," roared Lottie, her arms wrapped around Birdie's waist. "I'll *die* if I missed it."

"Yeah," chimed Birdie. "If there's no chicken left, I'm going to cut your fucking throat." She made a throat-slitting motion. All three girls started giggling and laughed themselves onto the floor.

"Birdie's been saying that all night," said Helen, delight plastered in her eyes as she wheezed with laughter. "She threatened to cut the throats of two bankers, grabbed one of their crotches like he was a bag of dough, and then he sent us home with his driver. In a Bentley!"

Looking at the three bombed and boisterous tenants, Sigrid, Cat, and Bess felt like elder stateswomen.

"You're in luck, you monsters. It's almost done; we haven't had a bite," said Sigrid. "Wash your faces, change your clothes, and drink water; then you can have dinner."

Helen wobbled over to the staircase, hiked up her silvery, cocoon-like silk dress, and began to undo the oversized straps on her block-soled jelly sandals. "I'm totally cool," she insisted.

Sigrid raised her eyebrows and pointed to the tangle of Birdie and Lottie, who were still slumped on the floor in hysterics. Birdie's legs poked skyward out of her coral Bermuda shorts; no one made a move to help her get up. Helen looked momentarily sheepish.

"It was just one of those nights, you know?" Helen said. "Everything was free." She yawned and stretched out, lying across the width of the staircase with her legs propped up against the wall. "We just need to have some water."

"Everything is *always* free," said Sigrid as Helen threw her sandals in the general direction of the hallway. "You have that distinct aura of youth. Men just *look* at you and they feel a vagina tightening around their penises like a phantom limb."

Bess's phone buzzed. "Hey, they 'grammed back."

@loch_ness_bess @ragebeauty looks like a custom blend, bring in for exam and we can tell u more. happy 2 help w #beautymystery for #RAGEdetectives

Birdie poked her head out from under Lottie. "What's the hash-tag mystery? *I'm* hashtag mysterious. Put *me* on the case."

Bess grinned. "The hashtag mystery is that we found a purse of Hillary's—"

"That *I'm* keeping," Cat interrupted before the terrible trio could get their hopes up.

"Cat is *trading* me for it," retorted Bess, "but that's not the point. It had this small bottle of drops in it from Bedford Organics and we Photogrammed them to find out what it is, but they didn't know from the picture."

Helen looked around for the bottle. "Is it small and clear and plastic?"

"Yes!" they rang out in reply. "What is it?" asked Bess.

"Eyedrops. Hillary was using them to make her eyes bigger or something. She said they made her look all manga." Helen was tri-umphant.

The oven timer beeped. "Chicken!!" shouted everyone at once.

"We still have to set the table and it needs to rest out of the oven. Girls, go get cleaned up, okay?" Sigrid, ever the den mother, was helping Birdie and Lottie up and pushing them toward the stairs.

The three girls bounded up the steps in cheerful thumps and bumps as they scattered to their rooms. Sigrid, Cat, and Bess looked at one another with knowing grins. Once upon a time, they, too, had stumbled through 170 Ocean's heavy wooden front door after parties, singing off-key and haphazardly shedding their clothes, Matt Keyes hitting the basement ceiling with a broom to acknowledge their arrival home.

"Should we text Matt, too?" asked Bess.

"I already did," Sigrid said. "He'll be up in fifteen minutes or so."

Cat and Sigrid finished the sides of carrots, potatoes, and a huge French-style warm salad, while Bess set the grand rose-wood dining table off the kitchen. Just as she was about to light some scattered votive candles, she heard the front door open, and a wry voice rang out.

"Hello, girls," Matt called as he locked the door behind him and walked through the dining room doorway. His downy white hair poked out of his head in ten different directions; his tan skin and boiler suit were spattered with paint. But he looked, as always, like the happiest person in the world.

"Bless this mess," he said jovially, gesturing to the table and setting down a bottle of Cabernet. "I brought some vino."

Cat and Sigrid popped in and hugged Matt simultaneously. Bess had a final moment of inspiration; she pulled the white ribbon out of Cat's braid ("Hey!" Cat cried) and tied it around a vase of hydrangeas into a textbook bow, worthy of any puppy.

"Bow classic," she said with a sigh. "The table is ready! Let's eat!"

Just after midnight, Detective Mark Hutton sat in his vintage Volvo, the door of the limestone at 170 Ocean fully visible through his rearview mirror, waiting for Cat to reemerge.

He hadn't *meant* to stake her out. After visiting Cooper, he'd headed back to the precinct to compare the original Whitney file with his notes. There were no factual discrepancies: everything Catherine Ono said matched what she'd said two months prior. The background checks on the women who Hillary Whitney had reported to—Paula Booth, Constance Onderveet, and Margot Villiers—had come up clean, and so had the checks on other staff members, Elizabeth Bonner, intern Molly Beale, and, finally, Whig Beaton Molton-Mauve Lucas, the interim fashion director. Catherine Ono had been open, accurate, and consistent; he had absolutely no reason to continue pursuing her, though he found himself replaying the afternoon out loud at his desk, repeating the things he'd already said to her, like a lunatic, while he chewed through an entire bag of sunflower seeds and tried to resist googling her.

All afternoon he'd gone through the other paperwork, including Hillary Whitney's credit report, most recent credit card statement, and phone records. Nothing stood out, but he shoved them in his briefcase anyway when he left the office at 5:00 p.m.

From there, Hutton went straight to the police gym, ran eight miles on the treadmill, doubled his ordinary weight-lifting circuit, and sat in the sauna for a while. After a postworkout beer in the Irish bar across the street, chatting idly with the other officers, none of whom he knew very well, he boarded the subway for home.

The train had been a mess. The air-conditioning was broken in the first car he boarded, so he changed cars at Twenty-Third Street, though pressing up against the glass at the end of the car wasn't exactly comfortable. At Union Square he saw a tall woman with black hair and black clothes board the same train through the car's filthy window, holding a large reusable shopping bag, her purse slung over her shoulder, reading a paperback as she leaned against one of the doors. When she reached an arm up to pull a section of hair away from her face, he realized it was Catherine Ono, and he felt suddenly self-conscious, though she didn't look in his direction once. Sweat dripped down her brow in the hot car; commotion ensued at DeKalb when a rat got on the train. Though she glanced briefly at the rat with disdain, she kept her eyes on her book, and Hutton kept his eyes on her.

She got off at Lincoln Road.

He got out, too, following her at a deliberate distance as she exited right, then turned left at the corner. He crossed to the other side of Ocean, ducking behind the park's stone barrier when she climbed the steps of a large and immaculate limestone, gold paint over the door reading 170 Ocean Avenue. She disappeared inside using her own key.

He sat on the first bench he found, only a block or so from his own apartment building at 60 Ocean; in fact, his car was just a few feet away. He *knew* this house, even though he'd been in the neighborhood only two months. *Everyone* knew this house. There seemed to be an effervescent fountain of youth within, hiccupping out an unending stream of stylish women onto Ocean Avenue every morning. It was noticeable even from within the running trails in the park, which was where he'd first spied what the barista at the nearby coffee shop called the "Honey Pot."

Hutton smiled to himself. *Of* course *she is connected to the Honey Pot.* He briefly wondered how many other men had sat on this exact park bench, watching that exact door, then considered his options. It was after eight and she'd had a Whole Foods bag: probably dinner. There was time. He walked to the Lefferts Tavern, ordering a plate of enchiladas and sipping a Lagunitas as he leafed back through the Whitney file.

Hillary's credit report listed only one previous address where she had resided from 2002 to 2011: 170 Ocean Avenue, the building Cat had just walked into. No apartment number, just the building. He pulled out his phone and searched the address. Google identified the last recorded sale in 1990 for $92K. *It must be worth millions now*, he thought.

RAGE had certainly been an aesthetically overwhelming environment, but the employees seemed productive and rational. Catherine Ono had left work at a normal-ish hour that evening, clearly had a social life, and appeared to be in good health, if a little pale. Cooper's tense environment wasn't a good enough explanation for Hillary Whitney's stress-induced heart attack, not to mention the postcard with a cryptic note sent the same day she died. There had to be something he was missing.

He finished his enchiladas, dropped a twenty on the table, and walked back out to the park, keeping his distance from the sidewalk as three women lurched out of a Bentley limousine that had pulled up in front of 170 Ocean. After a few tries they managed to unlock the front door. He sat down on a bench, slightly farther away than his previous perch, and waited. Later a thin, white-haired man emerged from the basement apartment holding a bottle of wine. He, too, unlocked the large front door with his own key. Multiple tenants of the same gender and age range on the upper floor in what appeared to be a single unit; an elderly man in a lower unit. It wasn't unusual to see so many people occupying the same space, not in New York, not now; but for women like Catherine Ono and Hillary Whitney to live all the way out here, in this house on the bad side of the park, as long ago as 2002, though they likely had the money to live elsewhere . . . he didn't understand, which meant there had to be something he was missing. Hutton considered his options. Realistically, what could be resolved by camping out here? He took out his notebook and jotted down *170 Ocean, no sale since 1990? (confirm rec.), keys owned by Catherine Ono, girl with afro, white-haired man in basement. known as honey pot, ask around, H.W. resident 02–11.*

Hutton pulled out a pack of Camels and lit one, taking a long drag. *What would Catherine do next?* Take a car service home, probably—he couldn't think of an easy subway route to Bushwick from here. He *could* contrive to run into her on the street, but it was probably already too late and too dark for that to work. There was no reasonable explanation for him to be on that part of the block; his apartment was in the other direction from the subway. Scaring her wouldn't help.

Hutton already had more information than he'd had three hours ago. *Time to give up.* He walked home, nodded to the doorman, and took the elevator up to his apartment. After flicking on the light switch in the foyer, he threaded his way through the half-empty-box maze left behind by his apathetic, single-serving attempt at unpacking, and settled down on the living room sofa, an extra-long sectional he'd picked blindly out of a catalog after determining it was long enough to sleep on and dark enough to spill beer on.

Hutton opened his laptop and loaded an old episode from season three of *The X-Files*, content to fall asleep there. He didn't care whether he slept in his bed, on the sofa, or upright in a chair; it was all the same to him.

But two episodes later he was still awake. He reached for his gym bag to pull on his running shorts and shoes before taking a whiff of his rancid T-shirt. The smell was perverse, unwearable. He balled it up and threw it in the corner.

Hutton told himself that he'd just hit the park loop once and then go to sleep. But after a mere five hundred feet of jogging, he saw that the parlor lights at 170 Ocean were still on, shadows crossing and filtering weakly through the frail wooden shutters.

The house beckoned.

His Volvo parked across the street, Hutton couldn't stop himself. He walked to the car, opened the door, adjusted his rearview mirror, and waited.

When the door of 170 Ocean opened at twelve thirty, he was bent across the seats pretending to rifle through his glove box, one long, muscular leg half out of the car. He retrieved a sheet of paper before stepping out and locking the door, then turned around to find five wide-eyed women staring at him from the stoop.

When the plates had finally migrated to the dishwasher, and Matt had long since returned to his garden-level studio, Cat checked the time.

"Does anyone want to have a cigarette on the stoop? I should call a car," she'd asked the group.

"I'm too tired," said Lottie, "but you guys go ahead. I'll see you later." She draped her body over Cat and Bess in a kind of hug, then wearily climbed the stairs.

When the women of 170 Ocean opened the front door, the old Volvo sedan across the street contained a very tall, mostly naked man. Clad in running shoes and shorts, he appeared to be rooting around in his glove compartment.

The women leered in unison at his back muscles, dramatically shadowed by the Volvo's weak interior lighting. One of his long legs stretched into the street—a smooth, perfectly shaped calf, twitching as he stretched farther across the car. His shorts rode up to expose the bottom half of his left butt cheek.

When the mystery exhibitionist closed up his car and turned around, Cat recognized him immediately. He started to cross to their side of the road, then looked up—just in time to catch the women staring with their mouths open. Startled, he stopped in the street, like an animal caught in the headlights of a moving bus.

"Ohmigod. Hot cop. It's the hot cop," Cat muttered quickly under her breath.

Helen had already seized the moment. "Nice night for a run," she called out before whispering, "What?" to Cat.

He walked closer, hopping onto the sidewalk in front of the stoop.

"Not bad," he said, flashing a smile at Helen, his teeth large and white. Cat didn't bother explaining. His eyes scanned the group before settling on Cat.

"Detective Hutton," she said. "Hi, it's me, Cat from *RAGE*."

His eyes widened. "Uh...Hi," he said a bit awkwardly. "I thought you lived in Bushwick."

All five women took note: *He knows where she lives.*

"I do. Dinner party," Cat said, gesturing to her friends. "We're wrapping up...but to my credit, *I'm* still fully clothed after midnight, and you're down to just running shorts."

"Not that there's anything wrong with that," said Helen in an exaggerated aside.

Hutton's smile came back. "I couldn't sleep," he said deliberately, looking only at Cat. "I went running to burn off the energy, and I had to grab something out of my car...I live down the block, actually."

"On Ocean?" Sigrid jumped in, unable to stop herself. "Do you live in the jazz dorms?" The building adjacent to the above-ground subway stop, 100 Ocean, was famous for the never-ending rotation of recent jazz school graduates who lived there, swapping

Berklee, UNT, and the New England Conservatory dorms for crumbling prewar studios where—thanks to the ambient noise from the train—they could play all night.

"No, but is that what you call the building next to the train? That's funny. No, I'm at 60 Ocean."

"Oh!" Sigrid looked shocked. "Are you subletting?"

"No, it's a family property," he said. "I only moved in two months ago."

"Oh. Okay, nice to meet you. I'm Sigrid Gunderson. This is my house," she said and pointed behind her. "I know everyone on Ocean, that's why I asked. I *love* that building. The units never go on the market, though." Sigrid could talk neighborhood real estate for hours. "I've been in a few of the apartments and they're all period prewar, original medallions in the ceiling, everything. Someone told me last year that both units on the sixth floor are still classic eights."

"They are. I'm on 6. Uh...do you guys want to see it?" he asked. In a different real-estate climate, this would have been an odd question coming from a shirtless man standing on the sidewalk in the middle of the night.

"Absolutely," Sigrid said as her face lit up. Birdie, Helen, and Bess were all bobbing their heads enthusiastically.

Cat froze. "*Now??*" she asked. "You don't want to have us over now..."

Hutton gestured at his body. "You've already seen it all," he joked. "I'm halfway through a renovation, but there's a full bar," he said roguishly, flirting with all five women at the same time. It was inappropriate, appallingly blatant, and it made Cat laugh.

"Okay," she said. "We'll come over to your apartment in the middle of the night, but only because I have your badge number, *Officer.*" Her emphasis on the last word was aimed at Birdie and Helen, who squealed and saluted.

"*Officer!!* We're Birdie and Helen, and that's Bess," they chimed in an untidy, alcohol-warmed unison, descending the stoop and sticking out their hands. He leaned up a step and gave all four women firm handshakes.

"I'm Mark Hutton," he said, "and yes, I'm in the NYPD. I met your friend Catherine today."

"We're just going to grab our things," said Sigrid. "We'll be right back out. Don't go *anywhere*."

Bess gave Cat a suggestive wink before filing back inside with Sigrid, Birdie, and Helen. Hutton climbed the stoop halfway and sat down; Cat folded herself down a step or two above him.

She looked down at his body and was unable to stop herself from ogling his suntanned skin, the tiny hairs running down his neck, the line where his shorts banded over his stomach muscles. The tattoo on his arm was a topographical map of something she didn't recognize. He wasn't very sweaty. He still smelled clean and sharp. *I bet he's one of those people who exercise for fun*, she thought, before realizing she was still holding her cigarette. She lit it, smoking almost unconsciously.

Hutton reached up and grabbed her hand. Her heart stopped.

He ran his fingers over hers and slid the cigarette into his own, then pulled his hand away, took a long drag, and held it up for her to take back.

The heat, heavy and still, suspended a thin ribbon of smoke between them. His fingers were long and *dexterous*-looking. She felt a sudden urge to put them in her mouth.

Instead she took the cigarette back and said—more aggressively than she meant to—"A runner who smokes?"

"I run so I can smoke," he replied. "I run so I can drink, so I can eat meat, so I can sit still and be lazy. It's my sole concession to health. What's your excuse?" Hutton, too, sounded sharper than he meant to.

"I'm completely, helplessly addicted," Cat said slowly, looking right into his eyes.

The front door opened behind them. Helen swooped down to grab the cigarette out of Cat's hand before dancing down the steps.

Birdie and Sigrid followed, each carrying a bottle of red wine. Bess walked out with her helmet strapped on; she reached down and hugged Cat while Sigrid locked the door.

"I have so much to do tomorrow. Love you, but I have to go home." Bess unlocked her bike and rolled it out to the street.

"Are you okay to bike?" asked Hutton, his voice stern.

"I'm good. Watch." With her helmet still on, Bess cartwheeled into a handstand and held steady.

Hutton gave her a nod of approval. She climbed onto her bicycle and pedaled away toward the Manhattan Bridge, while Sigrid, Birdie, Cat, and Helen followed Hutton up the street.

Chapter Four

Cat stood on the escalator promptly at 9:00 a.m. She'd been awake since six, when the sound of her building's fire alarm ripped her awake from the obscene dreams she'd been enjoying. After shuffling outside with the rest of the tenants while wearing an old pair of shorts that said "only $5 we write anything you want" on the butt and a heavily ink-stained men's flannel shirt for what turned out to be a false alarm, she was unable to go back to sleep.

She'd had a coffee before dressing carefully, trying to forget about the night before, to focus on her day, grateful for the chance to get to work early. Cat desperately needed to prep for the weekly editorial meeting that Paula Booth ran every Tuesday at eleven, and at today's meeting Margot would be back from Paris to make one of her increasingly rare appearances.

She smoothed her outfit, a red lace bodysuit topped with a starched and slightly oversized white Comme des Garçons shirtdress. Cat found herself imagining Detective Hutton reaching between her legs, unsnapping the gusset, and bending her over her desk; then she blushed so hard it looked like she was having an allergic reaction. Self-consciously she turned her face down to her white leather slip-on sneakers and let her mind run through the events of the night before for what already felt like the hundredth time.

When Sigrid, Birdie, Helen, and Cat had walked into Hutton's apartment, they had *lost it.* The apartment was indeed a true classic eight, but instead of the prewar medallions, crown moldings, and pocket doors that Sigrid had been expecting, they'd discovered the half-excavated remains of Lorelei Hutton's sixties bachelorette paradise. No proper widow's den this: the formal dining room had been transformed into two distinct areas of low seating on either side of a central river-rock fireplace, and of the five original bedrooms, only Hutton's and the master still fit their intended purpose; he showed them his room briefly as he pulled on a T-shirt. The other three bedrooms had been converted into a library-slash-reading-room, an elaborate closet, and a bar. Boxes and power tools were scattered everywhere between piles of wood and plaster dust. Hutton had updated many of the light fixtures, but he was clearly working on stripping the wood and reincorporating more traditional details throughout.

Most of the furniture had been removed and several of the walls were half destroyed, but the bar was pristine. It held a full bar top in polished elm, matching stools, and standing bronze ashtrays. Hutton led them directly in there.

"Sorry—this is the only room I haven't taken apart yet," he said. "But it's where everyone wants to be, anyway. Let's have a drink, then maybe one of you can tell me what I should do with the place."

Birdie nodded in agreement. She opened both bottles of wine and lifted five exquisite lead crystal wineglasses down from one of the bar's shelves, emptying the first bottle between them with a heavy pour.

"Is it hard for you to get your girlfriend to come to this side of Prospect Park?" she asked sincerely, dumping the other bottle into a decanter.

Hutton laughed. "Maybe that's why I don't have one. But my

grandmother didn't seem to have a problem, so I don't know, maybe it's just my personality."

"Did you spend a lot of time with her?" Birdie, a bartender, was highly practiced at ferreting out potential murderers, mama's boys, narcissists, and dilettantes. The other women sat quietly while he lobbed back the correct answer.

"Not until I was out of college. She wasn't hugely interested in children. When she died last year she left this apartment to me, and I moved in a few months ago. I meant to finish renovating before I got here, but . . . it didn't work out that way."

Cat was looking at the framed linear prints on the wall of the bar—*all signed lithographs*, she thought. There was a series of curvy lines that looked like a Lichtenstein; another, with straight lines, looked like the work of Donald Judd; and a series of triangles drawn in the signature style of Sol LeWitt.

"Are these genuine?" she asked Hutton. He handed her a glass of wine.

"I think so," he said. As he turned toward the LeWitt, Cat allowed herself to look at him again, to really stare at the muscles in his arms and legs, and she felt an urge to run her fingers across his skin. He looked back to catch her staring at him, openmouthed, for the second time that day—but this time he smiled.

"Cheers," he said, touching his wineglass to hers. "Nice to meet you."

An hour later the group was settled in the living room, nursing Calvados out of oversized brandy snifters. They all fit on the enormous sectional he'd wedged into the conversation pit, a tiny amphitheater that looked as though it had originally housed dozens of floor pillows.

Cat hadn't sat down right away. Instead, she'd wandered into every room, looking in closets and at light fixtures and asking about his plans for each space. Hutton had followed her around as she explored, eventually pulling on an old Hampshire College hooded sweatshirt.

"Bess went there," she said. "Did you know her?"

"Oh," he said, looking surprised. "No, sorry, I don't remember her."

She did learn that he'd been a member of the Peace Corps in Mauritania before going into Columbia's journalism program. Then, after five years working the night shift at CBS, trying to "make violence go viral" as he put it, he'd given up journalism and joined the NYPD.

"What prompted that?" she asked when they finally settled into the sofa with the others. "I mean, *I get leaving journalism*; it sucks, there's no money. It's a giant pyramid scheme where we make the Coopers and Martins richer by using our half-million-dollar educations to distill meaningful human experiences into regrams. But joining the NYPD seems like something a *Scared Straight* kid from Queens would do, not someone like . . . you."

"I'm a New Yorker," he explained. "This is my home. It's the biggest cliché there is, but I genuinely wanted to make a difference. I honestly think that law enforcement does that, makes a difference, keeps us safe," he said.

Oh no. He's a total idiot, she thought.

"Stop-and-frisk isn't keeping us fucking safe, it's putting another generation of young black men behind bars for *loitering*." She couldn't help herself. "And writing parking tickets is an important part of the municipal revenue structure, I'll give you that, but it's not exactly noble."

"Stop-and-frisk isn't technically still legal, but yes, it sucks," he said, agreeing with her. "Writing tickets is what robots are for, but that's not what I do all day."

"Not *all* day. Sometimes you flirt with girls," Cat pointed out.

"Okay, fine." He threw up his hands. "I'll give you an example.

Look at the Boston Marathon bombing. Five days after it happened, Tamerlan Tsarnaev was linked to a triple homicide in Waltham that happened *two years* prior. The *Times*, the *Journal*, CNN, CBS, everybody, asked the same question: Would the marathon bombing have happened if he'd been arrested, tried, convicted, imprisoned? *No.* Of course it wouldn't have. In that case, dragnet federal surveillance *didn't* keep us safe—good police work, two years beforehand, is what would have kept us safe."

"Okay. I'll give you that." She sighed, swirling her brandy. "My experience is more that guys like you join the NSA, CIA, or DIA, whatever is federal—they don't go civil. I feel like there's a—"

"Gigantic class division between federal, state, and local law enforcement? Yes." He nodded slowly. "But it doesn't change unless you change it," he said, gesturing at himself. "I believe in justice. I genuinely believe that we're all responsible for the parts we play in this great democratic republic of ours. Mine is law enforcement." He drained his brandy and leaned in toward her conspiratorially. "I *might* be getting the sense that you don't find the police to be totally effective," he said a bit archly.

Cat laughed. "You're the only policeman I've ever met who's impressed me, and let's be honest—you have the instincts of a journalist. Police work is just bloated, macho bureaucracy. People who can think critically are probably just as qualified as the police to solve crimes, if not *more* so."

"You think you could solve a crime?" he asked.

"Sure," Cat said. "I'm a good researcher."

"It's not really *about* critical thinking, though; that's what I'm saying. It's about drudgery, just drilling down on cases, grinding down on every piece of evidence without accidentally shooting someone along the way. It's about patience. It's not enough to know who did it—you have to be able to send them to jail *and keep them there.*"

"You need to be able to prosecute, you mean."

He nodded. "That's the magic word. The people I work with

may not have gone to graduate school—hell, half of them didn't even go to college—but most are smart enough to know how important the rules are." He reached over and tucked a stray lock of hair behind her ear. "Beautiful girls like to take shortcuts."

Cat swatted his hand away. "*I* don't take shortcuts," she insisted, pointing to herself. "I could be very good at being a cop. I'm very detail-oriented; I love to waste time; I love drinking coffee and filling out paperwork. I just happen to do something else, which I don't think you understand."

Hutton didn't give up. "So explain it to me," he flirted.

"You know what? No!" Cat laughed. "No. We were talking about you. Don't change the subject."

"Okay, okay. You want to know something else?"

"What?" Cat bit her lip.

Before he could respond, Birdie and Helen crashed on the floor next to them, crying "Timber!" Birdie's giggles were verging on turning into sobs.

"I think we're too drunk to drive," said Helen. "Can you take us home, Mr. Officer?"

"We're *bad girls*. We need a police escort," Birdie chimed in.

Sigrid stepped in. "Don't listen to these idiots. We can walk home just fine, it's all of one block."

"No, I'd be happy to," he said. "Let's go."

"I've got to order a car," Cat said. "It's almost two—I have to be in at ten." She pulled out her phone and summoned a car service. He looked incredulous.

"Ten? Man, you magazine girls really have the gravy hours."

"I'm not a *magazine girl*, thank you." Cat's tone came out a little bit defensive and sharp.

"Oh boy," he replied. "My bad."

"I . . ." Cat stammered, trying to be nice. "*RAGE* is more than that. It's . . . *important.*"

Sigrid, halfway out the door and towing Birdie and Helen behind her, yelled, "We're walking now! Thanks, neighbor. Byeee!"

The elevator doors opened and they piled inside, leaving Cat abruptly behind in the apartment. Hutton waved good-bye and shut the front door.

"How long until your car gets here?" he asked, moving closer.

"Three minutes," she said. "I should head out front, I guess."

"I'll walk you."

She retrieved her handbag from the bar. Hutton had turned off most of the apartment's lights and was waiting for her in half-shadow, keys in hand. He held open the door, and they took the elevator down to the elaborate art deco lobby in silence, where the car was waiting outside. Cat climbed into its cavernous backseat. After closing the door, she rolled down the window to say good night. He crouched down and leaned on the door, refusing to let the driver pull away. Cat's heartbeat picked up.

"You're interesting," he said decisively, his face just an inch or two away from hers. "And your friends are nice."

"I like to think so."

The driver coughed loudly and shifted into gear.

"Okay, honey, where we going?" he asked in a thick Puerto Rican accent.

"Can I call you?" Hutton asked. "I have some more questions, but I won't come to your office again, I promise. We can make it very unofficial."

Cat nodded. "Unofficial works for me," she said with a smile.

Hutton winked, let go of the car, and strode back to the curb. Cat waved good-bye, then hit the button to roll up the tinted glass.

"It's 239 Moore Street in Bushwick, please, between Bogart and White. You can take Bedford to—"

"To Flushing. I know, I know. I'm gonna get you there, don't worry. So you gonna go out with him or what?" He hit the gas. "I think you should. He looks like a nice guy."

She looked out the back window and saw Hutton standing on the curb, watching them drive away.

"He is nice, but he's a cop," she replied. The car veered around the corner. Hutton disappeared from her view. "What do you think about cops?"

"It's a good man who does a job like that. They make a nice living, too, but it can be dangerous," he said. "You make sure when you get married that he gets a desk job. Better than FDNY, they never get the desk jobs. But good for retirement."

Cat suddenly remembered Hillary's drops sitting at the bottom of her purse. *Shit.* Maybe she should've told Hutton about the bottle. They'd been too busy flirting and talking about him, about his life. Sigrid hadn't even mentioned that Hillary had lived at 170 Ocean, but then again, she wouldn't have—Sig was in full wingman mode all night, dragging them over to his place, bringing booze, leaving Cat alone with Hutton at the right moment. *You've got the best group of friends, Cat,* she thought to herself. *Hillary deserves your loyalty. Even if the police won't really do anything . . . don't let this go.*

She fell into a deep sleep as soon as she got home, dreaming about Hutton in flashes throughout the night. Now, as she walked toward her office through the maze of *RAGE*'s black cubicles, all she could remember of the dream's plot was an impression that he'd tied her up against a wall, somehow immobilizing both her ankles and her wrists. She had fleeting memories of a man's leather belt tightening around her arms; of Hutton's face floating over her; of his skin, so close to her when they'd sat on Sigrid's stoop. *How will I possibly get any work done today?*

She opened her phone and composed a text to the number from his business card before coming to her senses and deleting it totally.

When Margot Villiers entered Cooper, the building changed, deference rippling out in military precision as she passed through the lobby. Employees lowered their heads and sucked in their stomachs. Only the interns were dumb enough to look directly at her. Even the custodians, who'd been fully immunized to celebrity by ten thousand trash cans, paused as they cleaned, feeling gravity's tug toward the black hole of her particular type of power.

Margot was seventy-two years old and had stood at the helm of *RAGE Fashion Book* since its founding in 1985. A former personal shopper at Bergdorf Goodman, she'd happened upon the opportunity through her first husband, a cocaine-addled Wall Streeter who was a close friend of George Cooper, onetime CEO of Cooper House.

The apocryphal story went like this: George Cooper spent so many nights on the balcony of the Villierses' apartment in the early eighties, drinking scotch and complaining about the downward trend of his women's titles, that Margot stole his Filofax and penciled in a meeting for herself two weeks later, which his secretary found, confirmed, and added to his calendar.

She walked into that meeting with a full written assessment of the last year's issues for four of his titles, chronicling their faults and successes down to the final detail, along with an elaborate proposal for a magazine of her own: *RAGE Fashion Book*, a publication that would work *with* American manufacturers and retailers to reinvigorate an ailing industry in a way that the new workingwoman would recognize. *RAGE* would contain no recipes, table settings, or money-saving household tips; it would instead serve the women of the eighties, power-suited careerists who paid for their own thousand-dollar briefcases. Let their housekeepers read about housekeeping. Margot anticipated that the college-educated women of 1985 would want more from their magazines, and by narrowing *RAGE*'s demographic to educated women, breadwinners with money to burn and families to feed, their ad rates could skyrocket. She argued that guaranteeing exclusive product for the magazine from companies who, with their guidance, wouldn't be going out of business anytime soon, would in turn guarantee a natural advertising base and that the American-only angle would anchor their editorial stance in the otherwise rocky shoals of the cold war era's media landscape. "Women are the new men," Margot had declared to George Cooper, "with one big difference: they fucking *love* to shop."

By the end of the meeting, she'd founded her own magazine with a renewable contract for two years and a guaranteed staff draw from existing Cooper titles. She turned that two-year audition into the most successful publication the magazine industry had ever seen; betting on the better angels of the Western world's women had paid off, and she survived the tenure of not only George Cooper, but his younger brother Matthew as well. Their older brother Pete remained a mostly silent partner, and now George Cooper Jr. ran the show.

In the nineties, as Gap and Nike suffered enormous public relations crises over their sweatshops, Margot had pivoted the magazine's focus and moved from the patriotic to the humanitarian, banking on the living-wage appeal of luxury goods that required expensive production to ensure their value. "There are no fucking Gap jeans in *RAGE*" was an oft-repeated Margot quote, along with "We don't promote clothes made by children," a claim easy enough to commit to given the quality of the clothing they featured. Nineties-era *RAGE* was transformed from "American-made" to "living-wage, worldwide," with the clothes increasing further still in price. When confronted in 1998 by the *Wall Street Journal* about the astronomical costs of *RAGE*'s fashion editorials, Margot pointed out, "It costs a lot to look like you didn't continue a cycle of poverty for working women on the other side of the globe." Luxury brands touted their *RAGE* seal of approval, and the mid-level "designer" labels and luxury diffusion lines sold in department stores had to shift their focus to hold on to their cachet, lest they be branded as fascist fashion. *RAGE Fashion Book* flourished, and though it spawned multiple imitators, none matched the success of Margot's original.

But in the new millennium *RAGE*'s prospects had shifted, trend-

ing downward as technology made luxury accessible to people
Margot had never considered in ways she'd never dreamed. Street-
style stars of their own blogs, who subsisted on protein shakes while
Photogramming images of cupcakes, created their own advertori-
als faster and cheaper than magazines and got their kickbacks direct
from the manufacturers through Mania, a software application that
was now *RAGE*'s biggest competitor. Margot's specific ethics were
taken for granted, and her empire no longer cornered the aspirational market for women's luxury goods. The magazine's ad rates
had been forced into decline as they competed with Manhattan
teenagers willing to sell their lives, without any disclosure whatsoever, to the sponsorship of brands. Why pay $150K per page for an
advertisement in *RAGE* to reach four million American women—
once, on paper, without a resale opportunity—when you could just
throw some free clothes at a teenage girl who would sell them directly to her own twenty million global followers, while Mania
measured their clicks, engagement, and ROI down to the second?

The founders of Mania, four siblings, all born after 9/11, were
teenagers who'd started the entire company three years earlier as
a middle-school science fair experiment. The Bishop children's
initial app had allowed users to snap or upload a photo of any
object or article of clothing, then geolocate the nearest version
or substitute on sale. The results were sorted by price and their
"proprietary ethical rating," which compiled publicly available data
to determine the degree of "ethics" in the garment or object in
question, a notion so vague it gave Margot hives. Mania had over
a million downloads in its first week. In under a month venture
capital groups from Silicon Valley were competing over their first
round of seed funding. Within six months, they'd discovered a way
to gather user-generated content from the street-style stars who
worshipped the platform, and created an entire advertorial application from the clothing and objects they were already generating
revenue from. "Local, ethical, *radical*" was their slogan, a stab in
RAGE's direction. The software—open source from the start—

worked flawlessly, receiving constant updates and patches from the engineers all over the globe who were eager to help out a start-up, one that was made up of not only primarily female engineers but photogenic adolescent ones to boot.

It didn't have any editorial content—only user-generated images and advertising—but nobody cared. Now, two years later, Mania's content was created by their users and curated directly by their advertisers; they operated out of a warehouse in suburban Los Angeles, of all places; and they had a staff of just ten. They were lean, impossibly young, and successful on every available digital platform. Mania was everything that *RAGE* could never be—no matter how many times Margot flew around the globe to shower their advertisers with the glow of her attention.

George Cooper Jr. had made it clear he was less inclined than his predecessors to support *RAGE*'s insane budget, including the lobbying firms, labor attorneys, and global auditors who verified their living-wage-only editorial claims. Until twenty issues ago he'd been unable to do or say anything about how Margot ran the magazine, but now he'd made it crystal clear that if they didn't move forty-five million global issues by the end of the year, he'd be taking control of the magazine. His staff was checking their expenses line-by-line, and she felt Cooper's fountain pen swinging over her head, ready to drop and reduce her kingdom to nothing in a moment.

She stalked through the lobby, Paula trailing behind with her ever-present cellphone glued to her ear, before taking the escalator steps two at a time and striding confidently across the upper lobby. Paula hung back to finish her conversation. A handsome young man in a tuxedo—one of Cooper's doormen, his uniform designed by Margot herself in the late nineties, although *he* probably didn't know that—directed her to elevator B with perfect timing. As she rounded the corner into the elevator bank, the doors opened and the assembled crowd instinctively parted. She swept in and stared down at the black screen of her phone, incapable of making eye contact, until the doors parted on 46 and Margot glided seamlessly into the cavern she'd once built from nothing.

At 11:00 a.m. the editors of *RAGE Fashion Book* filed in and took their places around Margot's office, each unfolding one of the custom camp stools that were stacked next to the door. There were exactly enough stools for the twelve members of the editorial team, no more, no less: Margot's own foolproof attendance system.

The walls of the office, a twelve-hundred-square-foot glass rectangle that took up most of the building's north side, were lined with plants—hearty succulents, lush cascading ferns, potted trees, tuberoses, and even a lilac bush. A corner of the room was arranged with silk sofas, dressmaker's dummies, and sewing machines, but the empty space in front of Margot's desk was where Cat and the other editors placed their stools and sat in a semicircle.

Margot remained behind the lacquered pearl-gray slab she used as a desk. A single yellow legal pad lay on her blotter. Paula sat on the left, a laptop open beneath her narrow fingertips. Constance stood to the right, commanding a large rolling corkboard used to plot stories and issues.

When the group was seated—Cat let her dress fall around the stool in a perfect bell—Margot spoke five words in the dense Scottish accent she'd never shed.

"We are losing our edge."

No one responded, but Paula's narrowed eyes and embittered face showed the group all the emotion that Margot's blank visage so automatically repressed.

"Mania's outpacing us, has cornered us on every front, every platform, every angle. I need to hear stories that are original today. Nothing that is a retread. I want *new*. I want *the future*. I want you to give me *elegant full frontal*: provocative, exclusive, salable. We have to go all the way. I want ideas that the little children of Mania cannot even conceive of."

Oh shit, thought the editors collectively, each of them scrambling for a spin to place on their pitches by the time their turn came up.

Margot nodded slightly to Paula, who pointed at managing editor Constance Onderveet, a hawk-nosed, birdlike woman swaddled in Prada.

"Connie, go," Paula ordered.

"I got an update yesterday from Maddie Plattstein," Constance reported. "She's nearly done with her exposé on unregulated beauty products. In terms of the fallout, she takes retailers to task but manages to place a great deal of the blame squarely on Congress and on the manufacturers, so I don't think we'll see too much trouble—I can give a quick heads-up to Barneys, Bergdorf's, Net-a-Porter, and Sephora that they'll need to check newsstands and be ready to pull product. That should be sufficient courtesy."

"Issue and pages?" asked Paula.

"September, barring any hang-ups with research and legal. Four or five pages."

Janet Berg, the senior features editor, nodded in agreement. "It's solid. I don't anticipate too much trouble, but we'll turn it around in time no matter what."

Constance moved two yellow index cards—**I Stopped Using Soap** and **Heaving Bowls: Secrets of the Jockey Diet**—across the corkboard from September to October, replacing them both with another that read **Skin Deep in Their Pockets: The Big Business of Beauty Lobbyists**, before she ran down the remainder of her list. Upcoming pieces included a set of first-person essays from transgender students at three different elite men's colleges; a class-picture-style profile of twenty-one female Fortune 500 CEOs; a digital map of the New York and Paris Garment Districts; and an essay from a scientist who was developing the next big stain-resistant fabric.

Janet jumped back in and listed pitches she'd gotten in from freelancers. Margot voted yes or no with a simple nod or shake of her head, occasionally smearing her liver-spotted hands with hand cream as she stared out the window; everyone else remained quiet. During Cat's early days at *RAGE* they'd all spoken up excitedly during meetings, throwing ideas back and forth. Now everyone was treading on eggshells. Margot's management style—ruling with fear and absolute control, choosing the covers and coverlines mere days before each issue closed—had previously been motivational, but now... *now* it seemed to be paralyzing the room.

Paula pointed to her next victim, senior photo editor Rose Cashin-Trask.

Reading from a single sheet of paper, Rose robotically recited the shoot schedule and her various updates. As she spoke, Constance layered pink photo cards on top of the yellow story cards, Paula nodding in approval, while Margot's face remained blank and unimpressed. Cat didn't look up from the jellied Mary-Janes Rose wore, a slightly more sophisticated version of the ones Helen had on the previous night.

Lou was next. She read quickly from a sheet that Bess had put together for her, updating Constance on the status of the fashion layouts planned through December; it was efficient and logical. When she reached the end, she folded the paper in her lap and looked up, her eyes bright.

"I examined Mania last week and I think we still have something they don't. They're *accessible*. I think it doesn't matter how much couture you pile onto a seventh grader from Texas, or whatever; they're still just little girls playing dress-up. I think we should drill down on the biggest weapon we have in our arsenal. *Age*," she said enthusiastically, gesturing to Margot, to herself. "We have access to the world's aging socialites. I think we should play that card every month, you know? They certainly won't put their lives *online*, but I know they'll talk to us. And we can arrange compensation, sponsorship, anything. I know that hasn't been the standard in the past, but it seems prudent to open ourselves up to new budgetary approaches."

Cat's mouth dropped open. She'd never expected Lou to deviate from the script in the slightest, much less float ideas about how *RAGE* should structure their business practices. Everyone looked at Margot, who nodded her head carefully.

"What's the pitch?" Margot asked Lou.

"I want us to lean more on real women over thirty, on their real lives, every month. We could debut a new section, something that's 'at home with,' but really it's 'at one of their homes with.' The Hillary piece in September could kick us off, if Cat would be willing to expand it from tribute to memorial." She looked at Cat.

"Maybe." Cat shrugged, amazed by Lou's bravado. "What are you looking for?"

"Talk about her life—show her accomplishments, her depth, her taste, her friends. Really get into it. Especially photos. Do you have anything from school? From when you were younger? Let's see *everything* you can find. Her life *is* the editorial, it *is* the story. And then I think we should do it again in October but with, you know, someone *living*."

"Are you willing to be one of those women?" Margot interjected.

"If you are," Lou replied boldly, "but let's wait on that. I want to call Princess Sophie from Denmark. I think she has a property— it's a castle in Bavaria—that needs some updating. If we can convince some advertisers to sponsor, then we could probably get her to commit to a weekend shoot. She'll do it if we hire locally. I want to show women like her who are now in the positions, socially, that men used to occupy—women whose wallets manage to keep entire towns alive. The *benefactors*. The matriarchy . . . the new maternalism . . . is materialism? Is that making sense?"

Margot was nodding vigorously now. "*Matriarchy.* I love that. Older women ruling the world."

"Like you," Lou said to Margot. "The *RAGE* woman has always been a reflection of you. Let's not try to be something we're not. We're *you*. That's our strength."

"I want to see fifteen potential names on my desk next week," Margot said. "And I want you to reconsider the fashion editorials for winter in the eyes of older women."

"What if we started using older models?" Cat asked. "Or made a deliberate move to diversify—in terms of both size and age? I can start calling around."

"I don't think that we're quite ready for gray-haired models," Margot replied. A sneer rippled across her face so quickly that Cat thought she might have hallucinated it. "This isn't the J. Jill catalog. But maybe we can start using some bigger girls. I think that's not . . . a bad idea. It's where the market is going. Everyone's getting so *fat* these days."

Cat nodded, writing *have Molly call agencies for plus-size girls for Nov issue forward* on her legal pad. Margot stood up behind her desk and started to walk around the room, muttering quietly to herself. The editorial team remained on their stools.

"I want . . . okay . . . I want . . . to pivot. We will *pivot*. We will be a new *RAGE*, again. We will recapture the exact same women who bought this magazine for the first time thirty years ago; we will grow up with them, but we will not pander." Margot's voice grew louder as Paula typed furiously. "I do not want . . . older actresses advertising for yogurt that makes it easier for your aging bowels to take a shit. I do not want advertisements for condominiums in warm places. I want to see the most glamorous old ladies the world has to offer, and I want their most dangerous opinions. I want the fucking . . . Queen of England, shooting a handgun, drunk on sherry, saying she wants to dismantle the monarchy. I want the Empress of Saudi Arabia behind the wheel of a convertible, her headscarf flying *just so* in the wind, reading Christopher Hitchens. I want women in charge talking about who they pay and how much and why. I want to find icons. I need *icons*."

Margot turned sharply to face the staff. As she leaned on the porcelain autopsy table she used to water her plants, her eyes gleamed.

"Go back to your desks and pitch me something new, and how to do it here in New York with advertisers or sponsors footing the bill. We must be the critical *RAGE* we have always been, but for now we must clip some coupons. If we succeed, however, I promise you: I will personally fly the whole staff to Paris in October and we will *all* go to every show." She walked back to her desk and sat down. Cat's eyes grew wide: Margot sure knew how to motivate her team.

"Now get out. Go eat lunch. Make your minds strong. Each of you draft me a full wheat pitch for next week—no chaff. I want your best work." She nodded firmly, then took the laptop and turned away toward the windows. Paula picked up her cellphone and disappeared into a thicket of ferns. Bess, Cat, and the other senior and associate editors filed out of Margot's glass house and bolted back to their desks with new drive.

Chapter Five

Back in her office, Cat surveyed the PMS window and added "studded jelly with thick wool socks" to the plus side. The minus side remained intact.

She cracked open her computer, opened the document on Hillary's tribute, flexed her knuckles, and got to work. She'd been avoiding this file for weeks, but it was nearly due and now she had to expand on it, turning it into a full memorial and the first entry in MATRIARCH. She got to work, drafting copy for Margot to approve.

HED

Our Heartbreak: Hillary E. Whitney, 1979–2017

DEK

At *Harper's Bazaar*, *Vogue*, and *RAGE*, she made a brooding strangeness fashionable for all.

BODY

Hillary Edith Whitney, a longtime and beloved member of the Cooper House family and fashion director at *RAGE*, passed away tragically on May 15 of this year from a heart attack brought on by a long-term eating disorder. Ms. Whitney's trademark work revealed women and their homes together in spectral visions that stayed with you long after the page had been turned. She was the recipient of numerous awards, including the ASME section award for her monthly feature on totems and curios (*NikNak*) for three years running, and she received multiple commemorations from the Junior League for her work with the Dress for Success program. On behalf of Cooper House, we send our love and condolences to her family, friends, and colleagues in the industry, and we offer the following pages in a memorial to her wit, kindness, grace, and impeccable style—a life well lived, and well loved, despite the devastating illness that killed her. She is the first entry in our new monthly section, *MATRIARCH: women who rule the world*, and we hope her memory will inspire the millions of *RAGE* women reading these pages.

Sincerely,
Margot Villiers and the staff of *RAGE Fashion Book*

Cat opened another folder comprising dozens of numbered photos of Hillary from Fashion Week events, celebratory weekends, photo shoots, her Photogram account, and, eventually, though she felt a little morbid about it, Cat's own personal files. She couldn't figure out what to choose. *Caption as much as you can*, she told herself, though hesitation tugged at the corners of her mind. *You're being too emotional*, she finally decided, shoving her feelings into a cupboard under her stomach before starting at the top.

1996: Hillary pulling her first racing scull from the boathouse at the Sawyer School for Girls in Farmington, Connecticut. Go Fighting Sunflowers!
1998: Hillary Whitney, Catherine Ono, Bess Bonner, Sigrid Gun-

derson, Nora Bunting-Davis, and Olivia Dolman Fox shucking oysters on the beach at Menemsha, Massachusetts.

1999: Y2K! Hillary rings in the millennium from a balcony on Central Park West in a black Halston kimono.

2001: Hillary graduates from Parsons. Shown here with her long-time friend Oliver Delong.

2002: Hillary modeling a pair of bumsters, the original Alexander McQueen low-rises, at an Oscars party in Los Angeles.

Cat worked her way through another two dozen before she got to the past year. Hillary looked nearly the same as she had fifteen years earlier: still elegant, bone-thin and white-blonde, although her style had been updated from obviously gothic to pointedly ladylike, a look that Hillary herself referred to as "sophisticated villain." The photos showed a pale woman with dramatic freckles, no makeup, and huge green eyes. *Really* huge green eyes.

Cat found a close-up, a high-res shot taken front row at Fashion Week in 2014, and dragged it to compare with a Photogram from May. Hillary wasn't wearing eyeliner in either photo—eye makeup always looked a little bit crude on her white lashes and brows—which made the comparison simple. By placing the images side by side and zooming in, Cat could see that Hillary's eyes had nearly doubled in size in the later photograph, the pupils and irises enlarged to cartoon-ish proportions. The irises might be contacts, but the pupils were all Hillary's. It looked like she was on mushrooms. *What the hell?*

Cat googled "enlarge eye" and found only spambot articles from aggregators covering makeup tricks and tutorials on inexpensive colored contacts. She didn't bother to click on any of the links, but typed bedford organics into the browser and found the shop they'd exchanged Photogram messages with the night before. Cat punched their number into her Cooper landline.

"Bedford Organics."

"Hi, this is Catherine Ono. I'm a senior editor at *RAGE*. Is the owner available?"

"Ohmigod. We *loooove RAGE*. Unfortunately Vittoria's not here right now, but can I give you her cell?"

"I'd prefer to stop by the store. Could she be there in an hour, do you think?"

"I'll make sure she's here. Do you know how to find us?"

"At 400 South Bedford?"

"Yes! Ring the third floor any time after four and we'll buzz you up."

Cat thanked her and hung up. A Williamsburg-based beauty company without a street-level storefront? Real estate was obviously expensive everywhere in the city, but a semiprivate upper floor was more suited to Madison Avenue. Aping the luxury business models of Manhattan might *seem* like a fine idea, but Cat was surprised that a start-up beauty business could survive without traditional retail traffic. *They must wholesale*, she thought. *Maybe that explains why I've never heard of them.*

She grabbed a pen and made a to-do list on a plain white index card for the following morning:

WEDNESDAY

finish HW memorial
Delvaux promo lunch at Per Se
beet dyes in home upholstery—750 words (work with Lou)
follow up with Delvaux rep and ask to see factory

As soon as Cat set down her pen, a leathery, manicured claw reached through the crack in her office door and yanked it open. Lou stood in the doorway, wearing a gauzy tank dress made from multiple thin slips of cream silk. The tanks billowed in the slight breeze of the office air-conditioning, whipping softly around her Pilates-carved calves. Her veiny arms were coated in henna tattoos; fine gold bracelets cut into her biceps. An enormous crystal dangled on a brass chain from the spindle of her neck, and a streak of earthy red pigment had been painted across her left cheekbone.

"Kit-Ohhhhhhh!" Lou cried. "I have a new inspiration, and I think you're going to like it."

"Desert priestess," Cat threw out in reply, feeling kindly toward this motivated new Lou.

"*Close.* Pre-Columbian *jungle* priestess, but *with a twist*: she's the victim of a rift in space-time, wandering Fashion Week, discovering technology, using it for her own anachronistic witchcraft."

"Vaporwave Gaia," Cat tried.

"Yes? Maybe? Actually, no, I don't think I know what that is. What's *vaporwave*?"

"It's this thing that kids do where they put the Windows 95 logo over some computer-generated clouds and dance to remixes of Céline Dion."

"No. Not that."

"Hmm. Uh . . . *cyberpunk* Gaia?"

"Better. Are we both talking about the same kind of cyberpunk?"

"Cayce Pollard," Cat and Lou said in unison.

"I just think," Lou opined, waving her hands around wildly, "that we could take all these earthy resort clothes, and style a kind of priestess figure out of it, a sort of first-century jungle witch—"

"Because all the resort clothes for next season are just *so* natural, and *logoless*, and *earthy*, and how many fucking shoots can we do in Sedona? *Totally.* Let's get Bess and Molly to pull everything together. I'm busy tomorrow, but how about Thursday or Friday?"

"Friday I have to leave at noon. Let's board everything on Monday and we can pitch it to Margot and Paula next week."

"Can we use your office, since it's still empty?" Cat asked. "I don't want to go in the workrooms anymore, to be honest."

"I know what you mean. Guns don't kill people, workrooms do," quipped Lou, before turning bright red. "That was awful, I don't know why I said that, I'm so sorry—"

"It's fine," Cat said. "We have to start joking about it sometime."

"I know, but that was *tasteless*. I'm sorry, I'm just still this *stupid*

Englishwoman sometimes; we can be so rude. It's because we repress all emotions, we forget that other people have them." Her whole face contorted itself with regret.

"It's fine. *Don't* worry about it. And I'm not saying this because I'm offended, but I was actually just running out the door to check out a beauty company in Brooklyn. I'll see you tomorrow."

Cat gave Lou a quick hug to lessen her embarrassment, grabbed her bag, and dashed for the elevators.

When the M train resurfaced on the Williamsburg Bridge, Cat got a text.

> Mark Hutton here. Any chance you'd want to blow off work and get a drink?

She responded immediately.

> Already left, heading to Williamsburg now.

As the ellipses bubbles lit up on his side of the screen, Cat reached the Marcy Avenue stop. She shoved her phone into the pocket of her dress, hustled out the door, down the stairs, and through the turnstile onto Broadway, walking west toward the river until she turned left on Bedford.

She paused outside 400 Bedford to check her phone one more time.

> Leicester?

Leicester was right around the corner from where she stood. If she gave herself an hour at Bedford Organics, and another fifteen minutes to fix her makeup in their bathroom, maybe they could turn an early drink into dinner.

Love that place. 6?

See you there.

She looked up at the facade of 400 South Bedford. A small neon light shone through the window of the third floor: the letter *B* placed inside the letter *O*. She hit the buzzer. Seconds later the door vibrated. Cat pushed through a small foyer into a dark stairwell that hadn't been renovated or cleaned in years; no elevator in sight. She started climbing. When she reached the third floor, a short, dark-eyed Brazilian woman opened the only door on the landing and effusively kissed her on the cheeks.

"You must be Cat-er-inne," she trilled. "Meu nome é Vittoria. And this is my lab-or-a-tor-ee."

She waved Cat into a large formal parlor lined with custom floor-to-ceiling shelves. The room overflowed with merchandise packed into beautiful glass apothecary bottles nesting in matte paper boxes, wrapped with elaborate navy ribbons and handwritten labels. Cat didn't recognize anything in the store—she'd never seen these products *anywhere*. And yet there was enough stock in this room to suggest a healthy, growing business, with a full product line and daily shipments out.

"What beautiful packaging," she said, gesturing at the shelves. "How long have you been in business?"

"My family, we have been in bus-a-nees, oh, I think for fifty years, one way or the other, but in this space only three years. In Brazil it was my father's company. In America, we are called Bedford, but in Brazil we are Brasília Órgãos. It's, how you say, a play on words; it is both 'organ' like a kidney and 'organic' like *bio*. Everything we make, it's for the whole body, for everything."

"Who carries your line?" Cat picked up one of the amber

glass bottles littered everywhere; the one in her hands was labeled "Beauty Sleep" in an elegant cursive. It had a surprising heft to it.

"Nobody! *Nobody* carries us." Vittoria squinted at Cat. "We only do direct sale. We have our own customers. Everything is custom, special for each client."

"That's amazing," Cat responded. "Manufacturing *and* direct sale. Good for you. Like Poppy King."

Vittoria laughed, a throaty Portuguese vibrato. "Yes! *Exactly.* You understand. I'm an immigrant, you know? I'm cheap, I don't want a middleman. It's not good for us, it's not good for our customers. For a long time we were just in Rio, but now, with the internet, we can move to America and make everything here; no more customs, no more bullshit, ship domestic, no problem."

Vittoria certainly didn't *look* cheap. The pant legs of her navy silk Jil Sander jumpsuit were rolled up above a pair of spotless Chanel saddle shoes, and her only accessory was the gigantic emerald on one finger of her left hand.

"That makes sense," Cat said and nodded, pulling the bottle out of her purse. "I actually have a custom bottle right here. Can you tell me what it is?"

"Oh! You sent us a 'gram last night!" Cat passed her the plastic bottle, and Vittoria gave it a squeeze, pulling out the dropper and smelling the liquid. She shook her head.

"They are eyedrops, but everything is different for everybody. I might have to put the drops down, do some tests. Unless, do you know who is it made for?"

"Hillary Whitney, from *RAGE*," said Cat. Vittoria looked surprised.

"Oh my gosh, that was so sad. I saw it on the Page Six when she died. She come here a lot, we make a lot of stuff for her. She was sad. She was in love. Everything we make for her was about love. So what, you cleaning out her desk?" Her voice grew thin, suspicious.

"Not exactly," Cat replied carefully, seeing the trepidation on Vittoria's face. "We worked together at *RAGE* but we were friends for a long, long time—she was one of my first friends when I moved to America. I found the drops in a handbag she gave me. We used to trade beauty products all the time—but I'd never seen your brand before, so I thought it was a good excuse to come check out the store. Hillary was so beautiful that I *straight copied* her style whenever I got the chance."

Vittoria still looked suspicious. Cat pulled out her phone to show her old photos of Cat and Hillary, starting with the two girls side by side in their Sawyer School uniforms. Vittoria let out a few oohs and ahhs, then looked at Cat, satisfied.

"Okay, so if you her friend, then you gonna know who she was in love with."

Cat sighed and eye-rolled at the same time. "Robert Reid. What an asshole."

"He was never, *never ever*, never gonna leave his wife. Poor Hillary. She wanted to marry him, to have his babies. She always say to me, *I'm gonna be so beautiful that he won't want to live without me*. And I tried to help! I give her everything with a little bit of love in it, with extra energy so she can sparkle. She was uptight, you know, but these drops, these are special. They are based on an old recipe from my great-grandmother."

"What's in them?"

"Family secret. Some special plants from both sides, from Portugal, from Brazil. There's also natural preservatives, so this tiny bottle, it would last her forever. It looks like she must have spilled it, though. She didn't *use* all of it."

"What do you mean?" Cat was confused. Nearly half the bottle was gone.

"These drops, they are for special nights. For the nights when the moon is full, when there is magic in the air, when you want your lover to gaze into your eyes and stay up late with you. They *not* for every day, not for every week. We had a long talk about it when I gave her these. I said, *You can make him fall in love with you if you use these at the right time.*"

"Why is the bottle so big if the dosage is just a few drops?"

"Well, it's a liquid, so it does *eva-porr-ate*; like with an American whiskey barrel, the angels take their share. And we dilute it because these plants, they are very strong. It is very expensive to make, a long process, too, so it is easier just to make one bottle for one woman, for her whole life to have."

"How much are these?"

"This leetle bottle is nine thousand dollars to buy." Vittoria sighed. "I know, it is a lot, but it is a-hard to make!"

"Wow," said Cat, shock written all over her face. *A glamorous South American woman selling unregulated love potions for six times my rent. So that's who can afford to live on Bedford Avenue these days. I'm in the wrong business.*

Vittoria still held the bottle in her hands. Cat *definitely* needed to get it back. She softened her expression.

"Can you really make someone fall in love?" Cat asked, pretending to telegraph lovesickness of her own. Vittoria responded by placing the bottle in Cat's hands and folding her fingers around it.

"Yes. You keep them. You put two drops—just *two*—in each eye, when it is night, where there is candlelight, moonlight, music. You dance, you look into his eyes. You will shine; you will be at your best. Just a little polish is all you need. These are gonna help you."

"What *exactly* do they do?"

"They gonna make your eyes big, you gonna see him better, you will laugh easier. They're gonna make you more beautiful."

Cat looked around the store. Every single product was labeled only with the intended effects—no cutesy product names and certainly no ingredients. Stacked behind Vittoria she could see bottles that read "Happiness," "Clarity," "Long hair growth," "Nice hair texture," "Strong nails," "Fertility," and, most sensationally, "Bigger breasts."

"I actually have a sort-of date after this," she said. "I feel like I need all the help I can get. What else should I do?"

Vittoria squealed. "Oh, that's perfect. Kate already make samples for you, but now we try to find something better. Come here"— she pointed to an oversized peach velvet settee—"and sit down. You wanna tea? Let's get you a tea. Kattteee!"

Vittoria spent the next forty-five minutes fussing over Cat, brushing out her hair and massaging her face while she applied lotions, powders, and serums, all with a specific goal, some of them from beautiful amber jars. *For happiness. For the nerves. For the regeneration of the cells. For the glow. To soften the wrinkles. To fatten the hair follicle. To thin the fat on the neck.* She talked the entire time, her voice a melodic stream of stories about each product, about her family, about her own degree in botany from the University of São Paulo, about the natural fragrances she was so careful to mix—lily of the valley, rosemary, balsam, jasmine, juniper, honeysuckle, eucalyptus, apple blossom, lavender, tangerine, and rose water, among others.

Cat felt soothed and pampered. She'd walked into Bedford Organics red-faced and anxious as a fussy baby, but when Vittoria held up a hand mirror at a quarter to six, a radiant, breathtakingly beautiful woman stared back at her instead. Cat's skin glowed; her hair floated around her face, glossy and voluminous. Even her fingernails looked healthier—she could have sworn they were ragged and dry this morning, but now her nail beds were tidy and clean.

"You want to add the *mulher bonita* drops?" asked Vittoria. "It's gonna be a beautiful night. It could be a good night for these." Cat nodded. Vittoria gently tilted her head back, placing two drops in each of Cat's eyes.

She wrapped up Cat's dozen or so samples and a few full-size products in thick brown butcher paper, tying them together with a heavy grosgrain ribbon. Kate brought her a small Provencal-style woven basket with leather handles and placed the products gently inside, fastening the handles together with more ribbon.

"All of this, it's a gift for you. You try these out. And share! Make sure you share, okay?"

Cat nodded and ducked into the powder room, which was lined in Dupioni silk curtains, to apply some deodorant and a flamingo-pink lipstick. She felt *incredible*. The floor-length bathroom mirror confirmed it: Cat could see that she now looked more beautiful than she ever had in her entire life, almost as bewitching and ethereal as Hillary Whitney. When she stepped out to pick up her packages and say good-bye, Vittoria pressed her little body into Cat's to give her a warm, friendly hug.

"I'm so glad you come by today. Hillary was a lovely girl. You come by any time. You share these with all your friends, you give them my number; I make more, custom." She winked.

Cat thanked her as she took her bag of product, then floated down the staircase out to Bedford. The sidewalk pavement sparkled in the summer sun. Instead of the usual polka-dot pattern of old gum stains, she noticed the glimmering flecks of mica and granite embedded in the slabs; instead of tasting garbage in the air, she smelled the lavender and lily traces wafting off her own skin. Her sneakers felt unexpectedly light as she wove her way through the after-work crowd of pedestrians, all of whom seemed to notice her, to happily bask—just for a moment—in her glow.

She caught her own reflection in a shop window, found it in the next, and one across the street and then another. Surrounded by a prismatic army of her own form, their dresses starched and white like hers, she moved her arms to the sky and reached for the sun; they did the same. She put on her headphones, and the other Cats did, too. *Hello, Window Cats*, she thought happily.

She selected the Beatles' "Blackbird" from her playlist, skipping down the north side of Broadway and ducking down Driggs. Window Cats followed her wherever she went. The sunshine dripping on her arms began seeping into her body, filling her up from the outside in with a soft, airy gold. By the time she reached Leicester, tears of happiness were blooming on her cheeks, and she wiped them away with her fingertips. *You were only waiting for this moment to arise*, McCartney sang.

Hutton was waiting outside the restaurant wearing his work uniform of rumpled button-down, unstructured jacket, lightweight trousers, and battered brown oxfords. She barreled toward him, wrapping her arms under his jacket, feeling his muscles through his shirt, pushing her face into his chest, smelling his bell-pepper scent, listening for the big drum of his heartbeat.

"Wow, hi," he said, surprised.

Cat looked up, then stepped back, realizing what she'd done. She blushed.

"I just got the nicest facial. I must be relaxed. I guess that doesn't happen very often. What's new, Detective? Catch any murderers today?"

"No." He grinned, shaking his head. "Just crazy women." He stared at Cat, studying her. Her hair—long and loose in big, lustrous hanks—gleamed. Her skin was rosy and flushed, her brown eyes even more enormous than they'd been the day before. He could see a wide strap of red lace peeking out from beneath her stiff white dress, and she carried a big straw bag filled with boxes wrapped in brown wax paper and tied with navy ribbon. She had a magic, easy quality to her that hadn't been there yesterday, like she'd suddenly been unwrapped on the inside.

"*I'm* not crazy. I'm . . . investigating. Like we talked about."

"What do you mean, *investigating*?" he asked. A group of Italian tourists split and passed around them like a school of fish.

"Buy me a drink and I'll tell you *all* about it." She smiled as the chorus of melodic Italian voices swept over her. "Come on. Let's go. I love this place."

Cat skipped into Leicester. Her long limbs bent every which way as she followed the hostess to their table. The air between them became magnetic, a force field, and Hutton followed, inhaling her floral-scented wake with every step. *This is fun*, Cat thought. Vittoria had been right. All her inhibitions were gone. All her self-confidence had bubbled to the surface. *There's power in these jars*, she thought, feeling the heavy weight of the bag of product at her side.

After the waitress led them to a secluded wooden nook carved out of the patio in the ivy-covered backyard, Hutton ordered two gin cocktails. Just like the day before, when Molly had brought him coffee, Cat waited for him to give the beautiful and very young waitress an approving look, but he kept his eyes focused on the table's wooden slats when she returned with their drinks.

"Tell me about yourself," she demanded. "I want to know who you are."

"No, it's *your* turn," he replied, grinning. "All I did last night was talk. Tell me about you."

She twisted her mouth up in thought. "Okay," she said, nodding, "I'll talk."

"What's your first language?"

"It's Flemish. It's like . . . an antique Dutch."

"Can I hear it?"

"Dat is een ander paar mouwen," she said, reaching for his arms. She took out his cuff links and folded the sleeves of his shirt up and over his linen jacket.

"What does that mean?" he asked. "Your face is different."

"*Dat is een ander paar mouwen* means . . ." she said slowly, her face changing back, the muscles rearranging themselves to match the current of self flowing into her body, "'to have another matter.' *Paar mouwen*, 'to have a new *pair of sleeves*,'" she said insistently, tugging on his cuffs. "It's an idiom from medieval tournaments. The knights wore tokens on their sleeves."

She took the cuff links—two plain, silver knots—and set them into the sleeves of her own white cotton shirtdress.

"Are you stealing those?" he asked.

"It's not stealing," she explained. "It's borrowing. It's my new pair of sleeves."

"So you're the knight."

"I'm the knight," she said and nodded, laughing easily, her voice melodic and open. "You got it."

"Is it hard for you to speak English all the time?"

"It's not *hard* exactly. It's different. I do feel sometimes like I'm only playing with half the deck. I have to dive under the ocean, kind of, to speak English. Or, I have to dive back, maybe, now, to speak Flemish. It's one or the other. Not both."

"That sounds sad."

"It's not. I have lots of oceans this way. I . . . contain multitudes."

"I bet you do," he said, reaching out for a piece of her hair, holding it between his fingertips before he caught himself and pulled back.

"You know, I was investigating, earlier," she said. "Like we talked about."

"I still don't know what you mean by that." Hutton looked concerned.

"I think I got something," Cat said. "But . . . I'm wondering what you're gonna do with it."

"That depends. In the most basic terms, anything that's recorded as evidence *could* make a difference, but I don't know what you're going to say."

Cat smiled broadly. "Okay. That sounds good."

Hutton tapped her hand, a tiny reminder to keep going. She tried to look serious. "Before we saw you at Sigrid's, we found a handbag of Hillary's. It contained what turned out to be custom eyedrops from this company, Bedford Organics. I went by this afternoon to check them out, and they gave me kind of a makeover."

"Custom eyedrops? I don't understand what that is."

Cat didn't answer. "I still can't believe we ran into you last night on the street," she said, changing the subject. She stroked his palm with her fingers, running the edges of her pointed blue nails along his heart and life lines, looking up at him with a cartoonish expression, full of a happiness and longing that he found himself wanting to believe was real.

Hutton reached past her and pulled the Bedford Organics bag onto the table. He took out some of the samples and unwrapped them from their butcher paper. Cat watched his long fingers as he expertly untied the ribbons with a few strategic pulls.

"How much was all this stuff? It doesn't have any labels or price tags."

"It was free," Cat said, picking up one of the ribbons and tying it around her wrist.

"Is that common?"

"Sure. Beauty companies are always giving us free stuff, hoping that we'll put it in the magazine, put it on Photogram, whatever kind of association they can get. But this company is direct-sale-by-referral only. She didn't even ask about a feature, actually."

"That's interesting," he said, turning over some of the bottles in his hands. "Is that a viable business strategy?"

"I guess so." Cat shrugged.

"So which of these products was Hillary using?" Hutton's tone grew serious as he turned each sample over, looking for clues.

"Other than the eyedrops, I don't know." She dug the small bottle out of her purse and handed it to him, unconsciously obeying his officious manner. "What do they test for when people die?"

"A standard toxicology screen would look for opiates, amphetamines, barbiturates, alcohol, marijuana, check for any prescription medication found in the home or near the body to confirm the amount taken, and anything that the body was reacting to, producing antibodies for, basically."

"Would they have done anything else?"

"In her case, no. We didn't have any reason to—until now."

The waitress interrupted them to drop off another round of

cocktails. Once again, Hutton kept his eyes on Cat; she realized he was deliberately ignoring every other woman in the restaurant. His focus on her was so steady that she found herself wondering if it was a show for her benefit.

She filled Hutton in on the remaining details of her experience at Vittoria's shop in fits and starts, between poetic asides on the beauty of the ivy draped overhead, the beams of sunshine breaking through the spaces between the leaves—*Doesn't he see how beautiful it is?*

"I think I should call you a doctor," he said when she finished.

She looked confused.

"Cat, you're *very* charming. But you're not sober," he explained gently. "Whatever's in this"—he shook the metal tube of hand cream—"got you high. How do you feel?"

Cat felt a rush of blood hit her cheeks, pooling in bright round circles of embarrassment as it drained from the back of her head. *Holy shit*, she realized. *He's right.* Her jaw fell open slightly and her eyes grew even wider.

"Oh *shit*…I *am* high. Am I in trouble?" she whispered, her embarrassment turning to panic. "I…I didn't mean to…I would never…not on *purpose*, not in front of a police officer."

"I know," he said gently. "If it wasn't for this," he said, holding up the Bedford Organics bag, "I would have just thought you had a mood disorder."

She laughed, her embarrassment briefly alleviated. "I have flaws, but not that."

"Good," he said, smiling. "I think…I think I should take you home, though. Unless you need a doctor."

Cat shook her head. "I'll be fine," she said, feeling rejected and humiliated, despite his considerate tone.

"Okay, beautiful," he said, and he took her hand to help her up, knowing that he should take her into custody right now and get a blood sample. "I'm taking you home."

Hutton threw some cash on the table and shoved the Bedford

Organics products back into their bag before leading her out onto the street and hailing a taxi. She trailed behind him into the car's backseat and stared listlessly out the window as they rode silently back to her apartment.

After helping Cat into her building, Hutton caught the train back to Manhattan. He'd taken the whole bag of Bedford Organics products, despite Cat's attempt to keep the bottle labeled "Happiness" ("Please! I'm going to be so sad when this wears off!"), intending to get the case back in gear as soon as possible.

As he exited the subway and waited to cross Thirty-Fourth Street, he thought about Cat: the wide strap of red lace cutting into her shoulder, the ribbon she tied around her wrist, the way she popped the collar of her exaggerated shirtdress like a Japanese teenager imitating a frat boy. Her big brown eyes, both kind and sharp. He'd never met someone so . . . *studied*, who was *also* smart. He felt like she was daring him to solve a puzzle he didn't yet understand.

It was 8:00 p.m. The lab would be open until midnight. Hutton pulled open the double doors to the Midtown South Precinct, nodded to the patrolman on night duty at the desk, and buzzed his way through several more sets of doors before he arrived at his office. He divided the products, labeled them, processed requests for each analysis into the computer, and then ran them across the street where the lab assistant pointed wordlessly to a deposit tray.

Back in his office he searched for more details about Hillary Whitney that might help him gain access to her belongings. He punched her address into Google and found a current sale listing for the apartment from the Cormorant Group; it was still on the market. *Jackpot.*

He dialed the number on the listing. Though it was already after ten, a sharp voice answered right away.

"Betty Cormorant," a voice squawked after just two rings.

"This is Detective Mark Hutton, NYPD. I'm calling about an apartment you have listed for sale, from the estate of Hillary Whitney."

"You wanna see it? I can set something up for the morning. I think ten percent above asking and it's yours before noon."

"I need to see the belongings you took out of it, actually. Any chance you put a hold on the personal effects for the family?"

"Shit," she said. "Get a warrant."

"Listen, Betty, you know how it is. I got so much paperwork. I'll get the warrant, but first I need to know if the personal items are in storage. Can you take a look for me?"

"So what?" Betty snapped. "I just lost my seat at the bar to take this call. I thought you were a buyer. Paperwork sounds like a *you* problem."

"The next body I get in a good building, you're the first one I call."

"What precinct?"

"Midtown South. I got a few blocks of Park below Grand Central and all of NoMad."

"Deal," she said. "I'll call you right back."

Five minutes later, his phone rang. "You're lucky," she said. "The personal effects are all in a storage facility on the West Side."

"You got keys to the unit?"

"That I don't know. But I can give you the address and the contact. You're gonna have to make the warrant for the unit anyway or they won't let you in."

"I take it this isn't your first rodeo."

"How do you think we find listings in the first place? You're the third cop I've talked to this week."

He laughed and hung up, then spent the next two hours filing paperwork. At midnight he finally locked up his office and hustled down the stairs and out the front door of the precinct, hailing a cab within seconds.

"Hey boss," said the driver. Three separate cellphones were attached to his dash, all running different hailing apps.

"Hi. Good evening. Brooklyn, Lincoln and Ocean, please." The television screen embedded in the divider blared as a doe-eyed waif wearing an NYC-branded T-shirt pretended to eat a hot dog on the Staten Island Ferry. Hutton jammed his finger into the screen, eventually turning it off.

"Okay, no problem." The driver popped his earbud back in and resumed laughing and joking in a language wholly foreign to Hutton as he lurched and surged the cab over to Brooklyn.

He briefly fell asleep in the cab, waking up when his own phone buzzed.

> You free tonight?

He let the text from Callie Court—his longtime close friend and frequent hookup—float on the screen. Callie had lately been tending bar at three different places, singing in two bands, and working for the avant-garde and occasionally outré designer Jonathan Sprain as a "muse," in addition to her dwindling modeling gigs, and she had more energy than anyone he'd ever known.

Another text popped up.

> B/c I have an extra ticket to see guantanamo baywatch / hoodie & the blowjobs @ Grasslands, done with my shift in 20.

Shit. I would so go to that. But he desperately needed to go to sleep. He texted back:

> I need to sleep Cal, I'm two feet from bed

> Ok but set time is 1 am! So soon?

Before he could reply, the cab screeched to a halt in front of his apartment. Hutton pocketed his phone and dropped two twenties through the partition. "Keep the change," he said, hopping out the door. He waved to his doorman, climbed the stairs two at a time, and collapsed on the couch next to his laptop.

Chapter Six

While Hutton slept, Cat was perched in a makeshift toilet at King's Landing, the cramped bar around the corner from her apartment, using her keys to snort cocaine out of a tiny blue plastic bag she'd found in her closet. Sigrid leaned over the sink, reapplying a matte red lipstick. The walls that surrounded them were made from plywood sheets recently hammered into some two-by-fours; the door was a ribbed panel of plastic roofing with a large hole drilled for a handle. Swedish house music shook the room.

"I totally fucked it up," Cat was yelling. "Hot Cop looked so *sad* when he brought me home. I don't know if he believed me, you know? That it was an *accident*." She sniffed, tasting cocaine on the back of her throat.

"I almost don't believe it either, that you managed to get high from beauty products, but I know you. *You*, Catherine Celia Ono, get high *on purpose*," Sigrid said, blotting her lipstick on a square of toilet paper. "Either way, that's fucking hilarious."

Cat offered up a little pile of cocaine on a key. Sigrid pinched a nostril and huffed it back with a practiced snort.

"What do you think is going to happen to the bag of product from Bedford Organics?" Sigrid asked.

"Uh...nothing?" Cat replied hopefully. "*Fuck.* I don't know."

"Tell him you want to be anonymous."

"Right?" Cat agreed. "I gave him my bag of awesome free drugs. The least he can do is make it anonymous."

"I'm sure he doesn't want to get you in trouble. He totally likes you," Sigrid said confidently. "Send a cute text."

"I texted him twenty minutes ago and he hasn't texted back," Cat admitted, frowning.

"What'd you write?"

"Just, *thanks for taking me home, you're sweet. do-over?*"

Sigrid pinched her other nostril and took in another little stack of cocaine off Cat's keys. "That's not time-sensitive. He'll write back tomorrow. Don't worry. He's probably asleep." She passed the bag and key back.

Cat dipped her finger into the coke and rubbed it on her gums. "Thanks for coming up here. I was just feeling *so* mortified. And I was way too high to go to bed."

"Girl, I don't give a *shit.* I had a second audition today for that series on the CW and I *completely* fucked it up. Whatever, I'm too fucking old anyway to play a teenage lesbian." She wiped excess lipstick from the corner of her mouth with a practiced flick. "Let's get wasted."

Cat rinsed her hands in the dirty sink and wiped them dry on her jeans. She'd at least had the good sense to strip off her starched white dress. Now, clad in a pair of heavily ripped 501s and equally shredded black T-shirt, Cat was ready to throw the entire evening down the toilet. Sigrid was too—she wore a crop top screenprinted with the emojis for "I love roosters" over her usual high-waisted black cigarette pants and Bensimon slip-ons.

They squeezed out of the bathroom together and marched over to the narrow bar top. Two tattooed, bearded men in identical leather jackets and Buddy Holly eyeglasses were sitting at the corner of the bar, drinking neat whiskeys. They both had motorcycle helmets hanging under their stools and gave off a general aura of handsomeness, although it was difficult to assess how much was natural and how much came from their tough-guys-who-went-to-art-school costumes.

Sigrid turned to Cat and lowered her voice. "Place your bet: let's call it twenty bucks. I'm going for carpenters? Maybe fabricators. They went to SAIC or RISD. I bet they're in that studio around the corner that makes giant fake astronaut sets for Moncler and shit."

"Deal. Because you're *wrong*. I'm thinking...menswear, the two straight guys in their class at FIT, raw Japanese denim, and at least one of them is named Jay," whispered Cat.

"Let's find out." Sigrid stuck out her butt and leaned over the bar top, greeting the bartender with a kiss on the cheek. "Callie, can we get two of whatever those guys are drinking?" She winked at the two men, who immediately stood up and walked over.

"I'm Dave, and this is Jay," said the one with the Nazi Youth haircut as he pointed at the one with the man bun. Cat felt Sigrid laughing over the invisible tin-can telephone of their friendship. They all shook hands, the type of warm and friendly greeting that signaled the beginning of a group adventure—the kind you exchanged on hiking trails or ski lifts.

"Did you guys see those tires burning outside in the empty lot?" asked Sigrid.

"It's supposed to be an art installation. Some kids from RISD. It's bullshit, though."

"Kids from RISD are bullshit?" Cat pretended to be offended.

"We went there, we're allowed to say that."

That took all of forty-five seconds, she thought. "Oh yeah? When?"

"We graduated last year," said Man Bun. "How about you two? Let me guess: Pratt..." He squinted and pointed at Cat first. "You're majoring in industrial design, and you're obviously in fashion design."

Sigrid looked at Cat. *Play along, or tell the truth?* Cat gave her a smirk that said *walk the line*.

"Not bad," Sigrid said, pretending to be impressed. "Well, what year do you think we are?"

"Seniors, you're definitely seniors," said Nazi Youth. The two men had a focus like a laser beam, their pure and unadulterated youth aimed directly at Cat and Sigrid.

"That sounds fucking great," said Sigrid. "Let's go with that." Their whiskeys arrived on the bar and Cat and Sigrid raised them simultaneously, knocking the shots back and signaling for another round.

Five hours later they'd closed down Pillow Fort, a bar three blocks away where everyone always seemed to get roofied. James, the obscenely handsome bartender, had locked the front door, and he and Cat took shots off the bar top. Nazi Youth, Man Bun, and Sigrid were all making out in the corner.

"I'm just saying, I really just want to be on the sea, you know? I've been building boats all my life. It's time to really commit." *Shot.*

"You should totally fucking do that. Follow your dream! If *you think* you are a boatbuilder—"

"Shipwright," he interrupted. *Shot.*

"Right, *shipwright*, that's just who you should fucking *be*." She pulled out her pack of cigarettes. "Can I smoke in here?"

He nodded enthusiastically and pulled out a lighter. "Only if I can have a drag." His blond hair fell down over his face.

Cat climbed up on top of the bar, crossing her legs. He sat across from her and took the same seat, their knees touching. She held up her cigarette for a light, and he lit it before reaching over and pressing his forehead to hers. She held the cigarette to his mouth and he inhaled, their foreheads still touching.

"You're going to find *your truth*, James," she said, really meaning it. "I just know it. *You belong in the sea*."

"Cat, you're the best." He had the same youthful, sincere energy as Man Bun and Nazi Youth.

I get older, but they stay the same age, Cat thought.

She grinned and climbed into his lap. They kissed messily, the cigarette still between her fingers. Cat vaguely heard the sound of a glass being knocked to the floor but ignored it. Someone—probably Sigrid—turned down the lights and turned up the music. Cat and James took the cue and stumbled through the dark over to the tattered velvet sofa in the bar's back room, leaving Sigrid and her two men alone in the front of the bar.

Later that morning Hutton woke up to a series of text messages from Callie Court, sent throughout the night after he'd drifted off to sleep.

This set is amazing

Just met Hoodie and the Blowjobs

MADE OUT WITH HOODIE

We could be having a threesome with Hoodie right now

He checked the clock: it was 6:10 a.m. Confident that Callie would be passed out cold at this hour, he texted her back right away with what he thought was an impossible overture.

I was sleeping. Any chance you're still up? I could swing by before work.

He changed screens, about to reply to a late-night thank-you text from Cat, when Callie wrote back:

> Need to sleep soon but wanna get breakfast?

He looked around the apartment. His boxes, still mostly unpacked, were strewn around the edges of the living room; he didn't have any food in the refrigerator, and he was almost certainly out of coffee.

He threw on a clean pair of running shorts and a threadbare Battle of the Bands T-shirt, packing his work clothes and dress shoes into a backpack as he brushed his teeth. He texted Callie back.

> Taking a lap then coming by you, be there in 20, don't fall asleep!

Callie replied with a photo of her bed.

> Run fast

Hutton locked the apartment and looped the park once before sprinting up the westernmost trail of Prospect Park toward Callie's apartment, a converted turn-of-the century tenement studio on Sterling Place, just off Grand Army Plaza. After buzzing him up, Callie answered the door wrapped in an oversized Turkish towel, her dark-blonde hair still damp from the shower. She reached forward and scratched his beard by way of hello. He grinned and closed the door behind him.

Callie and Hutton had met in college and started sleeping together his senior year—her freshman year—and yet they'd never officially dated or broken up. Hutton's last relationship hadn't *exactly* ended because of Callie...but she certainly hadn't helped. It was hard to qualify her to anyone else in his life. Men usually thought he was stringing her along; women usually thought they were destined to change their minds about each other and get married. Neither judgment was accurate. He thought of their connection as a true friendship punctuated by bouts of what could only be referred to as breakneck fucking; it wasn't *romantic* per se, but it was still meaningful to them both. They'd had various on-and-off periods over the last decade, the most recent off when she'd gone to rehab, but they'd been back on, sort of, for the past four months, hanging out, going to shows, and fooling around.

"I'm so hungry." She yawned. "Give me two minutes."

"I'm gonna rinse off," he told her, and she nodded sleepily. While he showered, Callie rummaged through the antique armoire she used for a closet, pulling on her standard uniform: black lace underpants and matching bra, black Levis, and a plain white V-necked T-shirt. Hutton came out from the bathroom half-dressed, and she knotted his tie.

"Don't let me get coffee," she said, grabbing her keys. "I need to sleep after we eat."

"What did you do last night, anyway?"

"I had a shift at King's Landing until midnight, then I met up with Libby and Tess. We hit up that new North Korea–themed fried chicken place before going to Grasslands. The show was amazing. They're *so* good. Liza, that Indian girl with that cool neck tattoo I keep talking about, was running the bar, so we all went backstage after, and I *fully* hooked up with Hoodie. Like, *in Grass-lands*, like, *behind a curtain*. It was so fun. Then we played ping-pong in Joe's office over on Wythe and drained the keg. Then all of them started doing dope, so I left and came home."

"You know you're telling a cop that, right? And I seriously doubt your sponsor would think that it's okay to even be *around* drugs."

"I keep forgetting that I'm not supposed to tell you the truth any-more. You're so fucking weird, Mark," she said, slipping on a beat-up pair of leopard-print Vans. "I'll have you know that Josh, my NA sponsor, is fine with it. He says New York is full of drugs and you can't spend your whole life trying to avoid them; you just need to know that it's not part of *your* life anymore. I happen to agree."

He kissed her on the forehead, eager to change the subject. "Let's go get breakfast."

They left her building and grabbed egg sandwiches from the nearest bodega, eating them on a bench in Grand Army Plaza as the morning crowds of commuters surged around them.

"How's that guy you're hanging out with?" he asked.

"It's good. I mean, it's a job; it's not like we're dating. Hanging with Jonathan is *like* modeling, except nobody publishes my photo. He just lets me hang out and play around with the clothes. Sometimes he films me, too, but he doesn't show them to anyone. At least I don't think he does."

Hutton laughed. "That's the shadiest thing you've said yet." He took a huge gulp of coffee and raised his eyebrows.

"It's not shady. It's *better* than modeling, because I don't have to see myself all the time. It's like...everywhere I go, there I am, especially when I least expect it," she said, tucking her hair behind her ear with a self-conscious twitch. A bus roared by with Callie's image stuck to the side, though you couldn't *quite* see her face.

She had recently appeared in a Valentino campaign that was plastered all over New York's transit system. Callie was omewhere between a straight-size and a plus-size model, and the ad made her body look like a big fat girl had been squeezed into a child's wedding dress. Callie *hated* it. She watched Hutton watch the bus and thought bitterly about how quickly the thirty grand she'd gotten for the campaign had run out.

"That ad is like a Dalí tit-crease. I still can't believe it wasn't photoshopped. In fact, I *don't* believe it."

"I'm sorry you hate it, Cal. *I* think it's beautiful. You're the most beautiful girl in the whole world," he said sweetly as he shoved the remainder of his sausage, egg, and cheese into his mouth.

Callie balled up their sandwich wrappers and tossed them into the trash. "All right. It's almost eight. I have to go to bed. Go fight crime, or whatever."

They stood up and exchanged a warm hug good-bye.

"I'll call you later," Hutton said automatically before turning and heading to the 2/3 Line. Callie watched him walk all the way to the subway entrance before she turned to go back to her own building.

Cat's phone alarm was going off. She pressed the center button.

"SIRI, WHAT TIME IS IT?" she croaked.

"It's 9:14 a.m.," said Siri. *Oh fuck.* She couldn't be late twice in one week.

Cat felt a hand squeezing her butt. The handsome bartender was draped over her body, his breath a rancid cloud. She shimmied out from under him and leaned against the plywood headboard mounted on the wall, tucking the sheet around herself. It was *cold*—she'd left the air conditioner running on high again, too fucked up to remember to shut it off.

"Let's go back to sleep," he mumbled, pawing idly at an itch on his sculpted chest while his other hand groped the bed to find her body.

"You can go back to sleep, but you need to do it at home—I have to go to work." Her head was pounding. Her brain had constricted in size and was pulling away from the sides of her skull.

She reached for the two plastic bottles next to her bed, one covered in black gaffer tape and the other in cream-colored masking tape, and popped out two ibuprofen and two acetaminophen. Her tongue was dry and swollen. She wiped the sleep crust off her lips and searched around for her water bottle, but found only a half-empty can of beer. *Ugggh.*

James looked up at her with his big green eyes, looking extra young and extra pouty. "Can't I just sleep here?"

Cat was unable to mask her annoyance as she hopped out of bed. "No, I have a million things to do today, sorry," she snapped, shoving a commemorative plastic cup from a Mets game under the kitchen sink's shoddy aluminum tap.

"I'm going to take a shower, okay? Here"—she paused and downed her pills—"drink the rest of this water. It'll help." She passed him the Mets cup and ran into the bathroom.

Cat sat on the floor of the shower for ten minutes, the water as hot as she could stand. She washed her hair twice, scrubbed the smoke and beer out of her skin with a stiff agave-fiber brush, and combed through a leave-in conditioner. A pile of fresh towels—Cat's only concession to cleanliness was the laundry service that picked up her clothes and linens once a week—sat in a basket opposite the peeling cast-iron tub she used as a shower. She wrapped one around her body, the other around her head, and stepped back out into the loft with her toothbrush in her mouth.

James slipped past her into the bathroom, closed the door, and turned the fan on. *Double ugh. Whatever, she was finished in there anyway.* She towel-dried her hair and body, sprayed herself down with the sea water bottle, then applied a heavy coat of children's SPF 50+ sunblock.

She turned on the light in her closet and searched for the easiest thing she owned, a black silk T-shirt dress from Reformation that everyone constantly mistook for Dries Van Noten. It always looked good, no matter how wrecked she was in the face, and it was appropriate for any situation. Cat moved like a robot in high gear, automatically pulling on her dress, smearing a heavy-coverage cream from Korea all over her skin before lightly applying a swipe of mascara, a coat of clear lip balm, and braiding her hair in an inside-out Mohawk plait. She tried on a resin bead necklace, but the weight suffocated her. *No necklaces today*, she decided. *No bracelets.* She turned to a shelf of ceramic ring pyramids, pulled off a dozen gold bands of different sizes, and layered them on between the joints on all her fingers. *Good enough.*

For eyeglasses she chose a pair of thick, square tortoiseshell Tom Ford frames to distract from her face, applying Visine drops to the redness in her eyes. She found her bag hanging neatly on a hook near her front door. It was 9:50. James was *still* in the bathroom. She called out to him.

"James, I have to go to work."

His voice was easy to hear through the bathroom's cheap hollow-core door. "Okay, one minute," he said awkwardly.

She checked her phone. Still no text back from Hutton. Cat shut down the air-conditioning, and the air in the loft grew still. The sunbeams coming through the lead-cased windowpanes cast a tic-tac-toe grid onto her floor. She pictured ghost versions of the nine drinks she'd had the night before popping up in the sunbeam grid, like *Hollywood Squares*. The nine beers and shots sang to the tune of the *Golden Girls* theme song: *Thank you for being a friend, we traveled down your throat and back again, your liver is true, it's a pal and a confidante.* Little bags of cocaine sprinkled their fine-grain snow on top.

"Cigarettes, phone, wallet, metro card, keys," she said aloud, gathering the items from the apartment. The toilet flushed as she pulled her driver's license out of last night's jeans pocket. *Finally.*

James opened the bathroom door and sauntered proudly out into the loft. He wrapped his arms around Cat's body. She gave him a friendly pat on the back, her torso rigid. "Okay, babe," she chided. "Where's your shirt? I'm *so* fucking late."

"Oh shit, you really are dressed," he said, frowning, strolling back to the bed and slowly rolling his T-shirt back on. He tried to wrap her in a hug again, but she was already holding the door. She ran down the graffitied cement stairwell and out the front door onto Moore Street. He followed her and grabbed her hands, attempting to pull her into a kiss. Cat pecked him on the cheek and squirmed out of his embrace. As she flew down the block toward the L train, she yelled, "I'll call you later!"

They both knew she was lying. James sighed and shrugged his shoulders, then ambled toward the coffee shop on the corner to see who was around. After all: it was still technically his after-hours.

Whig Beaton Molton-Mauve Lucas stood on the wooden dock at the Seventy-Ninth Street Boat Basin, sipping her morning coffee and waving good-bye to her daughters. As the pair of towheaded girls hung precariously off the back of their father's catamaran, Lou prayed that their life jackets would keep them safe all the way to Montauk. They'd be there for three whole weeks, during which time Lou planned to completely throw herself into work. She hoped they wouldn't be lonely—she knew *logically* that they wouldn't be, but she always worried about them anyway, perhaps never more acutely than when she watched them disappear with their father into the world's vast oceans.

The girls faded into little pink specks. When she was certain they could no longer make her out, Lou stopped waving and turned to climb back up the hill into Riverside Park.

The sun was already beating down on her legs, bare and tanned beneath a pair of slightly oversized ivory crepe Bermuda shorts. By the time she scooted into the driver's seat of her customized electric Porsche Panamera, she had forgotten her worries, and she sped recklessly down Broadway, narrowly dodging pedestrians as she hit green after green. When she pulled into the service entrance of Cooper House and threw the car into park, an attendant opened her door and helped her out. Lou never parked her own car; it was too stressful.

"Thanks, Gina!" she yelled, pulling open the heavy glass door and waving her bag spastically in front of the aluminum pole that controlled the basement's elevator bank.

I'm going to make something of today, she thought, stepping into elevator G. She told herself that every morning. Lou was thirty-seven years old and this was her very first job. She'd spent her whole life as somebody's wife, somebody's trophy. Married first at seventeen to the ninth Earl of Southumberland, Charles Molton, who died four years later in a fatal Formula One racing accident; then again at twenty-five to Alexander Lucas, from whom she was just recently finally and officially divorced, this was her first real year as an adult on her own.

Up to now she hadn't minded; she'd never known anything else. Lou's mother, Aurelia Beaton Mauve, Marchioness of Dorset, had spent her entire life simply throwing parties, and she'd been more than approved of; she'd been downright *celebrated*. The Mauve family's greatest hope for Lou—with her horsey teeth and booming voice—had been to marry well and become as accomplished a hostess as her mother, ideally with someone who had far more pounds sterling in the bank than her own father. Well, *she'd done that*, and now that her own girls were old enough to head off to school, she'd been wondering if there was more to life than just spending other people's money.

The opportunity at *RAGE* had come at the perfect time. Her contract was just for six months, but now that she'd had a taste of shaping the zeitgeist, she never wanted to stop. Lou was determined to figure out a way to stay on the *RAGE* masthead—Paula had told her they intended to eventually promote Cat, but Lou was certain she could find a way to stay. Just before she reached the forty-sixth floor, she told herself: *You are not going to waste this opportunity. You're just as good as everyone else in this building.* The doors slid open. She marched purposefully through the marbled lobby and into the cubicle maze. It was time to get to work.

After Cat skulked into the office, she started on the to-do list she'd compiled the day before, barely making it uptown to Per Se on time for the promo lunch for Delvaux. She was so hung over that she almost couldn't remember what it was like to be sober. She left the lunch early and took a cab back to Cooper, locking her office door before crawling under the desk.

With the chair shoved out of the way and her sunglasses on, the underside of her desk wasn't half bad. She stuck her legs out, tried to assume corpse pose so she wouldn't overly wrinkle her dress, then promptly passed out.

Forty-five minutes later she felt her phone buzz on the floor next to her. *Shit. I'm sleeping on the floor*, she thought before looking at the screen. It was Hutton. *Dear Lord, please don't let him come storming in here.* Long gone was the fantasy where Hutton barged into her office and bent her over the desk. If he was at Cooper now, she would have to go outside, dig a hole, crawl into it, and die of embarrassment.

She managed to answer just before the call went to voicemail.

"Hello," she said through a sigh, hoping she sounded world-weary and mysterious instead of ready for her first AA meeting.

"How are you?" he asked in a voice that seemed clipped and neutral.

"I'm alive," she said. "I'm embarrassed, but I'm alive."

"That's good."

"Did you find out what was in the products?"

"Not yet." His voice definitely did not contain a single ounce of flirt.

"Am I in trouble?"

"No," he said, sounding distracted. "I'm going to have to call you back."

He hung up.

Well, I guess that's that, she thought. *He's over it.* She let her head fall back down onto the office carpeting. It smelled like vacuum cleaners, like the accumulated dust of a thousand and one boxes of printer paper. Cat let out a long breath and willed her body to expel every ounce of her hangover into the ether.

For a fleeting moment she became vaguely paranoid that Hutton had somehow found out she'd spent the night before boozing, snorting, and licking a bartender. Not that she was ashamed—far from it—but it seemed prudent to maintain a certain kind of facade with the kind of man who joined the NYPD to make a difference. *At least at first.* But the only person they could know in common was . . . *Bess*, she remembered. She reminded herself to bring it up in the future.

Her computer buzzed. Cat dragged herself into an upright position, trying to quietly roll the chair back into place as she awkwardly hoisted her body into it, catching a whiff of herself as she landed in the chair; god, was she sweating beer? She looked at the monitor, the bright screen hurting her eyes.

bess.bonn: hey, lou doesn't know how to use chat

catono: ?

bess.bonn: beet dye in home upholstery!

Fuck. Cat opened the CoopDoc marked "beets" and scanned the *very* brief notes that Lou had made.

positives: non toxic, very strong dye, easy to plant in a variety of climates, can adapt sugar beet plantations, doesn't pollute soil, no GMOs needed, a sustainable plant's sustainable plant, if you know what I mean.

cons: looks like period blood??

Cat let out a snort over the last line. *Well, if anyone can make me feel better, Lou probably can. Might as well do some work.* She punched Lou's extension into her Cooper landline and unlocked her office door. Within five minutes Lou had pulled up a chair beside her.

It took just forty-five minutes to hammer out the copy for September's page on eco-friendly fabrics from one of Lou's pet projects. RED IS THE NEW GREEN, declared their headline. "From the thread and dye, all the way to the packaging, this eco-warrior is using beets—one of the world's most renewable resources—to reimagine home furnishings." The accompanying photographs had come in that morning, and the subject of the photos, Lou's friend Criselda Johnson-Butler—former Photogram marketing guru turned eco-designer—looked like she hadn't eaten in days. Her arms were overflowing with beets.

"God, she's as thin as a feral dog," declared Lou. "I wonder what she's doing."

"I'd say 'eating beets,' but somehow I don't think food is involved," Cat guessed.

"I bet she got a lap-band. I hear they'll give it to anyone now."

Cat laughed. "That's horrible."

"It's not horrible!" protested Lou. "Some people just don't have any self-control."

"Yeah, *obese* people. Not size twos."

"Well, I support *whatever* elective surgery she wants. That, my darling, is what we call choose-your-choice feminism."

Cat rolled her eyes. "Yeah. That's exactly what it means. Like telling the bear performing at the circus that it can 'choose' its own tricycle to ride on."

"Poor bears." Lou wrinkled her nose. "Jane wanted to go to the circus last week, and Alex's new girlfriend—she's vegan, of course—insisted on giving her some literature from PETA. Jane is *six*. She can barely read, yet she understood enough to cry for an hour, and then she insisted we all sign an anticircus pledge. I pray to god that the next one doesn't teach her about vivisection."

"Does your ex-husband always introduce his girlfriends to the kids? Doesn't that...*annoy* you?" asked Cat, slightly incredulous.

"Honestly, it's not usually that bad. They're *so* sweet, even this PETA one—the problem is just that they're all completely witless," Lou explained. "They mean well, they do, but they're basically very expensive blow-up dolls. I don't think it's affecting my girls too much. I tell them the girlfriends are 'Daddy's assistants.' I do feel for *them*, though, these poor beautiful women who all think they're going to be his next wife."

Alexander Lucas, heir to a multibillion-euro industrial fortune protected fiercely by a variety of boards, attorneys, blind trusts, and two determined ex-wives with five children between them, wouldn't be getting remarried anytime soon.

"It's Claire's girls I worry about," Lou continued, her voice brimming with genuine concern. "They're in their twenties now. I wonder if they're going to have, you know, *daddy* issues. It was hard enough with me, although they came around eventually. It helps that their mum and I are so close."

"You and Claire are so cool," Cat said. "I was actually thinking that maybe we could do a piece on you two—maybe something for the holidays? Maybe the two of you could be a MATRIARCH piece together."

"I'll check with Claire. She's redoing the house in Tahoe to fit the whole gang with enough privacy—maybe she'll be open to shooting it. It's got ten bedrooms now."

Cat glanced at the clock on her computer. The afternoon was flying by. "Shit. It's almost four. Let's choose these shots already."

Their favorite was the one of Criselda pretending to eat a beet; she couldn't keep the look of wild hunger off her gaunt face with food so near. Cat was sure Margot would veto it, though— too real—so instead they selected a variety of images that showed Criselda in a glamorous white cotton suit reminiscent of a tampon commercial, directing her hardworking and mostly female staff.

After completing the copy and preliminary layout, they sent it off to Production.

"I have one more thing," Cat asked, pulling up the HW file before Lou could get out the door. "Can you edit this? We have to turn it in next week, and I'm done with my draft, I think."

Lou looked shocked. "But...I wasn't *that* close with Hillary. We went skiing together last Christmas, but that was with a *group*. I don't *really* think I should have the final say on her international

obituary. What about Constance?" Lou said kindly, referring to
the managing editor. "They seemed much closer. Maybe she's a
better fit."

"No, you definitely should." Cat placed her hand on Lou's arm.
"MATRIARCH was *your* idea. Don't give it up to Constance. All
of these shots are worthy. *Really*. You can't make a bad choice. But
somebody needs to cut half of them, and I just can't do it. It might
be a tribute, but it's also a magazine—I need an objective eye to
edit the best composition here. And society stuff is your *bag*."

Lou nodded. "Send it all over, and I'll work on it tomorrow."

"Thanks, Lou. I'm sure you'll make it look amazing."

Cat spent the rest of the day with Bess and Molly, researching
options for Lou's *RAGE* Gaia pitch for the November issue. Lou
gave intermittent aid between Skype sessions with Princess Sophie
and dialing for dollars over possible sponsorship of the elaborate
renovation Sophie's Bavarian summer castle would need. Cat's
hangover slowly wore off, and by the time she hopped on the subway at 8:00 p.m., she was nearly recovered.

When Cat got home the bell rang with a delivery; Delvaux had
messengered over their entire spring collection. *For Cat: Please take
a closer look. Yours, Ekaterina.* Her morning hangover must have read
as unimpressed. She smiled and signed for the box. There must
have been thirty thousand dollars' worth of bags in there. Cat unpacked it slowly, examining each piece with care. The briefcase in
particular was exquisite. She was pleased to discover it was already
stamped with her initials, as was the matching weekend duffel bag.

Cat lit a Diptyque candle and gathered her books from around
the apartment, tucking them back one by one into the wall-length
bookcase. Hutton hadn't called her back, she realized as she found a
home for a dog-eared copy of *I Have It All and So Do You*, Margot's
autobiography from a few years earlier. It was just a twenty-four-
hour fantasy, she reminded herself, fueled by booze and the way he
smelled and a whole bunch of crazy drugs.

Cat wondered how anyone ever managed to make it through

the awkward phases of dating into an actual relationship. Andrew, the only serious boyfriend of her twenties, had struggled through three years of long distance, flying into New York once a month while finishing his PhD in Chicago—until the day he was offered a full-time, tenure-track position at Pomona in California. Cat had flat out refused to move to Los Angeles. "I don't know how to drive," she'd argued. "I don't have any friends there, I'll be lonely, and you'll be my whole life."

"I want to be your whole life," he'd replied.

"Then move to New York," she'd demanded, unable to admit she was so jealous of his job it would eat her alive, and knowing that this was the end.

"You know I can't," he'd said. "You want me to give up my career for you? This is my shot, Cat. Pomona is a *really good* goddamn job."

"So *I* should move and give up *my* career? Sorry. *I don't think so.* Maybe if it was *Stanford*," she'd spit back.

After a few more phone calls and one very sad weekend when she flew to Chicago to help him put down his aging dog, they were done for good. Since then Cat's romantic life had been a succession of weird dates and six-week love affairs with men she respected but didn't actually like. Now that she'd finally found someone she definitely liked, it seemed that *she* was the one who wasn't good enough.

Just eat some dinner and go to sleep, she told herself. *It'll be better in the morning. It's always better in the morning.* She cooked a quick dinner of ready-made udon noodles and poached eggs before climbing into bed with a book. She managed to read ten pages further into *Welcome to the Desert of the Real* before falling into a peacefully deep and dreamless sleep.

Hutton hadn't expected Callie to come by his office after their early-morning breakfast, if only because she usually slept all day. But when she knocked on the doorframe—squeezing the shoulder of the dumbstruck officer she'd convinced to bring her through security straight to his office—he'd just dialed Cat, who picked up and said "Hello" at the exact same time that Callie purred out a "Hey there" in her low voice.

He pointed to the phone and tried his best to sound officious, keeping his voice steady and clear while Callie stood in the doorway obviously eavesdropping. Cat sounded exhausted anyway, like she couldn't wait to get off the phone either, so he hung up quickly.

"What's up, Cal?"

"I found your keys on my floor," she said. "I thought you might want them back."

Hutton reached over the desk and Callie dropped the keys into his outstretched palm. "Thank you," he said. "They must have fallen out of my bag. You didn't have to come out here. I could have met you on my way home."

"I'm actually going to Newark. I got an audition for a music video in Nashville and a new girl took my shifts for me." She pointed to the rolling suitcase next to her in the hallway. Hutton watched three of his colleagues stop behind Callie to stare at her backside, their hand gestures and facial expressions crude.

"I'll be back on Monday. Wanna hang out?" she asked. The trio spontaneously grew into a group of five. One of them held up a cellphone and took her photo. Annoyed, he stood up and motioned her into his office, wheeling her suitcase through the doorway. One of his colleagues flashed him a thumbs-up. Hutton closed the door in reply.

"I can't Monday."

"Tuesday?"

"Can't."

"Wednesday?"

"Can't. I'm in it, Cal. I think this case is big."

She stared at him for a second, then nodded and grabbed the handle of her suitcase. "See you on the other side," she replied. Callie opened the door to his office and walked through it without looking back, blowing through the cadre of leering officers down the hall like they were seeds on a dandelion.

Hutton stayed at the office until his warrant to search the Cormorant storage facility was approved. He picked up a pizza and a six-pack of beer, then spent the rest of his Wednesday going through Hillary Whitney's belongings until he found what he was looking for.

Chapter Seven

When Cat walked into the ladies' room before her Thursday morning production meeting, she turned on the tap and left it running as she walked to the handicapped toilet on the end.

Managing editor Constance Onderveet was attempting to vomit discreetly in the first stall. After a few awkward run-ins and knocks during her first month on the job ("Are you *sure* you're okay?"), Cat had learned to take her coffee mug into the restroom and stick it under the tap to "rinse" in order to drown out the noise while she peed. Hearing other people throw up inspired the same in Cat, but unlike Constance, she *truly* despised vomiting.

When she returned to her office, coffee mug in hand, Molly and Bess were waiting. The three women sat down around Cat's desk, which was littered with index cards, agate paperweights, a brick she'd spray-painted gold, and a half-dozen rose-tinted college-ruled legal pads.

"I can get you a clean coffee mug, you know," Molly said. "You don't have to keep rinsing the same one."

Bess laughed. "Cat rinses the coffee mug because she hates the sound of people doing...*bathroom* things."

"Who are you, Monk?" asked Molly. "What do you do in public, just hold it 'til you get home?"

"It's mostly the barfing," Cat admitted.

"Uh, you guys went to prep school, too," Molly replied. "How did you not get used to that?"

"Yeah, but we went to *Miss Sawyer's*," Bess explained. "We didn't have the performative additive of men on campus. We ate real food, played sports, spent a lot of time outside."

Molly looked confused. "That sounds like lesbian summer camp."

"I think it was healthy," Cat said.

"But how did you get into college?" Molly asked. "Didn't you need to be, you know, the best or whatever? I'm not saying bulimia makes you 'the best'; it's just, you know...a real type A thing to do. Like...being organized."

Neither Bess nor Cat had an answer for that. Lou knocked on the door and popped her head in.

"Are we set?"

The three ladies nodded, gathering up their notebooks and folios before walking into the conference room to meet with the production staff. They spent a few hours coordinating details for photo shoots in the upcoming weeks before heading as a group down to the cafeteria.

Bess and Cat both loaded up on salad and bread. Molly got a half-serving of sushi. Lou pulled her lunch out of her purse, grabbing just a coffee from the barista. After they swiped their cards to pay and sat down, Cat pointed to Lou's Tupperware.

"I didn't know you liked to cook, Lou."

"Oh! I don't, really. I did have cooking classes at school in Switzerland. It's all very Victorian over there—I can draw and play and sing and make soufflé. '*Don't worry: Britain's women can always entertain*,'" she said in her poshest baritone. "I didn't cook this. I have a service that delivers all my meals. It's *pure bliss*. This is some superfood with eight kinds of seeds and so forth."

She dug her fork into what looked to Cat like plain brown rice with red onion and carrot mixed in.

"Very practical," Bess commented. "I should be so organized."

Cat spread butter on her two baguette slices. "I can't bring my lunch. Every time I've tried, the Tupperware winds up rotting for months in the bottom of my desk drawer. I just had to commit to buying it every day."

When they'd finished eating, Cat collected all of their empty plates and containers, positioned them in a quadrant, and snapped a picture for her Photogram account, captioning it no food just plates #garfield #lasagna #cleanplateclub @loch_ness_bess @mollybeans @lou_lucas and tagging the Cooper House building.

Molly looked at her quizzically.

"It's my Photogram rebellion," Cat explained. "I want to remind everyone on the Cooper feed to go eat lunch. I'm daring them to consume carbohydrates."

"Even though we didn't eat lasagna."

"I ate bread. It's *basically* lasagna."

The women cleared their table and filed back up to the office. Bess and Molly started racking the clothes Cat had selected for the following week's shoot of **Dotty for It**, the Sylvia Plath–themed spread for October. Cat retreated into her office and set out a fresh legal pad; she still hadn't planned out all the shots.

Although her Tuesday afternoon adventure had taken her off the rails and completely embarrassed her, Cat was now feeling gratitude for the accidental trip. Her mind was loose; she kept noticing groups of colors where she hadn't seen them before, like a yellow car parked in front of a yellow bicycle chained next to a yellow rosebush; three red baseball caps in the crowd; the explosive green of the city's summer trees. *Maybe the world really is big and wide and open*, she thought.

She put on her headphones, turned her white noise generator to "Thunderstorm," and logged into the **Dotty for It** shoot's badge board. As she clicked through the clothes, moving and sorting the scans, Polaroids, and screencaps that made up the possible inventory, she had a moment of inspiration.

They could pose the model facing mirrors distributed throughout the background; get the angles right, and the model would be surrounded by prismatic images of herself. *Little armies, like the Window Cats that followed me down Broadway and Driggs. What could make you crazier than looking only at your own reflection?*

She remembered changing at her gym in Chicago and watching a passel of teenage girls measure the circumference of each other's thighs with the spans of their fingers as they stood in front of the mirror—*yours are the smallest*, they'd declared to their leader, who smiled in satisfaction. Cat's heart had broken watching them. She'd wanted to slap the girls, to scream: *You are prisoners in a jail you're too young to see. The images you see everywhere of tiny thighs are a lie. You are more than your bodies. Don't give in.* But at the time she'd said nothing; just looked out the window, gone back to her apartment, and doubled down on research. Deep inside, Cat thought that if she could just help people understand the images that were supposed to inspire them to spend all their money on their bodies instead of on their futures, she could break the invisible bars that held women everywhere back. She kept writing, sketching out the shots and sorting through the scout's Polaroids and notes to determine the order, and had just pinned a white index card labeled DOTTY to the sheaf of paper when Lou called Cat into her office.

"I'm a bit nervous, so you'll just have to tell me if this is wrong," Lou said, pointing at the InDesign file she'd prepped with Hillary's tribute. "Obviously Production will make it look better. I'm garbage at fonts."

Cat started clicking through it. The layout was *spectacular*. Through Lou's strategic crops, cuts, highlights, and pull quotes, Hillary's life appeared glamorous, effortless, and even—*timeless*. Cat barely recognized the person illustrated in front of her. Still, it would be the perfect premiere edition of the MATRIARCH section. She realized for the first time exactly how Hillary Whitney could fit into the pantheon of powerful American women: she was a strong, athletic, well-mannered woman from a good family—socialite classic in those respects—but her personal style managed to express cleverness without being whimsical or explicitly sexual. Lou had chosen all the right images and edited the chumminess out of Cat's voice in the captions.

"This is perfect, Lou." She clicked back to the beginning of the layout, scrolling through it once more. "Really, truly *perfect*. She's . . . she's an icon, just like Margot wants. You can send it in now, if you want."

Lou smiled with satisfaction. "I'm just going to let it marinate over the weekend. It either needs one more thing, or I need two days to forget that *I* think that."

"Thanks," Cat said softly as she ducked back into her own office. "See you tomorrow, Lou."

She sat down at her desk and got right back to work on **Dotty**, productive magic lulling her into a happy rhythm while the sun sank in the sky behind the PMS board. Soon Bess was knocking on her office door.

"It's almost eight. I'm going to that party for *DICKS* tonight. Wanna come?"

DICKS, the men's magazine for practicing consumers, threw parties in Williamsburg famous for their wild stunts, all-metal bands, designer drugs, and regrettable photography. Founder Dick Soloway, the neighborhood's preeminent pervert, was the kind of man who wore basketball shorts to business meetings and openly snorted cocaine at the ballet. His merry band of lost boys—metalhead dope addicts, amateur tattoo artists, and rich kids who were both—had become a cornerstone of the city's media scene. But instead of becoming more corporate on their decade-long journey from fringe to mainstream, they insisted on pushing the boundaries of transgressive bad taste, getting rowdier with each passing year. Cat had heard their last party was called "Literal Animal Sacrifice." A night with the *DICKS* crew was something to never, ever, *ever* remember again.

"Oh god, I forgot about it," Cat replied. "I don't know if I can handle that tonight."

"I'm not going to drink anything. I'm just going to 'gram from there for the *RAGE* feeds. I'll be an hour, max."

"Did you hear about the goat?"

"I heard the goat was *already* dead. Molly said it had a terminal illness and they were just pretending to kill the corpse."

"God, their poor interns: *Get me a dead goat.*"

"Yeah." Bess laughed and shook her head. "The things those boys can get away with is beyond." She shouldered her backpack. "Are we still on for tomorrow afternoon, by the way?"

"Absolutely. I have so many things to tell you, I'm really looking forward to it. I just want to smoke pot, bake a cake, and try on clothes. God, I love summer Fridays."

"Sounds perfect," Bess said, closing the door. "Catch you tomorrow."

Cat stayed in the office for another hour before heading home. After a tired walk from the subway, she hung her bag on a hook, microwaved old Chinese food, shed her clothes haphazardly along the floor, pulled up season three of *The X-Files* on her laptop, curled up on her velvet sofa, and inhaled her dinner at a land speed record. Queuing up another episode, Cat rotated her laptop on the coffee table to face the bed and crawled under the covers. Mulder's and Scully's voices were the last thing she heard as she drifted off.

In the past twenty-four hours, Hutton had discovered a raft of evidence—much more than he could have hoped for. He'd spent all day testing, confirming, and writing up his findings, and now, sitting alone in his office, he was certain that it would pay off: tomorrow, they were going to raid Bedford Organics, and it would be a success. The lab's assessment of the Bedford Organics products turned up varying amounts of cocaine; methamphetamine; MDMA; a variety of opiate compounds; and atropine, derived from *Atropa belladonna*—more commonly known as deadly nightshade—in all of the smaller samples, the ones with Cat's name written on them, and in the bottle of eyedrops she'd taken from Hillary's purse. The coroner's wife, a cosmetics chemist, informed them that belladonna had been used as a pupil-enlarging cosmetic by Italian women during the Middle Ages. The larger bottles, which he had guessed were sold off the shelf and then custom-ized later, contained nothing but garden-variety herbs and essential oils—hardly worth the price tags he found on their website. Two hundred dollars for a bottle of moisturizer that smelled like a rot-ting bouquet of flowers seemed insane.

Sergeant Roth, his superior, had immediately contacted the FBI and DEA with the good news: they had what looked like a multimillion-dollar drug operation on their hands. Hutton couldn't understand how Bedford Organics had kept their business under wraps for so long—unless Cat had been the only client to ever walk into the building without explicitly understanding what the products contained.

After he'd searched the Cormorant storage locker for the Whit-ney apartment, he'd found a bottle of contact lens solution that turned out to contain traces of the same ingredients in the eye-drops: more *Atropa belladonna*. Hutton theorized that Hillary Whit-ney had dumped half the small bottle into her contact lens solution, diluting it for daily use with the colored contacts she wore. The contact lens case contained the same solution, indicating that the lenses were soaked overnight—every night, he guessed—doubling or even tripling the daily dose she intended, which would have seeped into her eyes throughout the day. He suspected that all of the custom samples were intended to be used in the same way, to expand their effects over time, keeping rich women on a constant low simmer of wrinkle-free euphoria.

Hillary Whitney's body, cremated and crumbled into an ivory

urn, was unavailable for further autopsy, but the tissue samples held in the coroner's office, thankfully preserved in cold storage, had been retested. By midafternoon Thursday they'd concluded that Hillary Whitney had died from cardiac arrest prompted by an overdose of *Atropa belladonna*.

Hutton still wasn't sure what to make of the postcard she'd sent to the family cabin in Idaho on the morning of her death. Roth had chalked it up to the drug's effects, and pointed out that they didn't need a motive *or* a suspect, because their drug case now had at least one confirmed homicide and a soon-to-be-unimpeachable chain of evidence. The note might have started his case, but it no longer mattered, and Roth had encouraged him to forget it.

Whether she intended to or not, Cat had given the NYPD what they craved most: a case that was *prosecutable*. Someone would go to prison, the seizure would be in the newspaper, and other sophisticated drug traffickers—he was sure there were dozens of other schemes—would momentarily panic and shut down. Law and order would be enacted in public in real time. It wasn't a perfect system, but it worked, mostly.

"All you need is a statement from the girl to ratify the chain of custody," Roth had barked. "Get it done first thing in the morning."

Chapter Eight

On Friday morning, Cat woke up at 6:45 and laced up her sneakers. She jogged through Bushwick and up to Trout-man Street in time for her usual Pilates mat class. The workout was grueling, and Cat was determined to fully extend in every posture, pushing her muscles until they screamed as a personal penance for her party-heavy week. She ran home, showered, dressed, and grabbed the subway into the city for work. Today was a summer Friday, which meant the office closed at 1:00 p.m.; she had only a few hours of work to do, and then she and Bess could spend the afternoon getting stoned before finding out what the night had in store for them.

When she pulled her phone out to summon the Cooper elevator, she saw three missed calls from Hutton's cellphone, along with two text messages asking her to return his call immediately. She stepped to the side of the lobby and dialed.

"Hi," he said, picking up on the first ring.

"Hi," she said. "Is everything okay?"

"I need you to make an official statement," he explained. "You're not in trouble, but we need you to come in."

"I have a ton of work to do before I leave today," she said, annoyed. "Does this have to happen right now?"

"Yes. The precinct is on Thirty-Fifth Street between Eighth and Ninth Avenues. Ask for me at the front desk and someone will escort you up."

Cat sighed, agreed, hung up, and turned around to see Lou coming up the escalator.

"Hey, Lou, I have to run out," Cat explained quietly. "I thought I was fine, but now I definitely think I have a UTI."

"Oh, poor bunny. Take care of you, Kit-Oh. I'm back out in an hour, so I'll catch you Monday?"

"Thank you. Catch you Monday." Cat bounced back down the escalator and headed west toward the precinct, texting Bess to come straight to her apartment after work.

The behemoth concrete building surprised her from a block away; even in Midtown, the brutalist architecture of the Lindsay-era police precinct stood out like the butt of a handgun. She strode confidently through the glass doors only to run smack into a long line of irritated Manhattanites queued at the desk. *Fridays at the NYPD must be like lunchtime at the DMV*, she thought, *everybody pressing charges so they can enjoy the weekend.*

She tried to wait patiently, but the line didn't seem to be moving. She read the newspaper on her phone, considered posting to Photogram from inside the precinct—#badbadgirl—but thought better of it.

Time went on.

The line remained immovable.

The clock on her phone now read 10:26.

The line didn't budge.

She texted Hutton.

I got here at 10. I've been waiting in line at the front desk. Happy to keep waiting if that's the protocol but wanted you to know I'm here.

Nothing popped up on his side—no ellipses bubbles, no message. She waited two minutes, then checked her phone again. Still, nothing. She looked down at her cowboy boots and felt a self-conscious flush come over her cheeks.

"Ah-know," came a muffled voice over the intercom. "Ah-know to the window."

Cat looked up and made eye contact with the officer monitoring the line. She raised her hand meekly; he pointed to a bulletproof window on the side, where another officer leaned over and hit a buzzer. "Go through the door to my left and then stop."

She obeyed. He met her on the other side and gave her handbag a cursory glance before waving her through another set of doors. "Sit on that bench. Someone will be with you in a moment."

She nodded and sat, gathering her dress around her. Emboldened this morning by adrenaline and endorphins, she'd decided on an eggplant-toned silk and linen dress from last season's Phoebe collection that evoked Xena, Warrior Princess. The halter neckline dipped in an exaggerated curve, displaying a keyhole of flesh around her left rib, where she'd pasted a small strip of gold leaf; the open back was broken up by heavy silk tassels hanging from the strap around her neck. A rose-gold men's watch was her only jewelry. Her hair, brushed straight, hung in a black curtain across her pale shoulders, and her repainted nails—still filed into points—matched her matte tangerine lipstick.

She sure didn't feel like Xena now. When Hutton opened the door and stared at her dispassionately, motioning for her to stand up and follow him without so much as a hello, she wished she'd worn a burka.

Cat didn't say anything when he motioned her through the door—not even "*Hi*"—and he found himself sweating nervously as he led her down the Plexiglas-walled hallway to one of their interrogation rooms. He held open the door for her, and as she swept through it, a gust of sea-scented wind invaded his personal space. Hutton glimpsed a hole in the side of her dress and a streak of what looked like gold body paint. *Trouble. This woman is nothing but trouble.*

Cat sat down in one of the interrogation room's steel chairs and put her arms on the table, running her fingers over the handcuff loops embedded in the surface. Hutton picked up her handbag, took out her cellphone, pocketed it, then placed his recorder faceup in front of her.

"I need you to give a complete statement regarding the substance you found in the personal property of Hillary Whitney, and how you came to report that to the department."

She nodded.

"I did try to classify your information as an anonymous tip, but it wasn't ... possible," he continued, trying to speak clearly and deliberately. "Without a recorded chain of custody, we'll have a difficult time prosecuting. You're now technically a confidential informant. You may be called upon to testify in a court of law."

Cat shivered. The room was freezing, she realized, and her skin had turned paler than usual, almost green.

"I'm going to turn on the recorder. Do not state your name or any identifying details about yourself."

"Okay." Cat continued to run her fingers over the handcuff loops, betraying no emotion.

"This is Mark Hutton, NYPD, recording a statement from CI 25401, for case file Halo-Alpha-Niner-Niner-Seven-Oscar. Today is Friday, July 14, 2017. State how you came to contact the department and submit evidence."

"I found a bag of Hillary's with some drops in it on Monday, July 10. I contacted the company that made the drops and met with them on Tuesday, July 11. After trying the samples myself, I suspected that they contained illegal drugs. I gave Detective Hutton everything I had, that same day."

"Name the location and person or persons you received the samples from."

"Bedford Organics, 400 South Bedford Avenue, Brooklyn, New York, third floor. I met a woman named Kate and a woman named Vittoria, who said she was the owner."

"Were the samples that you received from this company in the hands of anyone else at any time?"

"Besides Detective Hutton? No."

"Did they come directly from the shelves?"

"Yes."

"How much product would you estimate is on the premises at 400 South Bedford?"

"Maybe a few thousand bottles? I couldn't really tell how deep the shelves were, but there was a ton of product in there."

"Did it look temporary? Like a storage facility?"

"No. It looked like a wholesale showroom. I would expect a lot of it to still be there."

"Do you know how Hillary Whitney came to possess the eye-drops?"

"No."

"Do you know anyone else who has purchased products from Bedford Organics?"

"Not that I know of. I thought about that. The moisturizers smell like dozens of other products. Anything that uses natural herbs and oils will have the same scents."

He turned off the recorder. "Thank you, Cat. I think that's all we need." He stood up and moved toward the door. Cat followed, but he motioned for her to remain seated.

"Can you wait here?" he asked.

"Love to," she replied.

"I'll be right back." Hutton slipped out the door, handed the recorder to a secretary, and checked his watch. Once the paper-work was complete, signed warrants could be generated by the department's vast post-9/11 security apparatus in a matter of min-utes. As he ran down the hallway to Sergeant Roth's office, Hutton imagined dozens of federal judges sitting at a long library table, rubberstamping pages over and over while a clerk walked around with a copy of the Patriot Act, calling out the relevant statutes over and over like a reader in a nineteenth-century factory. His supervisor sat casually at his desk, watching ESPN on his tablet.

"Carol's uploading the statement now," Hutton reported to his boss. "We'll have the warrant shortly."

"The DEA's been in the building for the last twenty-four hours," Roth said, barely looking up. "Keep track of her. We'll find you later."

Hutton nodded and jogged back down the hallway, but Cat was already gone.

After the nearest police officer had escorted her outside—all it took was a light hand on his arm—Cat hit the pavement and turned east, walking as fast as she could. She wanted to break into a sprint, but the crush of pedestrians on all sides forced her to move apace with the collective current, a tide rolling east. All her mind would do was endlessly run through everything she thought she knew.

One: *Something from Bedford Organics*, *probably the eyedrops*—although Hutton hadn't confirmed it—*had killed Hillary*. If she'd been dosing herself with their products for a while, that certainly explained all her bizarre behavior over the last few months of her life, and Cat had been too self-absorbed to ever call her out on it. Now Hillary was dead.

Two: Hutton had flirted with her, using the personable sleaze of a reporter, dressed up with the moral authority of a cop, then ignored her completely once he had a bag full of evidence. Cat should have known better. *So embarrassing.*

Three: Cat was now a key witness in a drug investigation.

The list echoed around her skull. *I'm a thirsty snitch*, she thought to herself. *Hooray. Somebody get me a pen, I have a bucket list to update.* She leaned against the nearest building, pulled a cigarette out of her bag and lit it, sucking down nearly half of it before realizing that he still had her phone.

Shit.

She walked back to the precinct, clocking Hutton when she was still half a block away as he leaned against the exterior wall, hands shoved into the pockets of his navy jacket, his battered brown oxfords crossed in front of him. Her breath quickened. She tried to ignore how attracted to him she felt. *Get over it, Cat.* He spotted her and walked in her direction, keys in hand.

"I need my phone," Cat demanded as soon as he was close enough.

"Sorry. I can't give it back to you until we're done with our raid on Bedford Organics." Hutton shook his head. "I'm parked over here. Get in the car." He motioned to the opposite side of the block and they crossed together to the bottle-green Volvo he'd been rummaging in on Monday night. She hesitated.

"I have to go to work," she insisted. "I have things to do."

"I can take you home or you can sit in the station in a locked room for an indeterminate period of time. It's for your own safety. It's up to you," Hutton said gruffly as he unlocked and opened the passenger's-side door. Cat sighed and climbed in. He closed her door gently before crossing over to the driver's side.

He started the car but didn't move it into gear. Instead, he reached across and put his hand behind Cat's shoulder.

She froze.

Time slowed to a crawl.

He pulled out her seat belt and clicked it into place without touching her.

Turned the dial to WNYC and pulled out into traffic.

Cat felt like an idiot.

An awkward silence filled the car. Cat punctured it by opening the window and lighting a fresh cigarette without asking. Hutton, after a beat, motioned to indicate that she should hand him one, too. She lit one and passed it over, their fingers remaining chastely distant as he opened his window. He cut through SoHo and cruised straight over the Williamsburg Bridge onto Broadway, weaving through the heavy traffic easily, never swearing or seeming even remotely flustered. He briefly took a phone call, but the only things he said in reply were "Yes" and "That's fine."

"How long am I supposed to sit in my apartment?" she finally asked.

"Just a few hours." He gave her a forced smile; though it was meant to be reassuring, she sneered in reply.

At eleven o'clock Bess was sitting in her cubicle, idly rubbing the bright-red-ink penis stamp off the top of her hand and clicking through the badge board for **Judy and the Technicolor House-coat**, when Constance Onderveet's face rose above the black plastic wall like a solar eclipse.

"Bess!" Constance barked. Bess jumped in her chair.

"How are you, Constance?" she replied steadily.

"Where's Cat?"

"She's at a personal appointment," Lou explained, walking out of her office with perfect timing and a huge monogrammed Goyard weekend bag. "Approved by *me*. But! It's a summer Friday, Coco. No one's doing *anything*! I'm catching a seaplane with Bitsy and Margarita from the East River in half an hour."

"No one but me." Constance half scowled at her friend. "I've got proofs to approve and freelancers to whip. Even Stephen went up early to go fishing."

Lou leaned in and left a big wet kiss on her cheek. "Well, I hope you make it tonight. Crumb and Cosmo got the whole Point and all the cabins across the lake, and they hired a gondolier collective from Gowanus to ferry us back and forth. It'll be marvelous."

Bess assumed they were talking about the weekend-long Adirondack nuptials of Cressida (Crumb) Popplewell and Cassiopeia (Cosmo) Groggin-Butz. Cosmo, a long-list potential heiress to the British monarchy who'd spent the last two years in New York giving away her first husband's frozen orange juice fortune to every cultural institution with a checking account, was on the outskirts of a social circle that *RAGE*'s former and current senior staff members seemed to dominate—a circle that had once included Hillary—and she appeared to be buying her way in with no trouble at all. Bess, too junior for membership, was usually included in these discussions only when they needed something from her, like logistical help or gossip. Lou hoisted her bag to leave, but not before Constance turned her glare back to Bess.

"Is Ella going?" Constance demanded. Bess's older sister Ella had been in the same class as Hillary at Miss Sawyer's, and though she was a serious person with a serious job—she had a law degree, but worked as a film and television agent—Ella had a reputation for consuming champagne like a Ukrainian teenager. Bess suspected that Constance was concerned she'd find her husband, Stephen, in the bushes with Ella, an annual ritual since they'd clerked together for Ginsburg. Hopefully, this time he wouldn't also be consuming Veuve Clicquot anally.

"I'm afraid so," Bess warned her. "Keep all lighters and matches out of reach, and make sure someone puts a life jacket on her. Last time we talked, she said it's been an extra-stressful summer, so I imagine she's due for a real rager. Have the gondoliers sign something."

Lou laughed. "This is going to be the best wedding of the whole year," she announced. Constance's face puckered.

"Is there another seat on your flight?" she asked Lou, who nodded. "I'll just grab my purse." Constance bolted back to her office.

"Thanks for all your help earlier," Lou said to Bess. "Someday I'll get this whole CoopDoc thing figured out! *And* the chat. I'm *dying* to understand the chat bit."

"No problem," Bess said, "but remember to change your password!"

Constance came running back with a matching prepacked Goyard duffel and a strained look on her face. Bess suspected that Stephen's so-called fishing trip consisted of just him and Ella.

"I'm so glad you can make it, Coco," Lou said to her nicely. "We'll have the best time. And Boots," she said to Bess, winking, "if you're as trousered as your sister this weekend, I hope you have *twice* as much fun."

"Not possible." Bess laughed. Constance and Lou headed for the elevators. Five minutes later, Bess saved her documents, closed up her computer, dismissed Molly, grabbed her bike helmet, and headed for Brooklyn.

As he drove through Bushwick, Hutton watched Cat's floaty purple dress ride up, exposing the full length of her bare legs. She didn't tug it down but instead smoked nervously out the window, her orange-tipped fingers twirling her hair when they weren't tapping the ash off her cigarette. When they got to her block, he pulled over and parked in front of the nearest hydrant, throwing a dog-eared NYPD parking pass onto the dashboard. Cat hopped out of the car the moment it stopped and marched toward her building, the dress hovering around her, the morning sun lighting up the veins in her otherworldly skin, her hair shaking in a glossy curtain across the bones of her back. Hutton locked the car and chased after her, but she ignored him completely, pulling open the building's graffitied metal door and taking the stairs two at a time until she reached the hallway and unlocked her apartment door with two separate keys. Hutton caught up as it was closing, grabbed the top of the door and held it open before she could yank it shut. He felt his phone ring in his pocket and declined the call without looking at the screen.

"Can I come in?" he asked.

She shrugged, pulled herself up to sit on her kitchen countertop, a cold-looking polished concrete, and poured herself a glass of water from the sink. Hutton took this as a yes.

"It's not that big a deal," he assured her, closing the door, turning the dead bolts, and setting his keys and phone on the coffee table before taking a seat on her sofa. "You don't have to freak out."

Cat stared at him but didn't speak. He watched the skin on her legs turn to goose bumps.

"You did the right thing," he tried.

She leaned back against the kitchen cabinets and stayed quiet, sipping her water and refusing to speak or make eye contact. Hutton looked around the loft. It wasn't any particular category that he could identify; it wasn't girly, it wasn't kitschy, it wasn't modern. It seemed purely functional. A king-size bed, velvet sofa, vintage armchair, coffee table, and a dining table that could seat a dozen people were the only pieces of furniture in the cavernous space. It looked like she used the dining table as a makeshift desk.

The kitchen was clean, but the wood cabinets she leaned against were flaking paint, the bargain-basement appliances at least a decade old. The apartment's two painted-brick walls were covered salon-style with framed pictures, prints, posters, drawings, and a huge, overflowing bookcase; the other two walls of the unit were nearly all lead-paned windows. Pale gray linen curtains hung near the bed. A metal IBM clock on the wall read eleven thirty.

"I'm sorry," he ventured. "I realize you weren't expecting this."

"Why did you lie to me?" she asked. "I thought I was just coming in and out. I thought it was . . . I didn't realize what was happening."

"I didn't lie," he said. "Things . . . changed."

"It's not great for me. I don't have room for this kind of thing, to be in a trial, to be a witness, to be vulnerable."

"I know."

"Cooper hasn't promoted me yet. I don't have a green card, so I can't get another job anywhere else. I've never done anything else, except graduate school, which I failed. My job is competitive. Anybody would take my place in a heartbeat. There's no room for mistakes."

"I know," he said again.

"Why are you still here?" she asked. "You got what you wanted." A wave of sea-scented air popped off her skin.

"I didn't." He stood up and walked over to the edge of the kitchen counter, two feet from her purple dress and long legs, realizing what he was doing but unable to stop.

"Cops can't act like reporters. You're supposed to have boundaries. You shouldn't fraternize with suspects or informants or witnesses or whatever I am to you."

"All of the above," he said.

"Lucky me," she said, though she no longer looked mad.

He moved closer, a foot from Cat, who now matched his height only by sitting on the countertop. Their faces were even for the first time. A smile tugged at the corners of her mouth. She pushed her cowboy boots halfway off her feet, revealing a pair of white cotton men's socks with athletic stripes, the silliness of which made him smile in return.

"You don't have to stay here," she said. "I'm not going anywhere. You don't need to keep an eye on me."

"Yes, but I want to," he said again, moving closer. The cowboy boots fell to the floor.

Cat finally broke into a grin. "You don't have to keep pretending to like me."

"I'm not pretending."

"Then why were you so rude to me on the phone? Or at the precinct?" She raised an eyebrow to maintain the now ten-inch distance between them. "Maybe you're the one with the mood disorder."

"No." He laughed and added, "But you're right, I'm not supposed to date you. It's unethical."

Cat snorted. "Dating me is unethical, but camping out at night in front of my friend's house is totally okay."

He blushed. "I wasn't camped out."

"You weren't sweaty enough to be running." She reached out and wiped a bead of sweat off his forehead. "*That's* sweat."

He reached for her hand, and she let him take it.

Cat took a deep breath when Hutton's fingers closed around hers, her heart racing. She reached out with her other hand and traced his jaw with her finger.

Hutton didn't hesitate. He moved between her legs and wrapped his arms around her; she bit his lower lip. He didn't make a move to kiss her in response but held still, looking into her eyes and leaning forward with just the right amount of his weight. He nuzzled her neck. Cat felt every single cell in her being pulsing with his.

"Am I still being rude?" he asked, kissing her shoulder.

"I don't know what you want."

"I want to rip your clothes off," he mumbled into her ear, pressing himself against her with more weight. "I want to make you come all day."

Cat found herself biting his neck, pulling his earlobe into her mouth. Hutton folded his legs and brought them both down to the cold floor of her loft, shifting her into his lap.

They kissed. The full taste of bell peppers and cut grass—the cleanest taste in the world—flooded through Cat as he lowered her all the way to the ground, his hands pulling her dress over her head, finding their way through her coral lace underwear. He pushed his fingers against her as she shivered, holding on to his mouth with hers, their tongues moving in beat with his hand.

He moved his fingers up and down as she pushed herself against him, finally releasing something she'd been holding in since the second he walked into *RAGE*'s offices. A scream let out from the back of her throat. He worked frantically to pull her underwear off.

Somewhere, his phone rang. *Loudly.*

And rang.

And rang.

It stopped.

She yanked off his jacket, unbuttoned his shirt, and fumbled with his jeans, pushing them to the floor.

"Condom," Cat demanded. "*Now.*"

Then his phone rang again. His voicemail beeped, then the phone beeped with text messages; one, two, three, four, before ringing again.

It rang.

And rang.

Cat felt his mouth move away from hers, his fingers slip out of her. He was pulling them both up off the floor with her legs entwined around his waist. She tried to keep up with him and planted her mouth back on his. In between their heavy kisses, he grabbed her hips, unwrapped her legs, and said,

"I

have

to

answer that."

Holding her hips with both hands, he lowered her to the floor to stand on her feet, holding her up against him. Cat stayed on tiptoe and looked up at him. His jeans were shoved down around his calves, his naked body pressed up against her as he looked around for his phone.

Then her apartment's buzzer rang.

"Are you expecting anyone?" Hutton asked.

"No," Cat said slowly as she leaned over and pressed the intercom. "Hello?"

"It's Bess," crackled the speaker.

"Oh. Right," she said to Hutton. "I'm expecting Bess."

He shook his head. "It's fine," he said. "I have to take that call."

Cat let go of him, threw on her dress, and hit the buzzer while he buttoned his shirt. He kissed her on the top of the head and wandered off in a daze. By the time Bess knocked, he was already across the apartment, mostly dressed and mumbling into his cellphone.

Cat opened the door. Bess chucked a joint at her. "Let's get stoned," she said.

"I can't," Cat said, pointing to Hutton. "The hot cop is here," she whispered. "I gave him Hillary's eyedrops the other night. This morning I had to give a statement about them at the precinct."

Bess looked shocked.

Hutton walked back over before she could say another word.

"I have some not-so-great news," he said. "We need you to buy more drugs."

Chapter Nine

Bess laughed in surprise and snatched back the joint from Cat's limp palm. "More than this?" she asked, lighting up and blowing the smoke through the apartment's still-open door. "I knew you were cool," she said to Hutton.

He shook his head in disagreement.

Cat took the joint from Bess and hit it once before running the lit end under the tap. She stored the remainder in an oversized mason jar filled with grains of rice.

"Bad Bess," she chided. "He's trying to be serious."

Hutton ushered Bess inside, closed and locked the apartment door, then ordered her to sit. "Give me your phone," he demanded.

"Yes sir!" She answered and complied. "The dirty pictures are all in InstaCRT."

"This isn't a joke," he said sternly. "I have to take you both to the Williamsburg precinct."

"Why, do they want to get stoned with us?" Bess asked.

"That's not funny," he said.

"Oh, it's funny," Cat agreed. Bess nodded. Hutton indicated that Cat should sit, too, and the two women folded themselves on the sofa. He grabbed a chair from Cat's dining table, flipped it down across from the coffee table, sat, and tried to look imposing.

"We've been planning a raid on Bedford Organics, but we're concerned that the owner may be out of town, or on her way out," Hutton explained. "No one's been in the building for the last twenty-four hours. We need you to call and set up a meeting for our undercover officers."

"That's crazy," Cat said. "She's not going to agree to see two random women. My crowd is pretty . . . *specific*. We're all googleable."

"Don't worry about that part. You need to call her and set up a time."

"No, I'm serious," she insisted. "They would need Photogram accounts, other forms of social media, something affiliated with Cooper."

"We can generate that."

"Seriously? They need *real* followers and tons of mentions. Good ones."

"We can do that in an hour. The digital team will clone accounts similar to yours as believably as possible, then manually update the top five pages of the major search engines."

"Wow." Cat paused. "That's fucked up."

"It's merely the *dawn* of modernity," Hutton equivocated.

"If that's true, I'd hate to see the sunset."

"You won't."

Cat laughed. "Isn't she going to know it was *me*, though?" she pointed out. "That I'm the tattletale?"

Bess nodded in agreement.

"Not if you get arrested," Hutton said. "They'll prep you for that, though it won't be a real arrest, not exactly."

"Oh." Cat swallowed. "Okay."

"Don't worry about that part. You need to make the call," Hutton insisted. "Then I'll take you both to meet the undercovers."

"Why me?" asked Bess. "I want to go to the park."

"I'm not letting you out of my sight," Hutton said. "This is serious. You showed up at the wrong place at the wrong time, Bess. I can't risk anyone else knowing about this."

Bess stuck out her lower lip. "Every time I come to Bushwick, something dumb happens. Ugh, remind me later to tell you about the *DICKS* party. It was called 'The Bush.'" She grimaced.

Cat and Hutton ran through what she should say to Vittoria. She practiced a few times with Bess, trying to sound genuine, though Bess kept laughing. Finally, Cat pulled out Vittoria's card and lit another cigarette.

"Now or never, right?"

Hutton nodded. "Just pretend you're telling the truth."

She made the call.

"Hi, Vittoria? It's Cat from *RAGE*...No, no, it *worked*. I mean, *really* worked...I'm definitely hooked...I'm good for right now, you were so generous, but could I bring some friends over later?... Yeah, other girls from *RAGE*...What time works for you?... Okay, I'll confirm with them. I'll call you if we need to cancel but otherwise see you later...Yeah, okay...and Vittoria—thank you so *so* much!"

Hutton called Roth as soon as she hung up. "It's done. Five p.m.," he said.

"That was good timing," Cat said. "She's squeezing us in on her way to Teterboro."

"Ready?" he asked, grabbing her purse and keys from the counter. "Let's go."

Cat paused. "What are the undercover officers wearing, if I may ask?"

"The secretary went to Zara, I think. Why?"

"We would never wear that," Bess and Cat said in unison.

"I don't think it matters."

"It matters," they said. Hutton looked skeptical.

Cat rolled her eyes.

Bess grinned at Cat, who nodded.

"We have an idea—" Cat said.

"They have to come over," Bess finished, her voice excited. "We should dress them."

"With what?" Hutton asked.

Cat flung open the door to the white box, where Hutton spied hundreds of pieces of clothing organized by color, most still in their plastic dry-cleaning shrouds.

"With this!" Cat explained.

Hutton considered the wrinkled polyester dresses Carol had snagged from Zara, which didn't look even remotely close to the same quality as Cat's floaty dress or Bess's, what was that, overalls and a printed top? Basic, maybe, but the overalls were a fine light fabric, the shirt probably silk. Her sneakers were spotless neon-yellow running shoes that he'd never seen anywhere else, and her jewelry was an oversized ring in the shape of an elephant's face whose trunk wrapped around her middle finger. Putting a middle-aged woman in an ill-fitting dress in front of either of them would only further serve to highlight how modest the police department's budget was.

He picked up the phone. "Mary and Pat need different clothes," he said. "Can you bring them to 239 Moore…Yeah…buzz Ono." He hung up. "They'll be here in fifteen minutes."

"Operation Lady Cop Makeover is a go," Cat said.

"This is the best day of my life," Bess replied, her face glowing.

Cat and Bess were still pulling what looked to Hutton like a hundred dresses out of the enormous closet when the buzzer rang. A minute later, a swarthy uniformed cop, presumably Sergeant Roth, and two sturdy middle-aged women walked through the door.

"Oh man…this is going to be good," Bess muttered as she and Cat walked over to introduce themselves.

"Hi, I'm Bess," she said, shoving her hand in the officers' general direction.

"Mary," said the short one. "Patricia," said the taller one.

Bess pointed to Cat, who shook their hands next. "This is Cat's operation, or whatever. But I'm helping."

Roth nodded at both of them but didn't extend his hand, so Bess and Cat nodded before stepping back to study Mary's and Patricia's bodies, firm and thick-waisted under their polyblend suits and striped button-downs. The two female officers accepted their professional scrutiny without flinching.

"Mary, Patricia, are you wearing vests right now?" Bess asked.

"Of course," the officers replied in unison. Everything separating them as individuals was removed from their appearance and affect—*understandable, considering their profession*, thought Cat. *You couldn't pay me enough money to be a female cop in this city.*

"Can you take those off? They're too bulky."

Roth spoke for them. "Go ahead," he ordered. Cat immediately hated everything about him. She pulled the elastic out of Mary's no-nonsense ponytail and ran her fingers through it, fluffing it out. Her hair was auburn, thick with a strong natural curl. *Not bad.* Bess, standing beside her, was already clipping Patricia's bangs back with an alligator claw she'd pulled from her own bun.

"How much time do we have?" Cat asked Hutton.

"About an hour," he replied, glancing at his watch.

Bess pointed to the white box in the middle of the room. "That's the closet," she said to Mary and Patricia. "You can change in there."

Roth laughed nervously. "I don't think you girls are the same size," he said.

"Oh, shut the *fuck* up," Cat muttered reflexively, rolling her eyes.

The room fell momentarily silent. A stunned Roth glanced at Hutton, who gave a tiny shake of his head. Bess smirked. Mary and Patricia stared at the ground. Cat ignored everyone and grabbed a tape measure from her wall. She held it up to Mary, measuring her hips. Patricia wasn't much bigger.

"Go into the closet, look into the blue tub on the floor," Cat barked. "Find the smallest full-body shapewear you can squeeze into."

Mary and Patricia filed into the closet and obeyed without question. Their gun belts hit the floor with a thud. Meanwhile, Cat chose a playlist on her phone and plugged it into the apartment's speakers, then walked over to the bathroom and turned the shower on full force before closing the door. She glanced around the room, then gestured to Hutton and Roth. "Sit at the table," she said. "Order takeout if you're hungry. This is going to take a while." The men sat down obediently. Danish electronica boomed out of the speakers, bringing the room's vibe up a beat.

Bess cleared the section of the dining table opposite from where Hutton and Roth sat. She opened a black hard-sided suitcase and started pulling out dozens of shiny cosmetics tubes and pots, then laid them out in neat rows on the table.

"That's a lot of beauty shit," said Roth.

Cat stared at him. "Do you *want* our help?" she asked.

"I'm just saying, it's a lot of shit. No offense. I'd rather spend my money on other stuff. That's just me."

She leaned forward, her eyes darting rapidly from side to side. "Is that a joke?"

He shifted nervously in his seat. "No, I mean, you gotta admit, it's ridiculous."

"No. I don't have to admit that. Pretending that women are blind narcissists, instead of self-aware pragmatists, is just... *dumb*," she said impatiently. "Let's not." She turned around and tried to ignore him.

Roth shook his head. "Like I said, I'm not trying to offend you."

"And yet!" Cat sighed. "Listen. I, too, would rather spend my money on 'other shit,' as you so politely put it. Whether or not you recognize the extent to which you're performing a sexist pantomime—the working-class guy who thinks ladies don't understand how to spend money—you're still doing it. And it's *still* offensive."

"Honey, if you want to be offended, go ahead," Roth replied. "I'm not trying to be sexist either. I just think, *it's a lot of stuff.* It seems kinda . . . over the top. That's all I was trying to say."

"Ohmigod. How else can I explain this," Cat said slowly, putting her fingers to her temples. "*Taste classifies. It classifies the classifier?* No? Okay. This"—she waved her fingers around the room, at her body and at Bess's body—"is a language. Today Mary and Patricia need to look like we look. It's not simple. This is a job I get paid to do, same as you. You may consider it frivolous, but it's profitable for a lot of people—people like the *drug operation* you're asking us to help you bust, so maybe try to take it as seriously as we have to."

Mary and Patricia had come out of the closet clad in matching robes. For the first time since entering the apartment their faces showed emotion: they wore matching smirks.

Roth cleared his throat. "Yes ma'am."

Cat turned back to Mary and Patricia without a word. "Ladies, can you head to the bathroom for the next twenty minutes or so? The steam will open your pores. What are your shoe sizes?"

Hutton was astonished by the sheer volume of clothing they'd managed to produce. Cat had rolled out two metal racks from behind the closet, along with an industrial steamer. A clear spray bottle marked "vodka" and a *very* large one labeled "Property of The Standard Hotel" hung on the steamer's rack.

"What's the vodka for?" Hutton knew *he* probably wasn't supposed to talk either, but he was getting curious.

"It's for anything that hasn't been dry-cleaned. Really cheap vodka—like, comes-in-a-plastic-bottle-cheap—takes the body odor out of anything. It's a theater trick."

She grabbed two tubes from the dining room table and ducked into the bathroom. He watched through the crack in the door as she applied a white goop with a thick brush to Mary's clean face, and a green goop with her fingers to Patricia's.

"She seems like a real bitch," Roth whispered, nodding his head in Cat's direction.

"You have no fucking idea," Hutton replied with a genuine smile.

Their masks applied, the female officers stood and followed Cat out to the dining table. Roth, occupied with his cellphone, refused to look up, but Hutton stared shamelessly; he was fascinated.

Bess used hot towels, dampened and heated in the microwave, to pull the masks off the female officers' faces before spraying them liberally with a large bottle marked "CARIBBEAN SEA WATER DO NOT DRINK." Hutton inhaled deeply, recognizing the base of Cat's sea-smell.

"Try on all the dresses we racked for you," Bess ordered, following the two women into the closet. Hutton listened in amazement to a dialogue he didn't understand—one punctuated with laughter and sarcastic comments and thoughtful *hmms*—until Mary reappeared wearing an oversized green shirtdress; Patricia was dressed in a pair of tiny pink silk shorts, matching jacket, and shiny gold top.

Bess and Cat fussed over the women's hair and faces, and eventually held up a mirror. Mary and Patricia looked ten years younger than they had walking in, and the women nodded approvingly at their reflections.

"How'd you know to do this?" Patricia asked Bess.

"It's daytime, so it would be too heavy to have both an eye and a lip," Bess replied. "Your milkmaid braid is kind of... wide-eyed Amish virgin, so I went with a more space-age eye with the ultramarine liquid liner to balance it out. I think your more classic Brooklyn party girl would go with a dark lipstick, but I wanted you to look a *little* more sophisticated than that. And with Mary, it's all about the hair," she continued. "Mary, you have *St. Vincent hair*. It's amazing. If you die today, I want you to know that I'm going to shave your head and make a wig out of your hair. From your dead body. Okay? So, anyway, we left the skin basically bare, but I added a little bit of lip stain to give your face some depth."

"I'm so Williamsburg," said Mary.

"I bet I can get three days out of this braid," Patricia noted.

Roth finally looked up from his phone. "Holy shit," he muttered. "I wouldn't have recognized either of you."

Bess checked the clock on her phone and interrupted before Cat could get another rant in. She really didn't see the point in trying to argue with a middle-aged, white, male *New York City police sergeant*. "Hey, it's already three," she pointed out. "What time are we leaving?"

"We'll all head over around four," said Roth. "You ladies go ahead and take the subway, get a coffee as you walk over, do whatever you would normally do. Act like you're going out tonight."

"Do we need to wear wires or anything?" Cat had become so focused on the makeovers that she'd forgotten to ask about the logistics.

Mary and Patricia laughed. "No," Patricia said. "We don't really *do* that anymore. The whole place is under surveillance already. They can record a sneeze from across the street. You just have to act like we work with you and try to have the same sort of conversation you had last time. Then we'll all get arrested."

Mary gave Cat's arm a reassuring pat. "It's easy."

"Okay, so this is the part where you teach *me*. I've never, ever been arrested." Roth looked shocked. "Do I...protest, act scared, what?"

"All the officers will be from the DEA. You won't know any of them. It will be legitimately scary—I doubt you'll need to *act* scared," Patricia replied. "The hardest part is pretending you don't know it's coming. Say no a lot. Like, 'Nonononononono, I can't be arrested. Where's my lawyer?' Things you would actually say."

"Okay. I can do that. You're saying it's like *Sleep No More*, but with martial law instead of public sex. Then what happens?"

"You'll get brought into the precinct, and you'll get your photo taken, fingerprinted, the whole thing. You'll be held for an hour, max. We'll have an attorney get to you quickly. Charges will never be filed, but it *is* an arrest."

Cat was confused. "Wait... what? I'm actually going to be *arrested* arrested?" Her tone grew serious. "I'm not a citizen. My status here is contingent upon my employment. I have a morals clause. Cooper is a conservative company. I can't risk getting in trouble, not legally."

"I can see why that would concern you," Roth said, a twinkle in his eye. "But at this point you really don't have much of a choice. You purchased and possessed large quantities of—even, perhaps, considered distributing?—some *very* illegal drugs. It's in your best interest to cooperate with us."

"That's such bullshit!" Cat snapped back. "I had that bag for *ten* minutes until I gave it to Hutton."

Roth smiled. "The fact that you turned the products over to law enforcement is something we are absolutely willing to consider. I don't see a reason to file charges or disrupt your status here in any way, provided, of course, that you help out today. I'd also like to remind you that we still don't know how Hillary Whitney became connected to Bedford Organics—the one person in her life connected to them, that we know of, is *you*."

I should have known better than to play games with policemen, Cat thought, suddenly feeling extremely bitter. *All they want is to dominate. If they can't do that, they don't even stay in the same room as you.* She glanced over at Hutton, who stared at the floor and refused to make eye contact. He didn't have any power here; even Cat could see that.

"Why do I need to be *arrested* arrested, anyway? Aren't I *bait*?" she pointed out, trying to pivot the basis of the entire argument. "Can't we just say, 'Hey, the jig is up'? It's not as though I'm trying to be a repeat customer."

"We're talking about a potentially significant amount of money,"

Roth said, his voice firm. "This company is an LLC. The shares could be owned by anyone. It'll be a series of shells within shells within shells. We don't know who these people are. I assure you that it's very much in your interest to suffer the potential embarrassment of detainment—it's a tremendously small price to pay for your own safety."

"So," Cat argued back, "you *don't* protect your informants *at all*."

"We *do* protect our informants," Roth replied, "by making sure no one ever knows they're an informant. And I mean *no one*— not my wife, not your employer, not anyone. It's really that simple. You have two choices today: Participate, and be arrested without charges. Don't participate, and I'll arrest you and charge you right here and now with possession and intent to distribute. It's up to you."

Cat felt tears well up automatically, which she resented almost as much as she resented Roth. The sergeant was so aggressive, so dominant, so satisfied; it broke her. *This man has no idea what he's asking me to do*, she thought. A fat tear streamed down her cheek. Bess looked horrified. Hutton whispered something to Roth.

"Just . . . calm down for a minute. I'll call the FBI about your visa. Let me see what they can do," Roth said before he turned around and began muttering into his cellphone.

"I know you cared about Hillary Whitney," Hutton said to Cat quietly. "These are the people who were responsible for her death. You have a chance to do something about that." He wiped the tears off her face with his thumb, a gesture both intimate and kind. Bess, Mary, and Patricia all looked away, momentarily embarrassed by the obvious closeness between detective and informant.

Cat shook her head. "No, of course not. I want to help; I . . . I hadn't realized what I could lose."

Bess waved her hands furiously, her face suddenly alight.

"*Hello* . . . what am I, chopped liver?"

All four police officers turned to look at her. "I don't give a *shit* about being arrested. I already work at *RAGE*, I'm a real human being, and the Bedford Organics people probably already know who I am because I run our Photogram feed—and most importantly, Cooper won't fire *both* of us, Cat. Honestly. We do *so* much work, but Margot is *so* particular about who to hire—they can't *fire* us because *they can't replace us*. I know we were going to pretend these two were freelancers or whatever—"

"*Were* going to? You still are," said Patricia. "It's obviously better to have you both in there, but we need an undercover officer in with you."

"Okay...fine," Bess agreed. "But I'm going, too."

"The FBI says you're fine to get arrested. They'll take care of it, no matter what," said Roth, putting his phone down on the table.

Cat took a hard look at Mary and Patricia. "I think we need to go with freelance stylists from Los Angeles," she said to Hutton. "They have that 'too many accessories' look. Can we invent credits for them somehow on IMDB?"

Mary nodded. "The FBI can add our names to anything that's online. Old photo shoots, celebrity profiles, literally anything."

In a matter of minutes, Mary and Patricia had an entirely new internet history that went on for dozens of pages.

"Cat? It's time," Hutton said. "I'm supposed to walk you all to the subway."

"We need our phones," she demanded. He handed them back, saying, "Don't do anything stupid with these, okay?" while Cat grabbed a pair of square black Prada sunglasses and ignored him. Patricia, Mary, and Bess were lined up next to the door. *Not bad*, Cat thought. *Nobody will mistake them for anything but party girls.*

On their way to the subway they walked past a mural of a robot sodomizing a pickup truck. Cat gave Hutton her phone and ordered the girls to line up. Patricia grabbed Cat's phone from Hutton and substituted her own.

"I'll post the original," Patricia insisted. "You can regram it. It'll look more real."

Cat smiled and felt her energy returning. "Okay. Let's make this look fun." She backed up and leaned against the mural, putting her hand on the robot's butt in an obscene gesture. The other three posed dramatically.

Hutton snapped a few images. Cat inspected them quickly. *Hmm. Fun, but uninspired.* She looked around for a prop. A plastic bag caught on the razor wire above their heads, errant medical waste from the clinic around the corner, read "*speculum: extra large*." She got back into her pose and pointed it out to the group, asking, "Did anyone misplace their bag of extra-large speculums, or is Brooklyn just an actual toilet?" right before Hutton hit the capture button again; the resulting photo had all four women laughing out loud, their bodies twisted toward the plastic bag flying above their heads. It was genuine, spontaneous, and actually funny.

Cat wrote the caption and posted it to Patricia's account, @patt_the_bunni:

> plastic bag reading "speculum xl" begging for us to play with it under this #throatneck mural. bk weekend with my @cooperny girls from @ragebeauty @loch_ness_bess @catono @mar_bear_stare #badgirlsgoeverywhere

"'Patt the bunny,'" Cat said to Patricia. "Is that *supposed* to sound perverted?"

"Yes," Patricia and Mary replied in unison.

"It's the FBI. You think Roth is bad, wait until you add an Ivy League education." Patricia rolled her eyes. "The smarter they are, the more disgusting they are. But whatever—the FBI's not in charge until they can prove this is organized crime. Right now they're just an amazing resource that's extremely annoying."

"You know what," Mary said, "fuck them. At the end of the day, I have my health, it's nice outside, and there's a gun in my purse. Let's go arrest some criminals."

At the L train entrance, Cat hung back for a moment and

grabbed Hutton's arm. Bess, absorbed in her phone, ambled down the steps without looking up.

"Can we get a drink after this drug bust?" she asked as soon as the other women were out of view. Hutton leaned her against the wall and wrapped his body around hers.

"Let's go back to your apartment first," he said before kissing her. "See you later."

"That's good enough for me." Cat grinned and turned away, dancing down the stairs.

Chapter Ten

Three hours later, Cat and Bess found themselves handcuffed in the back of a police car that was driving the wrong direction down the BQE.

"You're supposed to take us back to Midtown South," Bess said politely through the screen. "The Williamsburg Bridge is much faster than taking the Manhattan this time of day. You can turn around at the Wythe exit."

The freckle-faced officer driving the car ignored her.

Cat looked at Bess and shrugged. "So much for fuel efficiency," Cat said, loud enough for the officer to hear. "I guess he just wants to sit in traffic."

"Would it be possible to get the keys for these handcuffs?" Bess tried. "We're not *super* comfortable back here."

The officer continued to ignore them, raising the volume on the radio and turning on the siren as he sped toward downtown Brooklyn. The only time he spoke was when a squirming Cat tried to dig Bess's phone out of her pocket.

"Sit down and stop moving," he'd growled. "*Now!*"

"*Jesus,*" Cat said, turning to face forward before she could get Bess's phone out. "Give up the ghost, dude. We're not the enemy."

It wasn't until he skipped the exits for the Manhattan *and* Brook-

lyn Bridges that Cat started to get nervous. When he turned onto
Atlantic Avenue, she tried attitude.

"We don't want to go with you to Fairway," she said, referring
to the Red Hook grocery store famous for its aisles of olive oil.
"Take us to Midtown, or you're going to get in *huge* trouble."

"Ladies," he finally snapped, "I don't know what your deal is.
But in this city, when you have an outstanding warrant in Brooklyn, you go to detention in Brooklyn."

The officer pulled up in front of Brooklyn Central Holding,
threw the car in park, and escorted them inside.

Hutton couldn't believe his luck.

The DEA had seized over five hundred sample- and full-size
bottles loaded with illegal ingredients matching the samples already
in evidence. They'd also seized an additional thousand twenty-
four-ounce bottles of overpriced full-size creams, lotions, and potions that contained no illegal drugs and would be distributed to
every officer in the precinct—bottles smelling like flowers, fruits,
mint, essentially every kind of perfume imaginable. Rupert Whitney agreed to follow through on his donation to the policemen's
union. In a single week, he'd gained not only a career-making case,
but the gratitude of every single person at Midtown South.

The case was deeper than he'd thought possible. Vittoria Cardoso
owned just thirty-five percent of the shares in Bedford Organics,
LLC, a New York State entity that also purchased the building three
years earlier—a process requiring an attorney, whom they'd subpoe-
naed immediately. The company's visible assets totaled more than
$10 million, including the entire property at 400 South Bedford.
Once the NYPD discovered the names of the remaining shareholders, they'd have a money trail running a mile wide.

Bedford Organics, LLC wasn't just a legitimate business; it was a healthy, thriving direct-sale beauty manufacturer and retailer whose products had a relatively transparent production process, save for the final—and most profitable—"special blends" brought in on limited import from Brazil. Cosmetic products and ingredients, not subject to FDA approval, were given only a cursory and occasional inspection in customs to ensure that a box of moisturizer wasn't *really* a plastic bag of cocaine. An established business like Bedford Organics would have no trouble smuggling drugs in their own sealed and branded boxes of product.

Hutton's only real problem was Cat and Bess, who were still in Brooklyn.

At 6:12 p.m. on Friday, Cat, Bess, Mary, and Patricia had been standing near the parlor door on the third floor of 400 South Bedford with overflowing bags of product, all of it lovingly wrapped in blue ribbon and brown butcher paper by Kate the assistant while they had received their hour-long consultation with Vittoria. Their faces were flushed and glowing, their eyes sparkling, when five DEA agents barreled through the door with guns drawn.

At first they'd all feigned ignorance, protesting when their bags were snatched from their hands and the product on the shelves around them was shoveled unceremoniously into duffels. Vittoria had sighed and waited calmly behind the desk while Cat and Bess tried to convince the agents to let them leave, saying, "Excuse me, but we really need to get going," as though they were being detained by a waiter who was too distracted to bring the check.

Mary and Patricia followed their cues, acting slightly more wide-eyed and afraid when Vittoria and her assistant, Kate, were handcuffed. Cat and Bess transitioned from disbelief and irritation into full-on entitled outrage, screaming that their rights were being abused and they'd be suing the DEA for every penny the government had. Cat had to be dragged downstairs by force. When the agent struggling to get her into a Crown Vic bound for Midtown pulled her hair, Cat—high from her special facial—responded by spitting in his face.

That's when their luck changed. A rookie officer from the Ninetieth Precinct—who happened to be eating a bagel down the block at the time—had watched the entire arrest from the driver's seat of his car before stepping in and offering to transport the two women. "Cadet Lewis reporting for duty," he'd said to the DEA agent. "I can take those two off your hands." The agent, busy cleaning Cat's saliva off his face, nodded with exasperation before uttering the unfortunate words "They're not *my* goddamn problem." Cat and Bess incorrectly assumed that Cadet Lewis was their ride back to Hutton and allowed themselves to be shoved into the backseat of his car.

Zealous Cadet Lewis ran their licenses and turned up two outstanding warrants for Catherine Celia Ono and Elizabeth Folsom Bonner. He took them to Brooklyn Central Holding and processed them into the detention center with such remarkable speed and efficiency that by the time Hutton got there at 8:30 p.m. it was too late; they'd been shuffled into the thick stack of trespassers, drunks, vagrants, and loiterers whose triplicate paperwork was still filled out on old-school carbon-copy forms. Hutton was helpless to even locate them within the building, much less get them out before Monday without seeing a judge, the holding facility's *only* requirement for egress.

He prayed they'd be smart enough not to make any friends or tell anyone why they were there. He'd spent two hours trying to talk his way into the facility to retrieve them, but the bureaucrats running their borough's detention center had no interest in helping a second-year detective from a tony Manhattan precinct violate their only rule. Finally, so distressed that he could feel himself skirting the boundaries of unprofessional behavior, he gave up and drove back to Midtown South, where he attempted to convince his superiors to step in and interfere with the detention center on Cat's and Bess's behalf, but Roth was unwilling to make any moves that would indicate their cooperation.

"They'll have to sit it out," Roth said with absolute certainty.

"You can't risk interfering—it doesn't look good—but they'll be fine in there. Don't act like they're special, and they won't be."

Roth inclined his head toward Vittoria Cardoso's attorney. Donal Windsor, a senior partner at the white-shoe British firm Cavendish Crane, waited in the hallway with the patience of a man who made $2,500 an hour.

"You see that guy? He's a shark. I've met him a dozen times. He's never rude, never impatient, *nothing*. These people are so calm... I can taste the blood in the air, kid. We've got something big."

Mary and Patricia had been dragged back to the station in a car following Vittoria Cardoso and Kate, and Roth made sure they were seen getting thrown into an interrogation room down the hall from where Windsor sat with his beatific, compensated smile. They had sobbed dramatically, making a scene in the hallway, while Hutton watched Windsor give Mary's handbag an approving glance. Cat and Bess had dressed these women well; never in the history of the precinct had there been such perfectly attired undercover officers. The FBI's online cloning would ensure that their phony identities remain unquestioned until the trial, and possibly through it, depending on how liberally they might apply the Patriot Act. Cardoso's status as a foreign national gave them considerable prosecutorial leeway.

Prosecute. The very word made his dick hard.

Hutton spent the next five hours watching through one-way glass as various FBI and DEA agents tried to crack Cardoso, each without success. Around 1:00 a.m. her attorney finally entered the interrogation room and the team took a break. Roth told Hutton to head home for the night. "You did good, kid. Go home, get some sleep. Tomorrow we have a shitload of work to do."

Hutton practically sprinted out of the building, sticking the portable flashing siren on top of his Volvo to speed through traffic. He was exhausted. He'd been on pins and needles since the labs had come back on Cat's original samples, feeling jumpy, focused, terrified, full of anticipation, and neurotic all at once for days.

But this evening's denouement, when the woman he'd been naked with this morning was arrested at gunpoint at the exact moment his career soared, had pushed him in so many emotional directions that he was almost delirious. Nothing positive would come from returning to Brooklyn holding, so Hutton went straight home, poured himself a glass of whiskey, and crawled into bed, trying to repress how bad he felt for Cat and Bess.

Six hours later, he woke up to the sound of someone banging on his door repeatedly, a noise he tried to ignore until he was awake enough to wonder if the building was on fire. He quickly wrapped a towel around himself and ran to the front door, flinging it open only to find Sigrid Gunderson standing there in leggings and a hoodie, accompanied by a tall, clean-shaven young man in a spotless suit. She shoved past Hutton into the apartment. "This is Grant," she barked. "He's Bess's brother, and their lawyer."

"Grant Bonner," the young man said politely, introducing himself with the easy confidence of inborn privilege, his handshake held out at a side angle, a manipulative fraternity gesture.

"Mark Hutton," he replied, shaking Grant's hand with a crushing firmness before waving him into the foyer where Sigrid was already pacing.

"What did you do?" she asked. "Cat and Bess called me collect two hours ago from a pay phone in Brooklyn Central Holding. I made Grant come out here so you can tell him *exactly* what you did. They wouldn't tell me, but it's obviously your fault. You have to get them out."

"How did *you* get in here?" he asked. "Did you shoot my doorman?"

"I told him I was your ex-wife and that Grant was my attorney," Sigrid said distractedly. "He sent me straight up. I think you need to tip him better. But don't change the subject."

"I'm not," he said, yawning. "Make some coffee?" He pointed to the kitchen. "And we'll figure out what to do. Let me put on

some pants and brush my teeth. I'll be right back." He walked back
to his bedroom and shut the door before Sigrid could protest.

When he came back out, Sigrid and Grant were sitting at his
kitchen table. Hutton felt her vibrating with anger from across the
room.

"It'll be okay," he ventured.

"I don't think you understand how bad this is," she said quietly.

"It's not *that* big a deal," he scoffed. "They'll be out on Monday.
The story will blow over."

She pulled up Cat's mug shot on her phone. "This is not a joke.
You can't *make* mistakes like this after thirty. It's not cute or rebel-
lious: it's seen as irresponsible and unprofessional. This," she said as
she pointed to Cat's picture, "is how you become a pariah. And I
won't let that happen to my two best friends."

"Come on, Sigrid, they'll be fine," he insisted. "Everyone will
forget about this next week."

"*How do I explain this to you?*" Sigrid asked, her voice breaking.
"This is a *public shaming*. It's different for women. If you're not married and you fuck up like this—hell, even if you are married, let's
face it, in this day and age, your husband can still just leave you
with absolutely no consequences; someone else will climb right
back on in a heartbeat—you'll never be someone that somebody
wants to be with. New York is so competitive, for everything.
Who's going to hire two washed-up party girls? Who's going to
take them home for Thanksgiving? Nobody. *Nobody.*"

The room was quiet.

"What, no response?" Sigrid asked desperately. An awkward
moment passed until Hutton finally spoke, filling Sigrid and the
young associate in on the details of their arrest and the protocol
at Brooklyn holding. Grant finished up their discussion with professional courtesy, but an obvious distaste—*almost a hatred*, Hutton
thought—shone through his eyes, and Hutton knew then he was
an interloper: a bad-boy-bad-influence who had quite possibly ruined the lives of two perfectly nice women for his own gain. When

he shook Grant's reluctantly extended hand a second time and they
walked out the door, he felt truly ashamed of himself.

Cat and Bess perched awkwardly on the edges of two metal chairs,
their hands still cuffed behind them, while Grant Bonner sat across
from them.

"Are you okay?" he asked immediately.

Bess looked at him sheepishly. "We're fine, just uncomfortable.
Thanks for coming."

"I spoke with the DA," he replied. "They aren't pressing drug
charges pending further cooperation, but your custody was devi-
ated to Central Holding because of outstanding arrest warrants.
You both got tickets for biking on the sidewalk in April. Because
the fine wasn't paid, it turned into an arrest warrant."

"We figured that part out over the last *ten* hours," Bess said.
"When can you get us out of here?"

"The officer who originally arrested you both wasn't aware that
you were already cooperating with the department—he was from
a different precinct. He ran your licenses and took you here. I
checked with Citibank and they confirmed the payments went
through last Friday, but the NYPD's credit card processor hadn't
updated their system. We still need to get you in front of a judge
and show them the bank's confirmation before you can go home."

"What?" Their jaws dropped open.

"Yeah," Grant said, shaking his head and holding his palms to
the sky. "This is the system. You're in it now."

"You can literally show it to them on your phone," Bess pleaded.
"Let me log in."

"It doesn't matter if you show it to a guard," he explained. "You
need to show it to a judge, and there are no judges here between
5:00 p.m. on Friday and 7:00 a.m. on Monday."

"How much longer are we going to be here?"

"Again, the judges aren't in chambers until Monday at 7:00 a.m."

Bess thought she was going to burst out crying then and there. "That can't be possible. Today is Saturday. *We're not safe in here.* What if one of their henchmen decides to shank us or something?"

"You should be happy to know that nothing actually indicates this was more than a beauty company. Sure—they used Schedule I felony substances in the manufacturing of their products—but the organization appears to be pretty narrow. It wasn't a drug front so much as a clever business plan with a healthy revenue stream. Plus, the women in your cell are two old prostitutes, a pregnant woman who stole a car, and a nineteen-year-old from Park Slope who let her dog off leash. I think you'll be fine."

"Do the Bedford Organics people suspect anything? To be fair to us, they did get us pretty high before we got arrested."

"I doubt it. Someone videoed the arrest on Bedford. Bess, you were yelling 'They're trashing our rights,' whatever that means; and Cat, you hissed like an animal and spit on the officer who handed you off to the clown that brought you here."

"Matthew Lillard yells that in *Hackers*. It's all I could think of," Bess replied.

Cat was shaking her head and laughing. "I forgot about that. Verisimilitude, man. Look it up."

"You weren't exactly protesting in Birmingham." He laughed, too, but nicely. "You were arrested for buying face cream with ecstasy in it."

"Have you seen our mug shots?"

"Cat's is pretty cute, actually," he said, winking at Cat, who rolled her eyes. "Very defiant. Bess, yours looks like a class picture."

"Is there any way you can get them deleted?"

"No. They're already online."

An officer knocked on the door and called out, "One minute."

Cat started to panic. "Find Detective Mark Hutton and Sergeant

Peter Roth. They got us into this. They have to fucking get us out of here."

"I did," he answered. Cat's heart sank.

"Look," Grant continued, "I know it's frustrating, but you're in holding in Brooklyn, not in Midtown South. There's nothing anyone can or, frankly, *should* do until a judge releases you. This is all in your best interests. I'll be back first thing Monday morning. You'll be out in less than forty-eight hours, I promise."

Two officers opened the door, barking, "Time's up."

"I brought you some snack bars." Grant stood and held up a paper Whole Foods bag, which he handed to one of the officers. Cat and Bess were led back to a tiny cell, where they were given the bag after a cursory search.

Cat chewed on a bar as she sank to the floor, but she didn't cry.

If she started crying, she was afraid she'd never stop.

Paula Booth had planned to spend this rare and peaceful Saturday morning doing absolutely nothing. She'd turned off her phone, slept late, had her coffee in bed with her cats, and was considering taking a long walk across the street in Central Park when her doorbell rang unexpectedly.

She threw on a cashmere robe over her cotton pajamas and walked to the door, peering through the spyhole as she twirled her long white hair up into its signature bun. Both her assistants stood in the hall. She cracked the door open warily.

"It's *Saturday*, girls. My phone is off for a reason," she hissed.

Izzy and Liesl pushed right by her, coming all the way into the apartment and closing the door. "Bess Bonner and Catherine Ono were arrested last night," Izzy said, holding up a copy of the *New York Post* with Bess's and Cat's incredibly flattering mug shots on the front page.

Paula snatched the paper.

LIVING THE HIGH LIFE screamed the headline in hundred-point font, followed by *RAGE* BABES SNATCHED IN LUXURY DRUG RING.

> Last night's raid of a high-end drug ring on Bedford Avenue in Williamsburg swept up two *RAGE* employees buying beauty creams loaded with prescriptions from a Brazilian Doctor Feelgood. The business, Bedford Organics, had been under surveillance by the NYPD, DEA, and FBI for weeks in relation to an as-yet-unspecified Manhattan overdose. It was shut down last night when the DEA seized over two thousand pounds of creams, lotions, and serums that were allegedly loaded with street drugs like opium, ecstasy, heroin, ketamine, amphetamine, and cocaine.

The article went on to wildly speculate about the backgrounds of the six women who were arrested. The little information they did have about Cat and Bess was peppered with so much hyperbole and sexism that they were rendered as little more than caricatures of two slutty rich girls trying to get high on their beauty supplies. Their Photogram post from earlier in the evening was reprinted in full color. A Cooper House rep had provided a succinct "No comment."

Paula didn't recognize the names of the two other women, who were reported to be freelance stylists from Los Angeles. She checked her email. There was nothing from Margot. Paula would have to deal with this herself—as usual. She'd hate to fire Cat and Bess considering the sheer volume of work they accomplished, but this kind of public embarrassment was well beyond her comfort zone. Her first instinct was that *RAGE* couldn't support this kind of attention, not while they were in such a weak position. She started playing the voicemails that had racked up from Cooper's senior publicists asking for clarification, deleting them one by one.

Paula had been putting out Margot's fires since 1987. As she finished an MBA and intended to go work for IBM, her whole life was derailed, forever altered, by the speech that Margot gave at her commencement to the biggest graduating class of women that Harvard Business School had ever had. Margot had argued that without mandatory equal pay and a global economic floor for women, the leaders in front of her—these freshly minted uber-elite empowered feminists—would be nothing but a flash in the pan. *You have an obligation*, Margot had said, her voice resonating powerfully, *to the women of the world, because there but for the grace of God go you. You must use your privilege for good and for nothing else, because you will always be fine. You will always have enough; you will always be able to provide for your families. So you must be responsible, powerful capitalists, though there is no incentive for you to be this way aside from your own moral compass; in fact, the greater incentive is to disregard the costs of our values. As such, you must be the economic change you wish to see in the world, or it will fall apart. There is something very rotten at the core of a society that increases in its wealth without diminishing its miseries. Do not lie to yourselves. We have too much, while everyone else has too little.*

Paula had shown up at the magazine's offices three days later, résumé in hand and statistics about domestic production rates for polyester, lamb's wool, leather, cotton, and silk on the tip of her tongue. She'd argued that pushing an Idaho-based hosiery company to establish a minimum wage would ripple through the state's economy, and that the sock company's board members, who also had interests in a handbag manufacturer, could be tempted by a feature in *RAGE*. She'd advocated for a strategy of winning at all costs, for cajoling and bullying the world around them into meeting their requirements, and pitched the idea that would eventually become the system of auditors who doled out the *RAGE* seal of approval. Margot had hired her on the spot and fired her current assistant mid-sentence, forcing the young woman to clear out her desk and leave immediately so that Paula could have a place to stash her handbag while they continued that first exceptional conversation.

Her first two decades at *RAGE* had changed the world; the wage gaps between the cottage industries of Lake Como and the factories of Sri Lanka had been forced to narrow by Paula's and Margot's sheer forces of will, and their own employment policies, which included six-month paid maternity leave followed by paid child care for children ages six months to twelve years, had been aped by dozens of companies who were trying to recruit women of the same caliber as the *RAGE* staff.

But for the past twenty issues, *RAGE* had been in free fall, and now Paula faced a very specific choice: fire Cat and Bess, or figure out a way to use them to boost circulation. She read and reread the *Post* article before calling Maddie Plattstein, the author of the **Skin Deep in Their Pockets** beauty industry regulation piece they had scheduled for September. This plan *was* possible, Paula insisted to Maddie, rapidly calculating the hours to their production deadline for September. They could turn this around. She was certain. Maddie finally agreed, and they hung up.

"Izzy!" Paula barked. "Liesl! Make lunch. We have work to do."

At 6:00 a.m. Monday, the buzzer finally sounded in the dank cell where Cat and Bess had spent the last thirty-six hours. "Back away from the door," the intercom crackled. The door swung open.

"Ono, Bonner," said a female voice. A uniformed officer led them through a maze of hallways to a windowless waiting room where they sat with dozens of other male and female prisoners queuing to see the judge. The room's plastic chairs were badly scuffed and cracked. The air reeked of body odor, cigarettes, stale beer, and bad breath—the accumulated stink of a hundred people who had spent the weekend in jail without toilet paper or a shower.

Brooklyn was represented in full force. There were skinny college kids with ironic stick-'n'-poke tattoos who looked terrified;

shifty-eyed middle-aged men in shabby clothes who looked resigned; old women who looked disoriented; and dozens upon
dozens of young men.

Cat and Bess found two seats together and sat quietly, trying not
to make eye contact with anyone. Thirty minutes later, the first set
of names were called.

"Diaz. Johnson. Moses. Kwan. Ono. Bonner."

They stood up and made their way through the crowd to the
guards as quickly as they could without bumping or touching anyone else.

The guards waved their hands impatiently. "Let's go let's go let's
go, ladies, hurry it up," one said forcefully.

Grant was waiting on the other side of the door, where they
were uncuffed and directed down a hallway.

"Don't say anything unless you're spoken to by the judge directly," he said.

They walked into another windowless room with three metal
desks. An older woman in a pantsuit and black robe sat behind the
desk opposite.

Grant handed her two printouts. She looked over her glasses,
squinted briefly at Cat and Bess, then signed a third piece of paper
and handed it back to Grant before calling "Next!"

"That's it?" Bess whispered to Grant as he led them through another door.

"That's it," he replied. "Go sign for your things."

They waited in line at a window covered in bulletproof glass for
their handbags. Cat checked the contents; her wallet, phone, keys,
and cigarettes were all still there. She signed the release as quickly
as she could and Bess did the same.

"There's some photographers outside, but I have a car waiting.
Just walk straight behind me and don't speak to anyone," he said.
Cat and Bess turned to each other automatically, trying to wipe the
dirt and smeared makeup off their faces and hands.

Cat dug a full-coverage liquid foundation designed to cover up surgical scars out of her purse. "*Thank god*," she said, patting the opaque porcelain cream all over her face before handing it to Bess, who did the same. Grant tapped his toes and sighed.

"Let's go," he said impatiently as Bess clipped her hair into a top-knot.

"Well, this is some A-game hot mess," Cat said to Bess, ignoring Grant completely. "We are epic."

"Put your sunglasses on," Bess commanded, sliding a pair of oversized aviators onto her own face. "*Now* we can go." She set her jaw and marched to the building's exit, flinging the metal doors open while Cat and Grant tried to keep up.

A pack of photographers descended upon them immediately, snapping thousands of frames before they even got close to the waiting Suburban. Cat tried to keep the look of shock off her face but felt her jaw drop open. Both girls had spent their time in jail trying not to cry, not to make a scene, to be small and friendly to everyone they encountered; they'd deliberately avoided thinking about the real-world repercussions of what they'd done. Now, as the gaggle of men in cheap T-shirts and bedazzled jeans took their photos and screamed their names, Cat and Bess both felt their stomachs plummet. They fought their way into the SUV and slammed the doors.

Cat looked at her phone, which had miraculously stayed on all weekend and still had eight percent of its battery life. She had 49 missed calls, 23 new voicemails, 207 text messages, and 142 new emails. *Not good*. Cat realized, for the very first time in her life, that maybe it really didn't matter how much Berger she threw in anyone's face or how much theory she tried to bury inside the magazine; the rules of the world were real, and they were not hers to alter.

"We are so fucking fired," she said.

"No, we're not," Bess insisted. "This is totally to our advantage. You'll see."

Chapter Eleven

Monday evening Hutton stood on Sigrid's stoop, stabbing the pewter bell with his index finger. He peered through the channel of bottle-green glass lining the door but saw no signs of movement within. He leaned over and tried to see through the wooden shutters, but they were shut tight and the drapes were closed behind them. If anyone was home, they certainly weren't acting like it.

He'd spent the past three days chained to his desk transcribing statements from all the agents and officers present during the raid and interrogations, leaving messages during his breaks for Cat, Grant, Bess, and Sigrid. No one returned his calls, so he'd left the office at 5:00 p.m. sharp and come straight to 170 Ocean from the subway.

He pulled a thin piece of paper out of his briefcase and studied it. Roth had been thrilled with his work, even implying that he was sure to be promoted. But when Hutton had insisted that none of this resolved the problem presented by the note Hillary had mailed to Idaho—*the ribbon is the key to everything*—Roth had turned surly and told him in no uncertain terms to forget about it, that it didn't matter. Cardoso's status as a foreign national had given them a fair amount of leeway under the Patriot Act to manufacture a story that implied a long-term investigation. Not only did they no longer need the note, Roth pointed out, but its very existence could impact the prosecution of the case. He'd actually taken the note and thrown it into the garbage before sending Hutton back to his desk with a sneer.

When Roth had gone to the bathroom Hutton dug the note out of the trash, and now he sat on Sigrid's steps, smoothing the index card flat and wishing desperately that Cat, or Sigrid, or Bess, or *someone* who'd known Hillary would come out and talk to him about it. He didn't know what to do.

Finally Hutton gave up and walked home. He stripped off his work clothes as soon as he walked into the foyer, changing into his running gear. The July evening was sweltering—nearing ninety-five degrees—but he looped around the park three times, punishing himself, pushing harder on every lap. His sneakers hit the pavement until his legs shook and his T-shirt was soaked through. He slowed down each time he passed 170 Ocean, but the building remained dark.

After a long shower he tried to keep himself busy with unpacking between obsessively checking his phone. After two hours and two doses of scotch, he'd emptied nearly a dozen boxes, collapsing their corpses into a tidy pile by the door and roping them neatly with twine for the super. The apartment barely looked different, having swallowed his meager belongings into cabinets and closets without effect. He was finally moved in.

Cat still hadn't called back. He suspected she never would.

Why am I so obsessed with her? Why do I feel so responsible? She was just another magazine girl, he told himself; there were a thousand of them in the city, beautiful and shallow, obsessing over clothes and makeup all day, posting Photogram images of donuts they would never eat. All of them from good families, all of them educated and poised, all of them working at some job for $35K a year until they met a banker who would be proud to say "My wife used to work at a magazine" for the rest of their lives. Hutton could have his pick of any of them, he told himself.

Exhausted, clutching his phone, he crawled into bed and sent a text to Callie:

u back?

He fell asleep waiting for her to respond.

Callie Court was at that very moment having a late-night cocktail at Peacock Alley with Whig Beaton Molton-Mauve Lucas, who had very kindly insisted that Callie call her Lou. They were perched on velvet stools in the artfully darkened bar, sharing a charcuterie plate—well, Callie was, anyway—and drinking Negroni cocktails. The bartender loitered at the other end of the bar, reappearing only when Lou summoned him with a flick of her polished fingers.

When Callie had landed at Newark that evening, she turned her phone on to find a breathless voicemail from her agent. *RAGE* wanted her for an exclusive pre-resort collection shoot in early September—*during* Fashion Week. There was one caveat: the editor running the shoot wanted to meet her as soon as possible.

RAGE represented the first real opportunity to make her defining image something other than the Dalí tit-crease haunting her at every bus stop and subway station, so she had cabbed it home, showered, and changed into a simple black silk T-shirt dress, then grabbed another car back into the city to meet Lou. She'd waited at Peacock Alley—the bar inside the lobby of the Waldorf Astoria—for over an hour.

As she sat alone, drinking water and scribbling in the black Moleskine notebook she used as a diary, Callie wondered if Lou would really be as glamorous as she looked in all those spreads in *RAGE* over the years, if she'd be as tiny. If she'd have that look of expensive frailty, like an antique vase, that all terribly rich women wear like moisturizer.

Lou hadn't disappointed. She'd swanned into the bar around eleven thirty, begging forgiveness for her lateness in a filmy lilac georgette dress that had probably cost Callie's annual rent. Her tiny feet were banded into metallic Valentino sandals, and she wrapped them around the stool's legs like little vines. She ordered for them both—without looking at the menu—before launching animatedly into her vision. Callie just sat back and watched the show as Lou gestured and squeezed and winked her way through her pitch, her big booming voice still managing to be loud in a whisper.

"It'll be part public performance and part staged shoot," Lou was saying. "I want the background to be made up of boldfaced names, so we'll be doing this after the Dior presentation—literally everyone will be there. I need a girl who can really *act*, not just pose. Your agent did send your clips, and Jonathan texted me some videos he made of you, which were very compelling." She swirled her cocktail, the orange Campari casting a glow into the enormous stack of rubies she wore on her right hand.

Callie looked down, unconsciously covering the panther tattooed on her ring finger.

"I'd love to," she said with absolute sincerity. "I'll do whatever you ask. You don't need to explain anything to me."

"Well, I just wanted to . . . I'm sure you've heard about my colleagues," Lou said quietly.

"Yes," Callie said, surprised that she had brought it up. "I know them, actually. Not well, but Cat lives around the corner from a bar I work at, and I went to college with Bess."

Lou looked shocked—*I guess she didn't really expect the fat girl with the hand tattoo to intersect her professional circles*—but recovered quickly, pulling her face back into a sympathetic facade that Callie guessed was meant to telegraph seriousness.

"I'd love to. Really. I'm a twenty-nine-year-old plus-size model, you know? We work longer and we work older than straight-size girls, but I'm ready to take risks. I've done enough catalogs to last a lifetime."

Lou grinned, the bar's low lighting glinting off her enormous veneers. "That's settled, then. We'll have to get your measurements taken by our coordinator to start getting samples made in your size from the various houses. You're the first plus-size model we've ever worked with at *RAGE*."

Callie held up her glass to toast. "Cheers—I'm honored. Thank you for choosing me for this."

Lou toasted with a quick clink and hopped off her stool, half her drink still in the glass. She hugged Callie, squeezing hard, practically groping her. "I've got to run, darling girl. Talk soon." She whirled out of the bar in high gear, the lilac dress flowing behind her like a fairy cape.

Callie dismissed Hutton's text and called her agent. The bartender dropped off a black leather folio with a hundred-plus-dollar tab inside. Callie threw down her credit card as the phone rang and rang.

"I'm in, Roger," she squealed quietly when he finally answered. Peacock Alley—all chiaroscuro light and soft piano—wasn't the place to be rowdy. "I'm really going to be in *RAGE*!"

"We're getting you fifty thousand dollars for the shoot," he said. "They *loved* those videos you've been making with Jonathan. He agreed to release one right before Fashion Week."

Her stomach dropped. "Which one?" The bartender returned with the black folio, and she pocketed the receipt—her first *RAGE*-related expense, Callie thought with satisfaction.

"Probably the one of you eating an ice-cream sandwich while you do the dance from *Rhythm Nation*. It's basically your 'Cat Daddy.'"

Callie swallowed the rest of her cocktail in a single gulp. "Shit...Okay. I was *really* high when we made that."

"It doesn't matter. Nobody can tell. Are you ready to get famous, girl? If this shoot works out, it could be the *cover* of the

November issue. You know, *she* always chooses them herself," he said reverently, referring to Margot.

Callie climbed off her stool and grabbed her cotton tote bag, shoving her book into it as she made her way toward the Park Avenue exit. "I can't even think about that. Let's just get it booked and signed, okay?"

"I'm on it, sweetie. There's an NDA, too. I'll have it messengered over in the morning. You can't mention this to anyone—and I mean *anyone*—until the shoot's over. It's eight weeks from now. Fashion *omertà*. Okay?"

"Sure. That's fine. Listen, I have to run—I'm so beat," she lied. "Talk tomorrow?"

"Talk tomorrow," Roger said sweetly. "I'm proud of you, honey."

She thought about texting Hutton back, but...she burned with hurt and rejection. If he was going to treat her like this for the millionth time, the very least he could do was call. Or text during the day; she'd settle for that.

Callie walked out into the street. The city her oyster, she was alone, dressed up, had no plans, and now she had income to count on. *Should I treat myself to a late-night dinner at the bar at Balthazar?* she wondered.

No. She wasn't hungry; and besides, she'd just eaten an entire two-person serving of assorted meats. She needed... *to dance it off,* she realized. She hopped in a cab and headed back to her neighborhood, stopping into Outcast, the venerable gay bar around the corner from her apartment.

Outcast was packed tonight with shirtless guys—most of them embarrassingly young—and a lone bachelorette party getting sloppy drunk at the bar. Donna Summer's "Bad Girls" hit the speakers as soon as she walked in. Her friend Jared was behind the bar in a white tank top and extremely low-slung jean shorts. She lifted herself up onto the polished wood, elbowing two boyish blondes out of the way, and kissed him hello.

"Babe!" Jared yelled over the music. "Shots?"

She nodded. He passed her two ounces of tequila and she knocked it back without salt or lime, tossing him her tote bag to stash behind the bar.

"I have to dance!" she screamed over the music. "Come find me when you want to smoke!"

Callie fought her way through the dance floor into the middle, shimmying between couples. She found a two-foot circle all to herself and started dancing, throwing her hips around while her feet moved in complicated steps, a mishmash of the ten years she'd spent doing competitive jazz routines. The DJ mixed "Drunk Girls" into "Bad Girls," then sped up the beat and added some of the vocals from Brandy and Monica's "The Boy Is Mine" over *another* beat made up of Lil Wayne grunting. Callie never wanted it to end.

She stayed on the dance floor until she was soaked in sweat, then ducked out for a cigarette with Jared. They came inside for another round of shots and a little bit of cocaine; she danced more; they smoked more; did more shots; danced more; did more coke, then finally closed down the bar around 3:00 a.m. Callie grabbed her bag from behind the bar, walked over to the DJ—a platinum-haired waif crossing gender's Rubicon from one side to the other, though she couldn't quite tell in which direction—and kissed them full on the mouth.

"That was epic," she said. "Thank you. Do you have a card?"

"Anytime." The DJ winked, handing their card to Callie. "Let me know if you want me for *anything*."

Callie slung her bag over her shoulder and smiled. "Good night, you guys. That was so much fun. It was exactly what I needed."

She hugged Jared and walked the single block back to her apartment in the rain, collapsing into bed alone, the speaker buzz still ringing in her ears.

Cat lay in her bed on Monday night while a summer storm raged outside, the night flashing white with lightning as the raindrops beat a steady drum on her building's lumpy windowpanes.

She tried to plan an outfit for the next day while staring out the window. No suede in the rain, she told herself. No white. Tomorrow would have to be all black, she decided, something appropriate for her own funeral.

Paula had left a voicemail asking her to come in the next day, but Cat didn't know what that meant. She'd spent her whole life being a good girl, a hard worker. The very idea of being reprimanded at the *one* place where she'd managed success in her life made her so sick to her stomach that she'd spent the entire day in bed. Apparently Bess's mother had texted Cat's mother, Anais, a link to the *New York Post* story. Cat thought of the email her mother had sent her, the last thing she'd read on her phone before turning it off again:

Schate Katteke, hoe moeilijk. U besteedt te veel momenten zoeken naar je eigen mooie weerspiegeling, en nu: heb je het gevonden. Ik zie U graag, maar je bent niet op zoek naar de juiste dingen.

[Dearest little kitten, how hard. You spend too much time searching for your own reflection, and now: you have found it. I love you but you are looking for the wrong things.]

It was so easy for her to say that. Rijmenam—the Flemish hamlet that Takeshi and Anais Ono lived in just north of Brussels—wasn't just three thousand miles away. It was actual lifetimes, universes, galaxies away. The little stores open only from eleven to three, and never on weekends; her mother's two Clydesdale horses, rough and muddy and velvet-mouthed; the tidy little BMW that her father drove into town; the farming priest whose eggs they left a fifty-cent piece in the honor box for. It was all another world. When their butcher died, Anais had gone to his funeral, wept with his widow. Cat shopped at Whole Foods.

In the 1970s, her father had been sent to Brussels by Mikimoto to attend a European law school course, while her mother, an abstract painter, had been working extra hours at a country stables just off the train stop in Jezus-Eik, a small Flemish town outside the city.

Takeshi Ono had shown up one afternoon to the stables sporting brand-new jodhpurs, tall patent boots, an immaculately flocked helmet, and a spotless suede two-button sport coat. Nearly two meters high, thin as a rail, and perfectly groomed, he looked as though he'd simply gone into a riding store and asked for the best—which, of course, he had, after receiving an invitation for an afternoon of riding from one of his new colleagues.

He couldn't yet read Flemish well enough to follow the signs, so Takeshi wandered through a few stone archways until he reached a set of white stucco Tudor-style stables arranged around a dirt ring. A ruddy-faced girl with braids—the picture of rural health, practically an eighteenth-century painting—had stood in the middle of the ring running a pretty little painted mare in a circle. She'd looked at him and giggled at his new clothes. He looked like he belonged in a magazine.

"Anais est a la bas," she'd said in heavily accented French, assuming he'd have no Flemish at all. "Back," she continued in English. "Back by the horse sleeping," she directed, pointing to stables that made a hallway to another ring, that one covered. He nodded, gave a small bow in thanks, then strode purposefully across the dirt to the stalls.

At that very moment Anais Pieters, in a ripped pair of overalls and a stained T-shirt reading "Fuck Nixon," was trying to pick out the hoof of their new pony. Anais was backing him into the stall, but Chokotoff wouldn't go. She gave up on moving him and tied his bridle loosely to the stall door, leaving too much slack. As she ran her hand down the horse's leg, applying pressure at the knee to let him know she'd be picking up his foot, Takeshi appeared, hands outstretched to pet the horse, his destiny.

Chokotoff leaned forward to search for food from this dandy new stranger—and stepped down so quickly that he crushed Anais's middle finger.

The finger turned black in under a minute. Takeshi dropped his immaculate helmet to the ground and picked up Anais, the dust and mud from her overalls smearing his beautiful jacket. She protested in her own broken mix of English, French, and frustrated Flemish—*It is just a finger! I can walk! Why are you kidnapping me?*—until she saw the look on his face.

It was the most gallant expression she'd ever seen anyone make. She stopped struggling. She let him carry her out to the parking lot. He set her carefully in his little rented Fiat and with her pointing aid drove her to the town doctor. Dr. Thys drained the swollen finger, pulled out some bone shards, and set the remainder with a tongue-depressor splint. Takeshi watched him like a hawk the entire time.

A stupid mistake for anyone to make, it was especially humiliating for Anais: she'd been riding at these stables her whole life. She insisted on proving herself to Takeshi, teaching him to ride, jump, and control the horse with some basic dressage in twelve weeks.

They were married by the end of the year.

Takeshi then perfected not just riding, but skiing, baccarat, cycling, and skeet shooting—the collegial activities of the wealthy businessmen who moved in and out of the circles of power in Brussels, Antwerp, and Luxembourg—along with Flemish and Dutch, Luxembourgish and German, and French and English, enabling him to move up the ranks at Mikimoto with speed as they grew their business with the Antwerp-based jewelry industry.

Now, after only three weeks of retirement spent pacing around the barn, trying to boss Anais and the horses around until she forced him back to the house with the business end of a pitchfork, he had taken a job in the Brussels office of an NGO to coordinate EU aid into developing economies at a fraction of his previous salary. Taki said it was service to the continent that had taken him in.

Cat was pretty sure he just didn't know how to be a person if he wasn't working.

Anais had continued painting and riding, and she took care of Cat, too, until they sent her off to Miss Sawyer's in the ninth grade. Cat's prior education at the European girls' school had given her flawless English, French, formal Dutch, German, and Italian on top of her native Flemish, but despite the rigor of her education, the Onos had been concerned that staying in Europe would turn her into what her mother called *ijdele prinseske*.

Transliterated it was "idle little princess": many of the wealthy euro-brats she'd grown up with were already asserting their entitlement over the world. Their casual utterances—formed in the bedrock-deep continental racism that Anais had never questioned until it was aimed at people she loved—were painting her daughter with a constant wash of inferiority. As she entered puberty, Cat started to look at herself with an eye so critical Anais feared she'd never recover.

Anais and Taki could see the consequences of their choices happening to their little *Katteke*, and they didn't like it. They had wanted Catherine—whom they'd given a Catholic first name to help her fit in anywhere—to be like them but better; to be practical and dedicated and earnest and then happy. *That* was the formula. There would be no happiness in chasing the same ambitions of the upper-crust Europeans whom Taki mimicked but was, at his heart, decidedly *not*. "Never let the mask become the face," he would say, adapting Orwell for his own purposes.

Taki was always on time, always at her baseball games and swim meets, always a proud and loving father, but he had a million rules. No television. No store-bought toys. Homework before riding or archery or baseball or swimming. By the time Cat was in seventh grade her peers were getting cars and drivers, heading to Paris or London for shopping weekends with their mothers and nighttime trips to bars with flashy young men. Cat's own mother, usually covered in a mixture of horse shit and oil paint, preferred Danskos and denim; she did not understand Cat's concern for clothes, for handbags, for objects and *things*. She worried that Cat, unable to realize that people who love themselves will fit in anywhere, was trying to change *herself* to fit in.

So Taki and Anais had searched for a practical solution to help Cat find her confidence. A friend of a friend described Sawyer's as "a challenging school for hearty girls from nice families." Intrigued, they sent away for the admissions materials, knowing it might be too late for that fall but pleading with the school's office to send them anyway.

Anais had squealed with delight over their glossy catalog. The rainbow-nation photos of other multiethnic Sawyer girls—a rowing crew, and girls with dirt on their faces tilling fields for the school's then-unusual organic farm—could have been staged from her dreams. Taki studied the academics and Ivy League acceptance rates and was pleased at their high numbers. Cat liked that it was in America, in Connecticut, the home of Yale University and a Barbara Stanwyck movie she had on VHS.

She had to write an essay about why she wanted to go but couldn't think of anything good to say. *Because . . . my parents think I know too many silly girls, and . . . I think they are right? Because America is exciting? Because I want to be an American girl with her own convertible, at a football game, like Nancy Drew? Because I want to see New York City?* The day after the catalog arrived she had sat at the kitchen table until dark, her mechanical pencil poised to write a brilliant first draft. But nothing came out. Six languages and she had no words. Taki looked at her blank cahier page and shook his head.

"You'll try again tomorrow," he said in English. "You must sleep on it."

She'd run up to her room, thrown herself on the bed, and

sobbed loudly. She didn't fit in here, but she couldn't even articulate *why* she deserved to fit in somewhere else.

Her mother snuck in and stroked her head, something Cat had stopped letting her do a year earlier. She patted and finger-combed and braided Cat's big hanks of black hair until her red-faced daughter finally stopped wailing and looked up.

"The Onos are adventurers," Anais leaned down and whispered to Cat in Flemish. "It's in your blood. You must cross an ocean to discover your soul."

In the morning Cat rose with the dawn to watch her mother traipse out to the barn, then put on her school uniform and sat down at the kitchen table. She drafted her essay with a furious purpose. By the time her father appeared to make the coffee it was almost done.

"May I read it, little Katteke?"

She handed it to him proudly. He read it out loud, a barely suppressed grin on his face.

My name is Catherine Celia Ono, and I am an adventurer. Twenty years ago my father crossed the world from Hokkaido to Brussels to find his soul. He found his soul mate and they made me, and now it is my turn to find my place in the world.

I know that Miss Sawyer's is a difficult school. I am a very hard worker. To prove that I have passed advanced fluency in Italian, Dutch, German, French, and of course English and Flemish.

I want to see America. It is a place full of important women like Annie Oakley and Eleanor Roosevelt and Ruth Bader Ginsburg. I want to become a part of America, and I know that being a student at Miss Sawyer's—a school inside the fabric of the country—will show me the way.

In return I offer my dedicated work. I will not waste a

moment of time. I am eager to learn from the teachers and from the other students. Please consider my humble application and be assured that I will try harder than any other student you have ever had.

Sincerely
Catherine C Ono

Taki and Anais hadn't changed a single word. They sent the essay out that afternoon, and Sawyer's—thrilled to have a full-pay middle schooler who spoke six languages—admitted her just one week after her application materials arrived.

The Onos had been so proud of her as she graduated first from Sawyer's, then North Adams College, and went straight to the University of Chicago to begin a doctoral program in art history; and so disappointed when she'd given up on her dissertation to work for Hillary at *RAGE*.

It must be nearly dawn at the farm. Cat could feel their disappointment pulsing from the air, as though her mother's tears had washed from the river into the North Sea, across the ocean and up through the bedrock, evaporating into the rain that fell outside her windows. They were sad for her: sad that she had made a superficial life and would be judged superficially. They didn't think she had any real friends.

But Cat *did* have friends. She had best friends, people who understood her obsessions with objects and appearance not just as the anxieties of a foreigner, of a minority—which certainly, on some level, existed; she would happily admit that—but also as the anxieties of a philosopher, someone who lived *in* the world and sought to change it using the lingua franca of culture at large. She didn't live in Rijmenam. She lived in New York. *They would change, too, if they lived here.*

She didn't think she could speak to Hutton ever again. How could he have made such a terrible mistake—have let her rot in a detention center for three days? How could he have allowed her to be so humiliated?

These were your own choices, she reminded herself. When she'd listened to his voicemails last night they were so sweetly apologetic that for a moment she had a hard time being mad, until she remembered her mug shot on the cover of the newspaper—and about how manipulated she felt, how abandoned.

Cat had gambled her whole life—her whole self—with only a moment's hesitation. If she was fired or demoted, in this public way...how could she go on? Where would she live? How could she face herself, her family, her friends? How would she ever recover from losing her job?

Notorious.

What a terrible word.

But I haven't lost it, she reminded herself. *Not yet.*

Part II

September

Chapter Twelve

Cat turned to Bess in the adjacent seat of what they'd come to think of as "their" Suburban, a nine-seater Cooper had been letting them use since July, and bared her teeth for inspection. Bess wiped an errant fleck from Cat's brow bone, then nodded.

"Flawless," she said.

Cat's makeup was indeed literally flawless, her face a perfect mask shellacked to require no photoshop. It was flawless every day now; Cooper sent hair and makeup artists any time she would be expected in the office or at an event. Today actual gold leaf lined her eyelids, a fall of blue-black-colored hair had been sewn into the crown of her head, and matching gold leaf tipped her navy fingernails, all of it designed to complement the custom-made Dior cocktail dress she'd been stitched into. The stiffly tiered black crepe structure—paired with pointed suede ankle boots that faded from red to pink—was surprisingly comfortable, despite the rubber shapewear she'd been squeezed into beneath it. Still, she'd been able to sit upright in her seat in the Suburban, an increasingly rare opportunity. Last week Cat and Bess had been sewn into lace columns so tight they'd been lifted on wood planks one by one through the back door of the SUV, then pulled out ankles-first in an alleyway behind the venue.

The vehicle's perforated calfskin interior was littered with empty coffee cups from Starbucks, cigarette butts stubbed into Luna bar wrappers, Sephora bags full of emergency product, dog-eared novels, and a scattering of king-size pillows with clumps of mascara smeared into their Frette pillowcases. Cat and Bess found themselves spending more time in the SUV than in the office. It seemed pointless to clean up.

Bess pulled back her lips to carefully expose her own blindingly white veneers. "How about me?"

Cat examined her attentively. The double sets of fake mink lashes were still in place, the matte pink lipstick hadn't migrated onto her teeth, and the tiny ruby studs set on the apple of her left cheekbone—temporary microdermal implants—weren't smudged with foundation. Her dewy skin was coated with the dust of real South Sea pearls that Raphael, their favorite makeup artist, had ground up in a mortar and pestle the night before. "They were free," he'd explained, "from some tacky company who wants to sponsor you. Much better as makeup. And you're still *wearing* them, anyway."

Bess was *intact*: their new standard for achievement.

"You're a doll," Cat said reassuringly.

Jim, the hatchet-faced middle-aged driver assigned to them by Cooper, looked back.

"Ready?" he asked, sounding positive though his expression remained stony and emotionless.

"Ready!" they chimed. Cat dug a Klonopin out of the bottom of her purse, broke it in half, and held it under her tongue.

He walked around and opened their door. Bess got out first, leaping gracefully onto the gray carpet with Jim's arm as a banister. The flashbulbs exploded. Ten thousand frames—professional, amateur, iPhone—clicked off as she made her way over to the first step-and-repeat, her movements now fluid and practiced even in scalloped four-inch silk stilettos.

Today's event, the Council for Fashion Awareness Awards sponsored by British Petroleum, had been jammed smack in the middle of New York Fashion Week, and Lincoln Center was overflowing with skeletal women swaddled in precious yardage, tiny human bouquets of cigarette smoke and hair extensions. Companion hordes of plain-Jane handlers screamed into cellphones and headsets, hustling their charges from logo to logo for the audiences watching and clicking around the world. As Bess posed, a childlike brunette publicist waved her arms at Jim to send Cat up.

He helped her out of the SUV onto the carpet, propping her up with his wiry biceps as she tugged her dress into place. The photographers were still focused on Bess, who helpfully changed poses and looked over her shoulder, giving Cat ten whole seconds before anyone noticed her. She took advantage of the stolen moment to breathe (a ragged little hiccup as the cage of her dress resisted any true expansion of the diaphragm) and scan the plaza for a friendly face.

Nothing. Everyone was familiar, but these days, no one was her friend.

A boy in a porkpie hat with a camera bigger than his head and brand-new seafoam Prada loafers turned around and screamed her name, galloping toward her on his slender little legs. The other photographers followed suit. Cat moved her lips into a grin automatically and began taking mincing, robotic steps toward the first step-and-repeat board, focusing her eyes on the fish-in-a-gown logo as the swarm descended around her. They all called her by name, asking asinine questions about what she was wearing, what she was doing later, where she had come from. She didn't respond: just stared at the fish drawing and smiled vacantly, holding her cheeks up and swiveling into a position modeled by the childlike publicist.

The cameramen from *TMI* were the pushiest: asking who her boyfriend was, if she had an eating disorder like her friend Hillary. They *all* knew Hillary now. *RAGE's* September issue had come out four weeks ago, on August 20, with a close-up of Hillary's spectacular face on the cover. Her green eyes and white lashes were rendered in high-resolution gloss on every newsstand on the globe. BEAUTY KILLS read the cover in navy all-caps. In the year-old picture—a test shot from one of Reuben Avador's winter shoots—Hillary's skin glowed like a Swedish teenager's, her visage placed in the center of a lightly feathered vignette. Set just beneath her pore-less and freckled jawline: THE LIFE AND DEATH OF HEIRESS HILLARY WHITNEY.

After forty-eight hours it was their best-selling issue of all time. Maddie's feature, fact-checked within a single pixel, had slaughtered sixteen different beauty companies, five members of Congress, four retail chains, and the head of the Federal Drug Administration. Margot ran it all with an editor's letter read around the world:

Dear Readers:

We must never step away from the critical lens, even when it is turned back upon our own faces. There is nothing to fear from transparency. Only lessons to be learned.

Magazines like RAGE are the collective conscious. Surely after this issue Cooper will lose some of the advertisers implicated in Maddie Plattstein's astonishing work of journalism, which, plainly, means losing money. This means you may have to pay more on the newsstand—but isn't a dollar or two more worth reading genuine editorial content from a truly independent apparatus, instead of the discounted opinions our competitors offer, constructed behind-the-scenes by the advertisers whose products are choked down your throats? Or, like some of our competitors, delivering no editorials at all? Well, I hope this issue will prove that it is, indeed, worth it.

Fashion and beauty are not meaningless. They are not frivolous. They are not silly. They are multitrillion-dollar industries that employ close to half a billion people around the globe directly and indirectly. RAGE is not just a consumer magazine—we are the most

widely read trade publication in the world. We consider that a respon-
sibility to the women in Bangladesh who cannot read this page, but
instead earned just thirty cents today making your cheap T-shirt; who
will be poisoned by making your face cream in unregulated, unsuper-
vised laboratories and still be unable to feed their families; whose lives
are literally dictated by your purchasing power.

So let us look inward and to the future without fear. Be careful
how you spend your money, lest it be your own death.

Margot Villiers, editor in chief and founder of RAGE *Fashion*
Book

The issue's articles—all headlined under MATRIARCH, the
new name for the entire features section—were paired with 47
pages of photography and 283 total issue pages of advertising, a
Cooper record. Cat's collection of Hillary history ran throughout
Maddie's piece, a career-making work of journalism that wove
the threads of Hillary's life and her friendships with Bess, Cat,
and even Sigrid alongside a razor-sharp exposé of the wholly unregulated beauty industry. In addition to reporting on Bedford
Organics, Maddie had also dug up whistle-blower testimony from
inside three major international beauty companies, exposing their
own attempts to experiment with minor fractions of illegal drugs
and mood-enhancing supplements in products like body lotion and
skin oil, all of it marketed as "natural" and "organic." An internal memo from Esme Bowder, which owned no less than fifteen
global beauty brands, asked the question "we don't have to disclose
this, right?" over email to a member of the United States Congress,
who replied "not really. that's what trademarks are for ;)" in reference to a weight-loss cream costing $250 per ounce.

RAGE's subsequent tests of the trademark in question, expedited
by the DEA, found that *HypnoEnerSerum*™ was loaded with
enough stimulants to potentially stop the heart of a child or an
extremely thin woman. Hillary's designer death, Maddie Plattstein

argued, might have been custom-made in Brooklyn—but just like reclaimed wood walls and screenprints of water towers, it had been merely the precursor to what could be a national epidemic.

Photo editor Rose Cashin-Trask had outdone herself. She'd combed old party pictures from celebrity photographers, wire services, and Photogram for the most flattering and sophisticated images of Bess and Cat she could find, portraying them as hard-working mini-Margots caught in the wrong place at the wrong time. They'd played along as instructed, giving a mea culpa interview—an hour-long sit-down on-air with broadcast personality Anders Smith—exactly one week after their arrest in July, affirming their devotion to *RAGE* and their devastation over Hillary's death with convincing sincerity.

"It doesn't matter what I'm being called," Cat had said, trying to garner support from every woman who'd ever called herself a feminist. "*Party girl*—which we all know is tabloid-speak for 'useless, drug-addled slut'—is just a pathetic attempt to reframe the focus from what *RAGE*, along with Maddie Plattstein, who I think you'll agree is an *incredibly* well-respected investigative journalist, is trying to expose. Bedford Organics has opened a door into the beauty industry that we refuse to close. So if what comes out of this is that women across the globe learn about what constitutes healthy and safe in the products they use every day, that they feel *pressured* to use every day in order to be defined as 'good enough' by the society around them, then I'll gladly be arrested a million times. We can tolerate being made fun of. We can't tolerate promoting products that kill people, people like our friend Hillary."

"But why not tell the whole story now? Why apologize without an explanation?" Anders had lobbed them a big fat grapefruit of a softball.

Bess had replied with her most serious face, punting to promote the magazine as Paula had instructed her to do: "The article will be out in the September issue, on newsstands August 20. It's late for us, but it's the soonest we can get it out. In this day and age,

I know a lot of people think print doesn't matter—but it does. It's the best avenue for us to distribute this information as widely as possible. And frankly, it's still being fact-checked at this very moment, something that's very important to us, and certainly to the public."

"So you're confirming that there's more to the story?"

"Absolutely. Read the September issue," Cat had insisted. "*RAGE* is still a global feminist publication for everyone, and we're still committed journalists, even if what we cover is fashion and beauty. Did we make a mistake? Yes. *Absolutely*. But that mistake has led to a story that we—and Margot Villiers—won't drop."

"What does Margot think about all of this?"

"Margot's politics have shaped an entire generation of women," Cat replied, ready for her final sound bite, one that had come directly from Margot herself. "As you know, *RAGE* began as a magazine that showcased only American-made goods, but when globalization demanded that we change, we did. We've focused proudly on featuring only goods made with living-wage labor since 1994. I'm thrilled to announce we've added a new standard, and that is represented by the word 'sustainable': starting with this issue, we're transitioning into featuring only goods that are made with care for the planet and care for the people on it."

Bess took the wheel. "Anders, did you know that the textile industry is the world's third-largest overall polluter, and the second-largest polluter of our water supply after agriculture? Each year eighty *billion* garments are produced worldwide. The global production of cotton alone consumes one trillion gallons of water, thirty-three trillion gallons of oil, and twenty billion pounds of chemicals annually."

"We're starting with face cream that could kill you," Cat continued, "but we won't stop until you can be certain that the blouse you're wearing didn't poison someone's well water. When we rely on goods—beauty products, clothing, shoes, anything—made under conditions that violate our own moral and ethical codes, we become vested in the oppression of others. The American woman can change that with her dollar."

Subscriber issues were delivered worldwide at 4:00 a.m. GMT on the same day the September issue hit newsstands. Protesters had chained themselves to the Food and Drug Administration's headquarters in Washington, DC, by lunchtime; two members of Congress who had taken particularly lucrative positions on behalf of beauty-industry lobbyists resigned by 3:00 p.m. Four national pharmacy chains cleared their shelves of product from subsidiaries of Esme Bowder, Ruby Global, Calico Inc., and Raven & Co.— leaving just two brands of shampoo left in the bulk of their stores. The Dow fell 1,282 points before close.

Over the last eight weeks Cat and Bess had been promoted from their comfortable status as boldfaced names in trade publications like *Women's Wear Daily* to a full-blown international obsession, dissected daily in every corner of the internet. Their glamorous mug shots, salacious backstories, perfect pedigrees, camera-ready wardrobes, and Photogram histories had sparked a flame of curiosity in the public eye; Paula had no trouble convincing Margot that flame could be fanned into a frenzy that would burn to *RAGE's* advantage.

The first weeks of their ejection into the coliseum of public opinion had been merely an experiment. Cooper's publicists sent them to events throughout August, with full makeup, hair, and wardrobe, as food for the internet's gaping maw, and it had worked like a charm. After only a few days, Mania devoted an entire vertical and real-time interactive map to Cat and Bess, running it completely on user-generated content that pulled the GPS coordinates from any photo that was taken of them anywhere. Margot had been enraged. *Why aren't we the ones who are capitalizing digitally on our own fucking product?* she'd screamed at Paula, but it didn't matter. The map was just one of the pieces lighting the route of their new trajectory, and *RAGE's* subscriptions went up by half a million.

The amount of time Cat and Bess now spent preparing to be

photographed cut into their workdays significantly. They were no longer expected to attend meetings or even review copy. Other staffers, their workloads doubled, bristled with resentment; only Molly threw herself into their service, refusing to return to school for fall semester on the basis that they "obviously" needed her help. Bess was grateful for the loyalty and allocated Molly a stipend for the year, calling her a "contributing assistant editor." Molly picked up the slack without question and happily settled into the cubicle next to Bess's, where she arrived early in the morning and was the last to leave at night.

"Congratulations. You still have jobs here," Paula had said to Cat and Bess the morning they'd returned to the office after their release. "Right now your jobs are to go out and be the faces of *RAGE.* I'll let you know if that changes."

So they spent the rest of their summer showing up at factories filled with child slaves in Cambodia; they made appearances at the headquarters of Gap, Nike, Apple, and even Walmart to meet with executives about their living-wage efforts, factory conditions, and sustainability efforts. They opened stores and approved beauty products, doing each other's hair and makeup on live television as they chatted idly about what their favorite new brands contained, hosting behind-the-scenes B-roll at deeply vetted pharmaceutical labs, all the while providing the internet black hole with constant new images of themselves, sometimes five outfits a day, for perusal, assessment, commentary. The eight weeks between their arrest and tonight's event had gone by in an instant.

Occasionally when she was trying to fall asleep at night, Cat tried to calculate the number of dollars people were making on her name. *The Cat Economy.* She'd stopped counting once she multiplied the image licensing fees beyond $10 million.

She started running every day when she woke up, both to cleave any leftover meat off her bones—seeing pictures of her own body everywhere left her reeling with insecurities—and to burn the anxiety out of her mind. If she was tired enough to sit still by the time

Raphael and June arrived to do her hair and makeup, she'd be able to make it through the day, to complete the labor of rotating her polished alabaster skin toward whatever lens was watching. *You're changing the world*, she told herself. *You're forcing even* Walmart *to care about buying living-wage wholesale. You're the impetus for the first real beauty regulatory bill in Congress. You're someone. You're important.*

Bess stepped into her new position with an addict's gusto, reveling in the new clothes that showed up on her doorstep by the trunkful, considering the appearances and events merely the cost of doing business. She spent her downtime smoking pot and itemizing her growing collection of stuff in CoopDoc spreadsheets.

Each night was the same. They hopped into the Suburban after events, cut each other out of their clothes, and wiped their faces clean before retiring alone to their apartments where they'd scroll through Photogram, too exhausted from a full day of socializing to speak to anyone. Cat particularly loved a meme that pasted her unsmiling photos over pictures of puppies and kittens with the caption "ur not good enuf." Bess loved fan comments that displayed the same affinity for cataloging that she'd been born with, and spent her downtime happily confirming the tiniest details about her outfits—the color of her nail polish, the brand of her belt.

They'd briefly tried to make friends in this new world but discovered that anything and everything they said managed to get quoted the following day, often incorrectly, online. There was no one to trust except the people they paid. Other celebrities either ignored them completely—famous for eight weeks certainly wasn't famous enough for most—or simpered with a condescending excitement that served only to point out the novelty of their existence.

Their new lives affected everyone around them. Bess's sister Ella, the hard-partying film and television agent, had stepped in to negotiate their appearance fees and strong-armed several CEOs into meeting with the two girls. She was the one who had ensured Cooper would pay for the Suburban, the driver, the clothes, and the fees for their new entourage; she was the one who landed Wal-mart. Last week, Ella had hired two freelancers to keep up with the appearance requests and contract minutiae.

Cat emailed her mother once a week with an update about what she'd accomplished; Anais always wrote back right away, with "Ik zie U graag, Katteke," but not much more. *I love you, little kitten.* She didn't understand.

The October issue was due on newsstands in under two weeks and expectations were high. Cat and Bess were only vaguely aware of the contents, now that their days consisted solely of changing clothes and trying to keep up with their own insane schedules. Cat had done her best to update her CoopDocs for Lou with detailed notes and instructions. She prayed that **Dotty for It**, **Judy and the Technicolor Housecoat**, **Tea Party All Night: A Celebration of Suri Cruise**, and **Gone Yachting (A Gowanus Story)** had been shot correctly, but no one shared proofs with her anymore. She'd have to wait for newsstands to see if they'd worked.

As the Childlike Publicist motioned her toward the next step-and-repeat, Cat wondered what Hutton was doing right now.

She'd texted him exactly six days ago, her bruised ego finally and wholly faded in direct inverse proportion to her overwhelming loneliness. Hi, she'd written, late at night, alone again in her apartment, a little mew across the chasm built between them since her arrest seven weeks earlier. He'd texted back immediately. Hi. Can I call you?

She responded by calling him, her heart cracking when she heard his voice. They both fell over apologizing; him for putting her in jail, her for ignoring him for so long. *You were right*, she'd told him. *It was worth it. The September issue proved that.* Hutton allowed long silences to go between their words, the spaces knitting a new intimacy, before he finally admitted he'd knowingly pushed her into it; but that he was still crazy about her, and he was more sorry than he'd ever been; could she forgive him? *I already have*, she'd replied.

Since then they'd spoken on the phone every single night when Cat got home but hadn't yet seen each other again in person. Cat said she wasn't ready. Hutton had accepted her explanation without question. *That's fine*, he'd said. *I'll wait*. And he did; he waited patiently, getting to know her a little bit better every night over the telephone.

He'd been promoted to a unit in the Major Case Division and moved down to One Police Plaza, the NYPD headquarters in the financial district, to work with the senior team, whose members were continuing to investigate the sources of funding behind Bedford Organics. He was probably there right now, Cat thought, going over casework. She pictured him sitting behind his desk in his rumpled clothes, a pen in his long fingers, sorting stacks of paper. Her cheeks started to burn from smiling, and she suddenly very much wanted to be out of the spotlight.

She walked away from the step-and-repeat and ducked behind it into a white VIP tent, looking around for Bess's blonde curls. The tent was full of fragile women in expensive dresses looking pained, but none were Bess.

The Childlike Publicist appeared with a tall cane that collapsed into a chair, an object popular in nursing homes and backstage at fashion shows. Cat sank into it gratefully and wrote a quick text to Hutton; whatcha doing later, it said. No reply.

"There's just *two* more shots! We can be *soso* quick with those," the publicist squealed, her baby voice coming out in a rolling vocal fry.

"No, I can't," Cat said firmly. "I did two. I'm contracted for two."

"IknowIknow, but BP would be *soso* happy if you could help out. It'll be *so* quick."

"No!" Cat snapped, closing her eyes to avoid making eye contact.

At first she and Bess had worn themselves out trying to meet the demands of all the handlers, publicists, assistants, and photographers they encountered every day. Two weeks into their new life Ella had accompanied them for the day "just to make sure" everything was going according to plan. She'd barked fiercely at everyone, refused everyone, embarrassed them horribly—and reduced their fatigue by half. Over dinner that night at Farmer's Almanac, a new rooftop urban garden overlooking Newtown Creek in Greenpoint, Ella had lectured them on the value of saying no.

"My assistant sends you a summary every fucking morning, okay?" she'd fumed, waving away the gingham-romper-clad waitress who was trying to get her to stop smoking. "Disaster is my business. I can get you your lives back, but not if you give them away first. Just *say no*. Don't do more than they pay for. Ever."

Ella then put her cigarette out dramatically in a rhubarb Napoleon topping the passing dessert cart, threw back a thimbleful of grappa, and left. Cat and Bess soon discovered that she'd gotten their meal (a seven-course tasting menu with wine pairings) comped on the way out the door. They looked at the Mania map. Forty-six users had pegged them there. The next day the restaurant had been "closed to new reservations until further notice."

The following week's schedule was impossible. Ella and Paula had booked them into dozens of appearances in the days leading up to Fashion Week. Cat wasn't sure how she was going to handle it. She was getting increasingly uncomfortable eating in public. She missed having something to worry about besides how she looked.

The sapphire ring on her middle finger buzzed. It was programmed to alert her when Bess, Lou, Paula, Margot, Molly, her mother, or Hutton tried to contact her; all other notifications were disabled. She reached for her phone to see a text from Bess:

where are ya

white tent, in chair

ask someone to take you through the opera stage door

ok see you in five

Cat looked up from her phone and tried to orient herself among the center's three buildings. The publicist pounced at the opportunity to catch her attention and placed her little body squarely in Cat's eyeline.

"Feelingggg betterrrr?" the girl drawled out. "I know *I* get so *so* tired when *I* get all dressed up."

Cat wouldn't be coerced into a bonding session. "Please take me to the opera stage door," she said, trying to keep the resentment out of her voice. She put her phone back inside the black Lucite bag the stylist had given her earlier.

"Happy to!" the girl chirped, disappointment flashing briefly across her face. "I just want to say, though, you two are *So. Awesome.*" A manic grin stretched across the matte pancake of her contoured cheeks, the tiny pearls of her teeth gleaming with the taste of opportunity. "If you ever need an assistant, let me know, because I have *really* enjoyed working with you today." She cocked her head in a way that was meant to telegraph enthusiasm. Yet all Cat could see was a sentient bottle of drugstore foundation.

"Sure thing," Cat said, accidentally knocking the folding chair over as she stood up. "I have to leave now, though." She looked down at the chair, unable to even bend over to pick it up.

"Ohmigod of course . . . of course! Right this way." The girl left the chair splayed on the ground and wrapped her bony little fingers around Cat's arm, moving her briskly toward the Met and tugging her efficiently through the huddled masses of socialites, editors, handlers, bloggers, and photographers clogging the plaza. A bug hit Cat squarely in the face, but she didn't dare react—not with all the cameras nearby.

The publicist held open the glass doors of the opera, then ushered Cat through a series of velvet-flocked doors into the cavernous backstage area. Huge logos fabricated out of fiberglass were stacked neatly against the walls in the order they would be loaded; plastic craft tables were heaped with labeled crates and boxes for the following week's builds. Cat wound her way through a dozen piles of rope, curtain, scrim, and coiled electrical wire before she spotted Bess's blonde curls in the distance.

She tried to detach herself from the girl's grip, but her surprisingly strong fingers wouldn't budge.

"I have to get you to the car!" she chirped again, yanking Cat along with even more force. "That's my *job*!!"

Cat gave in and let herself be pulled through the hallway like a disobedient pony. She'd learned it was just easier to go along and get along. Ten yards later they rounded the corner into the loading dock, where Bess was being held in place by another teen.

"Get this fucking car here right NOWWWWW!" screeched Bess's warden into her iPhone, entitlement dripping off her like drool from a dog's mouth. "This is *important*," she hissed, winking at Bess, who rolled her eyes.

"Please don't yell at our driver," Bess said wearily, trying to take the girl's phone away. "It's really unnecessary." The publicist maneuvered away from her, putting down the phone but keeping the line open so the driver could hear her every word.

"He needs to understand you are *important*. *V-I-P-P*. That's what our firm does, we provide Very Important People for Parties. These drivers are just not *grateful* enough for these opportunities, you know? Honestly," she said, her tween face suddenly looking genuinely fatigued. "This is New York. We could hire *anybody*."

Before Cat could remind her that Jim was employed by Cooper, and not whatever their PR firm was called, the Suburban pulled into the loading dock. She exhaled: only one more costume change and event before she could finally go home, eat Chinese food, and call Hutton. She released herself from the publicist's fingers and tried to choke out a "Thank you" before fleeing down the loading ramp into the car.

Jim held the passenger side door open for them. "I'm so sorry about that," Bess said to him as he hoisted her up onto the seat. Cat climbed in behind her.

"I couldn't care less," he said kindly. "Don't worry about it."

"You're a good guy, Jim," Bess said once he'd walked around and climbed into the driver's-side captain's chair. "Thank you."

"Cooper?" he asked, obviously changing the subject.

"If that's what the schedule says," Cat replied.

Jim nodded, shifted into drive, and turned the radio to their favorite satellite station without comment as he sped his wards back to their Midtown barn.

Cat pulled up their schedule on her phone. They were indeed heading back to Cooper for an outfit change, scheduled to be seen walking into a brand-new Nolita restaurant in two hours with a pair of actors that *IQ*—Cooper's biggest men's title—would be putting on the covers of the November and December issues, respectively. Cat hadn't met either of them before, but she wasn't thrilled about going to dinner with two closeted narcissists wearing tinted moisturizer and lifts in their shoes. She showed their photos to Bess, who shook her head sadly.

"I hate, hate, hate actors," she said. "And what is this restaurant anyway? They only serve toast? Is that a joke?"

Traffic thickened and they pulled to a stop. Cat used her phone to change the car's satellite station from XMU to a twenty-four-hour internet channel of *Pop-Up Video*. LCD screens unfolded from the roof, playing the video for "It's the End of the World as We Know It" by R.E.M.

The two girls sang along quietly at first, but were screaming by the time they got to "Leonard Bernstein." Jim joined in on the choruses. Cat couldn't hear his voice, but she could see his lips moving in the rearview mirror.

For a moment, as the three of them sang in the car, she almost felt happy.

The song ended.

Traffic released.

The SUV pulled into the Cooper garage. They climbed out of the car with significantly less care than they'd used getting in; Cat heard stitches popping on her thigh seams, but it didn't matter. They didn't have much farther to go. The spider silk underlay of Bess's gorgeous cocktail dress, made over a period of years on the island of Madagascar, had come loose from its moorings and hung down haphazardly over her knees. Bess fingered it sadly.

"I bet we can get away with jeans tonight," Cat whispered.

Though it was 6:00 p.m., *RAGE* was still abuzz with activity. The cubicles were filled with at least a dozen women Cat had never seen before; she assumed they were permalancers hired to take over the workload that she and Bess had left behind. Through the glass walls of Margot's office they could see Lou, Margot, Paula, and Constance assessing a naked plus-size model who was currently halfway into a burlap evening gown, her face and arms obscured by the fabric ballooning over her head.

The staff had moved from their high-summer uniform of filmy silks onto that year's pre-fall theme of midi-length shifts in a mix of suede and sweatshirt material, a half-nod toward colder days. Many of the new hires wore eggplant tones; one of them even had eggplant-colored thigh-high kidskin boots so tight they could be stockings. Cat didn't recognize them, couldn't even guess the brand. She hadn't been to a showroom in weeks.

As they strolled through the cubicles on their way to the southwest corner, only Molly greeted them, giving both women a hug. She wore a navy boiler suit with "BEALE" written on the pocket in silver paint, having taken Cat's suggestion that she "find a work uniform in order to free up time in the day" rather literally. Still, on her twenty-year-old frame the polyester blend draped with some charm, and she'd rolled the sleeves and cuffed the legs *just so* above her platinum sneakers, which transformed her from overdressed college intern to chic insider, hair pulled back into a clean ponytail, two inches of blue remaining on the tips.

"Raphael and June are just grabbing some dinner, but they'll be back soon," Molly reported, holding open the door to Cat's office. They walked in.

Cat's office was a mess. The desk was covered with accessories and sewing notions; her Aeron chair had been removed and replaced with two makeup stools. Her books had been boxed up and stacked in the corner to make room for three dozen pairs of shoes now residing on the shelves.

Bess had tried to make some impact on the space, too, replacing the PMS board items with causes and buzzwords in the hope that it would rub off on anyone who came into the room:

+	—
nickel mines	diamond mines
Nile Valley	Silicon Valley
urine-powered batteries	cold fusion
child diplomats	child soldiers

Cat was the only one who paid attention to it, although Molly had eventually texted a photo of the board to Ella, who had rolled her eyes and deleted it. June the stylist had her own list tacked to the back of the door, dividing the city's designers into "lets us keep merch" and "demands merch back," undoubtedly more of interest to visitors to the space than the PMS board.

Cat rooted around on the desk until she found a tiny pair of scissors, which she used to snip the already-ripping side seam of her dress until it was loose enough for her to wriggle out of. She snapped the fabric of the industrial-strength rubber bodysuit that Raphael had insisted she wear underneath the structured cocktail dress. Her internal organs, sensing freedom was nigh, started to ache.

"I think we have to cut this suit off," she said.

"There's a hook on the desk somewhere," Bess replied, moving her hand through the debris until she found a coated vinyl shepherd's crook. "Stand up and turn around."

"We have to get it off or I'm just going to pee in it!" Cat cried, her stomach cramping.

Bess failed to budge the clasps.

"Hold on," she said. "I need more leverage." She took off her shoes, braced one foot up on the desk, and pushed against the wall. "Okay: I'm gonna pull!"

At that moment, Molly opened the door and the whole office got a glimpse of Bess in her orange spider-silk slip trying to yank the bodysuit off Cat: two giant swans bent half-naked over a desk, standing in a puddle of priceless clothes.

The permalancers sharing the nearest cube rolled their eyes. "Is *that* what they do all day? I have an MFA from Iowa and I'm still not full-time," one muttered to the other. "This is *horseshit.*"

"Tell me about it," said the other one. "I've been interning at Cooper every summer since the ninth grade."

Bess gave up, finally using scissors to cut it off, and the leotard snapped against the wall like a rubber band. Cat was too frustrated to laugh; huge red welts glowed where the seams had dug into her skin.

They both changed into comfortable clothing: plain black jeans and an ivory jacquard-knit top structured with a lace effect from Alexander McQueen for Bess; and leather leggings, a black crocheted zip-up hoodie from Adidas, and a pair of rattlesnake sneakers from Jimmy Choo for Cat.

As they were wiping off their makeup and reapplying moisturizer, Raphael and June walked in the door. Cat braced herself for a wave of criticism but instead felt the quiet joy of approval.

"I love this," June said immediately, pointing to their clothes. "Casual wear says, *we are comfortable* with each other. It's totally convincing."

"Cocktail dresses are for beards," Raphael agreed immediately. "Let's do red lips and clean skin."

"Every modern woman's fantasy: being an undercover beard." Bess sighed. "My mother will be so proud."

June looked down at Cat's sneakers. "I have one edit. The rattlesnake takes you from Patti Smith to mail-order Eastern European bride," she said, handing Cat a pair of black canvas Vans. "Switch and sit for makeup."

Molly packed their handbags—a pair of neon plastic cubes—with house keys, cigarettes for Cat, wallets, and their fully charged cellphones.

"I feel like my daughters are going off to prom," she said jokingly, looking at her two bosses. "I'm a cool mom! Call me if you need a ride! No judgment!"

Fifteen minutes later Jim drove them silently downtown to Paahtoleipä, the new Finnish toast-only restaurant on Mott Street. When they pulled up to the restaurant, Cat could make out five photographers waiting outside with bored looks on their faces; after Jim opened the door, she could hardly make her way through them while she and Bess posed against the restaurant's painted window.

Someone held open another door for her, and she found herself inside a crowded town house that had recently been converted into a junk-shop-slash-restaurant. *Editor-slash-model-slash-junk-shop-slash-urban-farmhouse*, she thought, wending her way to the back through tables that were shoved so tightly together she was sure her butt cheeks grazed several faces.

Chris Spruce and Jent Brooks stood up politely as soon as they spotted Cat and Bess. The two mid-thirties actors wore matching ensembles of dark, slim-cut chinos, simple button-down shirts, and light jackets, each with three days' worth of stubble beneath their fresh haircuts: stylish but not fashionable, poster boys for nonthreatening suburban masculinity.

The two women towered over their dates, but when she sat down, Cat kissed Chris Spruce full on the mouth as soon as their heads were even. He kissed her back dramatically. She heard cellphone cameras click around them. *Mission accomplished*, she thought. *Maybe we can leave after our first piece of bread*.

"I'm Cat," she said. "Sorry to spring that on you, but I wanted to get it out of the way."

"Nice to meet you, too," Chris whispered, pulling out her chair and helping her into it with a smile. "But you should know"—his voice grew even quieter—"I am the *gayest* man on earth."

"It's true. He had sex with a man less than an hour ago," Jent added as he helped Bess into her seat, running his fingers through his black hair. "But I'm straight *and* available if you're truly into short actors." He leaned forward with comedic suggestiveness, flipping Bess's hand over and stroking the inside of her palm.

Both women smiled.

"I don't think we're shopping in that particular aisle," Bess admitted.

"The tall ones never are unless they're in actual poverty." Jent sighed. "Only illiterate teenage models want to date short guys. But someday I am going to find a tall, smart, beautiful woman like the two of you who is going to let me climb her like a tree. It'll be epic. Minstrels will sing songs about it."

"We ordered the first 'toast course' for the table, by the way," Chris interjected with a snort. "Do you girls drink?"

"*Yes*," chimed Bess and Cat in unison. "What kind of wine goes with bread?"

"Traditionally I'd say that one might want a finer boxed varietal to wash down a loaf of Pepperidge Farm smeared with Miracle Whip, but maybe that's more an 'alone in my apartment' kind of thing," confided Chris. "Should we just ask which one has the most alcohol?"

"Definitely," Bess replied, signaling to the waiter, who slithered through the table maze around them. "Red, right?" The table nodded. "Can you please bring us your most alcoholic bottle of red wine?" she asked sweetly.

"That's probably"—the waiter looked up thoughtfully—"the '93 Comte Georges de Vogüé, from Côte de Nuits. A lovely pinot. The black cherry is a perfect complement to the buckwheat course that's coming up—adds some fruit to the nuttiness of the grain."

"Great," Bess replied. "Four glasses, please."

Two more waiters appeared with their first course, managing to squeeze around the table and lower all four plates simultaneously as though they were dining at Daniel. "Your first course," chirped one of them without apparent irony, "is a pan-roasted buckwheat and almond meal unleavened artisanal flatbread, brushed with quail egg whites, seasoned with house-made blackened sesame, and set in a bed of handpicked dandelion greens. Enjoy!"

The waiters disappeared as quickly as they'd managed to appear.

Cat looked down at her plate and stared at her food, dumbfounded. Nestled in the middle of a few limp leaves was . . . *matzoh*.

"Are these fucking *saltine crackers*?" Chris hissed to Bess. "This. Is. Not. Food."

"I'm so fucking hungry, I don't care," Bess replied, cramming the cracker into her mouth. It crumbled immediately, dusting her lacy top with particles of unleavened bread. She gave Cat, Chris, and Jent a look of terrified hunger and began snatching the crackers from their plates, shoving them into her mouth like a monster. Everyone's servings fit into her jaw in a single stack. Cat giggled uncontrollably.

The waiter reappeared with their wine.

"I see we're all *loving* this first course," he said enthusiastically, gesturing at their empty plates. A sheepish Bess covered her mouth with her hand while Cat, Chris, and Jent nodded to the waiter sincerely, trying not to laugh.

"It was amazing. Bring us five more just like that, except you can bring them all at once," Chris ordered.

"Ooh, are we switching to the tower? Wonderful. I'll let the kitchen know." He winked. "It's *just* like the seafood tower at Balthazar, but it's our own *grain-based* version. You're going to *love* it."

He poured at what seemed like a deliberately glacial pace. *Chris and Jent aren't so bad*, Cat thought, but she was so bored: bored with the elaborate presentations, bored with the showcasing, bored with her own overdetermined life. She was bored with sitting here and pretending to care for the waiter's sake about what the waiter was so effectively pretending to care about for the customer's sake, all because someone, somewhere in her orbit, had been convinced that this restaurant's gimmick was worth supporting with the faint currency of her identity. She was a penny passing through a vending machine, through a thousand change dishes, tumbling through a thousand fingers. Eventually, Cat was starting to realize, someone would drop her on the ground and it would be bad luck to pick her up again. They'd leave her for the next passerby. And maybe—just maybe—she'd be kicked into the sewer before anyone spotted her.

The waiter finally finished and turned to take the bottle back to the bar with him. "You can leave that on the table," Cat pointed out quickly, making space next to her plate. "Thank you."

"Well done," said Chris. All around them, diners nibbled on their own meager toasted slices of bread and stared indiscreetly, a few tables still snapping photos of the foursome. Bess and Cat might be Photogram-famous in the right downtown circles, but Chris and Jent were truly on their way to genuine multiplex celebrity.

"You guys are nice and all," Cat said, swallowing half her wine, "but this place is a disgrace."

"I think—and correct me if I'm wrong—but the executive producer on Jent's last movie's current girlfriend's ex-stepson is an investor," Chris said slowly. Jent nodded.

"Can you imagine having a child who is so stupid that they'd put your money in something like this?" Cat asked.

"Or so *cynical*," Jent replied, gesturing to the packed room and the crowd that had formed outside. "They're making a fortune on flour. I don't know about you guys, but I'm from here, from Staten. And I don't mean to be one of those people, but this is insane."

"I'm from Tribeca," Bess piped in. "I was born at St. Vincent's. I miss specific years in specific New York neighborhoods the way amputees miss limbs. I'm so nostalgic for the West Village in 1997 that it literally hurts, you know? Or Williamsburg in 2000. Or Bushwick in 2004. It's the most bittersweet thing in the world. God, someone brought up Monkey City the other day and I almost *cried*."

"I *loved* Monkey City," Jent replied, giving her an approving look. "I remember sitting on the floor in 2005 watching the Dalí movie where someone gets stabbed in the eye and eating the best polenta of my life."

"I just can't imagine a world where someone feels that way about this toast restaurant," Bess said. "The waitstaff here. Is this honestly not absurd to them? Is this a real memory, an indelible part of their New York history? Will it *hurt* to remember it?" Just then, a server appeared with a multiplate tower of breads and crackers, which he dramatically placed in the center of their table.

"Okay: *this* is the tower," he said with a flourish. "Let me walk you through it. We have a nine-grain biscuit that's been wood-fired with Hudson Valley cedar and seasoned with anchovy crumble; a spelt and buckwheat pancake wrapped in a rice-based phyllo dough; a buttermilk johnnycake dusted with house-made arti-sanal toasted coconut flour; four petite almond meal loaves proofed in locally grown corn grain alcohol from our neighboring urban farm; and of course our signature rye rieska, a Finnish specialty, with a small side of cured lutefisk processed in the traditional birch ash, along with a selection of our house-made mustards."

It was basically indistinguishable from the bread basket at Olive Garden save for its massive size. But the waiter's sincerity as he searched their eyes for criticism and approval was, in fact, genuine. The group realized they couldn't bear to hurt his feelings or deni-grate his livelihood, no matter how absurd, with even the slightest eye roll.

"Thank you," Bess said kindly.

"This looks amazing," added Jent, his tone generous.

The waiter smiled in relief, having successfully delivered a $400 basket of the simplest food on earth, and retreated back to the kitchen.

"*If thou gaze long into an abyss, the abyss will also gaze into thee*," Cat said quietly to herself, staring down the bread in her palm.

"To be fair, this is, like, the *best* bread I've ever had in my life," Bess replied as she finished off a johnnycake and started on one of the miniature almond loaves.

Chapter Thirteen

The meal at Paahtoleipä finished up uneventfully, but Cat, still hoping to hear from Hutton, wanted to leave right after dinner. Chris obviously didn't mind. Jent was polite enough about it. So the group ate their bread, Photogrammed some behind-the-scenes pictures of themselves with the chef, and parted ways a few blocks from the restaurant. On busy Bowery no one noticed Chris and Jent hopping out of the Cooper SUV, their good-night kisses merely friendly pecks on the cheek.

Once they approached Delancey, traffic stood still. Hutton still hadn't replied to Cat's text from earlier. The doors were unlocked. This was her chance.

"I'm walking home," Cat announced abruptly, opening her door while they were stopped at a light. "See you tomorrow."

"Seeya," Bess, busy texting, replied dreamily, while Jim was disapprovingly unresponsive. *Whatever*, Cat thought. *I don't need a babysitter. I can go where I want.*

Her feet hit the pavement flat—*oh, sweet sneakers!*—and Cat pulled her hood up as she hustled over the Williamsburg Bridge, down Broadway, turned on Driggs, and slid sunglasses onto her face before walking into Leicester.

It didn't do much good. At least three people spotted Cat and took her photo while she waited for the hostess; they were using Mania, she was certain. The first user to flag Cat and accurately tag her clothing would get five Mania points, good on any form of merchandise in their online store, a juggernaut that was fast becoming the Amazon Prime of clothing.

"Hiya! How many?" asked the hostess.

"Just one," Cat said. "Outside, with an ashtray."

"Right this way," the hostess said, to the obvious exasperation of the four groups who had been waiting up front.

"I'm Yelping this," grumbled a man behind Cat, just loud enough for her to hear. He clearly meant the comment to be threatening—that Cat or the restaurant would quake at the internet wrath of another predatory credit-rich white male being denied his god-given right to go somewhere and spend spend *spend* as soon as he'd read about it in *New York* magazine—but Cat, her stomach grumbling, found herself so irritated by him that she actually lit her cigarette, turned around, and exhaled in his face before walking outside after the hostess. Then she ordered a double tequila on the rocks and a Pacifico, keeping her sunglasses on and the cigarette dangling from her lip while she drank alone.

She scanned the restaurant, looking for Hutton, but he was, of course, nowhere to be found. Leicester was a dozen miles from his apartment. They'd been here *once*. It wasn't exactly the top of the Empire State Building or anything, just a nice bar with a nice patio with good service and small-batch liquor, one of hundreds in this part of Brooklyn, here to serve you, to meet your needs, to provide a bistro-lit backdrop to your romance, any time after noon and before 4:00 a.m.

There could be hundreds of me, she realized suddenly, *sitting in hundreds of bars, just like this, alone in a crowded place, famous and not, trading one thing for another, winding up with nothing*.

Talking to Hutton over the past week had kept her spirits up, but at this moment, she started to think the whole thing was a bad idea. He'd admitted over the phone that his professional ambitions were priority A1; he'd already proved to her that the only thing he was interested in was getting ahead, and, worst of all, he'd used her to do it. It didn't matter how many times he apologized.

I've tried so goddamn hard, she thought, her mouth suddenly dry. She'd spent her whole summer getting dressed, being viewed, taking criticism about her body and her choices and her background, about her facial expressions. She'd powered her way through hundreds of conversations with strangers, forcing them to listen to her ideas about labor when really all she was doing was encouraging them with her very presence to worship at the altar of consumerism. She'd sacrificed her very personhood in the last two months, becoming nothing but a show pony in the process of trying to save her reputation from that train wreck of a week in July.

And the worst part was that all of it had happened because of how she felt the first time she met him, that she needed to prove to him she had more substance than he thought she did. To force him to pay attention to her, she'd playacted being a detective and wound up staining her own life with indelible ink. It had all been so stupid, and it was all her own fault, and she probably wouldn't even get the guy in the end.

Cat checked her phone one more time.

Nothing.

She absentmindedly circled her left wrist with her thumb and forefinger, measuring the size of her rapidly reducing arms. Cat hadn't intended to get so thin, but each pound washed away in a cascade she couldn't stop, a tide beyond her control. She took a fat book out of her handbag—*The Man Without Qualities* by Robert Musil—and sank into it gratefully, letting the words wash over her while the alcohol washed through her.

The waitress reappeared and asked if she wanted anything to eat. Without looking up, Cat shook her head and raised her now-empty glass for a refill, but instead of taking it from her, someone reached out and grabbed Cat's wrist with a set of huge, bony fingers.

"What the—?" Cat muttered as she looked up—and found Grant Bonner grinning down at her. She couldn't help but smile back. The Bonners were the closest thing Cat had to family in this country, and she hadn't seen Grant since he'd bailed them out of jail eight weeks earlier. He was a real, honest-to-goodness friend—even if he *was* nine years her junior and basically her opposite. Tall and lanky, with close-cropped hair, a clean-shaven face, and dark green eyes, his clothing was boyish and boring; he wore a nondescript gray suit and a striped banker's tie, the knot loosened and the jacket thrown over his arm. It was refreshing as hell.

"Hi," she said happily. "You're a sight for sore eyes."

"Can I join you?" he asked.

She scooted over on her bench and made room for him next to her, while he thanked the waitress and ordered two more beers. "What are you doing here?"

He held up his cellphone. "I think you've forgotten that there's a map devoted to your every move."

"You're stalking me?" she asked, arching an eyebrow.

"Not really," he said. "I was around the corner watching the baseball game at my buddy's house."

"And *then* you stalked me."

"To be fair, it was a *very* convenient stalk, but I've been meaning to call you. I got an offer to work out of the Brussels office."

"Really?"

"It's a back-and-forth job between here and there. Technically it's a promotion."

"Do you have a choice?" she asked. Their beers arrived.

He laughed. "Probably not."

"Then I think you should take it. Brussels is *fun*. It's not very big, but the two million people who live there come from all over the world . . . it's sophisticated, really, in its own way. Cheers."

They toasted glasses a little harder than she'd intended, and foam spilled over the cold glass onto the wooden table.

"Do you get to choose where you live?"

"I don't think so. It'll probably be a charmless corporate apartment."

"You have to go to my parents' house for dinner. And my mother will take you riding in the *bois*."

"The bois?"

"It's a bluebell forest. You'll like it."

"You want me to ride a horse through a bluebell forest? Cat, I was in a fraternity at *Emory*."

"Then it'll be the brony fantasy you've been longing for."

He laughed. "How are *you*?"

"I'm...honestly, I'm tired. We've been doing a *lot*. Fashion Week is almost over, then I get two weeks off. I'm just trying to make it through until then."

"If you ever need a chaperone, just say the word. I'm a very good date. Your life looks pretty fun from the outside these days."

Cat snorted. "From the inside, it sucks. Ugh, I'm so sick of myself. Actually can we talk about something else?" She scanned the room. "Want to play Scrabble?" she asked, pointing to a stack of board games on a bookshelf near the small outdoor bar.

"Sure," he said, walking over to grab the game. "But you're going to be sorry you asked that."

They spent the next hour playing Scrabble, and joking, and laughing, big, real laughs, and it was the most fun Cat had in ages. She built a real humdinger on the triple-word square, but wordsmith Grant won with 455 points. While they played, she forgot about work, forgot about Hutton, forgot about how she looked. Grant ordered fries and burgers for them both; she wolfed the food down without even thinking.

She forgot about Mania, too.

The next morning, the first thoughts to run through Margot Villiers's mind were wholly negative.

The October issue was a mess.

They'd be lucky to sell a global million on newsstands next week, *nothing* compared to the seventeen million issues they'd moved last month. October's biggest problem was that its photo shoots had been totally reimagined by Lou, who had fashioned **Judy and the Technicolor Housecoat** into a fun-looking but rather soulless story; just another dumb spread of models jumping up and down, pretending to look happy. Nothing to write home about. And **Dotty for It**, the shoot set at the Scoria Vale sanatorium, wound up making a mockery of mental illness. Lou followed Cat's notes to the letter, but in the end, it lacked the gravity that it had originally been pitched with; the photographer hadn't used the right lenses, and the prism effect looked badly photoshopped.

Irritation built up with every moment Margot spent thinking about it. The record-setting sales of their September issue hadn't been enough; they still needed to sell another fifteen million issues before the end of the year, or *RAGE* would change according to whatever George Cooper Jr. had in mind. *RAGE* stood on the precipice of real and total failure, and Margot with it. George Jr. had *laughed* at her pivot toward sustainability, actually, physically *laughed* in her face.

"That's the most expensive thing you've ever said," he'd scoffed.

"It'll make us money," she'd replied.

"We'll see," he'd responded coldly. "You have through the December issue. Publish pornography for all I care. But make some goddamn money."

Margot increased the speed and incline on her treadmill, picking up the pace on her morning workout. Twenty minutes and three miles later, her pink leotard soaked front and back in sweat, she jumped off the treadmill and started the forty-five-minute barre routine she punished herself with several days a week.

"You can choose either the cardiologist or the orthopedic surgeon," she always told her children, none of whom had ever joined her in her exercise studio except for the two months before their weddings, panicking about the state of their upper arms. But her hard work paid off. At seventy-two, Margot looked fifty, the same age as her oldest daughter.

She hopped into the shower and donned an oilcloth shower cap. After a quick rinse, covering her body in a tangerine-scented bodywash from an unlabeled bottle, she combed her hair back out and twisted it into a neat bun. In her carved mahogany walk-in closet, dozens of racks were hung with freshly pressed couture dresses arranged by color and by season; a wall-length set of narrow drawers held her underclothes and accessories. A huge upholstered bench dominated the center of the room. Virgin-white cashmere carpet, the wool harvested from goats perched atop the highest mountains in Mongolia, cushioned her knotty athletic feet as she wandered the room.

After opening a velvet-lined drawer, she wiggled into a silk crepe camisole and underpants before selecting a pale gray glen plaid suit from Vivienne Westwood. The oversized legs of the suit's trousers had been ironed and starched to a knife-edge drape. She ran her fingers down them with satisfaction, choosing a set of heavy brass neck rings from Kenya that she'd purchased at an estate auction from a minor Rockefeller.

Next she wandered into her gray marble bathroom, plastered a thick coat of moisturizer over her face from a small amber-colored apothecary jar, and tamped down the shine with a light dusting of translucent powder. Finally she applied a single swipe of Chanel lipstick and two of mascara, slipped a monogrammed kidskin wallet into her pocket, and walked out the front door of her Park Avenue penthouse into her private elevator.

Grinding her teeth, Margot read and replied to a crop of early-morning emails on her way down. The most interesting one was from Paula; it seemed that the remaining *RAGE* staffers were expressing outright resentment toward Cat and Bess.

She wrote back and authorized Paula to spend whatever she had to on Margot's personal credit card. Get them tickets to Paris like I said. The staff need to be motivated, she typed. And we can't let them think anything's wrong. Let's give them something to look forward to. It'll be great publicity. Ask Lou if you can get a discount at that hotel her ex-husband owns.

Fifteen million copies.

RAGE's future rested in the hands of the November and December issues.

Margot tried not to think about it.

Callie Court yawned and stretched out in her bed, tossing the dove-gray linen duvet aside. She kicked her legs up into a bicycle pose and stared over her soft, round belly at the lumpy plaster ceiling. The last eight weeks had been a whirlwind. Her agent had dropped the fact of her *RAGE* contract in all the right ears, omitting the name of the magazine but implying that it was one of the top three women's titles—either *RAGE*; *Frenzy*, the pornographic German monthly; or *Cinq a Sept*, the chic French quarterly—and she'd managed to pick up two runway shows for next week along with an "inner beauty" campaign from Raven, a cosmetics conglomerate trying to bounce back from allegations made in the *RAGE* article. Raven alone had kept her busy for the last three weeks. Callie had to give away all her bar shifts, too: the Raven contract didn't allow her to drink, lest she finally ruin the peaches-and-cream complexion she'd been born with and steadily abusing for the last decade.

She let her legs fall back down on the bed and breathed out in a long, slow whistle. Today was the day that Jonathan's camp would release her *Rhythm Nation* video online. In it, she wore only a sequined bikini bottom from his spring collection as she took tiny bites of an oversized ice-cream sandwich that melted and dripped down onto her body while performing the military-style dance routine from the 1989 Janet Jackson music video, something she'd spent countless hours rehearsing as a teenager.

The background was a crudely spray-painted scene of palm trees. Glitter exploded halfway through the video out of a cannon and stuck to the melted ice cream. She completed the dance by doing the splits, laughing hysterically, a banshee. FIN, it said, fading to white, STARRING CALLIE COURT / COSTUMES BY JONATHAN SPRAIN.

Tomorrow was Callie's *RAGE* shoot, and she was supposed to spend today relaxing, doing yoga, and staying out of the sun, so she finally rolled out of bed and walked the five steps to her kitchen to put the kettle on for tea, then walked over to the antique armoire where she kept her clothes and took down an old Vans shoebox.

It was full of photographs. The oldest ones had been taken with cheap disposable cameras: an out-of-focus Mark laughing on the quad in front of Dakin House, shaggy-haired Mark playing a guitar while she sat next to him in a ratty papasan chair, naked Mark lying in the bed of her freshman dorm, trying to hide his face.

Around 2005 the photos became mostly Polaroids. Mark in a tuxedo at the Central Park Boathouse, at the wedding of a couple now divorced. Mark wearing an aviation suit before they jumped out of a plane together in New Jersey. Mark holding a puppy in Prospect Park. Mark looking hung over in her apartment. Twenty-six-year-old Mark drinking a beer in Park Slope. Mark captured midair in the pit at a punk show downtown somewhere. Mark covered in body paint for a Bushwick party.

Around 2012 the photos turned into square printouts from Photogram; there were only a half-dozen of these, their time together less frequent during his relationships with the condescending horse-faced lawyer and the pointy-headed ballerina. Still, she had a photo of Mark standing in front of CBS in Midtown, clowning around during a lunch break; Mark drinking coffee out of a paper cup at Grand Army Plaza; Mark holding up a bowling ball at the derelict alley she loved near the Lincoln Tunnel; Mark doing a shot in his first NYPD uniform. Mark and Callie together on the Coney Island Cyclone before it was torn down.

They hadn't spoken since he'd dismissed her in his office, blowing her off for his "big important case," and his feeble late-night texts the following week had dropped off after just four or five days of no reply. After that he hadn't called—so she hadn't called. It wasn't exactly a breakup as far as Callie had been concerned: she'd thought of it as more of a détente.

Everyone who'd seen it assured Callie that the *Rhythm Nation* video was the sexiest, funniest thing they'd ever seen. That even if Janet Jackson forbade the use of the music—which she would never do, Jonathan claimed, because they'd gotten wasted together in Nashville once and she was sure to love it—they could put anything over it, even just a drumbeat. *It'll kill*, they said. *It's guaranteed viral. It'll get a hundred million views in a day.*

But all she cared about was whether or not Mark would see it. "You're my best friend, Cal," he'd said to her a thousand and one times. "You're the sexiest girl I've ever known," a thousand and two. They'd had momentum this summer—she knew they had—yet somehow it had disappeared in a single afternoon. She kept trying to remind herself of how he'd looked when he'd blown her off that day in his office: apologetic, but not in love. He hadn't looked at her with *love*. And somehow knowing that didn't seem to help her to let go permanently; it only gave her the strength not to call.

She had tried so hard over the years to forget him, to get over him, to love somebody else. It never happened. His big laugh and easy smile, his puffy hair that always looked so silly; the way he ate a sandwich, drank a beer; moved his big arms and legs around; all of it felt to Callie like he was designed just for her and her alone, like God had molded someone from her rib, her only complement in the universe, a soul mate.

An email sat in her drafts folder that she'd edited and rewritten a hundred times. She pulled it up on her phone just to look at it. Just to *think* about saying it was enough—that was how much she loved him.

I love you. I want us to be together.

I'll get my shit together and be your perfect wife.

I'll have a million of your babies.

I have forgiven so many things: The time we screamed in the street on my birthday. The time you made me hide under the bed. The time you came over to my apartment on Carroll Street and ignored me for three hours, then told me you never wanted to see me again. I will never run out of room to forgive you or out of room to love you more. I belong to you.

I want you to belong to me.

Yet—just like every other time she'd read the email—she hit Cancel and put down her phone.

Another day, she thought. *Maybe tomorrow or next week. He'll see the video, and read about the shoot, and he'll call, and we'll get back into it, and then maybe I'll finally send it, once we get our momentum back. That's the play. Don't plead for commitment out of the gate*, she told herself. *Get him back in your arms first.*

But Mark Hutton would never get to read it, because Callie Court died the next day.

Chapter Fourteen

Lou Lucas woke up at 4:00 a.m. without an alarm, springing out of bed to make the first cup of coffee. As the kettle heated up she changed into a pair of spandex underpants and matching sports bra—the type worn by elite marathoners—and searched for her favorite padded socks. She grabbed her headphones and stuffed them into her ears, her caramel-colored locks set in place the night before with a series of pins and foam rollers. She wrapped an Hermès scarf around her head to keep it all perfect, then coated her dry hands with cream.

The kettle whistled, and she poured the steaming water over a porcelain Hario set atop a thermos, then laced up her sneakers and tucked her house key into her bra. When the coffee finished brewing, she screwed on the thermos top, then sprinted out the door and darted across the street into Central Park for a quick five-miler to and around the reservoir before her day really began.

This would be a career-defining day for Lou: months of planning finally realized, which she now knew they needed desperately. October, out on newsstands this week, was a piece of shit. Paula and Margot had made it clear the blame rested squarely with Lou; her half-digested versions of Cat's work had come out just plain boring, their efficacy cut in half because Cat hadn't been there to help her understand what she'd meant to do. The October issue seemed a pale imitation of the high-concept high fashion that *RAGE* was known for, and Lou was, frankly, embarrassed—and furious with Cat for leaving her without any help.

But that wouldn't matter. Today's shoot would put the November issue over the top, and they'd be back on track; the visuals, of earthy, logoless garments, seamlessly matched their new efforts to promote sustainably made clothing; all the fabrics Callie would be wearing were undyed, a small step toward adjusting fashion's position as the world's second-largest polluter of drinking water, thanks to the chemicals required to dye and treat most textiles. Lou's tanned legs pumped up and down with energy and she couldn't keep a reasonable pace, ripping through her miles, passing every runner she encountered and even lapping a few. She felt her legs go numb, the muscles and sinews swelling with use and adrenaline. Sweat poured down her back in rivers and she grinned, taking a huge swig of her coffee. *Yes— today will be my day.*

She checked her watch, a thin little slip of platinum from Cartier, and realized she would need to turn back now and get changed if she wanted to be at the Museum of Natural History to greet the crew at five thirty.

She turned back and let her legs loosen, her gallop slowing to a canter when she reached Central Park West and spied the facade of her building. She nodded to the doorman, leaped into the elevator, and rushed back into her apartment for a quick shower, furiously scrubbing her skin clean.

After she hopped out and slathered herself with alternate layers of jasmine- and honeysuckle-scented lotions, Lou felt focused and calm—completely ready to tackle the most challenging day of her life. She surveyed the three outfits she'd set out the night before and felt her instincts pull her toward the middle one: the pair of cuffed, slightly oversized jeans she'd been wearing the day she got into Cambridge, though her first husband had eventually convinced her not to go; a pale blue shantung tank top; and a gauzy cream sweater from Japan, the stitching full of artful holes.

She pulled her running sneakers back on—today she'd need stamina, not style—and searched for a bag big enough to carry everything she'd need, settling on an old single-strap WWI RAF rucksack that had once belonged to her grandfather. *You're a survivor*, she thought, staring at the bag. *Me too.* For the first time in years, Lou didn't bother to apply any makeup; she didn't want to think about it today. *You're going to look old*, a nagging voice told her. *At least put on some concealer.* She turned and looked in the mirror, but as soon as she saw her own face—tanned, healthy, glowing—she thought, *I look beautiful. It's fine.* She resisted the urge to smash the mirror on the ground.

Lou untied her headscarf and pulled the pins and foam rollers from her hair before brushing out the curls with a handmade wooden brush. Her hair floated around her face, the fine, honey-colored strands shining with health and vitality. She snapped a hair tie onto her wrist and dumped the contents of her handbag into the backpack on her way out the door, adding some bottles from her personal supply—a heavy, shiny cream and a lighter, sparkly body milk that contained actual gold dust.

Today was the first day of the rest of her life.

Hutton hadn't intended to keep stalking Cat.

Not really.

But Mania made it really, really easy. He didn't even need to leave his apartment.

The night before he hadn't seen her text—whatcha doing later— until he'd already checked Mania and seen photos of her kissing an actor in some kind of Finnish restaurant that served only crackers. He'd been on the verge of responding to her when more photos showed up of her laughing an hour later with Grant Bonner, Bess's preppy lawyer brother.

After that he didn't see the point in responding—not now, and maybe not ever. It wasn't that his feelings were hurt, he told himself; she was welcome to kiss anyone she liked. No, it was the quickness with which those kisses made their way online.

It would be humiliating enough for Hutton to admit almost anything about his life to his colleagues at the NYPD: that he'd gone to Hampshire, a college that didn't have grades, or to an Ivy League graduate school, or that he now owned a five-bedroom penthouse apartment on Prospect Park when his *boss* could barely afford Staten Island. He'd done such a good job of keeping his background hidden. If he dated Cat, that anonymity would be gone, and not only would he lose the respect of his team, he'd never be promoted again, and he'd probably get suspended for dating a witness in an ongoing investigation.

She sure is a beautiful girl, though, he thought, scrolling through picture after picture of her, for an hour longer than he intended to, smiling in spite of himself when he spotted any photo where she looked annoyed, or frustrated, or suspicious, or bored. Those were the ones he couldn't stop looking at.

But Hutton knew, deep down, that he didn't want to lose any ground in the career he loved. He didn't have any hobbies; he'd left a tsunami of broken friendships in his wake when his last girlfriend had caught him sleeping with Callie not once but a truly unforgivable *four* times; and Callie . . . he didn't know how that was supposed to work out. They hadn't spoken in months. Hutton's career had become his entire world.

So when his new boss in the Major Case Division called ten minutes later and asked if Hutton was still awake, if he could make it to a crime scene down in Battery Park City, he said *no problem, on my way*—then closed Mania and deleted it from his phone, as well as all the texts they'd exchanged over the past week.

I'll just have to get over it, he told himself.

Lou counted the shots in her head. They had thirteen—no, *fourteen*—incredible shots so far of Callie Court as their very own *RAGE* Gaia, each more special than the last. The earthy, logoless clothes that Lou styled her in before each take had a magical quality that was both past and present, simultaneously formidable Anasazi warrior and intrepid Mars colonist. Lou knew they'd captured not only the November cover shot, but an entire feature that would get ripped out around the country, posted equally in teenage scrapbooks and on production designers' inspiration boards. She very nearly burst with pride. They had only one more shot to go.

The day had started at the American Museum of Natural History, where Callie had "woken up" inside one of the dioramas in the Native American wing, breaking the glass—they'd been allowed to install a temporary sheet of breakaway—using just her fists. As the glass rained to the ground, Callie's face showed a terrible rage. At that moment Lou had known that this extraordinary model would carry the day, that it would make both of their careers, that she was about to be a privileged witness to magazine history. She let the girl take the lead, stepping in only occasionally to coat Callie's gleaming skin with layers of the shiny lotions she'd brought from home.

As Callie strode through the museum, tracking the progress of human evolution, they'd captured her riding the elephants in Akeley Hall, sobbing beneath the blue whale, devastated that someone would take it so far away from the ocean, and lying on the floor of the Hayden Planetarium, her eyes as wide as a baby's. Paula had stopped by briefly, and she seemed impressed.

Their next stop had been the Central Park Zoo, but en route Callie had spontaneously scaled the walls of the Belvedere Castle, looking every inch the conqueror—another spectacular shot. She'd rolled down a hill with a group of children in their prep school uniforms, *bam*, another one. She dived into the remote-controlled boat pond; touched noses with a tiger at the zoo; rode the carousel; stepped in for an at-bat on the baseball fields; and smashed a tea set at the Plaza Hotel, her face dripping with queenly disdain. She had changed unself-consciously in public between every shot, stripping down without a single glance to see who was watching.

Then she shoplifted from the MoMA store, slipping nonsense into her pockets with the deft hands of a practiced thief while Lou had casually paid for it all at the register, before hailing a taxicab and convincing the driver to let her ride on top as though the cab were her horse.

She'd peed in the Columbus Circle fountain, kissing the police officer who tried to reprimand her, and marched up Broadway to a Sprinter van filled with three hair and makeup artists waiting to apply her final look.

Lou now sat in the driver's seat, examining Callie through the rearview mirror. Their work was almost complete: the model wore a leather bikini, handmade in Japan from Kobe beef hides, underneath a linen-blend cape that appeared to be equal parts beach blanket and queen's robe. Her hair had been braided with huge extensions into waist-length braids, their girth ridiculously large. Her face and body were coated in dirt held fast by the heavy lotion.

"Are you ready?" Lou asked.

Callie smiled. "Absolutely," she replied. Lou jumped onto the sidewalk, where she watched Callie leap from the van and run straight toward Lincoln Center.

There were huge crowds in front of the various sponsor tents, but Callie forced her way through as Lou and the camera crew followed breathlessly, waving their badges and elbowing strangers out of the way.

Callie stole the first cellphone within three minutes, rotating her cape around and using the corners as an ad hoc burglar's sack. In the following ninety seconds she scored over a dozen, snatching them with ease from the plaza's population of human mannequins, who were all so aware of being watched that they didn't respond at all. But the crowd responded as crowds do, instinctively forming a circle around Callie's zigzags to give her an arena.

Standing in the middle of the plaza, the model looked around with satisfaction at the hordes of strangers watching her. She wrapped up the cellphones in the cape and threw the bundle on the ground, pulling Lou's solid-gold Dunhill lighter out of her bikini top before setting the edges of the cape on fire.

"People of Earth!" she yelled. "Free yourselves! Throw your phones on this fire!"

A few moments passed. No one did anything at all.

Lou stepped forward to give Callie her cellphone and tablet. "Here," she said. "I don't want these anymore."

Callie hurled them toward the cape, where the first cellphone was starting to catch fire. It popped dramatically, the cover flying off in a rather impressive miniature explosion, and suddenly another woman stepped forward—an editor at *IQ*.

"I don't need it anymore either," the editor said. "I'm so goddamn sick of Fashion Week."

"Me too," said another woman in a black cocktail dress. She handed her tablet to Callie while the second phone exploded. The crowd flinched.

"Then take off all your shackles," Callie ordered the woman. "Give me your dress."

The woman in the black dress looked around. Tired, a little drunk, and extremely overheated, she was tempted to give in to this random performance—to finally take part in one of the spectacles that had surrounded her all week. *It's your time*, the woman told herself before unzipping her dress and handing it to Callie.

The crowd cheered. Callie kissed her and threw the dress into the fire. The woman felt loved.

In moments it became an epidemic. Dozens of women unzipped their dresses, throwing them into the fire while the crowd around them raged, their cheers turning to chants in the space of seconds. Someone pulled the BP flower sculptures out of the fountain and threw them on the pile, turning it into a real bonfire. Callie's face, lit by the flames, was simultaneously beautiful and terrible, a Homeric sibyl made real. Forty women, all of them boldfaced names, were standing in their slips and bras watching their clothing and cellphones burn. The very air of the plaza sizzled with the iron taste of menace while cameras flashed, and flashed and flashed.

And all of it was because of Lou, because of *her* vision.

Lou heard the shutters going off, and she visualized the fifteen shots that only *RAGE*'s photographers would have, including the last, of Callie running into the crowd before anyone noticed her.

Lou smiled. Her huge teeth gleamed, the orange flames reflecting in miniature on their bright surface.

She was *so* pleased.

Chapter Fifteen

Cat woke up after her night out with Grant and felt like herself again. The first thing she did was text June and Raphael to relieve them for the day; she wasn't in the mood to be poked and prodded and costumed. Cat did her own hair and makeup for the first time in months—plain face, thick black eyeliner, hair brushed and left down—before donning a floor-length black dress, the neckline cut in a rectangle across her collarbones. She threw an oversized black blazer and brass necklace on top, and wore the biggest, chunkiest eyeglasses she owned, then attended a whirlwind of fashion shows, promising herself that she'd take advantage of the next two weeks. Maybe she'd even write something. Constance, Paula, Margot, and Janet would all be in London and Milan, so Cat, the most senior employee after Lou, had no real reason to continue being out and about. There was plenty of work to do in the office. She resolved to bring it up with Lou if she saw her today.

The first official afterparty for New York Fashion Week was uptown on the ivy-lined terrace of the Howard Hotel. After a day of shows, she went straight there to meet Bess and found her flirting with Jent Brooks. "*I'll tell you later,*" Bess whispered. All anyone else had been able to talk about was Lou's insane bonfire—

the Gaia shoot—and the gorgeous, previously unknown plus-size model who'd started it all. Cat realized how close she was to losing her own place in the *RAGE* hierarchy.

It didn't take Bess and Jent long to sneak out early, and Cat found herself suddenly alone. She checked her phone for the hundredth time; no text from Hutton, but she did have an invitation from Lou. Impromptu celebration at my place for RAGE staff, it said. Get your buns over here: 150 Central Park West penthouse.

There were easily three hundred people milling through the apartment by the time she arrived, including most of the *RAGE* staff, a group of models, and various hip-looking young people. Lou's now-infamous plus-size model was at the center of it all, surrounded by admirers and hangers-on in a corner, wearing a textured, strapless burlap gown.

Cat spent most of the party on the terrace smoking cigarettes and trying to catch up with her coworkers. She managed to work her way into a lively conversation about the mayoral race with Janet Berg and Rose Cashin-Trask. During a brief lull after everyone agreed it might be nice to have Bloomberg back for a fourth round, Lou strategically appeared.

"More *wine-o*?" Lou boomed, her jaw unhinging and jutting forward as she grinned.

"I can't. I'm so partied out," Cat explained. "Besides, I think I need to start changing gears. I'd really like to get back to the office," she said, putting Lou on the spot in front of the two colleagues who'd had to pick up much of her slack.

"Oh, it hasn't been all bad," Lou replied. "We're paying you to party and wear beautiful clothes! Don't be a Deborah Downer," she chided in a fake American accent. "That used to be my whole life. You can't fool me. It's not very hard, partying all the time, being the center of attention." She winked, elbowing Rose and Janet in an overly jocular way.

"Oh, it's been lovely, really it has," Cat agreed. "But I'm sure my colleagues want to get back to doing only their own jobs," she persisted, using the people around her as graciously as possible.

Janet and Rose—both of them four glasses of wine–deep—nodded enthusiastically.

"You can say that again," Janet had replied. "Honestly, if you don't bring her back permanently, I'm going to ask for double the salary." Her voice was steely.

Lou, still just five months into her very first paying job, looked shocked; she obviously didn't know how seriously to take Janet's comment.

"Me too," said Rose, holding up her glass in a toast. "To more money or more Cat!"

"Cheers to that," Cat said, clinking her water glass.

"Well, I'll see what I can do," Lou said quickly before hurrying off to another group.

"I think we got her," Cat whispered conspiratorially, feeling the tension between them finally dissipate.

At that exact moment, the now-famous model in the burlap gown stepped out onto the balcony, a small plastic bag in her hand. Cat watched her tap out a pile onto the hollow next to her thumb and take a surreptitious sniff.

A second later the woman's eyes rolled back into her head. Her balance wavered.

"Excuse me," Cat said to Janet and Rose. "I'll be right back." She hurried over and grabbed the model by the arm, steadying her while she pried the bag out of her hand.

"Are you okay?" Cat whispered, hiding the bag of brown powder in the pocket of her jacket.

"It's none of your business, Cat," the woman said, her voice trembling slightly. She stumbled as her ankle rolled underneath her. Cat looked at her face, finally, and realized who she was—Callie, the bartender from King's Landing.

"I think you need to sit down," Cat said.

"Okay," Callie agreed, allowing Cat to lead her inside and down the hallway into the apartment's private quarters. Cat opened the first unlocked door she found. It looked like a small library, the walls lined in bookshelves and the only furniture a button-tufted chaise longue upholstered in delicate gray linen. She helped Callie sit down on it. The girl lay back right away before closing her eyes and passing out.

Cat sat on the floor next to her for a few minutes trying to figure out what to do. She still had the bag in her pocket. *Get rid of it*, she told herself, standing up and walking to the adjacent powder room. The little plastic bag disappeared down the toilet with just a single flush. She sat down and peed, trying to think about how to help Callie get out of the party without anyone seeing her, before flushing the toilet a second time and walking back into the study, where she stopped, shocked.

Callie was sitting up, grasping at her throat.

Her beautiful face was turning purple.

She was choking.

Cat climbed onto the chaise and wrapped her arms around the model's body, trying to force air out of her throat in a Heimlich maneuver, but the girdle beneath Callie's dress was too tight; it wasn't possible to exert the needed force through the undergarment. Callie kept choking, her face so desperate and terrified that Cat didn't give up. She used all her strength, squeezing in sharp hugs, trying to find some leverage, between screaming for help. Callie squirmed, grabbing Cat's long black hair and tugging on it, trying to communicate. She managed to pull out a fistful before she went back to pawing at her throat, the strands interwoven between her fingers. Cat tried to push Callie over the edge of the chaise, but she wasn't strong enough and they stayed locked in an upright position.

After the longest minute of Cat's life, Callie fell limp.

"Nonononono," Cat screamed at the model, leaning her back on the chaise. "Don't you dare. Don't you fucking give up."

She grabbed the model's jaw, then shoved her fingers down Callie's throat and tried to dislodge whatever was in there, screaming the entire time, screaming herself hoarse, trying to open the door with her foot. Cat failed on every count. Nobody came to help. Callie didn't move. She felt her fingernail break off somewhere in Callie's esophagus.

Eventually Cat let go, because nothing helped. She looked at Callie's face and watched the life disappear from it.

Callie was dead. A moment later Cat was sitting on the floor calling 911.

Five minutes later, the model's body remained on the chaise longue. Her eyes were still open, looking toward the ceiling, and Cat's hair was still wrapped in her fist. Tears had run down her face as she choked to death, streaking her eye makeup into watercolor ribbons that slashed across her cheeks.

A blank space hung in the air. Cat supposed it might be the distinction between life and death, between the atmosphere generated by a soul and the mere physical presence of a corpse. Time had slowed to a nothing, though the party raged on around her. Voices from the party mumbled senselessly as the stereo's bass vibrated the room's peach silk lampshades.

Her call to the paramedics had been surprisingly calm. "Hello, my friend has choked and she's not breathing, and I can't get it out," she'd said. "Please come to the penthouse at 150 Central Park West right now. We're in the library, I think."

As she sat on the floor next to the body, Cat reached out and grabbed Callie's hand. She didn't know what else to do. Peals of laughter bubbled up through the din. The air smelled like a Christmas tree.

Five more minutes passed.

An odd stiffness, a rubbery quality, passed through the girl's fingers, but Cat didn't let go.

Eventually someone barged in. There were flashing lights; the party dissolved; someone made her let go of Callie. The police kept trying to ask her questions. But Cat couldn't speak. She didn't have anything to say.

She found herself sitting on another linen sofa in the apartment's parlor, facing a paramedic. The world came back into focus.

"What did you take?" the paramedic was asking. Cat stared over his head at an oil painting of a ship. It had big foamy waves and a yellow sky, like a Turner. *It probably* is *a Turner*, she realized.

"I didn't take anything," she said. "I had a glass of wine earlier. But I didn't take anything."

"What did your friend take?"

"I don't know. She sniffed something and threw it out on the balcony. I brought her in here to see if she was okay and so that she wouldn't embarrass herself. I went to the toilet and when I came back, I found her like that. She was grabbing her throat. I tried to stick my fingers down it, to get whatever it was out. I tried to push on her stomach. But I couldn't do anything. The girdle was too tight, I think. I called 911. She died right in front of me. I couldn't help . . . " she said, trailing off.

Out of the corner of her eye she saw Lou speaking to a police officer, showing him her ID. She looked around the room for her handbag and found it folded in her lap.

"We need to give you a blood test," the paramedic said.

"Okay," Cat agreed. "Go ahead."

He took a sample from her left arm; rubber tourniquet, needle, cotton ball, bandage.

Cat felt herself dissociate completely from the scene around her as her mind retreated to a comfortable space far, far away from here, in her mother's barn. *The smell of sweat when you take off a saddle; the way dust comes up from a currycomb. The fur of a foal, matted and wet and new.*

She remembered the time they'd had to euthanize Fielt, their squat Brabants trekpaard—thirteen hands, a runt for his breed but strong—who had broken the lower shin of his left foreleg, the cannon bone, plowing a neighbor's field. The break grew infected and they had to put him down in his stall a week later. She'd held his face while he died.

Her mother hadn't cried at all.

Cat had been so angry, but Anais had insisted that leaving him to suffer for another moment in pain would be the only thing that could really hurt him, that Cat's anger was misplaced. *Putting him to sleep is a gift we can and must give*, Anais had insisted, but Cat had been only eight years old. She hadn't understood.

She remembered the heavy strands of his forelock, each one thick as dental floss, and holding the hank of it in her hands. The milky whites of his huge eyes, wild and glassy, and pained, until they were blank, and, finally, the size of the needle they'd used to inject morphine into his haunches. Cat remembered it as the size of a drinking straw.

She suddenly felt very, very tired.

After a while—when it became clear that she wasn't going to speak—someone walked her out of the apartment, into the elevator, through the lobby, and helped her get in a cab. She settled in and blankly gave the driver her address. As they pulled away, she caught a glimpse of Callie's body, zipped into a thick plastic bag, being loaded into the ambulance.

Two days later Hutton sat on the floor of Callie's apartment looking through a shoebox of photographs she'd left on the floor. With a flash of his badge and a copy of the death certificate, he'd had no trouble getting the super to let him right in.

The photograph in his hands showed a lighter-blonde Callie wearing a tattered black Hank Williams T-shirt while she smoked a cigarette in front of Dakin House. An equally youthful version of himself stood behind her, a rolled cigarette between his thumb and forefinger. He remembered when she bought the T-shirt in a thrift store out in Williamsburg, on an afternoon they'd spent drinking and shopping after waking up on somebody's sofa. *Whose party had that been?* He tried to remember. It must have been something in Bushwick, he thought, maybe McKibbin, back when it was still deemed habitable, before the rat infestation had forced the city to permanently evacuate the building.

There were so many photos of him, of the two of them together. Every photo forced the same set of recollections: what day of the week it had been, where they had been going. He spent an hour going through the box. She'd loved him. They'd loved each other. He knew that. But it wasn't enough. They'd never worked out.

When they'd met she was a naive girl from Ann Arbor who'd never had anything stronger than the so-called 3-2 beer they sold at midwestern gas stations. First it had been mushrooms and pot, then a short spell with cocaine, and then five years ago: heroin. *Dope*, she always called it, like she was a character in a Tom Robbins novel.

He didn't know when she started using, but he remembered the first time he'd seen it. He'd stopped by Callie's apartment just to see if she'd wanted to fool around, and found her listening to Depeche Mode and painting her fingernails with two of her spacey girlfriends from some bar.

"Want some dope?" she'd asked—her eyes huge, her voice so cheery, like it was anything else, like she was offering him a cocktail or a cigarette or a frozen mini-quiche. Too shocked to express his own horror, he'd just said *no thank you*, and hung out for a while until it was clear that everyone was so fucked up they wouldn't notice if he left. He stopped calling her for a while after that, but he could never cut her out completely.

After a year or two of using she'd gone to rehab. Hutton had asked her to. She'd given in way more easily than he'd expected, happily grabbing her ID and getting in a cab to the airport, docile as a puppy. Later he realized how high she'd been. It took her two tries to get clean, and a long stay at home with her parents, but she eventually did it, a period during which he also left CBS and joined the NYPD. Hutton had paid for the whole thing without ever telling her. She thought her meager insurance, a long-expired hundred-dollar policy from her first modeling agency, had covered it.

By the time she came back Callie's problems had—frankly—been too much for him to bear.

"I want you to be clean for yourself," he'd said at the time. "I'll always be here for you."

"I am clean for myself," she'd insisted. *But she hadn't made the changes she needed to make*, he realized now. She'd kept the same group of friends, kept partying.

It was never my job to keep her sober, he reminded himself. *It was never my job to tell her how to be. It was never my job to be her only lifeline*; he knew all of that, and yet the guilt washed over him in a tidal wave, replacing all the blood in his veins.

He kept looking through the photographs. They'd been so young, and so beautiful, and so stupid, once upon a time. He could barely believe they'd survived. *She didn't*, he suddenly remembered, in that way that you have to forget and remember and forget and remember and forget and remember—when people are very newly dead—that you'll never ever see them again.

He'd been the one to call her parents, from the morgue on the Upper West Side the day after she died; a detective there who knew him had recognized Hutton's name in Callie's contacts. He'd tried to explain that yes, she'd been at a party, but he didn't think it was that kind of party. No, he'd had no idea she was using again.

She'd choked on a piece of gum in the penthouse apartment of 150 Central Park West, at a party for *RAGE Fashion Book*. The drugs had relaxed her muscles, delaying her gag reflex when the gum she'd been chewing had slid down into her useless, weakened throat. And Catherine Ono—*Cat!*—had tried to save her, but the coroner found that the girdle Callie had worn to fit into her dress was so tight that Cat's attempts at the Heimlich maneuver had failed. They'd found one of Cat's fake fingernails stuck to the gum. But ultimately there was no explanation that could satisfy the exceptional grief of two people who had lost their only child, a person they had made and raised and loved.

Hutton checked his watch. The movers he'd hired to pack and ship Callie's things to her family, to spare them the pain of it, would be here in twenty minutes. He wiped his tears, stood up, then looked through every drawer and cabinet trying to find anything she might not have wanted her mother to see; notebooks, videos, photographs, anything. He found a hard drive, another box of photographs—most of them nude—and her laptop, which was password-protected. He put everything in a duffel bag and told himself he'd have the electronics wiped the following week. He searched for the little black notebook she'd carried everywhere, but he couldn't find it. *The notebook must have been in her purse*, he thought. The police would have released her belongings with the body. It was probably in a coffin on a plane right now. Her mother might read it, but he'd done his best, he told himself, even if it was too late.

Lou Lucas had spent the last thirty-six hours in a state of complete exhilaration, communing fully with her computer as she wrote with a fury she'd never known possible. At 5:00 p.m. on Saturday she was still in her office while Molly and Rose scoured wire services, catalogs, agents' records, and photographers' archives. Lou was nearly done with the text for the November issue, which would be closing the next week; all that was left was to present the whole thing to Paula and Margot.

After Callie had overdosed in her apartment on Thursday night,

Lou momentarily considered jumping off the terrace. Watching the coroner examine the girl's body—*that stupid, thoughtless girl dying in Lou's own office*—all she could think was, *They'll never make me staff.*

There is no way RAGE *will be able to run the shoot I worked so hard to produce*, Lou had realized, shaking with fear as she watched the police invade her beautiful penthouse. It would be repellent to run the photos after Callie's accidental death, purely and openly exploitative; she wasn't, frankly, well-known enough for her "final photo shoot" to be seen as a celebrity story, and so, November would tank. Come December Lou's contract wouldn't be renewed, and she would have officially failed. She nearly threw up right then and there but swallowed the bile back down, holding herself together long enough to instruct the caterers and servants to clean up.

She'd paced nervously in front of the office, watching the officers like a hawk. When they found a small black notebook behind the chaise, she'd claimed it immediately, for no reason other than wanting them out of her apartment as soon as possible. "It's mine!" she'd snapped. "This is my office. So are you done now?" They'd rolled their eyes and stayed put for another hour.

When it finally looked as though everyone, including the police, the domestic laborers, and the last phonily sympathetic gossip hounds, had finally gone, Lou had poured straight vodka into a tumbler, walked out onto the terrace, and opened the barbecue drawer where she kept her secret spare pack of Sobranies, fat, gold-tipped cigarettes packaged in a heavy rectangular box.

She smoked half of one and finished her vodka before she remembered the little black notebook she'd claimed as her own. She refilled her drink and examined it.

The notebook, Callie's diary, covered the last three or four years of her life, and it was surprisingly well-written, chronicling her professional successes and failures, her weight fluctuations, her feelings about her body, and her ongoing, on-again, off-again relationship with a policeman named Mark. It turned out Callie had been the woman in the Valentino campaign that had been plastered all over the city for the past six months, that she had a Raven contract, that there were more videos that would come out from Jonathan Sprain. This woman was an absolute volcano of content.

Lou found herself out on the terrace with the bottle for the next hour, smoking and drinking and reading the entire diary in one greedy gulp. When she was done, she picked up the phone and called Margot.

"I think I can resolve this whole fucking thing," Lou sputtered as soon as Margot picked up. "I think I've got it. We don't need to trash the photos. There's a story. We can keep them."

"That seems unlikely," Margot had responded, sounding almost bored. But Lou managed to convince her. "This is a story about feminism," she insisted. "This is a story about a woman betrayed. This is a story about a woman doing everything she can for the attention of one man who could care less, a woman whose career was, sadly, about to take off. There's oceans of content around her. We're just the first to break it."

"Let me ask you a question," Margot replied. "Do you want to be on staff at *RAGE* permanently?"

"Absolutely," Lou replied earnestly. "That's the *only* thing I want."

"Then I'd appreciate it if you could explore this, in five thousand words, by Monday morning. It needs to be compelling."

"I'm on it," she'd said to Margot. "You can count on me."

So Lou had spent the last two days in her office, fueled by a half-dozen bottles of cold press from the old Coke machine and some Adderall that she stole from Cat's desk drawer, composing a glorious and elaborate obituary for Callie Court, weaving the strands of Callie's love affair with Detective Mark Hutton as if it had been her own. *Who was to say that Callie hadn't told these things to Lou herself?* No one would ever know the difference, and Cooper's lawyers would surely be satisfied with the diary as her unnamed source.

Cat wouldn't be happy about the article, seeing as how it ended with her breaking a fingernail off in the girl's throat—a fact that hadn't yet made it out of the police department—but that woman had long ago sacrificed her right to a personal life, Lou thought, done it the second she agreed to put her personal photos of Hillary Whitney in *RAGE* after her "friend" had died so horribly; done it the very first time she put on a dress and stepped in front of a camera on *RAGE*'s behalf, eager for the attention. In fact, she'd done it the second she posted her first image on Photogram for the whole world to see. *Yes: Cat has done it all to herself*, Lou thought. *What difference will one more issue make?*

For the impoverished working women of the world—working their little fingers to death in some sweaty country in the East—whose incomes are protected by feminists at RAGE, *feminists like me*, she told herself as she typed, *it will make a huge difference. It will all be worth it.*

Part III

October

Chapter Sixteen

Cat stared at herself in the mirror of the cramped restroom on the plane that was flying them all to Paris. She rubbed her hand back and forth over the top of her head, relishing the soft bend of the remaining stubble. The clean whites of her scalp matched the wan tone of her pallid cheeks. Two weeks ago, the morning after Callie died, she'd cut off all her hair in her bathroom at home, shearing it half an inch from the skull before informing Paula and Margot via email that she wouldn't be making any more appearances until Paris, but that she'd be in the office if they needed anything.

Raphael and June had shrieked with joy when she'd walked through the Beinecke doors the following day. "We can wig you so much more easily now," June had said happily. Cat just sighed in reply and tried to get past them to her office, where she'd closed the door and spent the next two weeks prepping content for the December issue.

After the disaster that was October—it had done a mere half-million on newsstands globally after being eviscerated online, and Cat guessed they wouldn't have anything for November, either, now that the cover girl was dead—Margot had assigned Cat to oversee a photo shoot that Hillary had originally proposed for the

December issue, titled **Bridle: The Exquisite Ties That Bind**.
The shoot intended to showcase the nation's ten best-selling mass-
produced wedding gowns.

Hillary had put together a proposal to update those dresses using
high-tech, sustainable fabrics whose sheen could approximate that
of small-run Italian silk satin or handwoven French lace, with the
help of the latest 3-D printing and laser cutting techniques. She'd
sourced the quantities needed for the manufacturers in question
to update their stock throughout the entire North American retail corridor, including a thirteen-yard-*wide* section of fabric made
from a 3-D printing lab in Los Alamos, which Cat realized must
have been the spool of "ribbon" she'd died next to.

Margot had put the shoot on pause once Hillary died, but now
that *RAGE* was focusing on sustainability, it was worth a shot, and
so to sweeten the arrangement, Paula had spent the last two weeks
directing *RAGE*'s attorneys and their lobbying firm to negotiate a
ten-year import deal with Customs and Border Protection for each
of the participating manufacturers. All that was left was the shoot
itself, now Cat's responsibility; it had originally been assigned to
Lou, but given the remarkable failure of the October issue, she'd
been yanked from the project entirely.

The handmade samples were in the cargo hold below. The shoot
was scheduled for two days from now, the last free day before
Paris Fashion Week officially started. **Bridle: The Exquisite Ties
That Bind** was a feature that would hopefully prove to be both
high-fashion and high-minded. Most importantly, it could break
RAGE's politics into the wedding market for the very first time,
an industry so wildly profitable that *RAGE* had never made an iota
of impact. Women everywhere, manipulated by the complex retail
politics of "their day," had always been happy to shell out thousands
of dollars for what were, in the end, mostly synthetic rags made in
brutal East Asian sweatshops with astronomical profit margins. On
lower- and mid-priced wedding dresses, everything from the fabrics to the stitching were usually fabricated by actual children, little

girls who must have looked at the plastic lace and faux pearls that they sewed on so carefully with a particularly grotesque sense of fate's cruelty.

Cat finally understood why those last six months had been so important to Hillary, why her friend had been so concerned about *RAGE*, about their jobs, about their stability as a team: Hillary had seen that *RAGE* would need to pivot before anyone else did. Mania's "proprietary ethical rating" had oversaturated their moral high ground over the last three years, and readers officially no longer cared about the difference between editorial and advertorial, not when they perceived each to hold the same values. It was time to find a new tower to shout from.

Cat had wanted to discuss the shoot with Hutton the moment Paula handed her Hillary's notes. Her friend had *died* next to that box of "ribbon," something so trivial and odd that he'd asked her about it in their very first conversation. *No one will know*, she'd tried to tell herself, attempting to rationalize violating *RAGE*'s famously complete non-disclosure agreement. Yet in the end she hadn't said a thing about the shoot to Hutton—because he'd never called her or texted her again. Detective Mark Hutton had completely disappeared from her life.

When she returned to her seat, Bess was already snoring across the aisle, a sleep mask banded over her eyes, moisturizing gloves and socks on her hands and feet. *She must be exhausted*, Cat thought. Bess had been handling their appearances for the last two weeks all by herself.

The gamine air hostess was nearly done making up Cat's lie-flat bed with real goose-down pillows and a puffy, oversized duvet. She smoothed the sheets with a flick of her red-gloved palm, turned down the lights, lightly misted the pillowcases with lavender linen water, and motioned to Cat that it was ready before gracefully moving on to the next berth.

Cat climbed in, eager to get some shut-eye before they landed in Paris for what she hoped would be her final few weeks as

RAGE's very own live-action marionette. Margot had been out of the office for the last week, supposedly meeting with their international editions on a round-the-world tour, so Paula, seated in the next section up in one of the four suites of the risibly lavish Premiere Classe, had been at the helm. Cat had worked up the courage three days earlier to ask her about returning to the office permanently; Paula had put her off. *We'll discuss after Paris*, she'd said.

This week would begin with a few events and Hillary's shoot, followed by nonstop shows and meetings with European brands, mostly in public and always on behalf of the magazine. It was just ten more days, Cat told herself. All she had to do was make it through the next Sunday, and maybe, if there was time, she could go see her parents before flying back home. She slid in a pair of earplugs, popped a Klonopin, washed it down with some white wine that tasted faintly of rancid nail polish, and passed out.

Six hours later a red-gloved hand rested lightly on her shoulder. Cat blinked awake in the still-dark cabin. "Petit déjeuner, madame?" whispered the air hostess; Cat nodded, feeling dazed. "Café noir, double, s'il vous plaît," she whispered back before grabbing her toiletries and making her way to the bathroom.

By the time she returned to her berth someone had magically removed all her linens and remade her seat into a chair. The outfit she'd brought had been steamed, pressed, and hung in the narrow cubby above her ottoman, and her breakfast—a perfect double shot of espresso and two plain slices of toast—had been laid out on a table folded down from the wall and covered with a thick white tablecloth and heavy silverware. As Cat settled back into her seat, Bess yawned across the aisle and pulled her sleep mask over her forehead.

"Are we there yet?" Bess asked in a childish singsong, her face still half-smushed into her pillow.

"Forty-five minutes or so," Cat replied. "Want some breakfast?" Bess smiled and nodded.

Cat signaled for two more coffees. Bess yawned again, stretched her long limbs like a puppy, then wandered up to the bathroom in her flannel pajamas for her own toilette while Cat nibbled on her toast and started her second double espresso.

Soon the whole cabin was awake and chatting genially while they ate their customized breakfasts—fresh avocado salads, granolas, sausages, roasted grapefruits. Cat watched a chèvre-salmon-dill omelet go by and felt her stomach recoil. Lately, so achingly tense that she could barely stand to eat anything, Cat stuck to the pediatrician's standby, BRAT: bananas, rice, applesauce, and toast. She said a silent prayer for the day that her anxiety would subside enough to actually digest meats and cheeses again. For the past few weeks, Cat had been feeling a combination of dread and the same nonstop adrenaline that had dominated previous major escarpments in her life: her junior year of high school, her last year of college, the six months before she'd taken her graduate school comps, her first year working for Hillary.

But anxiety wasn't the only thing that kept her from eating. Cat was now so focused on the way she fit into clothes that she'd become obsessed with herself, unable to daydream about anything except the hollows between her bones. A few days before she'd caught herself staring with envy at the slenderness of what turned out to be a child.

Cat knew these feelings were wrong.

She knew they were a sickness. A capital-P *Problem*.

But when she felt the slender breeze of other people's envy: the moment they watched her pointed elbow rest on a table, or when their eyes slipped down to the pockets developing behind her clavicles—oh, it was a *rush*. The thinnest woman in the room proved her discipline and power just by being herself. It was akin to being a queen or inheriting a billion dollars. Nobody could take it away from you. *You could only take it away from yourself.*

She swallowed the last of her espresso and returned to the restroom to change into the Albert V. outfit the cabin staff had so thoughtfully hung out for her.

Cat had made an effort her very first year at *RAGE* to profile all the employees of Albert's Paris boutique, including the cleaning lady, who naturally wore a custom pair of Albert V. overalls. Albert sent a friendly thank-you note, and she'd sent a funny card back; a half-dozen letters and a few very brief in-person chats and years later, Cat received this mystery box via messenger with a note— *won't you wear this when you arrive to Paris?*—in his long, fine scrawl.

She held it up. The base layer was a crisp black cotton mid-length dress with a full skirt and neckline that plunged in a narrow rectangle to the bottom of her rib cage. Next, a wraparound belt cinched her waist and created a curve where none had previously been visible. The shoes he'd sent were slip-on sandals, heavily fringed, their leather thin and flat as paper; the matching jacket was short—cut just under her armpits—to show off the hard work accomplished by the dress.

With her shorn hair, thick black eyeliner, blocky sunglasses, and the rectangular leather backpack she'd brought as a carry-on, Cat looked like a terrorist sent from the future. She nodded at her reflection, then found her way back to her seat.

Bess had changed, too, in the restroom opposite, and now looked every inch the all-American sweetheart. She wore very pale blue jeans, a white cotton dress shirt, incredibly high striped stiletto pumps, and a thin rose-gold chain. Her hair had been blown out and pinned before the flight to give studied volume and shape to her otherwise-unruly curls, now the very color and quality of honey. She smiled broadly at Cat. A rust-colored suede trench, also coated in fringe, lay folded in her lap. Her handbag was an embroidered American football.

"I think I'm actually excited," she said to Cat, who tried to smile. "Did you see this Virtue coat they sent me? I'm dying over it."

Bess's wardrobe had increased tenfold over the past few weeks, beginning the day after Bess and Jent Brooks had been caught sneaking out of Portmanteau, a pop-up speakeasy housed in a train car inside the long-abandoned subway station at Worth Street. Virtue had been the first brand to get in touch. Bess had agreed but insisted that she be allowed to keep everything she wanted; they'd balked and tried to back out. Ella had stepped in, and after three days of negotiations, during which Bess and Jent were captured sailing on the Hudson, making out in the backseat of a yellow cab, playing shuffleboard in Brooklyn, and, the real coup de grâce, looking at a West Side townhome with a huge Sotheby's "For Sale" placket out front, Virtue more than caved. Not only would she get free clothing, she'd get fifty grand a year to wear it.

Jent was short. There was no getting around it; with shoes on he was barely eye-level with Bess. Without them she had to lean down to kiss him. If they actually got married, she'd never have to wear heels again, she realized, feeling a mixture of elation and devastation as she thought about the rows and rows of shoes currently occupying the built-in bookshelves of her West Village apartment's parlor. *At least*, she told herself, *they'll remain perfect forever—you can't ruin shoes you don't wear.*

But Jent's height had turned out to be inversely proportional to his other traits, the biggest of which was his sense of humor. He made Bess *laugh*, big, deep belly laughs, and he was also cynical, confrontational, ambitious, practical, thrifty; everything that Bess, sweetheart straight-A pothead peacekeeping hoarder, was not. She flat out *loved* it. He acted all the ways she had always thought about acting, said all the things she'd always thought about saying. He was brave and strong even though he wasn't tall, and, best of all, he rode a motorcycle, a beat-to-shit Honda café racer from the late seventies, a sporty, badass bike—loud, fast, and in constant need of repair. Bess was instantly fond of the way he looked sprawled out on the floor of his Bushwick loft, covered in grease and surrounded by parts.

The night they met at Paahtoleipä he'd reached over and punched his number into her phone when no one else was looking, texting himself right away with the words Jent, it's Bess, I love you. She'd laughed at the bravado of it and when he texted later that night—I love you too. Want to get married today?—she'd replied immediately, demanding, Take me to dinner tomorrow. Real food, no bullshit.

He'd picked her up on his motorcycle and driven her across the bridge to Staten Island, taking her to a tiny restaurant in St. George called Enoteca Maria, where every night the kitchen was run by a different old Italian grandmother. They'd spent their first real date eating chicken feet while a ninety-year-old woman, her body made mostly of bosom, screamed at Bess that she was too skinny before presenting her with a single cheese ravioli the size of a bagel. It was everything that Bess never knew she'd always wanted, and the past few weeks had flown by, the appearances and events a mere blur between dates and free clothes.

The landing gear growled up through the carpet as it kicked into place. The women buckled themselves in. A few short minutes later, they were pulling up to the gate, grabbing their coats and carry-ons, pulling out their embossed passport holders, and moving through immigration in a daze.

Molly came out from coach and helped them stack their suitcases onto an aluminum cart, and the trio made it through customs without incident. Luckily the crowd on the other side was made up of only bleary-eyed families waiting for their loved ones, instead of photographers waiting to capture them carrying their own bags. The cameras, Cat knew, would be waiting outside the hotel.

A slight man with dark hair and eyes held up a card with "ONO/BONNER/BEALE" written on it in marker. He walked them to his Peugeot, a half-minivan, half-SUV, and somehow loaded their bags into the tiny trunk and back row of seats.

They turned onto the Avenue des Champs-Élysées and rode the magnificent boulevard all the way to the Place de la Concorde, then rounded the Tuileries to Hôtel Le Narcisse, the venerable five-star situated on the north side of the gardens. A bellman in a sharp navy uniform, including a tiny hat trimmed in gold tassels banded onto his head, escorted them inside.

Le Narcisse, formerly owned by the Sultan of Yemen, had been the subject of a boycott for years until the sharia-law-loving sultan was forced to relinquish many of his assets to a class-action lawsuit for his USVI-based LLC initiated by over five hundred sex workers who claimed they'd been held by him against their will for periods of three months up to five years.

In a magnificent twist of fate, the sex workers—both men and women—now collectively owned Hôtel Le Narcisse and the Plaza Greque in Paris, Hotel Genesis in Rome, the Beverly Glen Hotel in LA, the Boston Hotel in London, and a half-dozen other exquisite properties. The entire Boston Collection, as it was known, was now managed for them by the Diogenes Group; and Diogenes, in turn, was a subsidiary of Lucas Holding, BV—the massive and privately owned company inherited by Lou's ex-husband Alexander.

The remainder of *RAGE*'s full-time staff would arrive tomorrow and stay through the weekend, a delivery on Margot's summer promise, and Lou had helped Molly arrange a takeover of the fifth and sixth floors at a significant discount. Cat prayed for a room of her own, but she thought it was probably unlikely, given how distant and awkward Lou had been with her lately—it had been weird after Callie died in Cat's arms at Lou's apartment, and then just plain *bad* once Cat had been given Hillary's December shoot. Thankfully, Lou wasn't due to arrive for several days, claiming obligations with her children until the end of the week.

As Cat had expected, dozens of photographers were positioned across the street from the hotel. The men leaned against the iron fence of the Tuileries as they awaited the arrival of the incoming flock of editors, models, buyers, designers, and socialites who were in Paris to buy, talk about, think about, covet, reject, and obsess over clothing. This industrial whirlpool of stuff would suck them all in while the men in the background counted their money—because all the labels Cat would see this week, the forty-plus "top" luxury brands that would "compete" during Paris Fashion Week, were owned by just six companies, all of them privately owned and commanded by men.

Cat rotated a few times for them before saying, "Au revoir—un plus juste'avant le dîner," swirling her finger to indicate she and Bess would be back and dressed in new outfits before dinner.

"Merci, mesdames," the photographers responded politely.

As soon as they entered the elaborate lobby, its ceilings hung with crystal chandeliers and the damask furniture in the style of Louis XVI, a small man with polished black hair and a perfectly fitted navy suit appeared.

"Bonjour, mesdames, Mademoiselle Ono, Mademoiselle Bonner, Mademoiselle Beale, bienvenue à Hôtel Le Narcisse." He switched to English. "We are so happy to have you. We have a special treat for you. Our best suite, if you can perhaps take some photos of your stay?" He mimed taking a selfie. "Yes?"

Cat, Bess, and Molly all nodded.

"Okay, wonderful, here we go."

He made his way across the marbled lobby and led them to a private elevator. They rode up to the seventh floor, where the doors opened into a cavernous marble entry hall. The concierge moved quickly, his polished dress shoes tapping sharply on the floor, and brought them through an elaborately carved and painted wooden door into the most decadent hotel room Cat had ever seen.

"No wonder they got their heads cut off," Molly said under her breath.

The windows looked out over all of Paris between casements of gilded, handcarved molding. A white grand piano, a painted antique harpsichord, and a scattering of silk sofas and chairs were placed around the enormous living room. The floors were carpeted in alabaster wool so fine that Cat was afraid to step on it. Tasseled white and beige Persian silk rugs had been placed underneath all the furniture, carved and polished woods that had the delicate, dollhouse look of the final French monarchies. Every single object in the room had been either gilded or inlaid—or both. *A kennel of one's own*, thought Cat.

"Mesdames, this is the Eurydice Suite. It has three bedrooms. Mademoiselles Ono and Bonner, you will be sharing a very nice bath; Mademoiselle Beale, you will be in the pink room. This suite is the crown jewel of Hôtel Le Narcisse. It is done in a Charles X style, the penultimate king of France. Follow me, please."

He brought Cat and Bess to the first of their adjoining rooms, painted an opulent royal blue with a canopied king bed. "Mesdames, in here?" They peeked into the enormous wood-paneled closet and marble bath that adjoined it with its exact twin, another king bedroom done in green, then nodded enthusiastically.

"I'll go green," Cat said, walking through to the other side.

"Very good. Mademoiselle Beale, follow me," the concierge continued.

Bess kicked off her shoes, hopped up on the blue bed, and started jumping. Cat saw her and laughed. "Get down!" she yelled. "He's gonna catch you!"

Bess winked, bounced up and down a few more times, then sprang onto the floor. "Come on," she said, running into the green room, grabbing Cat's hand and leading her into the marble bath. She climbed fully clothed into the empty tub, a Jacuzzi-sized marble pool that could easily seat six, facing the domes of Sacré-Coeur through the window.

"I'm going to pass out in here later," she declared. "This is ridiculous."

Cat sat on the tub's edge, picking up bottles of bath products by Panacea, a boutique brand from the UK. They each uncapped one labeled "Tangerine Dream" and breathed in the bright scent.

"I was hoping we might get upgraded, but I never imagined this," Bess said.

At that moment, the little concierge appeared again, perching at the door and clearing his throat loudly. "Mesdames, what can we get for you?"

"A full breakfast for three, please," Bess ordered before Cat could get in a "Rien, merci." "Coffee, juice, pastries, fruit, everything you can put together, and some champagne as well. Thank you."

He nodded. "Someone will be back with that right away, mesdames. Enjoy your stay." And with that, he backed out of the space and disappeared.

"Bess, we just had breakfast on the plane," Cat chided.

Bess rolled her eyes. "I'm on jet-lag hours. I can't control it. Besides, it's exhausting being us, and Margot's paying for everything. Let's order lobster and steak and caviar later when we're drunk." She jumped out of the tub, yelling, "Molly! Where'd you go?"

Cat wandered through the suite, marveling at the chef's kitchen, the dressing room, the beautifully appointed living room, and the foyer. She found doors leading onto the enormous private terrace, a wraparound 360-degree platform from which she could see all of Paris. It was so opulent and sumptuous that Cat half expected to see Caesar wander out of the kitchen and vomit into a velvet bag. She gazed down at the Tuileries, the gardens that were the centerpiece of Paris Fashion Week, and took in the crowds of fashionable people milling along its wide paths and circular ponds. Even the tourists looked good from up here.

Paris was home to the ten official members of the Chambre Syndicale de la Haute Couture, most of whom would be presenting their prêt-à-porter lines in the various palaces surrounding the Tuileries, so-called ready-to-wear collections that would be snapped up by buyers for stores like Barneys, Bergdorf's, Ikram, and Harrods. *RAGE* would cover as many of them as they could. Cat, in addition to making front-row appearances at the shows and presentations, would try to negotiate exclusive image rights to some of the dresses for upcoming shoots, while Paula met with their European audit team for the annual assessment of various local labor practices. Their first required appearance was tonight, at a dinner catered in the Tuileries on behalf of Cy Bianco, an American jeweler who had relocated to Paris in 1994. Tomorrow they would attend a luncheon for LVMH, which was an unofficial presentation for an up-and-coming designer from Algeria, and then prep the shoot; Thursday morning they'd be up bright and early to shoot **Bridle**. Then: Fashion Week. It was overwhelming.

Bess wandered out onto the terrace. Molly followed and immediately positioned the women against the edge of the terrace for a Photogram of Cat and Bess with the Eiffel Tower in the background. Bess grinned and jumped up in the air for the shot; Cat pulled down her sunglasses and glared. Bess captioned it, #goodgirlbess & #badgirlcat have landed...on your shoulder, PARIS! who wants to show us around?? before tagging the hotel and uploading it to the *RAGE* feeds. Within minutes there were thousands of replies in dozens of languages.

"Let's go out," Cat suggested. "I need a walk and some fresh air."

"What about breakfast?" Bess asked.

"Let Molly eat it. We can grab something as we walk."

"Sure," Bess agreed, grabbing her handbag. "I'm game."

They left Molly behind to unpack their bags; all the clothes for their upcoming events would need to be steamed and hung out before their first appearance that evening. Bess and Cat spent the next four hours, their only real free time on the entire trip, walking in a triangle to the east and back. They strolled through the Marais and the Bastille toward Place de la République; down cobblestone alleys and big crowded high streets, taking in the people and the clothing and the stores, the air and the noise and the smells, both good and bad. Their Photogram feeds kept lighting up with suggestions from fans the world over—stop here, stop there, you're close to my favorite store in the world—and they happily followed as many of the tips as they could. A small crop of photographers kept pace, staying ahead of them and just behind as they entered shop after shop; but they didn't mind—this way they never had to pay for anything at all.

Five minutes after they walked back through the door of the Eurydice Suite, their two local makeup artists for the week arrived.

Bibi and Edith—two little brunettes with skin so clear and hair so stylishly filthy that Cat immediately trusted them—rolled in with huge suitcases of product chatting a mile a minute about how much they loved *RAGE*. Half of their sentences were in French or *verlan*, a kind of inverted Parisian slang, the other half in extremely broken English, and they descended on Cat and Bess with a fury.

Bibi rubbed Cat's head like it was a bowling ball, smiling broadly and cracking her gum. Edith started pulling on the ends of Bess's hair and poked her earlobes, then lit a cigarette without bothering to look around for an ashtray.

"I love it," Bibi said to Cat in halting English, her accent thick as cheese. "Votre crâne est un rêve." (Your skull is a dream.)

"Merci, eh?" Cat replied automatically, her accent perfect. "Mes cheveux étaient le cauchemar." (My hair was the nightmare.) Cat signaled Molly for an ashtray. Bibi and Edith squealed.

"Thank fucking Christ," they replied in French simultaneously.

"Our English is so bad," Edith said, with relief and absolutely no embarrassment. "We didn't know if you spoke French. We were so worried."

Bibi nodded her head and took a drag of Edith's cigarette. "Let's talk details. What are you thinking for tonight?"

"I don't even care. Let me just hop in the shower," Cat volunteered. "I need ten minutes. You can choose," she said, pointing to the area where Molly had been diligently steaming and hanging potential outfits. Edith pursed her lips and sighed.

"Okay, we'll figure something out."

"Should I get in the other shower? Do you guys want me to wash my hair?" Bess asked Bibi and Edith, who screamed "NON!" in reply.

"This is Paris; clean hair is for ugly people," Edith followed up in her broken English. "Just a . . . " She gestured, at a loss for the words, pointing to Bess's armpits. "When you make a quick soaping? For the efficiency?" Suddenly, the answer dawned on her. "Whore! Whore's bath! Yes? You understand?"

"Yes." Bess laughed. "It's my favorite kind. I'll be right back."

Edith gave her a thumbs-up, then lit a fresh cigarette off the old one and dropped the butt in the nearest vase. Bibi cracked her gum again.

"New York City," Edith said in a fake John Wayne–style American accent as she stared at Molly's boiler suit, this one upgraded to a thick navy crepe from the mechanic's poly she'd worn a month ago. *Beale* was stitched on the pocket in elegant script. "She looks like a janitor, no?" to Bibi in French.

"They love that shit," Bibi pointed out. "They are obsessed with the proletariat. The men in New York look like dockworkers. Think about the jogging pant they're wearing. *Athleisure.* So silly. Crass."

Molly, who understood only "New York," "le jogging," and "athleisure," pointed to a stretchy silk crop top she'd selected that had a kind of athletic appeal.

"Non non non non non!" Edith snapped. "Opposite."

Molly held up an extremely small dress. Edith nodded. "Better," she said. "Comfortable doesn't look good."

"Beauty is, how you say, full of pain," Bibi insisted.

Molly nodded in reply, though she wasn't entirely sure anymore that this was true.

Chapter Seventeen

Lou Lucas perched on the edge of a green metal chair in the Tuileries Gardens, yellow dust clinging to her platform Skechers, and watched the entrance of Hôtel Le Narcisse through her birding binoculars. She wore huge plastic sunglasses, a cheap straw fedora from Canal Street, and a sweatshirt depicting a cartoon of a tabby cat sitting on the Golden Gate Bridge over tight bedazzled jeans, along with brown lipstick and chipped pink nail polish.

She had gone incognito.

Despite the hordes of photographers stalking the square kilometer around her, she hadn't been—thus far—noticed by anyone at all, not even other tourists. She sipped from a venti Starbucks paper cup with "double caramel latte whip" written on the side, though it held plain black coffee without sugar or milk; her zip-top plastic tote bag, emblazoned with a rhinestone version of the Eiffel Tower, had "La Vie en Rose" written on it with purple glitter. *Yes*, she thought, fingering the tacky rhinestone rings she'd picked up at the airport, *it's as good as wearing an invisibility cloak.*

The November issue would land on the doorsteps of their subscribers in ten days and on newsstands in two weeks; slightly late, but better late than never. Not a single person had seen the complete article, save for Margot, Paula, and Courtney Sacks in Legal, all of whom had seemed fully satisfied by Lou's hard work.

Luckily, no one else seemed to care about November at all; they'd written it off completely after Callie died, and now the entire *RAGE* staff was far too caught up packing for their trip to Paris. All thirty of them would arrive here the following night, to see the shows and sights on Margot's dime.

It won't take long, she told herself, *for everything to start falling into place.* The November story really was the most salacious thing she'd ever read in her life. She could barely believe she'd written it. The words had come out practically in a dream. She'd never felt so empowered.

Lou pulled a vanilla-flavored Ensure out of her purse, inserted a straw, and consumed her lunch with the birding binoculars still pressed to her face. She watched hordes of socialites pour into the entrance of Le Narcisse. *No*, she thought, *it wouldn't be long now.*

She drained the can with a loud throttling noise, threw it and the straw toward the nearest trash can, then felt the sudden lethargy of digestion take over. Eager to combat the unwelcome fatigue, she took out her hand cream and rubbed it vigorously into her papery skin. Her heartbeat increased and her lethargy disappeared. She put on her headphones, selected Wagner from her playlist, and let the music wash through her as she continued her stakeout.

Detective Mark Hutton, camped out in his office, rifled through the final set of boxes of New York State filings, all of them filled with tax ID numbers associated with Bedford Organics, LLC.

Bedford Organics' annual tax returns had—as expected—listed the shareholders as a set of shell corporations. After filing a request for the returns of those companies, and then the companies that made up those companies, and the companies that made up *those* companies, Hutton was finally getting close to the center of the matryoshka doll, though now he faced almost a thousand corporations that had been somehow associated with Bedford Organics. He still marveled at the fact that Cardoso had run it as a legitimate entity; without Cat's involvement, no one would have ever looked twice at what seemed to be a law-abiding, tax-paying small business. Vittoria had hidden in plain sight. He was hoping everyone else who'd owned shares in the LLC had done the same.

The biggest money, he reasoned, would have been the start-up capital. That's what Hutton was *really* looking for.

He'd instructed the team of junior FBI agents tasked with aiding his document review to look for three things: One, a corporation that owned shares in multiple entities leading back to Bedford Organics, LLC. Two, an incorporation date that was similar to that of Bedford Organics. Three, a New York City address. He was certain the start-up money was local. It had to be, since the business had run only on word of mouth.

Only a few dozen corporations fit his requirements thus far. They had sixteen more boxes to go.

He poured himself another cup of coffee and got back to work.

As Bibi put the finishing touches on her eyeliner, Cat found herself feeling drowsy. She was stunned at how powerful the jet lag seemed to be on this trip. After getting out of the shower she'd been overwhelmed by a combination of euphoria, nausea, and adrenaline; balancing on the edge of the tub, she'd primed her airplane-dry skin with lotion and tried to pull herself together. But the longer she sat in this stuffy hotel room, with Bibi's cigarette smoke and the scent of burning hair coming from Edith's straightener, the sicker she felt.

Cat stood up and darted toward the terrace. "I just need some fresh air," she yelled in French, throwing open the doors and lying down on the nearest patio lounger. She closed her eyes and let the sounds of Paris come up around her. Her head was swimming. The light was starting to take on the pink tinge of the city's iodine-tinted streetlights as dusk fell on the streets around the Tuileries, and she blinked weakly, feeling as though the light were moving through her.

Bess stood up and walked out to Cat, who was practically passed out. "What do you need, Kit-Kat?" she asked sympathetically. "Have you eaten enough today?"

"I had toast and that *pain aux raisins*," Cat replied.

"That was hours ago. I'm gonna order you something," Bess said decisively, walking toward the Dalí lobster phone that had been placed on top of the piano. She punched in a zero.

"Hello," she said in French, "I would like some steaks, rare please, with salad and bottles of fizzy water. Yes, as soon as possible. Thank you."

"Maybe I need a cigarette," Cat wondered aloud.

Bibi handed her a Gauloises Blonde, lighting it with a plastic Bic adorned with the phrase "*Don't Stop the Party*." She pulled up a chair.

"Edith and I have made a very good look for you tonight," she announced in her broken English. "Ready?"

Cat nodded in reply. Bibi held out her compact, a weighty gold disk lined with mother-of-pearl, and snapped it open loudly.

Cat gasped. Bibi had managed to elongate her lashes, brows, and eyes without any makeup lines appearing at all, and her lips had been stained a brownish mauve, but the color almost looked natural—there was no trace of product. Her skin was whiter and smoother than ever, as though they'd been able to sandblast and bleach it into perfection.

"Bibi, it's so French!" she exclaimed.

"No-makeup makeup," Bibi replied proudly. "But with a little bit of this monarchy shit"—she gestured toward the suite's Charles X decor—"thrown on top. White face, dark lips, like Marie Antoinette."

Bibi looked at her watch. "Time to get dressed," she said force-fully, clearly accustomed to corraling temperamental clotheshorses. She stubbed out the cigarette and dragged Cat back inside the suite.

"You better go to the toilet," Edith commanded them both. "It might be your last chance."

While Cat sat in the bathroom, she idly coated her fingers in the beautiful, thick eucalyptus-scented hand cream that had been placed on the back of the toilet. *I'm getting old*, Cat thought. *I need to start taking better care of myself when I travel.* She rifled through her cosmetics bag and chewed half an Adderall, hoping the am-phetamines would jump-start her lethargic body. As if by magic or psychosomatic expectation, she felt an immediate boost.

When she returned from the bathroom, Cat was unceremoni-ously squeezed into a hateful rubber bodice, to lift what was left of her breasts and smooth over the rocky vertebrae of her back, the sharp angles of her hipbones. After that she was stitched into an astonishingly tight dove-gray suede dress that ended mid-calf, the neckline laser-cut in triangle shapes, as though it had been hemmed with the world's biggest pinking shears. Bibi fitted Cat's feet into bleach-white patent leather stilettos, while Edith pinched Bess into an ecru minidress—made of the same fine suede as Cat's dress—that barely covered her buttcheeks. Bess's long legs ended in a pair of sculpted greige suede open-toe heels, held fast to her an-kles with nearly invisible PVC straps.

As Cat stared into the gilded mirror they'd dragged into the liv-ing room, she wanted to laugh at the irony of it all: *I'm completely fucking immobilized, a dictator's mistress, tits pouring out of my dress, everything I always hated.*

But after a moment passed, Cat didn't laugh after all. The look was part Antwerp avant-garde and part real-life princess. *If only twelve-year-old Cat could see me now*, she thought, remembering the stings of adolescence, *she'd be so excited to grow up.*

Bibi drew a seam on the backs of Bess's legs, as though it were the 1940s and stockings were scarce, while Edith picked out their jewelry: piles of gold and diamond necklaces made by Cy Bianco, the designer being honored at tonight's dinner. She piled them first onto Bess, and then Cat. The necklaces felt like a pair of reins looped around her neck. As they walked to the door, the bell rang: their steaks had finally arrived. "Right away" in France meant at least an hour.

"Shit," Bess exclaimed. "I don't know if there will actually be *food* at this dinner. Do you want to eat before we go?"

"I'll eat when I'm dead," Cat said dismissively. "Let's just get this over with."

Chapter Eighteen

Still at the precinct, Hutton was just finishing a late lunch of cold takeout from a Styrofoam package, blindly shoveling forkfuls into his mouth between opening file folders. His hard work was paying off: there was only one more box to go through. He cut it open with a penknife and tossed out the folders to the four junior FBI agents who had spent their entire morning in his office.

"Read carefully," he said before picking up the pile of possibles. "I'm going to get started."

He read through the deliberately vaguely named corporations, one by one.

CostCompany Limited. Version Holdings Inc. Spatula Fork Productions. Triangle Limited. Brown Jones Inc. Lilac Futures Limited. Creative Solution Company. IdeaPark. Twentieth Street Limited.

It went on and on; they all seemed the same. He pulled up the spreadsheet that cross-referenced the companies in his pile with those they'd already examined, a document he'd spent the last ten weeks compiling. It had been aggressively tedious, but gut instinct told him it would eventually pay off.

Sorting by column gave him three companies that owned the most shares in what would eventually be Bedford Organics, LLC. Suddenly, a name caught his eye.

Donal Windsor, Esquire, a partner at Cavendish Crane and Vittoria Cardoso's attorney, had been the registered agent for the original formation of Lilac Futures: a New York State Limited Liability Company located at 1131 Broadway, apartment 2250. He punched the address into his computer and found the website for a large rental complex.

He picked up his cellphone and dialed.

"Detective Hutton," Betty Cormorant yelled into the phone. "Whatcha got?"

"Fifth Avenue, two-bedroom. But I need another favor first," he told her.

"You're a real pain in the ass, you know that?"

He laughed. "I know."

Hutton fell asleep on the precinct's plastic sofa waiting for the records to appear, but he woke up in the middle of the night to find them in his in-box. When he finally found the name of the applicant, he almost threw the computer across the room: James Burton, Esquire. Employer: Cavendish Crane.

Hutton typed the man's name into his computer and found, as expected, that he worked as a senior associate and had litigated alongside Donal Windsor. It was an ouroboros, an endless loop of scales and vertebrae made from corporations and lawyers and lawyers and corporations, processing their secrets into dust, until there was nothing left to find. Still: there was one legal route left in his playbook. He picked up the phone, dialed the IRS, and started the process of recalling every single form that had ever been filed in relation to the profits of Lilac Futures.

Two hours into the sit-down dinner, Cat was finally starting to feel *good*. The Adderall had kicked in, you could smoke cigarettes inside the tent, and there was a seemingly inexhaustible supply of Louis

Roederer Brut in generous, bell-bottomed flutes. There still, however, wasn't any food—not that she cared. *Food was for the birds.* She
downed glass number four in a swallow, grabbed glass number five
from a tray, and teetered mincingly toward the dance floor where
a live band had started playing Louis Armstrong covers with lots
of verve—then stopped, aghast. The band was in *blackface*, something she hadn't realized from across the room. ·The whites of their
crooked smiles gleamed unnaturally behind the heavy black paint
coating their faces. She backed away quickly and prayed that they
could get out of here before this got online.

She scanned the room for Bess and spotted her surrounded by
a crowd of admirers in the corner. Cat tried very hard to remain
upright as she made her way over.

"Bess," she hissed. "The band has *blackface* makeup on. We have
to go."

"Oh, c'est génial, eh? Comme Josephine Baker!" said an idiotic
woman who overheard her.

"No, it's not *génial*," Cat snapped. "We have to go *right now*."

Bess turned around and stared at the band. "Wow," she said simply. "I honestly never thought I would see that in my entire life."

"Welcome to France," Cat explained, swaying slightly. "The
country where Galliano literally *praised Hitler* in the Jewish quarter and got a job running Margiela three years later." She
grabbed Bess for support. "*Fuck.* I think I had too much champagne."

"This way," Bess said, picking through the maze of raised cocktail tables toward a back entrance. "I keep seeing the waiters go out
here."

The two women brushed through a narrow hallway filled with
plastic crates and made their way past a set of heavy polyester curtains before finding themselves ejected into a small dirt circle filled
with cigarette butts and diesel generators.

"Shit," Bess said, seeing no way out. "Let's try cutting through
the kitchen."

She grabbed Cat's hand and led her through another maze of crates into the party's makeshift kitchen, where the cooking staff whooped and whistled at their arrival.

"Merci, au revoir," Cat slurred.

"You're really fucked up, Cat," Bess said, yanking her through the kitchen. They finally found a side exit closed off by another set of heavy curtains. Cat nodded, her brown eyes closing without permission. Bess looked around quickly and pulled the curtains shut. She pointed to the nearest plastic crate.

"Catherine Celia Ono, I order you to barf your brains out into that box before anyone sees you."

"Nooo," Cat whined, almost crying. "I can't. I hate throwing up *so much.*"

Bess spun her around, and before Cat knew what was happening, Bess had shoved her manicured fingers right down Cat's throat. Cat gagged and vomited right into the plastic crate.

"See?" Bess said kindly. "That wasn't so bad." She searched for a clean section of curtain and wiped the tears off Cat's face. "Okay. Ready?"

"I hate you," Cat replied, her voice soft and not very mean at all.

"I know," Bess answered, laughing. "But you'll be thanking me in twenty minutes." She checked Cat's face, straightened their dresses, and flung the curtain open. The two women made a mad dash for the nearest hedge, but after ten seconds of walking as quickly as their heels would allow, they both came to a stop. There was no point in rushing. Not a single person was waiting on this side of the tent—all the hubbub was at the front of the party, where Cy Bianco had just arrived. Bess looked around for the park's green metal chairs, and pulled two up behind a hedge to shield them from the rest of the garden, just in case.

Cat lit a cigarette. She was starting to feel a teensy bit better, though her right toe was numb from the pressure of the narrow stilettos Bibi had jammed her into. She stood up and started walking, slowly at first, then found her stride near the end of the hedge they'd been hiding behind, and turned back to look for Bess, who was still in the chair and hunched over her phone.

"I'm ready," Cat pointed out, gesturing to her upright body. "You were correct on the barfing front. Let's go back to the hotel." She leaned against the prickly hedge, its sharp leaves pressing their pointy, waxy angles into her skin.

"Fuck that," Bess said. "We need to have our picture taken somewhere before that disgusting blackface shows up on Mania." She held up her phone to Cat; notifications lit the screen one after another. "We've been invited to a hundred parties. Pick one," Bess insisted, her speech rushed, like she couldn't quite get the words out quickly enough.

"Great idea," Cat agreed slowly, tapping her cigarette's inch-long ash dramatically onto the gravel. The little gray log fell to the ground perfectly intact, like the molted skin of a snake. Cat wanted to step it into nothingness but after staring at it for a few beats decided to let the wind erode it. They scrolled through the invites before they found one from a group of mimes begging Cat and Bess to come join them a few blocks away, in an afterparty for Jonathan Sprain's runway show, held on the fifth floor of an empty office building.

"That's the one," Cat said happily, while Bess summoned a car. They snuck down the line of hedges and out of the gardens before tumbling into a waiting Mercedes.

Paula Booth sat in the lobby bar of Le Narcisse, nursing a glass of wine and working away on her laptop on the final layout of the November issue. She frowned as her finger hovered over the Return button, then let out a long breath.

A mousy-haired woman to her left who had been trying unsuccessfully to signal the bartender turned, mistaking Paula's sigh for an expression of exasperated camaraderie.

"Am I doing something wrong?" she asked Paula plaintively in English.

Paula looked at the woman, who wore a huge bead necklace, a tweed blazer, and brown jersey trousers over a pair of orthopedic clogs. "It's Fashion Week," she explained. "They're trying to take care of all the people who are here on corporate accounts."

"My corporate card is as good as anyone else's," the woman scoffed. "Note to self: France is exactly as expected."

"Is this your first time here?" Paula asked. Something about the woman—she was so plain, but she had eyes like a hawk—reminded Paula of what she must have looked like once upon a time, during her own first visit to Paris, and she felt sympathy, maybe even empathy for her: a pair of feelings that bubbled up into Paula Booth's consciousness very, *very* rarely.

"Is it that obvious?" The woman sighed, her middle-aged hands, pale and soft, holding the beads on her necklace. "I'm chaperoning my daughters."

"What do you normally do?" Paula asked, trying to engage her on a positive subject.

"I'm a college professor," the woman said flatly. "Experimental chemistry."

"Experimenting in what?"

"Fluid dynamics, propulsion, that kind of thing."

"You're . . . a rocket scientist."

"Well," the woman said, a smile appearing on her face, "we don't say it exactly like that. But, yes. Among other things."

"You must be horrified at this whole spectacle," Paula said, gesturing to the scene around her.

The woman laughed. "It's not what I wanted for my children. But they want what they want."

"Let me help you," Paula said, signaling to the bartender with a flick of her fingers. "Treat them like servants—the French worship *hauteur*. What are you drinking?"

"What are *you* drinking?"

"I was drinking wine, but I'd change to something stronger. Scotch?"

"Absolutely."

Paula ordered two double Laphroaigs, neat, in her imperfect but forceful French. The bartender complied almost immediately, and moments later the two women held matching tumblers.

"Thank you," the woman said, holding her glass up to Paula's.

"To your children," Paula said. They each downed an enormous swallow of scotch.

"You love them and all they do is disappoint you," the woman said wryly. "Do you have any?"

Paula raised an eyebrow. "No. It didn't work out that way."

"I have *four*. Enough for both of us. Cheers." The women clinked glasses again and another shot went down the hatch, their tumblers now nearly empty. Paula signaled for a refill.

"Are all of your children here this week?" Paula asked.

"No, no. Just the two oldest."

"What agency are they with?"

"Agency?" the woman asked, confused. "They have a small business."

And it suddenly dawned on Paula with whom she was speaking. "You're Dr. Bishop."

"Yes," the woman said, looking frustrated by the recognition. "I don't speak for them," she said quickly, shaking her head. "I'm just their mother."

"You're more than that," Paula replied. "You're on the board."

"Yes," the woman said uncertainly. "What outlet are you with?"

"I'm not a reporter," Paula explained. "I'm Paula Booth. I'm Margot Villiers's deputy at *RAGE*."

A very large silence descended between them as the name sank in. Paula let a beat pass before she extended a palm, her boardroom manners irrepressible in any situation. "It's very nice to meet you," she said genuinely. "I'm sure I don't need to tell you how impressive Mania is."

Dr. Bishop shook her hand with an enthusiasm that Paula hadn't expected. "And I don't need to tell *you* how influential *RAGE* has been," she replied immediately. "It's an honor to meet you. Of course I know your name. You've been the coauthor of what, forty-five white papers on the garment industry?" she gushed.

"A lot of that work is done by our lobbyists. I've only been the catalyst," Paula said graciously. "But . . . it's been my whole life." She gestured to her own outfit, a simple knee-length black tunic and polished boots. "I'm not much of a fashionista."

"You don't need to downplay your work to *me*. I'm in the chemistry department," Dr. Bishop explained, "but at UCLA I work with the Future Materials Institute. It's basically rocket science meets survivalism. We've used a great deal of data from *RAGE* to support our studies."

"I'm glad you've found value in it," Paula said, throwing back her drink as the bartender approached her with the bottle. "It might not be around much longer." He filled her glass back up to the top.

"What do you mean?" Dr. Bishop pointed to her own drink.

"I mean that your children are putting *RAGE* out of business." Paula tried not to sound bitter, just matter-of-fact.

"My children aren't doing that. The market is." Dr. Bishop could be matter-of-fact, too.

"Only because this generation fundamentally doesn't understand the distinction between editorial and advertorial," Paula snapped.

"Maybe, but who can actually tell the difference?" Dr. Bishop asked. "I mean that sincerely. It all has the same breathless promotional quality—'Buy this product; buy into this idea.'"

"The difference," Paula insisted carefully, "is that we've always made sure our breathless editorial copy was *truthful*."

"Truth and transparency are different things," Dr. Bishop

replied, surprising Paula with her candor. "Look, if I've learned anything from what my children are doing, it's that this generation considers it an *honor* to be chosen by a brand—to them, a brand is a business that somebody built, put their blood, sweat, and tears into. Young people *value* entrepreneurs. They don't need an editorial middleman to tell them what's okay and what's not. They want to choose, to be the curators themselves, actively and publicly building their own taste profile."

"You're saying that young people don't want to just imagine themselves being rich people; they want to *be* rich people," Paula said, thinking out loud.

"They want the same things your editors want, except by connecting brands directly to consumers, Mania is completely transparent where *RAGE* is not. My kids argue that transparency is the *new medium* of media. Print, digital, it doesn't matter. Honesty is the future," she insisted. "Companies like yours are in bed with every advertiser that's ever cut you a check and you know it—the difference is that you've been able to layer it in so many yards of privilege that you thought nobody could tell."

"I suppose we labored under the assumption that the audience valued our privilege and held us to a corresponding moral standard," Paula replied thoughtfully. "Let me ask you a question: How will your audience ultimately ensure that the products Mania promotes really are, as you say, local, ethical, and radical—'ethical' being the key word here. *Whose ethics?*"

"The market has taken care of that. Ethical manufacturing is a *requirement* now. You saw to that," Dr. Bishop said confidently.

Paula nearly spit out her drink. "The second that we go out of business and I personally stop visiting factories and bullying retailers and manufacturers, that ends. Have you ever *been* to a garment factory? This isn't academia—there are no moral actors in this business. There's just me and there's Margot, and we've had to behave like fascists to get things done our way. Pardon the comparison."

"I've never been to any kind of factory," Dr. Bishop admitted.

"But how quickly can labor conditions possibly change? The workers wouldn't allow it. This is the twenty-first century. That's what *transparency* is all about."

"Transparency is subjective. Let me show you." The November issue would have to wait: this woman had a billion dollars in the pocket of her Chico's jacket. Paula knocked back the remainder of her drink and summoned a car.

Cat leaned against a bookcase on the fifth floor of a desperately tacky eighties-era office building while the loud, sticky mob of the party swarmed around her. A tall mime, his face painted white and lips painted red, offered her a small bag of white powder.

"Turtally," she murmured happily, assuming it was cocaine and hoping it would sober her up. She snorted some up her nose while Bess, sitting across from her in the laps of two other mimes, sipped from a plastic cup.

Someone passed Cat a drink; she drank it.

Someone grabbed her hand and brought her out onto the dance floor; she danced. An orange-bearded man wearing a Carolina Panthers Starter jacket was in the center of the room, playing two keyboards, and everyone was jumping and screaming in his direction. Cat closed her eyes, raised her arms, and let herself fall in with the crowd.

Somebody else's sweat coated her arms.

Somebody else's hair whipped into her mouth.

Someone, a mime, maybe the tall one, kissed her, and she kissed them back.

Her heart sped up, and up, and up, and the mime carried her to the side of the room, where they made out in a long-empty plastic cubicle. She felt breasts that weren't her own under her palms, which made her laugh, until the mime pushed up against her, so she stopped laughing, the whole thing a mess of damp skin and pulsing lights and speakers so loud that she felt the bass in her bones.

"Cat!" she heard Bess screaming from somewhere far away. "Your tits are out!"

"Great! Let's be *free*," Cat cried out.

"Pull up your dress!"

Cat looked up and saw a phone pointed at her. *Dammit*. She peeled the mime off her body and hoiked her dress up as far as it would go. The mime smiled happily and danced back into the crowd.

"I want to be in bed," Bess yelled over the music. "Can we go?"

Cat stood up and immediately swayed sharply to the right. Bess caught her. "I'm taking that as a yes," she said, dragging Cat out of the building and wedging her into another waiting Mercedes.

Inside the car, Cat looked disoriented. "I think something was in my drink," she mumbled. "I should not be this fucked up."

"You whiffed some Molly, Cat, that'll do it," Bess insisted.

"Oh . . . whoops. But not *that* much," Cat said as she slumped into the seat.

When they pulled up to the hotel, two photographers waited outside. Inside the privacy of the car's blackout windows, Bess slapped Cat hard across the face. "Wake up!" she snapped. "Walk straight back to the little gold elevator. You can do it."

Cat nodded. She managed to walk through the lobby without falling, but her dress was covered in the mime's handprints and her face was smeared with lipstick, so the men took her photo with obvious delight. When they got up to the Eurydice Suite, Bess dragged Cat into the bathroom and dumped her onto the floor of the shower, turning on the water and forcing Cat to wash off the paint with the hotel's bodywash before drawing a bath for herself and doing the same. But the water didn't make Cat feel better—only worse. She felt something rise up in her throat and vomited for the second time that night, onto the shower's tiled marble floor.

"Cat! Are you okay?" Bess shouted from the bathtub across the room.

Cat raised herself up and pushed the vomit toward the drain with her fingers.

"I'll be fine," she insisted. "I feel much better now." Cat stood up, rinsed herself clean, and grabbed a towel. It was warm and fluffy and soft.

"I have the worst headache of my entire life," Bess complained as she climbed out of the tub. Cat nodded in agreement, her skull crackling with pain, like she'd been hit with a hammer. Yet, somehow, both women managed to stumble onto their silk beds, piled high with duvets and heavy goose-down pillows.

"Night, Cat," Bess called out, half under her sheets.

"Night, Bess," Cat called back.

When they fell asleep, it was straight into a black hole.

Chapter Nineteen

olly Beale stood over Cat's bed, panicking.

Cat was facedown in a pile of pillows, a towel wrapped haphazardly around her naked body. Bess was passed out cold in her own room. Their two beautiful suede dresses (on loan to *RAGE* from the designers) were soaking wet, covered in paint, and discarded on the bathroom floor, completely ruined. Molly tried shaking Cat. Nothing.

She grabbed a remote and hit Play. Emerson, Lake, and Palmer's "Hoedown" blasted as loudly as the suite's speaker system would allow.

Bess bolted out of bed first. "Oh my god, oh my god, make it stop," she screamed, until she saw Molly, at which point she laughed weakly and grabbed a sheet. But Cat still wouldn't budge. Molly turned the music off. She dug in her handbag for a compact and held it under Cat's nose; it fogged up, but barely.

"Something's wrong with Cat," she said to Bess, her voice shaking with fear. "She won't wake up."

"Oh my god," Bess said, running toward her friend's apparently lifeless body. Molly raised her hand to slap Cat and her palm connected, *hard*, but Cat still didn't stir; the only change was a faint red mark on her cheek. Bess ran to the bathroom and filled a tumbler with cold water, dumping it on Cat's head. Still: *nothing*.

"Call an ambulance," she told Molly, still shaking Cat. "Call one right now."

As Molly picked up the phone, Cat finally rolled over and pulled her towel up. "I'm awake," she said groggily. "I'm fine."

Lou Lucas, wedged on a plastic folding chair next to the rented apartment's lead-paned windows, scowled through her binoculars. They hadn't left the hotel all day. Had she gone too far? *No. They'll still be ruined tomorrow*, she told herself. It wouldn't be like them to skip tonight's event. Even if they had the mother of all hangovers, Cat and Bess would try to get out, she was certain.

She stood up and looked around the apartment, a high-ceilinged attic space with broad beams and thick plaster walls that she'd found online. From this aerie set high on the hill of Montmartre and facing the river, she could see all of Paris and its tangled mess of alley-sized streets. Copper windows winked in the sun, terra-cotta chimneys popped up by the hundreds, and colorful laundry lines stretched all around her, their bounty swaying gently in the breeze, while horns honked, teenagers laughed, and smoke drifted up from cafés. It was positively cheerful. Lou forced herself to be optimistic.

This time next week, she told herself sternly, *you'll have everything you want*. A bit tricky, to be sure. But everything that was truly valuable had to be earned. Nobody would *give* those things to you. You simply had to do what everyone else did: take it by force.

An exhausted Cat, propped up on the dirty steps in front of the Paris Opera, tried to stay awake as they waited for the Phoebe show, an unofficial presentation by an upstart local brand, to begin. She'd been sewn into a long column from Albert V., made from a blend of vicuña—a Peruvian wool so fine that it came in only one color, a nutty golden tone—and ivory artificial bee silk grown in a lab at MIT, and she strained at the discomfort of the tight stitching. A single rope of emeralds hung from her neck and looped down her back; she wore no other jewelry, carried no bag. Her fingers had been varnished with flakes of real rose gold. With her bloodless face coated in a snowy powder and her lips painted the palest of blush tones, Cat was a gift fit for a king.

Behind her, a perky Bess, her hair clean and worked into a braided updo by Edith, twirled for the cameras in a taffeta affair whose knife pleats lifted and separated to reveal themselves as the world's thickest fringe. An underlay of dreamy gossamer floated beneath. She smiled and giggled for the cameras until they suddenly stopped, the photographers' attentions dissipating as quickly as they'd arrived. Cat blinked in confusion while a commotion flared up rapidly in the street. Bess's face fell.

Two of the four founders of Mania had arrived, Keira Bishop and her identical twin, Karoline. Until now, the only photos of the Mania team on their own map were usually based in their office, plain and casual Photograms taken while they sat at their computers. This was the girls' first public appearance.

The twins wore matching pleated dresses in pastel shades that resembled upside-down flowers; the hems were sewn under to further emphasize the upended-tulip shape, and the oversized armholes revealed clear plastic bodices beneath. Their hair had been brushed out in huge disco curls and floated down their backs in big puffy clouds. Both girls wore real pink silk ballet slippers and walked *en pointe* with ease, flopping up and down and twirling as they walked into the opera.

Cat and Bess stood, openmouthed, and fell into the crowd that followed the two girls, who danced their way down the aisles and onto the stage. Everyone filed slowly into their seats while Keira and Karoline moved to the edges of the black stage. Nearly fifty models streamed from the wings and arranged themselves presentation-style, each one wearing ballet shoes and a variation on the looks sported by the Mania girls. The models didn't really look like *models*, though; they were muscled, and stringy, and short, and very *very* good at ballet.

"I think that's the corps," a surprised Bess whispered as they took their seats in the front row. Cat nodded. One of the Bishop girls caught her eye and winked. Cat smiled back; she couldn't help it. The girls were clearly so excited, and she felt a proxy of delight on their behalf.

Sounds came up from the orchestra pit: strains of violin, harp, piano, xylophone; blasts of trumpet, oboe, flute. Drums sputtered out a handful of heavy taps. When the entire audience was finally seated, the lights dimmed and the orchestra played a suite from *The Nutcracker*.

The ballerinas danced their way offstage one by one and through the crowd, passing by the front row and down through the aisles, each one taking a moment to solo onstage before leaping off again. The Bishop twins remained posed at the back of the stage, each standing perfectly still, like little robots.

A dozen cameramen wandered through the space, pointing their lenses and zooming. The show was probably being broadcast in real time on Mania, tags appending to the images of boldfaced names mere seconds after they appeared on-screen.

Then the room went pitch-black.

Cat felt a shiver run down her spine. Bess squeezed her hand.

A few moments passed before the ballerinas—still packed into the aisles—turned on flashlights previously hidden all around the theater. The corps performed the remainder of their dance, holding their own spotlights on one another, while the orchestra played with gusto in the background.

As Cat smoothed the impossibly soft fabric of her dress, as she watched the dancers, she immediately found herself wondering how much of a gain for Mania tonight would represent—and how much of a loss for *RAGE*.

I have to nail *tomorrow's shoot.* Cat felt the pressure with a deep certainty. Until now she'd dismissed Mania, thinking that their advertorial strategy didn't have half the magic *RAGE* produced in their editorials, but . . . they'd participated in a glorious spectacle that had been tasteful, creative, effortlessly coordinated, and, perhaps most importantly, wholly unmarketed in advance. They weren't desperate. At this moment, Mania was soaring toward the sun on their successes, while wretched *RAGE* tried to stiffen its own melting wings, the ground coming up beneath them in double time.

Sweat broke out under her armpits. She panicked, worrying about her career and the delicate fabric of the dress in equal measure. *What if this is how it will be for the rest of my life?* What if she got so far away from editorial work that she'd find herself begging for the appearance fees at energy drink launches, her assets dwindled and her fortunes reversed? What if, with each dress she put on, each RSVP she sent out, she was inadvertently scooping another shovelful of dirt out from under her own feet?

Cat didn't pay attention to the end of the performance; she smiled blankly, always, now, aware of the cameras lurking nearby. Bess pulled a container of the hotel's hand cream out of the handbag she'd hidden beneath the pleats of her dress and mindlessly rubbed it into the backs of her hands.

"Let's get out of here," Bess whispered as she dropped a dollop of the cream into Cat's palm. Cat nodded and felt her heartbeat rise again with pure panic. When the crowd stood to applaud the presentation, they edged toward the stage door and slipped out into the alleyway.

"Holy shit," Bess said. "I think I'm going to have a seizure. What a nightmare."

"I thought it was kind of genius," Cat replied.

"Are you serious?" Bess asked, her tone sharp. "That was ridiculous. That was designed for children with absolutely no attention span."

"Wow, tell me what you really think," Cat replied sarcastically.

"I think it was a spectacle. It didn't have any value."

"That's condescending," Cat snapped back.

Bess rolled her eyes. "You don't have to be rude about it. So we disagree. *Whatever.*"

"Look, I know we've had a long day," Cat said, "but you don't have to be mad."

"I'm just expressing what I actually think for once, Cat. You constantly bully me with your opinions. I'm finally expressing my own. *You're* the one who's being a . . . *bitch*," she hissed, the word falling between them like a bomb.

"Wow. *Bitch* . . . I didn't think we called anybody that, ever, especially not each other. *Fuck you very much, Bess*, because you have *everything*," Cat retorted, her voice edging on nasty as she jabbed her finger toward her best friend, counting each indignity: "You have a home, and a boyfriend, and a family who loves you. You don't need to have opinions."

Bess looked hurt and a little bit stunned before transitioning into total and complete shock. She looked into Cat's eyes.

"Are my pupils dilated?" she asked urgently.

Cat, annoyed and hurt, tried to walk away down the alley, carefully holding the hem of her dress above the pools of oil and gravel. "I don't know and I don't care."

"I'm serious," Bess yelled, chasing Cat down and grabbing her shoulder.

Cat stopped on a dime and looked at her friend, whose blue eyes were dominated by big, inky pupils. "Actually . . . yes."

"You too."

"We're high," they said at the same time.

Cat looked down at her $75,000 dress. "We'd better get back to the hotel," she said, "before I destroy this one, too."

Bess nodded and ordered a car. Ten minutes later, they snuck into the side entrance of the hotel, avoiding all the cameras. As far as the Mania map was concerned, Cat and Bess were still inside the Phoebe presentation.

Chapter Twenty

Hutton had been refreshing his email repeatedly for hours when a reply from the IRS finally appeared. There was only one Schedule K-1 that had been turned in for Lilac Futures, the taxes paid on time every year. The name wasn't familiar. He ran it through the database. Nothing. The junior FBI agents ran it through theirs.

"She's six years old," one of the agents said.

"Fuck," Hutton swore. That meant it was stolen. "You can go," he said to the agent, who nodded and disappeared. Hutton dropped his head to the desk and groaned, then went back to his computer and stared at the form. It took him a few minutes to notice the address associated with the child's name, but once he did, time stopped.

He noticed the flickering of the fluorescent tubes above him, their buzzing, the way the thick gray paint sat on the concrete walls, the beating of his own heart.

He felt a pressure build up, then remembered to inhale.

"It wasn't stolen," he said slowly to himself. "It was *borrowed*."

He darted out of his office, jumped into the nearest squad car, and threw it into gear. He looked at his watch. It was 3:00 p.m. He turned on his sirens and drove like a maniac, weaving in and out of traffic. When Hutton was just a few blocks from Cooper, he turned them off, double-parked on Thirty-Ninth, got out, and strolled confidently into the Cooper garage.

He smiled at the door attendant before flashing his badge. "Hi, I'm Mark," he said flirtatiously, standing a little too close. "My girlfriend Catherine Ono works on 46. Mind if I head up?" He took out his ID and handed it to her.

Gina couldn't help but smile right back at this tall, gorgeous man. "She didn't go to Paris?" she asked him. "That sucks."

"What?" he asked, confused.

"Oh," Gina said awkwardly. "Everybody's in Paris, for the shows. The whole magazine." She looked at him with pity.

Fuck. He wanted this arrest so badly he could taste it burning in his mouth like a handful of pennies, could feel it roiling in his stomach, next to his grief. He couldn't tell the FBI their suspect had left New York; they'd begin the extradition process and the case would be officially removed from his jurisdiction. He thanked Gina and walked back to his car.

He sat in the driver's seat, closed his eyes, and gave himself sixty seconds to meditate, allowing thoughts to move freely through his mind without judgment. When he'd counted to sixty, Hutton opened his eyes, sat up, opened his phone, and booked a ticket to Paris. On the way to the airport, he reinstalled Mania.

When they got up to the Eurydice Suite, Bess repurposed the cut-crystal vases in the kitchen into very large water glasses and filled them each with an entire bottle of Perrier. She picked up the lobster phone from the piano and ordered more steaks and salad, but this time appending a "rapidement, s'il vous plaît," sharply to the end.

"Tres bien, Bessoo," Cat said as she collapsed on the couch.

Bess flopped down next to her, grabbing a pillow and holding it in a hug. She checked her phone. "Molly's out on the town, I guess. How you feeling?"

Cat squinted one eye. "Not great. You?"

"I need to eat, I guess. Let's get out of these clothes." They cut each other out of their dresses and hung them up carefully in the closet.

"I'm gonna take another shower," Cat said. "Can you start making a list of who might have slipped us something?"

Bess nodded.

Cat stepped into the shower and felt nauseous. She reached for the open bodywash on the shelf but slipped and sent the tiny bottle flying. She gripped the door and steadied herself, then tried to uncap a second one without falling over. After a few tense moments, she managed to squeeze the scented gel into her palm. Cat nearly smeared it onto her body before her mind flooded with recognition. She *knew* this smell. It was the same scent that Vittoria had smeared on Cat's face not once but twice at Bedford Organics, the one that said "For Happiness" on the label. She let the gel fall out of her palm and down the drain.

The room spun, the water fell over her head, and she opened the shower door, focusing only on the three remaining sets of Panacea products scattered around the bathroom. She scooped them up in her arms and ran naked into the dining room.

"Bess!" she cried. "It wasn't our drinks. *It's Bedford Organics*," Cat exclaimed, tossing her the juniper bottle. "Smell that."

Bess uncapped it and recoiled in horror. "How is that possible?" she asked in amazement. "How did we not smell this already?"

"The ones we had before smelled like tangerine. Vittoria didn't use it on us," Cat said. "Who could have put this here?"

"Bibi? Edith?" Bess said.

"My instinct is no. Why would they want us to get sick?"

"Molly?!? She *wouldn't*. She loves us . . . doesn't she? Or . . . did she want us out of the way? Did she want to take over the shoot?"

"No...no," Cat insisted. "She worships us. I don't think she would harm us."

They sat there dumbfounded. Cat slumped onto the floor.

"I am so fucking high right now," she complained. "And so fucking tired. And so fucking hung over."

"I can't think right now either," Bess finally said, her head in her hands. "I need to eat something. Get dressed. I'll make coffee. The food is on the way."

Cat walked into the closet, pulling on the first clothes she found, black leggings and a white cotton T-shirt. She caught her reflection in the mirror. Her leggings were baggy and wrinkled—like when she was a child—and the shirt dwarfed her, her arms and neck poking out of the holes like wire hangers. Cat felt a rush of satisfaction at the sight of her emaciated frame. *I need help*, the rational part of her mind screamed. Another part sighed with happiness, telling itself *Now* that *is a textbook thigh gap*.

The doorbell rang. Cat marched over to the oversized wooden front door and opened it. A tiny waiter with a waxed mustache stood on the other side, pushing a wide cart loaded with silver-topped dishes. She ushered him in, and he laid out the plates rather ceremoniously, setting the table with fine linens and polished silver.

Bess immediately sat at the dining table, shoveling steak and salad into her mouth. "No excuses," she mumbled through a mouthful of meat. "You have to eat."

Cat rolled her eyes but sat down on the upholstered dining chair, crossing her legs underneath her. She plunged her knife into the fillet, its center so rare it glowed purple, and cut off a small piece. The beef felt fleshy, alive; when she put it in her mouth she nearly gagged, but she forced herself to swallow the bite—and the next, and the next, and the next after that.

Half a dozen bites later the steak was nearly gone. Cat found herself luxuriating over the peppery, winey fat coating the sides, and took forkfuls of salad in between the few final bites in order to sustain the meal. Bess pointed to the plate on the other side of the table.

"Go ahead," Bess said with evident joy. "I ordered that one for Molly, but she's obviously still out and about."

Cat stood up and walked around the table, where she sat down at the opposite seat and repeated the process, devouring Molly's steak with a pleasure she hadn't known for months. It was real food, not just a half-cup of rice consumed alone in her apartment with a dash of hot sauce. The blood from the meat drained down her throat, its fat melted on her tongue, and the salad leaves bloomed in her mouth; by the time she'd polished off the second plate, she felt alive for the first time in weeks—and deeply exhausted. Cat looked up and across the table. Bess smiled and popped a final bite of steak into her mouth like it was a piece of popcorn.

"So. Who drugged us?" Cat asked, her mind finally clear.

"Who else has access?" Bess responded.

"Who gains from hurting us," Cat said thoughtfully, "is maybe a better question. Hutton told me in the summer that solving a crime is about drilling down on the details. What would happen if we kept using all those products without knowing what's in them?" She opened a window and lit a cigarette.

"We'd ruin the shoot tomorrow," Bess said slowly. "Somebody else would have to take over."

"Who?"

They sat there for a moment while Cat smoked, each thinking to themselves, until they both spoke at the same time:

"*Lou*," they said together.

"Her ex-husband's company manages this hotel," Bess said. "She has access."

"I'm sure she thought this shoot was supposed to be hers," Cat realized. "She wants it back." She exhaled a long, thin stream of white smoke.

"But," Bess asked, "just to play devil's advocate here for a moment, is that really worth *poisoning* your coworkers? Let's be re-alistic. She has *so* much money. She doesn't have to work." She shook her head. "I agree that she wants you, both of us, out of the way. I'm sure she wants to take credit for our work. But I just don't understand *why*."

"Maybe it's not hers, you know? Rich people never have their own money. It's always tied up in investments and overseas accounts and whatever." Cat took a long drag of her cigarette and lit a fresh one from its burning embers.

"Lou *is* a permalancer," Bess replied thoughtfully. "It's basically like being an undocumented worker. That's certainly motivating. But if Lou knows October and November were both flops, why does she still think there's a staff job waiting at the end of the rainbow? Why is she *bothering* to come to Paris?"

"Because this is her *first job*," Cat realized. "She must not understand. *Nobody* in her family works. *None* of them. What is it they say on Lake Como: the grandfather starts the business, the father builds it, and the grandson goes snowboarding? Lou is a seventh-generation snowboarder."

"That seems awfully naive, though. Even for Lou."

"November isn't out yet. Maybe her hopes are still high. What was it they put on the cover instead? Princess Sophie's Bavarian castle—*where Bormann slept*?" Cat spit with disdain. "What's next, Leni Riefenstahl's gown collection?" Skillfully imitating Lou's posh Home Counties accent, she continued, intoning, "Here is the Schiaparelli worn during the award ceremony for *Triumph of the Will*: a crepe-and-satin gown cut on the bias, with genuine ruby beadwork along the collar and repurposed baby teeth sewn onto the bust."

"I don't know," Bess realized. "Nobody's mentioned anything about November. We never even had a meeting about it. I didn't even *think* about it. Honestly . . . I've been preoccupied with Jent."

"I've been working on December and January. I didn't think about it either. I didn't want to." Cat stubbed out her cigarette.

"Let's find out what Lou's been up to," Bess said, grabbing her laptop off the counter and cracking it open.

"I already checked Photogram," Cat said. "Nothing."

"No. At work. Her password is 'password,'" Bess said, laughing.

"She told me when I showed her how to use CoopDoc. Let's see if she has any pitches."

Cat pulled up a chair to Bess's side of the table. They didn't find any pitches, but they did find an email to Margot, Paula, and Courtney Sacks from Legal, marked with the subject line THE FINAL DAYS OF CALLIE COURT.

When they finished reading the attachment, Bess cried.

"Callie went to Hampshire. We hung out a few times freshman year, she lived on my floor," Bess said. "We drove to a party at Bard once, and he was all she could talk about in the car. I had completely forgotten."

"This is the cruelest thing I've ever seen," Cat agreed. "Look at Margot's stone-cold response. She called it 'perfection.'"

"How could they publish this?" Bess asked. "I mean . . . *Jesus*, her poor parents."

"It'll move," Cat said sadly. "People will buy this. They'll love it."

Bess looked stricken. She suddenly looked up and met Cat's eyes. "I just realized something," she whispered. "What did Callie smell like before she died?"

Cat paused and tried to remember.

"She smelled like juniper," she finally said. "Just like Christmas."

Lou, clad once again in her incognito cat sweatshirt and Skechers, waited in the dwindling crowd outside the Mania presentation. She'd been looking for Cat and Bess for the past hour but couldn't see them. *They must have slipped out*, she realized. *Off to another party.*

Her muscles twitched. *Time for bed*, her body screamed. She started walking swiftly back to her apartment, and recalled how Cat and Bess had looked the night before, lurching around their bathroom, with a deep satisfaction.

Stocking the room had been the easiest part. All she'd had to do was tell the concierge over the phone that she was thinking of investing in Panacea, the heritage brand from the United Kingdom used by the hotel the past hundred years. *Would he mind switching out the bottles of what they had in stock with another, slightly cheaper option the Panacea board was presenting her with?* She wanted to know if anyone could tell the difference, she'd insisted—and if anyone could, it would be the staff of *RAGE*. It was to be their little secret. *I'm sure you understand.*

He happily obliged. *Anything for Madame Lucas.*

So there was now a *very* potent mixture of uppers and downers in the bath gels, the shampoo, the conditioner, the moisturizers and perfumes, the linen sprays, the shaving cream, everything. Lou laughed just thinking about how easy it had been. She'd put more energy into choosing this stupid cat sweatshirt. She was so grateful for Bedford Organics. What had started out as a mere investment had gone on to pay dozens of dividends, not the least of which was an enormous profit.

"It has *real* cocaine in it," Bitsy Peters had whispered to Bettina Simpson-Travers, Lou, and Ilsa Ravenshall. "It's this woman that I played tennis with in Portofino last summer. She's from Brazil, but she's opening up shop here. She's going to make a *billion* dollars."

Lou, still married at the time, had just caught Alex getting pegged by a cocktail waitress in their guest bedroom during Jane's third birthday party. He'd apologized with some sincerity, but in the end Lou's attorney at Cavendish Crane had needed to step in to resolve it.

Now, thanks to Donal Windsor, Esquire, Lou—or rather, the LLC registered to a storage unit in Jane's name on the west side of Manhattan—owned four percent of Lucas Holding, BV, free and clear. The shares, a payment for that onetime forgiveness, were hers to do with what she liked. She'd been looking for ways to invest and—*bam!* Bedford Organics and its marvelous hand cream—so much better than a cup of coffee, no calories whatsoever—had fallen right into her lap.

So Lou sold a tenth of a percent in Lucas Holding, BV, and used Donal to invest anonymously in Bedford Organics. She'd paid $6 million to buy five percent of Vittoria's company, then watched her fellow socialites get hooked left and right, while Vittoria slowly bought her shares back from Lou at nearly double the price. *Vittoria was just another single mother trying to make it in the world*, she'd rationalized; who knew how long Lou's own marriage would last, or what would become of her when it was finally over. She would need her own money someday, so that she could really and truly be *set free* with an investment that Alexander couldn't touch. Vittoria had been the perfect opportunity: someone who had just as much to lose as she did. For nearly three years Lou was very careful never to actually touch Vittoria's product, enter the premises, or call her on the phone— until the day she started working at *RAGE*.

Lou simply hadn't anticipated how stressful it would be to *work*. After day one, she definitely needed a little pick-me-up, but she felt self-conscious about asking her doctor for a prescription. Surely this kind of stress was something she could handle on her own. So she'd asked Donal to contact Vittoria, who enthusiastically messengered over *everything*—dozens of boxes of the entire line for her mystery investor to choose from at her leisure. Lou had squirreled it away, storing the boxes in the panic room that Alex had once built into their apartment, taking out two bottles once a week and a tube of hand cream every other month: the jasmine lotion for energy, the honeysuckle for happiness, and the wonderful eucalyptus hand cream to suppress the appetite, and sometimes the juniper, just at night, for comfort.

"Is it possible to overdose on this stuff?" Lou had once overheard Hillary ask Constance Onderveet at Hillary's ski cabin back in Idaho, through the door of a bathroom that reeked of jasmine and honeysuckle. They had all flown there for a girls' weekend last March.

"*Margot* gave it to me," Constance had assured her. "It's perfectly safe. It's simply South American."

Three days later, Hillary had been so gloriously high that she'd told Lou all about her wedding dress idea for the Christmas issue, about the special 3-D printer she'd found. Lou had thought that was simply *marvelous*, and she'd also felt a teensy-*weensy* bit jealous that Hillary just *really goddamned had it all*—beauty, brains, respect. Lou hinted to Hillary that she'd *love* to work at the magazine, too. *Just a thought—if anything opens up, I could really help with the wedding shoot; we could use my hotel in Paris.* That kind of thing. And they'd made a deal to use the hotel, but then, months later . . . Hillary died.

I know where she got that face cream, she'd whispered to a jasmine-scented and red-eared Margot at the funeral. *Do you think it had anything to do with her death?*

The following week, Lou had Hillary's job, though she wasn't a staffer. *Look, you've never had a job*, Margot had said. *I can't make you staff right away, everyone else will resent you. Work with me here. All I can do is give you the chance to earn it.* Come the end of her contract, Lou thought she might be able to leverage it into a staff position, but then Bedford Organics had gone tits-up in July, and Lou had very briefly felt *depressed*, though she'd already made back double her initial investment. After a quick call to Donal—who assured her that her company was a shell within a shell within a shell, that Vittoria had never known her name, that the only way to associate her would be for him to break attorney-client privilege, which would *never* happen—well, then she'd simply put the whole thing out of her mind. It had been easy to pretend to herself that none of it had really happened, that none of it was connected to her or to the lotion she slathered on every morning—and by September, every night. The whole office depended on it: Margot and Constance Onderveet had reeked of jasmine all summer, Rose Cashin-Trask of honeysuckle, and Janet Berg of both, with some juniper thrown in. They all pretended together. It was easy.

The panic room where Lou kept her stash was concealed behind a bookcase in her private study. When Callie had died *right there in front it*, she'd been simply *terrified* that they'd somehow find her cache, that it would get taken away, that she'd lose her job and go to jail, that she'd be *shamed*.

But Cat had fixed it all; *I saw Callie sniffing drugs*, Cat had reported. *And I saw her choking.* Nothing anyone could do. Certainly nothing about the bookcase and nothing about the juniper-scented lotion.

When Lou got back to her apartment, she checked the Eurydice Suite one more time, just to be sure, but the lights were off. The girls were still out somewhere, embarrassing themselves. *Perfect.* Lou coated herself in her evening application and climbed into bed.

Detective Mark Hutton sat in Premiere Classe berth number 4—the last seat available for purchase on the entire goddamn flight—and stared at Mania. There were hundreds of pictures of Cat on the map. She looked increasingly thin and disoriented, including a series where she was covered in paint and kissing—were those mimes?—yes, kissing mimes. The photos made him uncomfortable. He knew this wasn't like her. Something was wrong.

But there was no way to resolve this on the flight, and so he clicked off the phone, cracked his briefcase, and opened envelope after envelope, trying to distract himself with a backlog of banal paperwork. He flipped the pile over and started from the oldest first, adding his signature to dozens of hardcopies bound for inter-office mail upon his return before filling out an updated insurance form and reading through two new manuals on handgun protocol. It was meant to be reassuringly tedious. He looked at every scrap of paper in the briefcase, including the white index card covered in Hillary Whitney's handwriting:

the ribbon is the key to everything

He traced the handwriting with his fingertips. The amount of belladonna-derived atropine present in Hillary Whitney's body—built up for so long that she'd stopped producing antibodies for it—had been enough to give her recurrent hallucinations, the coroner had said when Hutton showed him the note, enough to make her deeply paranoid. *Maybe the note really didn't mean anything*, he told himself.

Hutton opened his computer and connected to the airplane's Wi-Fi to begin sorting through the emails he'd received in the past few days. Most were work-related, but after a few minutes, a new message appeared at the top of his in-box from an anonymous re-mailer, the subject line reading "urgent re: callie court." He opened the email to find an attached PDF. As the document downloaded, it was *Callie's* face that appeared inch by inch, her gray irises glowing with a violet tinge, her face smeared with mud, flames licking behind her head.

The text below her face read THE FINAL DAYS OF CALLIE COURT—apparently he was looking at the cover of the November issue of *RAGE*. Next, a series of photographs of Callie from all over New York—the most beautiful pictures of her that he'd ever seen—loaded, followed by an accompanying text that was four solid pages long. The byline read "Whig Beaton Molton-Mauve Lucas."

As his eyes adjusted to the small print, he saw the same three words right there in black-and-white—written over and over and over: "Detective Mark Hutton."

His heart stopped for a moment. Thinking the plane had suddenly nose-dived, he looked up, expecting to hear screaming, to see smoke and flames, but the plane was quiet and calm, trucking along at 38,000 feet, level and pressurized.

Hutton scrolled to the beginning of the article and started reading. It was a lurid tale of a small-town girl in love with an indifferent city boy, using details from their relationship that even he barely remembered. In the story, the girl turned to drugs to forget him and then modeling to attract him. The climax began with a blow-by-blow account of the shoot responsible for the photos throughout the article, the author praising Callie's fearlessness and bravery—"As she scaled the walls of Belvedere Castle, a passing runner remarked that she must have a death wish"—and heavily implying that she'd committed suicide.

The final paragraphs were so ludicrous that Hutton laughed out loud before remembering that it was his own name on the screen.

Callie didn't think anyone at the party would notice her stuffing gum into her mouth and heroin into her nose. She grabbed the couture-clad arm of *RAGE* editor Catherine Ono and dragged her into a private room as she choked.

Ono tried desperately to save Callie's life, even breaking a nail on the wad of gum in her throat as she tried in vain to dislodge it. Before she knew it, Callie was dead and she was being interviewed by an aggressive pack of NYPD officers. And now? The world would have already forgotten Callie Court—if it wasn't for *RAGE*'s bravery in publishing this story.

Feminism cannot be about lifting yourself up while your sisters are trampled behind you. It is a movement for all of us. We must be united. We must be one. Women of the world: we must stop throwing ourselves upon the altar of male indifference. Like the logoless clothing worn by Court in the accompanying photo shoot, we must stop branding ourselves with the names of people who don't deserve us— a lesson she learned too late.

If Callie Court—fashion's most beguiling muse of the last twenty years—couldn't love herself enough to survive loving someone else, how will *we* ever survive? How will the rest of us ever love ourselves if we don't love each other?

I offer a simple solution: Be the matriarch. Find your feminism. Live in sisterhood.

Hutton actually snorted when he read the last line. He felt blood rushing to his face, and he pulled at his collar, peeling off his sweater and unbuttoning his shirt. The feeling in his stomach— a combination of shame, surprise, fear, and adrenaline—was quite possibly the most unpleasant thing he had ever experienced. He wanted to smash the file into pieces, though he knew there were millions more, probably being stacked on newsstands at this very moment; he wanted to burn down the world. Hutton recalled a phone conversation from September, when Cat found her name in the newspaper while they were talking and cried because the article was so mean. He'd told her to get over it and changed the subject. *How stupid was I?* he thought. *I had no fucking idea what I was talking about.*

He scanned back through the article, this time highlighting details only Callie would have known—the day he went to her apartment in Carroll Gardens and spent three hours working up the courage to tell her he'd met someone. Or two years later, their six-hour dinner. Her scarf had burned on the candle. He only vaguely recalled laughing in shock, the waitstaff laughing, too, as he simultaneously put out the fire with a damp napkin and ordered another round of drinks. They'd talked until the restaurant closed.

She'd worn that scarf every winter for the rest of her life, the article said.

Who would she have told all of this to? Callie didn't have friends like this, not people she poured her heart out to like they were her . . . *diary.*

It was, he suddenly realized, *taken straight from her diary*, the one he hadn't been able to find. That she "crashed against his indifference and broke every bone in her body"—that was true, he realized, recognition bubbling up so fast he nearly choked on it. "Your indifference is tearing me apart," she'd told him once.

As he read the article for a third time, he became certain that it was a mixture of her diary and the extrapolations of a salacious narrator, their heavy prose stitched onto hers with the drool of a tabloid screenplay.

Hutton read the lines that were meant to describe him over and over. Was he really a "self-involved playboy whose handsome face and bottomless wallet kept him safely insulated from consequences of any kind"? No. *She wouldn't have said that.*

Callie Court had been a lot of things, but she wasn't hateful— she was simply trapped by an emotional birth defect, a hole in her heart that she filled unsustainably, with parties, with sloppy, dramatic friends, with drugs. It stopped her from growing up. It had kept her living a decade behind Hutton. *I didn't want a ward*, he'd reminded himself, had no desire for a woman who would follow him around like a puppy, who needed to be cared for and monitored and chastised and cleaned up after. He'd wanted a partner. *It's not wrong to want to be with someone who faces the same challenges*, he tried to tell himself, repeating the mantra he'd adopted since the night she died. *You didn't betray her. You didn't abandon her. You moved on. It's not a crime.*

The photos made him deeply sad. In one of them, Callie was doing an exaggerated bend while wearing a rough cloth gown the size of a house, tears streaming down her face. She was positioned underneath the whale that hung from the ceiling in the Museum of Natural History, the background blurred behind her. The next page showed Callie lying practically naked on the floor of the planetarium, fake starlight dotting her skin and a large straw hat covering her torso. The next had Callie jumping from Belvedere Castle, her skirt swirling up around her as two very real-looking firemen stood below with a trampoline. On and on it went, each image more imaginatively implausible than the last.

Halfway through them Hutton felt tremors of grief cross his chest. He closed the laptop and shoved it in his briefcase. He wished the windows opened so that he could throw it out, and he imagined breaking one; saw the cabin depressurizing as his eardrums broke and anything not strapped down was sucked out the insatiable vortex of the tiny window—then blinked his eyes and returned again to the calm, blank space of Premiere Classe, the laptop and its contents corralled only by the thin leather walls of his briefcase.

Envy is the fuel of the capital engine, Cat had told him once over the phone, when he'd asked point-blank how she could possibly take her job so seriously. *It's both literally and figuratively a beautiful woman. You'll do anything—get a job, wear a suit, take her to dinner—so that you can fuck her brains out. Beautiful women are the fire upon which the world burns.*

That's desire, he'd argued at the time, *not envy.*

Same difference, Cat had replied.

Hutton grimaced at the memory.

The sun, burning a thin yellow through the quilted gray skies of Paris, was just starting to hoist itself over the horizon. Lou's phone beeped—*time to get up*—but she didn't need the alarm. Every fiber and sinew told her it was time for her morning application. She rolled over toward the opposite nightstand and grabbed her tubes of lotion, squeezing thick white lines onto her legs, arms, hands, and feet, mixing the eucalyptus hand cream and the jasmine lotion, along with a teeny-tiny dose of the juniper night cream on her face, to keep her perfectly balanced. She lay still for a few minutes and waited for it to dry.

Lou stretched her limbs, threw back the scratchy white duvet of her rented apartment with joy, and peered quickly through her binoculars to the Eurydice Suite; the curtains were still drawn. *They must be passed out. Perfect.* She marched into the living room, temporarily transformed into a closet, where three nearly identical day dresses were draped over the sofa, all of them custom couture that she'd ordered on a whim from the shows last year when she'd still been married to Alexander Lucas and his bank account. For the first time in months she didn't need to dress down—to look like Lou Lucas, a hardworking mummy doing her best on the alimony she'd been given, for whom any one of these $25,000 dresses would have been an absurd extravagance—no, no, no. *Not today.* Today she would be Madame Lucas again.

She dragged her fingers over the fabric of each dress: the first, bloodred handloomed silk cady; the second, a virgin-white broderie anglaise cotton; and the third, a flowery 3-D-printed plastic. They were all ladylike, hems dropped below the knee, waists belted appropriately, and sleeves extending below the elbow, but they were varied in tenor. The red silk was fluid and sexy, the white cotton overtly feminine, the printed plastic futuristic and strong. *That* was the one. She pawed through her suitcase for a high-waisted pair of opaque briefs and matching bra to wear underneath the semitransparent dress.

She selected a pair of ruby suede stiletto boots, their color a perfect match for the smattering of flowers melted through the bodice of the dress, added a huge cuff bracelet resembling a mermaid's tail, and sighed with satisfaction.

She stopped in the bathroom, brushed her hair, and rolled it up into hot curlers, then walked back into the kitchen, poured herself a cup of strong coffee, and popped open a snack-sized can of chocolate Ensure. A sudden surge of energy gripped her, and she responded to it by dropping to the floor for twenty push-ups and a two-minute plank. When she'd finished, her coffee was the perfect temperature, and she knocked it back while applying her makeup and a light swipe of deodorant, though the sweat glands in her armpits had been surgically removed for convenience.

After completing her face—black liquid liner, tangerine blush, flamingo pink lips—she dressed, stepping into the nude briefs and bra before zipping and belting herself into the plastic dress, its wide skirt undulating in Jetson fantasy waves beneath the 3-D-printed flowers.

All she needed was a handbag. Lou rooted around in her enormous suitcase, throwing skirts and pants onto the floor until she found a circular clutch plated in 14-karat gold, the iguana–leather strap designed to hold the bag in her palm like a discus. She filled it completely with a full tube of the eucalyptus hand cream and walked out the door.

Nestled safely in the backseat of a silver Audi, Lou checked her phone one final time: 9:55 a.m. Perfect. The shoot in the Le Narcisse ballroom should be springing to life at this very moment—and, thankfully, Cat and Bess wouldn't be anywhere near it.

It was time for Madame Lucas to save the day.

Chapter Twenty-One

Hutton found himself standing inside the lobby of a petite
Versailles, waiting patiently for the Poirot-shaped desk clerk
to finish a phone call. He shifted his weight and tried to catch the
man's attention, only to receive a raised finger in response; *one moment*, the finger said. Hutton nodded and forced himself to wait,
standing a few feet back from the counter. He looked at Mania
again, at the photos of Cat—dirty, thin, wild-eyed, her hair shorn
off—stumbling into this hotel two nights ago. She hadn't appeared
on the map for over twelve hours. Though he ached with impa-
tience, Hutton didn't want to embarrass her any further; he'd done
that enough for one year. He tried to remain calm.

Suddenly, a chime rang, echoing loudly off the polished walls
and floor. The brass doors of the elevator at the far end of the lobby
parted to reveal a dozen shellacked and perfumed sculptures.

Many of them appeared to display a permanent smile, huge veneers glowing ultraviolet beneath the stretched skin of their rosy
lips and wet eyes. It was a cluster of statues, he thought at first,
until suddenly—one *moved*, and they all moved behind it. It took
Hutton several moments to recognize them as human women, so
carefully had they been cosseted and finished.

The horde descended upon him, making their way toward the

front doors of the hotel in formation, their voices glancing off the marble ceilings and walls in an unintelligible cacophony. He closed his eyes and listened. Once he'd parsed the syllables—Russian and Mandarin, mostly—he became aware, finally, of their youth.

Some were impossibly young, *barely legal*, though each member of the pack had enormous diamonds hanging from their ring fingers. Ropes of gold banded the prominent sinews of their necks. When the first—a brunette, eighteen if she was a day—passed him, she turned her painted lashes up flirtatiously and let her mouth go slack, parting her lips. He tried to look away but found it impossible, and so he moved, to make his way past their bodies to the counter, but they insisted on passing him closely. Each one touched his jacket or brushed his arm. Hutton closed his eyes again and waited for the clacking of their heels to meet the whoosh of the revolving door at the front of the hotel.

When the last one had exited into the throng of photographers waiting outside, Hutton opened his eyes to find the mustachioed desk attendant staring at him with bemusement.

"Monsieur?" he asked.

"I'm here to see Catherine Ono," Hutton explained, showing his passport. The Premiere Classe ticket was still jammed into its pages, and the desk attendant smiled a twitchy little grin. "It's a surprise," Hutton explained lamely, though the concierge did not hesitate; this was a place where first-class men received first-class service.

"*Bonjour*, welcome, you must take the private elevator over there," he replied, handing Hutton a key and pointing to a small gold door at the end of the lobby. "Thank you, enjoy your stay."

Hutton dashed toward the elevator. Moments later, he stepped into a huge foyer and found himself facing a very large door. Hutton waved his key over the lock and ran inside to discover a room so elaborate it made the lobby look like a dentist's office—where Cat and Bess sat calmly sipping coffee.

"You're okay," he said, surprised, anxiety leaving his body.

"Hutton?" Cat said in disbelief. Shocked, she stood up from the table. "How did you get a key to our room?" she asked warily.

"Bad security," he said. "I found out who's funding Bedford Organics."

"Lou," Cat and Bess said together. He looked surprised again.

"She tried to poison us," Bess said.

"We're fine, though," Cat explained quickly. "We were discussing what to do."

"Don't do *anything*," he said firmly. "I'm here to arrest her." Both women smiled. "Where is she?" he asked.

"I would guess that she's on her way to the hotel," Bess answered. "Do you need us to find her?"

"Could you?"

Bess glanced at Cat, then nodded, shut her laptop, and walked past him. "I'll look for her. I'll be back," she said, then closed the door behind her.

The room was empty except for the two of them. Hutton stared hard at Cat with an expression she didn't understand. She rubbed the top of her shorn head self-consciously. "I cut my hair."

Unexpectedly, Hutton grabbed Cat and pulled her into his body, holding her so tightly that she thought he just might squeeze all the air out of her. He rested his chin on her head and she felt his chest heave. She tried to look up at him, but he wouldn't let her move. The air around them shifted. After a minute passed, she relaxed, resting her sallow cheek against the copse of gray and white and golden hairs on his chest, and she was so glad he was here. Though Cat had saved herself, Hutton had finally shown that he cared, first and foremost, about Cat's personal safety.

"I'm so sorry," he finally said, and she understood that he was apologizing again for the arrest, and for what he'd learned about her role in Callie's death, for her pain, for disappearing from her life. "I'm so, so sorry." He meant it.

"I'm sorry for you," Cat replied. "I didn't know about you and

Callie. That must have been really hard," she said, her voice small. "I'm sorry for your loss, I truly am."

He pushed his cheek against her head and went quiet again. A nearby church bell chimed the hour, the bells ringing ten times, loud and clear, until he relaxed his grip and let her go before kissing her on the mouth.

Cat reached up, wrapped her arms around his neck, and kissed him back. He still tasted and smelled like cut grass. Their kisses grew frenzied. She dragged him into her green bedroom and shut the door tightly. He peeled off her dress. She shoved him against the wall, leaning over to grab a condom out of her bag.

He picked her up. Cat dug her fingernails into his back and bit his shoulder—hard—before he moaned and put his mouth back on hers. They moved together until her face contorted and her cunt shuddered. With his face buried in her neck, Hutton gripped her body so tightly that Cat thought her ribs might snap.

"I have to find Lou," he said into her ear. "But I want you to know that everything is going to be okay, Cat. I won't screw up your life this time."

She leaned back and looked into his eyes, shining with the same sincerity she'd seen on the day they met. "I know," she said decisively, using her bare fingernails to trace the line of his jaw through his golden stubble. "But tell me your plan anyway."

Molly had been up since well before dawn, working with a set of local construction workers to transform the historic ballroom of Le Narcisse. Scaffolding had been erected above each of the seventeenth-century murals that lined the room—each one depicting a different scene in the Narcissus myth—so that the models could be hung from above, floating on air for each shot. Hillary's sketches and notes for the shoot envisioned the models as marionettes. The inspiration board was covered with images from a

Valentino campaign that had been plastered all over New York during the previous spring: a young woman's abundant body, her face cropped out, was squeezed and wrapped into a tiny wedding gown. Laces split and pearl beadwork popped off as the model's velveteen skin brimmed over the fabric, a vagina and a breast and a dress all at once.

Molly watched a construction worker climb down from the final set of scaffolding. "Fini," he called out. "Mercieee," she called back, then checked her watch. This was getting ridiculous. Was she expected to begin the shoot without them?

Cat and Bess had been sleeping when she'd left the suite, but Molly had scheduled their wake-up calls for over two hours earlier. The models were nearly done with their hair and makeup. The remaining *RAGE* staffers had arrived on the morning flight, and they stood over the breakfast buffet, drinking coffee and chatting. Molly smiled awkwardly at Constance Onderveet. Constance did not smile back. It was almost eleven. Molly sent her tenth frantic text message to Cat and Bess.

"Beans!" a voice echoed behind her. Molly turned to find Lou Lucas zooming across the room on her plastic Barbie-doll feet with astonishing speed.

"Hello, darling dear," Lou yelled, kissing Molly on the cheek. She practically reeked of a floral bouquet; jasmine, honeysuckle, juniper, and eucalyptus followed her in a rotten cloud. "Isn't *this* just the fur knickers." Lou grinned approvingly at the room. "I really do love this marvelous fucking hotel."

"Nice to see you," Molly said politely.

"Well." Her yell became a stage whisper. "Kit-Oh and Boots have a case of the old Mumbai handicap. They've sent me to run things in their stead. Girls will be girls, I suppose." Lou winked one of her starry eyes conspiratorially.

"What?"

"The trots, darling. The scoots. Saltwater cleanse?"

Molly still looked confused.

"Bad tummies, darling. Bit of a party tax."

"Oh." Molly blushed. "Of course. I'd better go check on them. Can you keep the models from getting restless?"

"Oh no no no, Beans, you're not going *anywhere*. These lazy Gauls will try to knock off at lunch, so we'd better get started. I think the girls need to be a bit shinier. Really *gleaming*. I'll order some of the hotel's moisturizer—it's simply the best. Bring me the shot list."

Molly frowned. "Sure thing," she said. "Let me just pull that up." As she pretended to search for the shot list, she texted Cat and Bess one more message:

DID YOU SEND LOU?!? SHE'S TAKING OVER!!

Bess, who had watched the entire scene from behind a luggage cart in the doorway, wrote back right away:

We're fine, but don't tell anyone. DO tell Lou she needs to check the hem on Alisa and set last looks on Yza.

Molly looked around, dumbfounded, and repeated the message; Bess folded herself between two garment bags and kept watch.

When Cat checked her phone, she found a message waiting from the exact person she'd intended to call: Paula Booth. Come up to the PH, she wrote back before changing into the dress that Molly had marked on her calendar, a calf-length Albert V. with thin straps that crisscrossed her shoulders. When Paula knocked five minutes later, Cat ushered her into the living room. Behind them, a click came from the front door as Bess let herself back into the suite. After seeing Paula, Bess sat quietly in a chair by the door.

"You do realize he's going to sue you," Cat said. Paula looked confused, until Hutton waved from the sofa.

"That's true," he offered, getting up. "I'm Mark Hutton. Though I imagine that you wouldn't go to print without approval from Cooper Legal, am I right?"

Standing behind Cat, he towered over both women, yet Paula stared him down with confidence. "That's correct. Cooper is not particularly concerned with defamation in this case."

"I'll try for copyright, then. I know you used Callie's diary."

"I see," Paula responded evenly, looking around the room. She waved her hand toward the sofa and chairs arranged by the window. "Do you mind if I sit down?"

Hutton responded without blinking. "Of course," he said politely, showing them both to a pair of chairs, though his tone was glacial. "Let's sit."

He lowered his frame onto the sofa across from Paula and Cat, who were seated in matching armchairs with a small walnut occasional table placed between them. Paula looked at him expectantly.

"All I'm telling you to do," Hutton said confidently, "is to cut the text. Obviously, I think the photos are in poor taste, but you're clearly welcome to publish those."

"I can certainly appreciate your perspective," Paula said, "although I'm afraid you may find a copyright suit against a billion-dollar corporation to be...difficult." She turned to Cat before continuing, her posture tall and firm. "But that's just my opinion. I'm afraid it's not really up to me," she said. "I'm resigning next week. I'm going to work for Mania. And I'm hoping you'll come with—both you *and* Elizabeth, actually. I'm not here to fight. I'm here to offer you a very good job."

Cat's eyes bulged with shock. "Why?"

"Because they look up to you," Paula said simply. "You're very hard workers, Catherine, both of you. I know you'll do well there. You'll be their most important employees—'maniacs,' I believe, is the term they plan to use. And you don't have to live in

Los Angeles, obviously, or even New York. You could live anywhere you wanted to."

Cat, openmouthed with disbelief, stared at Paula. "No, I mean, why would I take that job?" Her eyes narrowed.

"Well. That is what I'd like to discuss," Paula said kindly. "Margot Villiers isn't coming back to work—not next week and not ever. *RAGE Fashion Book*, as we knew it, is very much dead. I do realize that allowing Lou to write that article was insensitive. It was probably a mistake. It wasn't very good, either, though it was—and I do hate this word—titillating. Margot's judgment has not been the best this year, and while I have to give it to her—she really did pull out all the stops—nothing worked. Margot had a heart attack last week. She's been unresponsive in the ICU for six days."

Cat and Bess both gasped. Paula paused briefly to acknowledge their shock, then continued, "I've been handling her email. I've realized that it doesn't matter to me anymore if *RAGE* survives, not if Margot's gone. I don't think she'll be coming out of it."

"But you took advantage of me," Cat said quietly in a whisper gilded with contempt. "You *used* me. *And* my friends. And you made me become . . . this." She gestured at her body, indicating her now-public identity.

"Nobody *made* you do anything," Paula replied slowly, genuinely perplexed. "You did all of this"—she pointed to Cat's emaciated frame and to her cellphone to indicate the Mania map—"all by yourself."

Cat's horrified face fell. "But I would have *lost my job* if I hadn't done what you asked," she said. "It was an impossible position."

"That risk is where the rubber meets the road, isn't it," Paula agreed. "It's hard to know your worth, or what to leverage and when to leverage it."

"You're telling me—after all the pressure you and Margot put me under—that I should have just *quit* if I didn't like it?"

"Yes," Paula said, agreeing again, "that is *exactly* what I'm telling you. It was my job to put pressure on you," she explained gently.

"I'm sixty years old, Catherine. I came up in this business when men called me 'Sweet Tits' to my face. I might be tougher than you," she said, shrugging her shoulders, "and I might play the game a bit harder than you happen to think is fair, but that doesn't mean you lack agency."

Cat leaned back in her chair, folding her legs up under her arms and resting her head on her knees. As she looked at Paula's face—her expression unexpectedly kind and clear—Cat realized how right she was. *I should have quit months ago*, she thought, should have quit the very second they asked her to write a memorial to Hillary and put their personal photos in the magazine. But she'd stayed, and she'd posed for a million pictures, and she'd let her whole life become a product.

"You can do whatever you want, Catherine," Paula said simply. "Know your cards."

"I want..." Cat let the silence hang in the air. "I want that story gone," Cat demanded. "I want a hundred grand more than I made at *RAGE*, and I want the same for Bess. And I want my green card sponsored. No more of this H-1B bullshit." The sentences had come out of her mouth so quickly, and so sharply, that she could hardly believe she'd said them—but looking at Hutton's astonished face, it was clear that she had. His thick eyebrows were hovering an inch above his eyeglasses in shock.

"Agreed," Paula replied, smiling. She held out her hand, and Cat shook it.

"I want it done now," Cat said.

"Do you have a computer?" Paula asked.

Bess dropped her laptop on the table in front of her. Paula logged into the Cooper network with Margot's credentials, pulled up the November file slated to be sent out to the printers, then handed it to Cat—who deleted every single line of text that had originally accompanied the photos of Callie.

"Don't delete the photos," Bess said. "Her family receives payment in full if they run."

Cat left the images and handed the computer back to Paula, who saved and sent the file out to the printers.

"Done," Paula reported. "I feel good about that."

"I want my deal in writing."

Paula turned back to the laptop, where she updated the Mania contracts with Cat's requirements. When she finished, Cat picked up the lobster phone and called down to the front desk. "I'm emailing you a document," she snapped in rapid-fire French. "I want four copies printed and brought to the ballroom. And pens. Bring pens." She slammed the phone down and rose from her chair.

"Ballroom?" Paula asked.

"He's not here for us," Cat said simply. Paula nodded, and a corner of her mouth pulled back in a kind of smile, but she said nothing. Cat wondered how much she already knew. They gathered their things and headed for the door.

"Can I ask you something?" Hutton asked Paula, taking advantage of the moment as they waited for the elevator.

"Possibly," Paula agreed warily.

Hutton pulled Hillary Whitney's note out of his pocket:

the ribbon is the key to everything

"Can you tell me what this means?" he asked.

Paula read it, then passed it to Cat. "It's about the shoot that Catherine is working on today. Hillary sourced a synthetic, non-toxic fabric that can be 3-D-printed up to thirteen yards wide; in the manufacturer's parlance, thirteen yards is a *ribbon*. That's a huge leap for the garment industry—to have safe, cheap, easy manufacturing on such a large scale. Margot rejected the proposal the morning Hillary died. She was, at the time, afraid of running up *RAGE*'s resource bill any further. I think that rejection . . . well, it pushed Hillary over the edge."

"Why'd she mail it?"

"That, I don't know."

"I do," Cat said. "It's something we did in boarding school. We sent postcards with inside jokes, quotes, things like that, to each other's houses so we could read them at the end of the year. To remember what mattered."

The elevator's golden doors opened, and they walked out into the lobby.

Hutton trailed behind Cat and Paula as they strode toward the ballroom. The two women were opposites: one of them was tall, young, and nearly bald; the other, sixty, with her white hair in a conservative bun, but they had the same look in their eyes—determination. They were well matched, he thought, whether Cat knew it or not.

He'd been appalled when he first walked into the suite. Though he'd always thought of Cat as slender, in the last two and a half months her body had faded away, dissolved. She looked like she belonged in hospice somewhere as she stared at him, holding her coffee in her twiggy little hands, her clothes baggy on her bony frame. Still: he wanted her. Fat, thin, didn't matter. Her attitude was endlessly appealing.

The odd part, as they walked through and around a fresh horde of overpainted young women—though it could have been the same horde from earlier, Hutton realized, he could hardly distinguish one girl from the next—was that *nobody else* looked at Cat like she was sick. Instead they looked at her with obvious approval, at the pointed bones of her shoulder blades and hips with plain, unvarnished envy. He felt it wash over the both of them, the glow of approval, of *worship*.

She marched them to an opulent ballroom. There were models everywhere, wearing wedding dresses and hanging from scaffolding all around the room, and a passel of pointy-faced older women stood in the corner drinking coffee. A teenage girl dressed like a mechanic ran over to them. "Cat, heyyyy," she said anxiously. Cat held a finger to her lips. They walked past, to Hutton's surprise, several large posters from Callie's Valentino campaign.

Lou Lucas stood in the middle of the room, surrounded by *RAGE* employees, models, assistants, and photographers. Sausaged into a weird plastic dress, she was anxiously rubbing her hands together like an insect cleaning its antennae. As the group—Hutton, Cat, Bess, Paula, and Molly—descended upon her, Lou's face went dark. The *RAGE* staffers, sensing the discomfort of one of their own, fell silent and turned to watch. A mixture of delight and confusion appeared on their faces as the tall, handsome police officer held up his badge and showed it to Lou Lucas.

"Hello, I'm Detective Mark Hutton, NYPD," he said pleasantly, looming over her.

She looked up with shock. "Hello," she replied uncertainly.

"I know about Lilac Futures," he said. "I found the money."

She moved quickly, trying to slip past him, and he grabbed her arm. Cat and Bess stepped around him, blocking access to the lobby.

"I'm going to take you back to New York," Hutton announced to Lou, "and you're going to turn yourself in."

Lou snorted. "Why would I do that?" she asked.

"You will," he said plainly before taking out his phone to show a picture of her daughter, Jane Lucas, walking into school on the Upper East Side, her face cheerfully oblivious to the undercover NYPD officer taking her photograph from across the street. "You registered Lilac Futures in Jane's name. We can arrest and charge her. It's . . . *unusual* to have a six-year-old in juvenile detention, but it does happen."

"You're not going to jail a child," Lou replied flatly, though she was clearly panicking. Her skin was turning bright red beneath the plastic dress.

"We can and we will," he said, as honestly as he knew how. "If you don't come back to New York, we have the ability to keep her in juvenile detention for up to three weeks. The facilities are…brutal. Whatever happens to her will absolutely, one hundred percent be your fault."

Lou stared at the floor. "Why are you doing this to me?" she asked before looking at him with hatred. "All I did was tell the truth about you."

"This has nothing to do with the magazine," he continued. "As the primary shareholder of Bedford Organics, you financed and conspired to distribute Schedule I narcotics, resulting in at least one fatality. Possibly two. We'll be looking further into Callie Court's death."

Cat noticed a tiny ripple of terror passing through *RAGE*'s staff. In a fraction of a moment, Constance emitted a strangled noise, Rose stared hard at the ground, and Janet bit her lip with enough force to draw blood.

"Those *bitches* are *not* on me," Lou snapped, referring to Callie and Hillary with unvarnished contempt. "They were adults. *Americans.* They had total control over their own lives."

"You're certainly welcome to argue that in a court of law," he said. "Here's what's going to happen: I will escort you back to New York, right now. You will turn yourself in. That gives you roughly ten hours to figure out how to tell your children and arrange their child care after your arrest, not to mention contact your attorney. That's much more than most people get."

"If I don't?"

"Your daughter will be taken to juvenile detention."

"My husband will stop that," she insisted.

"I'm afraid not," he said, holding up his phone again and showing her Alexander Lucas's Photogram account: #betterthandavos, it said beneath a picture of him toasting champagne with two former United States presidents on the deck of a sailboat. "He's somewhere off the coast of Greece. We can be back in New York tonight."

Lou opened her cellphone to dial her attorney, but Hutton used his huge hands to pry it easily from her bony fingers.

"You can have it back once we're sitting on the plane," he said.

"Fine," Lou hissed, her eyes darting around the room as she obviously strategized ways to get away from him—but Hutton reached over and zipped a cable tie around her wrist, connecting it to one on his own, before she could stop him.

"You can pretend we're holding hands," he said, smiling.

Lou looked like she was about to cry. "No, that's not okay," she pleaded. "I . . . can't."

"You mean because of the story?" Hutton stepped back to let Paula, Cat, Bess, and Molly move into the foreground. The three young women looked at Paula expectantly. Constance Onderveet and the rest of the *RAGE* staff had gathered behind them and could hear every word.

Paula opened her mouth briefly, and then turned to Cat. "Go on then."

"Lou, your November story is dead," Cat said, "and you're fired."

"You ungrateful scabs!" Lou replied defiantly. "You've all used me. All you little strivers. I can't believe I fell for it. Well, you can keep your tacky magazine! You'll certainly be hearing from my attorney."

Constance, Rose, and Janet's faces turned bright red.

"Nobody *used* you," Constance insisted, unconsciously scratching her arms, while Janet and Rose stood trembling behind her. "We have no idea what you're talking about. You're just some crazy woman we should never have let into our lives."

"You *killed* Hillary Whitney," Cat added firmly, rising to her full height. "I think you killed Callie, too. And I know you tried to poison us. I'll be pressing charges."

"Bloody little addicts," Lou hissed. "Pills to stay thin, pills to be smart, pills to sleep, injections, bootcamps, surgeries. It's a wonder there weren't *more* corpses at the rate you lot were going. The office smelled like a bleeding perfume counter."

At that moment, the twitchy concierge appeared, with a handful of pens and four printed copies of Cat's and Bess's contracts.

"Madame?" he offered. Grabbing the papers, Cat turned on her heel and walked to the craft services table, sweeping a basket of croissants out of the way as she signed her two copies and passed them back for countersignature. Paula signed them before turning to Bess, who didn't move a muscle. Cat looked at her friend expectantly.

"I can't," Bess said. "I don't want to work at Mania. Sorry. I couldn't get a word in earlier. I hope that doesn't mess things up."

Unexpectedly, Paula smiled at her. "That's okay," she told Bess. "Do what's right for you."

Cat felt all the blood draining from her head—felt her fingers and toes go slightly numb. She stared at her friend. It had never occurred to her that Bess wouldn't always want what Cat wanted.

"I'm not the same as you," Bess said gently. "And you don't need me."

"It's not because of our fight—"

"No," Bess said sincerely. "I'm comfortable at Cooper. I know who I am there. I'm not like you, Cat. But please don't let me stop you."

"Okay." Cat exhaled and squeezed her friend's hand. Bess looked back toward the throng of *RAGE* employees hovering in the middle of the room. In an instant, Cat took in the opulent ballroom—the sunlight streaming in from the high windows, the cigarette smoke she could smell from the front door, the traffic honking on the street out front—and watched as her friend's posture shifted ever so slightly, as if Bess finally stepped into a pair of shoes that fit. Was this where their paths divided?

"If you'll excuse me," Bess said confidently, "I want to finish this shoot. Even if *RAGE* folds after this issue, you and Hillary put a lot of work into this. I don't want it to go to waste."

"Thank you," Cat said simply.

Bess smiled. "You're welcome."

"Don't forget to quit," Paula interrupted.

"Okay," Cat said automatically. She'd spent half a dozen years obeying Paula Booth, assuming that she was *really* listening to Margot Villiers, but perhaps it had been Paula speaking the whole time. Cat turned, broke through the crowd of gossiping *RAGE* staffers, and went directly to Constance.

"I quit," she said, holding out her hand and shaking the damp, skeletal palm of an astonished Constance. "And give Bess my job," Cat ordered. "She earned it." *Even if* RAGE *disappeared in the next year, having "Senior Editor" on her résumé would help get Bess anywhere she needed to go.*

Constance nodded limply.

Cat turned to Hutton and leaned in close, whispering in his ear as he held Lou at a distance. "See you in New York," she said, trying to sound nonchalant. He wrapped his free arm around her and kissed her—a long, searching kiss, one that embarrassed everyone around them.

"Come home soon," he said to her. "We'll pick up where we left off?" Cat smiled in reply, let go of him, picked up her handbag, and dropped her contract in it as she headed for the door.

"What are you staring at?" Bess yelled at the stunned room. "We have twelve shots to pick up. Let's go." The group slowly broke apart, and everything returned to normal for everyone except Lou.

Hutton could feel her hands shaking through their plastic bracelet chain before she passed out, her head hitting the wall behind her with a very loud smack.

Dammit, he thought, checking her pulse and trying to find a way to discreetly loosen the thick plastic casing she'd squeezed into, *don't these women* ever *eat?*

Epilogue

Cat sat in a second-class compartment of a high-speed train bound from Paris to Brussels, sipping coffee from a paper cup and turning over her new camera in her hands, a Canon 5D she'd purchased on her walk from the hotel to the Gare du Nord.

In under an hour she would be back home. Though it had been a decade, she knew it would be the same: the farm, with its damp ground, was a place of unshakable rhythm. While she was home, Cat and her mother would wake at dawn every morning to feed, water, and groom the horses before completing endless farm chores until nightfall, when they would eat bread and cheese and meat. When the sun rose, Cat would meet her mother in the barn with a thermos full of coffee and everything would start again. That was farm life. It was rigid, but it needed you.

She stared out the window at the passing countryside, absentmindedly circling her wrist with her fingers, and let herself eavesdrop on the French and Flemish conversations happening throughout the train car, realizing, for the first time in years, how hard it had been to go without those sounds, to live without this air. She felt herself diving deep under the surface of her consciousness, swimming away from her American, English-speaking world and, finally, reappearing on the long-forgotten shore of her Flemish self.

She was suddenly *so tired* of trying to fit in. All she wanted was to lie in the yellow grass of the farm's fallow fields, to go to sleep without worrying about tomorrow, to feel loved, to feel that she belonged.

For the first time in a very long time, Cat thought that she just might be able to.

Acknowledgments

Thanks to:

Julia Langbein, for all your help, edits, creative and emotional support, for suggesting Hutton's final line, and for being my high-water mark. Laura Pettitt, who made me feel like I was writing *The Count of Monte Cristo* for the over-thirty wine-and-Capri set, for happily debating the finer points of it all. Abbe Wright, who lugged a printed 8.5x11 version of this book in a binder to the ob-gyn and read it in the stirrups (the platonic ideal of an attentive audience), for being so supportive.

Emily Griffin, for being my guiding star and for bringing my book to Grand Central; Maddie Caldwell, for stepping up to the plate with so much enthusiasm and dedication; and Rose Tomaszewska, for all your insights and hard work on this book and for taking me overseas. I've never had a trine of editors before but it was truly a special experience, and I'm so grateful to all three of you. Many thanks, as well, to the teams at Grand Central and riverrun for all of your hard work, and to Lisa Forde in particular for making this book so beautiful.

My agents, Victoria Sanders and Bernadette Baker-Baughman, for your unwavering confidence and positivity, and for your excellent work on my behalf.

Carol Stack, Siri Hellerman, Jane Orvis, Patricia Van der Leun, Jasmine Oore, John Guari, and Alex Yanofsky, for your feedback and encouragement on early drafts and chapters, and to both of my parents.

Everyone I've cribbed from, a likely incomplete list: David, thanks for letting me borrow some of your weekend in jail, which I maintain was not my fault, no matter where you were headed. Clifford Owens, thank you(?) for referring to Bushwick as "The Bush"; Alfred Bridi, for steering me from cars to jewels; Jent from The Watch and Wait, for your awesome name.

There were several books about fashion, magazines, labor, and the garment industry that I devoured while writing and editing this book, and I highly recommend the following, in no particular order: *Overdressed* by Elizabeth L. Cline, *Bad Girls Go Everywhere* by Jennifer Scanlon, *Deluxe: How Luxury Lost Its Luster* by Dana Thomas, *Wear No Evil* by Greta Eagan, *Asians Wear Clothes on the Internet* by Minh-Ha T. Pham, *Sex and the Single Girl* and *Having It All* by Helen Gurley Brown, *Love and Capital* by Mary Gabriel, the essay "Distinction" by Pierre Bordieu, and, of course, *Ways of Seeing* by John Berger; thanks specifically to Penguin for providing permissions. And, in "preparation" for my own wedding, I was reading *One Perfect Day: The Selling of the American Wedding* by Rebecca Mead, along with her piece "Precarious Beauty" in the *New Yorker,* when I wrote the very first sketch of this book, so to Mead I owe a serious debt of inspiration—thanks for everything you write.

And to Ian for everything.